Ella Kingsley is the pseudonym of a women's fiction author. Before embarking on her writing career, she worked in publishing and retains her obsession with perfect punctuation to this day. Ella is in her twenties and lives in North London. At the karaoke mic, she has been known to sing 'Ice Ice Baby' all the way through with huge conviction, if not talent.

Praise for
Confessions of a Karaoke Queen

'A fizzy, funny, brill girl's-night-out of a book'
Jenny Colgan, author of *Meet Me at the Cupcake Café*

'Ella Kinglsey's riotous novel has all the ingredients
of a great karaoke night with the girls – dubious singing,
laughs galore and a reminder of the fun to be had
when you don't take things too seriously'
Jane Costello, author of *Bridesmaids*

'As sparkly and feel-good as a glittery disco ball.
Ella Kingsley is such a fresh and funny new voice.
Pass her the mic, we want more!'
Carmen Reid, author of *New York Valentine*

'I found myself lying in bed needing to be asleep and
saying "just one more chapter", then reading one more
chapter and dutifully laying the book down and turning
the light out . . . but then immediately turning it on
again. I couldn't put this lovely book down'
Lucy-Anne Holmes, author of *50 Ways to Find a Lover*

Confessions of a Karaoke Queen

ELLA KINGSLEY

sphere

SPHERE

First published in Great Britain as a paperback original in 2011 by Sphere

Copyright © Ella Kingsley, 2011

The moral right of the author has been asserted.

A CIP catalogue record for this book
is available from the British Library.

ISBN 978-0-7515-4594-4

Typeset in Caslon by M Rules
Printed and bound in Great Britain by
Clays Ltd, St Ives plc

Papers used by Sphere are from well-managed forests
and other responsible sources.

MIX
Paper from
responsible sources
FSC® C104740

Sphere
An imprint of
Little, Brown Book Group
100 Victoria Embankment
London EC4Y 0DY

An Hachette UK Company
www.hachette.co.uk

www.littlebrown.co.uk

For Caroline
Friend, editor and mic-wrecker extraordinaire

Acknowledgements

Huge thanks to Caroline Hogg, my brilliant editor – this book belongs to both of us. Thanks to my agent Madeleine Buston and all at the Darley Anderson Agency for their guidance and support.

To Jo Dickinson and Viv Redman for everything they taught me. Also to David Shelley, Manpreet Grewal, Andy Hine, and all the team at Sphere.

Finally, to the original Friday night karaoke queens: Vanessa, Rowan, Sarah, Donna, Katherine, Caroline, Suz and Cat. Nobody does it better.

1

Total Eclipse of the Heart

I can't sing.

There, I said it. I, Maddie Mulhern, raised by wild-haired parents on the exotic plains of Eighties Synth Pop, where colourful beasts roam the borders of Kaftan and Eyeliner, cannot sing a note. Maybe it's because I've grown up with a one-time-famous mum and dad, whose sole chart-topper gets played at weddings across the land. (You do know it: you'll say, 'Oh god, not *that* one?') Maybe it's because I'm 'eclipsed' and I need to 'own my own stage' (this is what my best friend Lou says – and she's taking a Psychology degree). Or maybe it's because my private apex of horror is a memory of my eighth birthday party, where my parents did away with the conventional freak-all-the-children-out clown and instead delivered their own freakish performance piece to Jean Michel Jarre's 'Oxygène'. Aside from anything else, that song is forty minutes long.

My mum and dad are . . . well, they're characters. Everyone reckons their parents are weird, but mine actually are. I love them, but they embarrass me. Does that sound bad? OK, so picture this: flicking channels on the telly and landing on *Top of the Pops 2*. It's 1987. George and Andrew (and the two girls, but I can never remember which one's which – and besides, it's all about George) are clad in white tracksuits and booties, their hair coiffed like the curls of butter you get in posh restaurants. Yep, Wham!'s all good. And then, just as you're wondering where it all went wrong – has he really been arrested *again*? – the song ends and another set of familiar chords strike up. Pineapple Mist (you did hear right) have taken to the stage, number three for the fourth week running! Mum's dancing about like some kind of shoulder-padded maniac, and she's got on this pair of bloated white leggings that make her look like the Stay Puft Marshmallow Man at the end of *Ghostbusters*. Dad's got dreads. *Dreads*.

Other people have frown lines; I have cringe lines. Honestly.

For a while they tried to get me in on the business – not like super-pushy tennis parents or anything, but because they thought it had to run in the genes. And up to a point, I guess it does: I've loved music since I can remember and I've always wanted to get into something media-related – but definitely, *definitely* behind the scenes. That's just as important, isn't it? Where would Boyzone be without Louis Walsh?

Spice Girls without Simon Fuller? What would Rick Astley be doing now without Pete Waterman? Er, actually, forget that one.

I'm an organiser, a planner and, I hope, a support. But no, I most certainly *don't* sing.

And that might go some of the way to explaining why I'm standing in the grey rain at Baker Street tube, listening to my boyfriend dump me.

'We're just . . . different, Mads,' Lawrence says, leaning against an advertisement for cruise travel. He's got a pastel-pink jersey knotted loosely round his neck, the sort orange-skinned men wear while smoking cigars on Capri. 'I think I need someone more . . . out there.'

'Out where?'

'You know. *There*.'

I fold my arms, feeling sick and trying to put this down to having just dropped sixty quid in the bar and brasserie Lawrence wanted to go to for lunch (when the bill came he realised his debit card expired last month), rather than the fact I know what's coming.

'Are you breaking up with me?' I ask, part of me wanting to stall the whole disastrous conversation and another conceding it better to just get to the point, like ripping off a plaster. There's a hurting blob in my chest that feels dangerously like tears.

He makes a sad face, as if he's about to explain something basic but inevitable, like the death of a hamster, to a child.

'I'm a performer, Mads,' he says, pushing a flop of dark fringe from his eyes. 'I need to be out on stage, doing my thing. That's the way it is for people like me.' The rain is

3

coming down in earnest now and he lifts his coat above his head like the wings of a great bird. I notice he doesn't offer me shelter, but I suppose that could be mixing messages.

I wait for him to elaborate but he doesn't, assuming this explains everything. Yes, Lawrence is an actor – a good one, in my view – but somehow this single fact seems to have permitted him a long line of concessions. I think back over the past ten months: the melodrama, the lack of money, the selfish behaviour. Suddenly I'm angry.

'I know,' I say tightly. 'And I've done nothing but help you out. You can't pretend that's not true.'

Now would be a good time to appear beautiful and windswept, like Kate Winslet in *Titanic*; instead I'm more drowned rat in a pair of Accessorize flip-flops. My suspicions are confirmed in the windows of a passing bus. I'm wearing this cross-strapped floral dress I picked up in the sale at Warehouse, which is flapping wetly against my skin like a piece of boat tarpaulin. My hair's stuck to the sides of my head *à la* the ears of a King Charles Spaniel. I curse my decision not to bring my little red anorak, even if it does make me feel like the dwarf at the end of *Don't Look Now*.

Lawrence does a sort of snort, and for a moment I'm convinced he's made the same observations. Then he says quietly, bitterly, 'You think I *enjoy* doing that sort of thing?'

He's referring to a gig I got him through the voiceover agency where I temp a few days a week. Admittedly it was a dubbing job where he had to talk over a wincing German in an ad for haemorrhoid cream, but beggars can't be choosers. Lawrence hadn't had a decent wage in months.

'Hang on a minute,' I say. 'It's not like you were turning

down the new Scorsese. What would you have done if I hadn't sorted that?'

He yanks the coat tighter. 'Oh, I don't know, Maddie, *not pretending to be crapping myself?*'

I should probably point out what I've been doing with this man for the best part of a year, since I'm aware I'm not painting him in a particularly favourable light. Lawrence and I met through mutual friends at a party last June – his best mate was someone I shared a Media Studies seminar with at uni – and at first he was sparkly, fun company. He was also an extrovert raconteur, in turn allowing me to assume a comfortable role in the background. He also told me I looked like Rachel McAdams 'in that dress' (this continued to bug me: just in the dress? What about out of the dress? What about out of *any* dress?) but I didn't know who she was at the time so I went and rented *The Notebook* and spent most of it wondering if I could convince my maybe-new-boyfriend to grow a beard like Ryan Gosling. (Although Lou says it makes Ryan's eyes look tiny, like currants in an Eccles cake.)

Anyway for six months it was amazing – we even talked about setting up together: I want to get into management and Lawrence could be my first big breakthrough – but the past few have been, well, rubbish. The hard reality of the industry set in and as the jobs became fewer and further between – especially for the north-London posh-boy: curse that new Doctor Who – and the money even thinner on the ground, his self-esteem followed suit. I've remembered this: Lawrence's tantrums aren't born out of malice, they're born of frustration. It's awful not to meet your potential.

My voice softens. 'Look, why don't we have a break for a

couple of weeks? Give us each some time to reflect on what we want.'

He shakes his head and spits '*No*' with such vehemence that a group of school kids shuffling past on their way to Madame Tussauds turn to look at us. 'I need to branch out,' he goes on, quieter now. 'I'm sorry, Mads. It's over. Don't call me, OK?'

I can feel the hot spill of tears threatening to push free. Why am I crying? I knew it was going nowhere with Lawrence, but in spite of this it's still horrible. Getting dumped is *horrible*.

'Fine,' I say, mustering my dignity. My feet are soggy. Why the bloody hell did I wear flip-flops? Those cork-soled ones, too: I might as well have sponges strapped to my feet.

Lawrence tries a no-hard-feelings smile. The rain is pit-patting on the coat strung between his arms, and for the first time I notice the slogan on the cruise poster behind him: BEST WATER TRAVEL. The material obscures each end of it, leaving the letters T WAT hovering just above his head. I decide to bank this image for the dark days ahead.

'Goodbye, Lawrence,' I say proudly, choosing not to return the smile. I shall walk away with my chin up, my shoulders back, hoping he remembers that I once looked like Rachel McAdams. I shall disappear into the London crowds like a ship at sea. I shall leave him in my wake, looking on at my departing back, brimming with regret. I shall. I shall.

At the swarming entrance to the tube I do a quick look back, just to verify all this. He's already bolted.

It's only as I'm stood, depressed, on the escalators that I realise Lawrence is one of the few people in the world who knows my real name. My *full* name. The one my parents gave me. The same parents who named their band Pineapple Mist.

Oh Jesus. Oh dear god, no. I've just got to hope that my ex-boyfriend searches the depths of his soul, the pit of human decency, and resolves to do the right thing, the only thing: to take my secret to the grave.

Breaking up with someone takes identity protection to a whole new level.

2

I Should Be So Lucky

'He's an idiot,' says Lou, rummaging around under her desk for a pair of size fives. It's useful to have a best friend who changes her shoes at least once a day and thus has a shop floor's worth of them within reach for occasions such as this.

Just minutes ago I stumbled back into the Bond Street office, bedraggled and tear-stained, eliciting gasps from the entire female contingent of Simply Voices. By some weird intuition they all seemed to know what had happened. Clearly twenty-five-year-old women don't stand out in the cold on showery April days unless they're breaking up with someone.

Cue lots of kind concern and offers to make tea, and the magical appearance from somebody's drawer of a box of Mr Kipling's chocolate fingers with sticky icing.

'Maybe,' I grumble, patting my soaked hair with a freebie beer mat a client sent us last week.

Lou surfaces and tosses me a hideous pair of those super-calf-toner trainers, the type with suspension better suited to a four-by-four. There's a two-inch-deep chunk of bright white sole, curved like the belly of a sailing boat. Not what a recently dumped girl in doubt of her own desirability needs.

She clocks my expression and laughs. 'Just take those wicker things off,' she instructs, nodding to the sorry wet flip-flops hanging off my feet. 'The trainers are comfy.'

'He implied I was holding him back,' I say, doing as I'm told. 'Do you think that's true? I mean, maybe I've been sub-consciously preventing him from reaching his goals as a way of maintaining my own sense of—'

'Maddie, shut up,' says Lou, coming over and putting her arms around me.

'You're the psychologist,' I mumble.

'And you're a big wally. Lawrence doesn't know what he's lost.' She kisses the top of my head, even though it must be like putting her face in a wet dog. Lou's the best.

And these trainers *are* comfy. They're really . . . bouncy. I have an urge to spring to my feet and run a million miles, like Forrest Gump. I'll run far away from Lawrence, from my dead-end temping job, from everything. I'll run so far and so fast that I break some incredible record and everyone decides I should do a marathon or something for the Olympics and then Lawrence will come crawling back and I'll forget it was him I was running from in the first place and then perhaps . . . Oh, as if. I hate running. And anyway, these trainers do pinch a little at the toes.

Lou perches on the side of my desk and bites into a Granny Smith. 'Look,' she says reasonably, tucking a lock of bobbed blonde hair behind her ear, 'the way I see it, you and Law were never that suited.'

I frown. 'You never told me you thought that.'

She shrugs. 'Of course I didn't. But I always knew you'd break up some day and then I'd be able to tell you. So while it was a bit of a fib, it was like an IOU fib.'

'Right . . .'

'Anyway, my point is that you're bound to feel like shit right now, but sooner or later you *will* see that it's the best thing. You're too good for him. I promise you.'

I smile at her.

Jennifer, the boss's PA, strides over with a cup of herbal tea. 'Drink up, sunbeam,' she commands, plonking it down and giving my shoulders a rigorous and borderline painful rub. I shoot Lou a worried look and she stifles a laugh. Jennifer is lovely, but she's about as delicate a masseuse as a tattooed trucker. Sadness is something to be treated in much the same way as an especially tenacious bout of athlete's foot. Efficient sympathy, if such a thing exists.

'Why don't you two take some time out' – she waves to the kitchen – 'ten minutes should do it?'

'Ten minutes should be ample time to sort out Maddie's life,' Lou agrees.

Jennifer nods once, satisfied, as Lou grabs the tea with one hand and my arm with the other, dragging me towards the little area where we make coffee in the morning and read *Heat* magazine. In these trainers I'm about nine feet tall.

'Do you want my diagnosis?' asks Lou, shoving a cup under the new cappuccino-making machine. It spits furiously and Lou yelps, before it settles into that smoothing *ahh* and a rich shot of caramel-coloured froth streams out the nozzle.

I take a pew on the side counter thingy and sip my own drink. 'Go on then,' I say gloomily.

'He didn't get you, not like your friends do.' Lou adds sugar and comes to sit next to me. 'Which is common enough, I guess – boyfriends don't always see the side we do. But with Lawrence it was like he wasn't ever that bothered.'

I must look hurt, because Lou quickly clarifies: 'Not bothered about *being* with you; just bothered about getting to *know* you. The real you.'

'Maybe.'

'And it was always about him, always. You were for ever going out of your way to mop up his various disasters. Every time I called he was having some crisis and you had to go running over to give him a shoulder to cry on, or an ear to bend, or lend him money for a cab – why can't he take the sodding bus like everyone else, by the way? – or talk him down from whatever precipice he was on that particular day of the week—'

'OK, OK, I get it.' I tip the rest of my drink down the sink. Tea's not going to cut it.

I give my mug a quick rinse and open the staff fridge, pondering what Lou has said. She's not quite a psychologist, but is two years into her degree at UCL and reckons what she's learning gives added gravitas to any relationship advice dispensed to friends in need. (I like to think she's right, as her

11

verdict post-relationship is strictly Anti-Ex.) I recommended her to Jennifer when Simply Voices were recruiting for more part-time bods but we've known each other since we were six. It's funny, but we sort of fell out of touch as we got older then became tight again. I don't think it's possible to lose someone who's truly your best friend.

'Plus he's anally retentive,' she adds.

My thoughts are dragged back to Lawrence and I sigh unhappily, wondering whose Tupperware box this is with blocks of millionaire shortbread inside.

'I suppose,' I concede. 'He was always pretty uptight about stuff.' I search the lid for a name. 'Like when I accidentally used his organically sourced mystic-bamboo-root soy sauce as Baby Bio.'

Lou raises an eyebrow.

'Or that time I said I fancied Darius and he had to go for a walk round the block and didn't come back for two hours.'

Lou shakes her head. 'No, I mean *literally*. All the times I had you guys over he never once went to the loo in my flat.'

Shocked, I turn to face her. 'Really?'

She lowers her voice. '*Never*. After I got the idea into my head, I never stopped noticing.'

I prise open the Tupperware and cheekily nick a couple of biscuits. Lou holds out her hands and I chuck one over. There goes our vinegar diet (Lou's latest weight-loss idea: douse everything in balsamic vinegar and it suppresses the appetite; plus, apparently it's got some clever enzyme that breaks down fats, or something). Probably wise, as I was beginning to feel a bit sour.

'That's weird,' I say as we stuff our faces.

For a minute we sit in silence. It's impossible to chat with a mouthful of shortbread – it gets thicker the more you speak.

'I think he was intimidated,' Lou observes when she's finished.

'By what?'

'The whole Pineapple Mist thing.'

I can't help but laugh. 'Come on, Lou – that's absurd.'

'Why?'

'Because . . .' I search for the words. 'Because Mum and Dad are many things, but they're *not* intimidating. They're . . . manic, and strange, and silly, but they're not intimidating.'

Lou shrugs. 'It's not them as such – it's that they made it. Once upon a time, OK, but they still did: they *made* it. How many people can say that?'

I make a face.

'Pineapple Mist was *the* hottest thing in the charts. Fine, it was '87, but even so. And you got to grow up with all that. Someone like Lawrence is *bound* to get jealous. It's all he's ever wanted, that kind of attention.'

'But he was never even fussed about seeing them!' I exclaim. 'I practically had to force him to meet them in the first place.' A shiver ripples down my spine at the memory. 'They made us sing "Love Lift Us Up Where We Belong".'

'Ooh,' says Lou. 'Did you do Joe Cocker?'

'They had to drag me to do anything at all – you know what I'm like when I get down there. It's like descending into the bowels of Hell. Hell with a mirror ball.'

At this point I should tell you what my parents do for a living these days. I say 'these days', but we're talking major

nineties throwback here. Sometime last year they had a journalist call up doing a Where-Are-They-Now?-inspired feature,
tracking down people like David Van Day and some bloke
from Haircut 100. They must have got a shocker when they
arrived at Sing It Back, where Pineapple Mist had solidified
into more of a gooseberry fool.

Sing It Back is my parents' Soho karaoke bar, a flagging
flagship of eighties-slash-nineties memorabilia, a hopelessly
outdated den of sordid serenading where the most cutting-
edge pop numbers are 'Mysterious Girl' and several flops by
Billie Piper. It's got a certain charm, if you like that sort of
thing (I don't), and you're drunk (if ever faced with karaoke,
I do), but it's in need of a serious overhaul. The biggest selling point is my parents' names – Rick and Sapphire have
become as recognisable as Pineapple Mist – but even so, their
market is fairly niche: retro-thrill-seeking twenty-somethings
on the occasional hen do or their usual Saturday night crowd
of bar staff's friends and a guy who sits in the corner doing 'Bat
Out of Hell' on repeat and calling himself simply 'Loaf'.
(Don't worry, it's not really Meatloaf. We don't think.)

'Come on, it's a cool place!' Lou grins, as ever leaping to
their defence. Her own mum and dad are separated and she had
quite a tough childhood, so she's close to my parents like that.

'You only say so because you fancy Simon,' I tell her, referring to the cute barman – Lou's had a crush on him for, like,
ever.

'I do not!' she huffs, glowing pink.

With a grimace I remember the stack of emails awaiting
both of us. 'Come on, we've got to do *some* work this afternoon.'

'Are you sure you're OK?' she asks, and I can tell she's glad to change the subject.

'I will be.' I smile weakly. 'There's life after Lawrence. Thanks, Lou.'

'Indeed there is.' Lou nods decisively, taking my arm. Then she says more quietly, 'It's not as if you told him your real name or anything.'

I cringe.

'Maddie, you didn't!'

'It just slipped out!'

'Something like that doesn't just *slip out*!' She steers me full circle and back into the kitchen, her this-is-a-code-red-crisis face on.

'Well this did.'

She shakes her head. 'You're done for, Maddie. If that ever, *ever* gets out . . .'

Great, now I'm crying again.

♪

Back at my desk I've got an email from Big Ideas, the celebrity management consultancy I applied for a placement with last month.

Maybe my luck's about to turn around, I think excitedly as I slip into my chair. Maybe the three years I've spent faffing around since uni are about to move up a gear. I might actually be about to *do* something with my degree. Maybe the break-up with Lawrence has come at just the right time, because I'm actually on the cusp of becoming a shit-hot celebrity manager and then he'll realise what a terrible mistake he's made and beg me for a second chance.

Eagerly I click on it.

```
Dear Ms Mulhern,
Thank you for your recent application
to work with us as a graduate trainee
manager. Competition was fierce, and I
regret to inform you that the position has
gone to another candidate . . .
```

Fuck!

I can't be bothered to read the rest. Crossly, I hit Delete and sink my head into my hands. Could this day *get* any more shit?

As if on cue, my mobile rings. It's Mum.

I resist the urge to ram my head repeatedly against the wooden desk until I pass out. Instead I force myself to pick up.

As soon as I hear her voice, I know something is wrong.

'Poppet,' she says, breathless. 'Thank god I made it through. This is urgent. I need you at home *right now*. Something's happened.'

3

Bad

The journey to my parents' flat seems to take forever. In reality it's only ten minutes from the Simply Voices offices, but that's when you're travelling on something that's actually moving. My bus sits in traffic outside M&S for a small eternity, so, quitting that, I attempt to hail a rickshaw. I swear these hard-pedalling guys actively swerve around me, a stricken-looking girl wearing a short damp dress and massive breeze-block trainers, shouting, 'I'm light! I'm light!' They probably think I'm some sort of religious fanatic.

Now, I'm running – and, like a bird of prey with wings unclipped, these trainers are finally soaring. This has got to be a revolutionary feat (feet?) of engineering: it's like I'm *flying*. But flying or not, I think as I catch my swooping reflection in the window of John Lewis, little takes away from the reality of looking like a complete berk.

Still, I might even be enjoying myself if it weren't for this hollow dread I've had in the pit of my stomach since Mum's phone call. What's happened? Is Dad ill? Is there something wrong with Mum? Is somebody dying? Fuck, somebody's dying. Somebody's dead. Is it my grandma? My aunt Sylvie? Sylvie's cat, which has bad breath but I love? Is it my great-cousin Jim who lives in New Zealand and we only see once every five years? (I hope it's him. No, shit, that sounds horrible. It's only if there *has* to be a death, obviously.)

I force myself to take deep breaths. It'll be something anodyne, like Dad's livid-purple Bentley got a puncture or Mum's eye make-up's melted because she left it on the windowsill in the sun again. It wouldn't be the first time they'd had a huge drama over something totally inconsequential.

Lifted by this, I practically bridge an entire pedestrian crossing with one boingy step. Moments later I enter the maze of Soho streets, past the John Smith pub, past the curry house with the best naan bread in London, past the hairdresser who once gave me a 'step' and I couldn't sleep for a month (on top of the nightmares, the back of my head was about a foot off the pillow). And, finally, I'm at Mum and Dad's.

The first thing I notice is that the car is out on the street. You can't miss it – it's the colour of black grape juice, with a big bright silver grille and broccoli-green interior. The second thing is that the car is overflowing with boxes. OK, now I'm properly worried. What the hell is going on?

I push my way into the building. The karaoke bar is in the basement but even so I get a chill as I clock the chipped SING IT BA K sign with the C that's been missing for ever. It's the same bright pink type as on the poster for Tom Cruise's *Cocktail*, and when it lights up at night it flickers sickly in the dark. Just around the corner are two more karaoke places – Mum and Dad maintain they had the first in this block, but I don't know – but the word 'rival' doesn't apply any more. To be a rival you've got to at least be competing, and Sing It Back hasn't competed in years. I know that in a few hours' time it'll limp into life for yet another Friday evening, and the knowledge gives me a sudden and unexpected pang of sadness.

Just inside there's a girl stacking crates of bottled beer and ticking off boxes on a tatty old clipboard. It's Sing It Back's only barmaid, part-time actress and one of my closest friends.

'Hi, Jaz.' As in Jasmine. Not Jazzy Jeff, as Lou originally thought.

Jaz looks up at me, wide-eyed, from the frame of her wild red hair. She's got huge blue eyes that appear even bigger because of her tiny size – but what she lacks in stature she makes up for in attitude. Jaz wants to be the Next Big Celebrity and her current obsession is with Lady Gaga: last month I saw her serving drinks in the bar wearing nothing but an outfit made of gaffer tape and a pair of slatted sunglasses you could pull like an IKEA blind. Apparently Simon started calling her Lady Gaffer and she got quite upset. Not as upset as she must have been removing the tape. Ouch ouch *ouch*.

'Hey, Maddie,' she says in her soft American lilt. Absorbing my panicky expression, she frowns. 'Are you OK?'

I catch my breath. 'Not really,' I say, slumping back against the wall.

She puts down the clipboard and rubs my arms vigorously, like mums do when their kids have been out in the cold.

'You're freezing,' she says, and a sweet smell wafts off her like cinnamon. Jaz always wears nice perfume – she's forever telling me off about my clutter of half-used £1.89 cans of Impulse. 'In fact . . .' She looks me up and down. 'You look *terrible*. What's happened?'

Jaz says it like it is – you'll get used to it. She's a total livewire, but she's fiercely loyal, too. She came over from the States three years ago after a doomed relationship broke her heart, and she's been a faithful part of Sing It Back ever since. Even though she can't be making pots of money, or be finding the bar work particularly stimulating, she just really likes my parents. Mum and Dad have that effect on people – you want to be with them, I guess, because everything feels more exciting when you are.

'That's the thing,' I say, worried. 'I don't know. Mum just rang and she was freaking out, saying there was some emergency and I had to come round straight away. Any ideas?'

Jaz shakes her head. 'Beats me.'

'And the car's all packed. Something's up, I know it.'

We're interrupted by a scuffle behind one of the crates. Jaz bends down and makes a kissy-kissy sound, clicking her fingers. I try not to appear too disgusted when her pet guinea pig, Andre, scrabbles into view. This is the result of Jaz's desire to own one of those toy dogs, the sort Paris Hilton carries round in a pink satchel, its worried face peering out from behind a gauzy peephole. On further investigation, however, apparently 'they smell', so the guinea pig got the job. Today he's wearing a tiny French maid's outfit with a little white cap and frilly sleeves, his itchy-scratchy feet poking out the holes.

'Come on, Andre,' she coos, gathering him into her hands. I don't get the French thing. Maybe he's having an identity crisis – in a world where giant rodents get their nails painted, anything's possible.

'Don't sweat it, Mads,' she says easily, getting to her feet and tickling Andre's head. 'You know what they're like, it's probably nothing.' She smiles encouragingly and pulls a cigarette out her red mane of hair. God only knows what else she's got in there. Can of Coke? Volume of Larkin poetry? Foothigh bearded acrobat?

Cigarette in mouth, she steps past me. Andre squints at me with small, accusing eyes. 'Nice shoes, by the way.'

The door closes behind her and I turn to look up the stairs. Why do I feel like something awful is waiting for me up there?

♪

Something is.

Mum and Dad's flat is a gaudy nightmare of eighties memorabilia. Photos of Pineapple Mist adorn one wall, along with gold awards for Best Single ('What You Do (Ooh Ooh)' – see? I told you) and Best Video (not that one where they're hanging out in the Laundromat in orange shell suits, surely), and signed bits and bobs from their UK '88 tour. A favourite picture of the famous duo takes centre stage: Dad's sporting one of those long thin plaits Jordan Knight used to have and Mum's got some amazing kingfisher-blue eye shadow on, her hair tied back tight like the women in the video for 'Addicted to Love'. On all sides a circus of familiar faces gazes out: Neil Tennant, moody in tin foil; beautiful Boy George wrapped in a Pineapple Mist sandwich (a new level of disturbing); Sting with his arm draped round Mum's shoulders; Chesney Hawkes in a too-tight T-shirt with worryingly good hair . . .

The facing wall is covered in purple-tinted mirrors, so the images are reflected all around in a slightly queasy hue. Everything is themed, from the little musical note coat hangers just inside the door, to the armchair in the shape of a great big concave cello.

'Mum?' I call, kicking off the trainers and throwing my borrowed coat on the table. 'Dad?' The light is dim and there's a faint sweet smell of baking. *Baking?* Clearly something is seriously the matter.

There's a loud thump. *'Blast!'* comes my dad's voice from the kitchen. I follow it and what I find there is frankly bizarre: Dad's on his hands and knees with his head buried in a cupboard, and on the floor there's a cardboard box filled with open packets of biscuits.

'Dad?' I wring my hands together. 'What's going on?'

Dad emerges from the cupboard, banging his head in doing so. He's still a good-looking man: tall and blond, only slightly balding, with a naturally happy face. He's got an iPod in and as one of the earphones springs free I can hear Prefab Sprout. This upsets me further.

'Maddie!' He gets up, holding his arms out. Unlike Mum, he actually listened when I told him I wanted to shorten my name. 'How's my favourite girl?'

I gesture to the floor, like, Please can *someone* explain?

'Oh!' He laughs. 'Your mother's adamant we take enough to eat. For the journey, you know. It could be a long time on the ferry, you never can tell. And she does like her fig rolls . . .'

I hold a hand up. 'Hang on a sec. What ferry?'

His face falls. 'Sapphy didn't tell you? I thought she rang this afternoon.'

'She did,' I say. 'She told me to come home and then she hung up. It was like this massive panic so I had to leave work straight away. I get here and the car's all packed up and you're shuffling about in all these biscuits and I'm freaking out now a bit, Dad . . .'

A pair of musk-scented arms wraps around me.

'Rick and I need to have a quick word with you, poppet,' Mum says, turning me to face her. She looks amazingly well, I notice. Her cheeks are glowing and her normal bush of dyed black hair is brushed and sleek. 'Come and sit down.'

Oh god, I think. Oh god oh god oh god. They're pregnant. Hence all the biscuits. She's *hungry* – she's got cravings for Malted Milks and Marmite, or something. And all the boxes in the car aren't going; they're *coming*. It's baby stuff, like a musical mobile that plays Spandau Ballet, and dummies in the shape of mini microphones . . .

'We're going away,' she says once I'm perched nervously on the edge of the couch.

I'm confused. 'What? Where?'

My parents exchange a look. It must be a holiday, I decide. Yes, it's a holiday.

'For three months,' she adds.

'A three-month *holiday*?'

23

Now it's Mum's turn to look puzzled. 'It's not a holiday, darling. It's work.'

'*Work?*' This is even more absurd.

'Yes,' Dad huffs, lifting his chin with pride. 'We're touring again.'

My mouth drops open.

'That's right.' Mum smiles. 'Rick and Sapphire are back. Pineapple Mist' – wow, she really savours saying that – 'are back.'

I still haven't had a chance to comment before Dad's straight in there.

'It's a revival tour, Maddie,' he says excitedly, darting on to the sofa next to me. 'Do you know what this means? Pineapple Mist is getting a second chance!'

There's a brief silence.

'Like that programme Tony Hadley did?' Of all the questions I need to ask right now, it is this I cough up.

'That's it.' Mum nods. 'A nostalgia tour. "One Hit Wonderful." We'll be touring Eastern Europe for the next few months with some old friends' – she gestures round the room – 'though I think your father's hoping something more permanent will come of it . . .'

'Something will, Sapphy!' He gazes adoringly at her. 'Just think about it: you and me out on stage, the crowd screaming our names—'

'What about everything here?' I interrupt.

They both turn to look at me.

'That's where you come in, darling,' says Mum, kneeling down and taking my hands. 'This is a wonderful opportunity for you.'

I frown.

'We were thinking, you see,' interjects Dad, putting his arm round me, 'about how this might work out for you. We know you're not too happy at Simply Voices, and this could be the platform you need to move on to bigger and better things.'

I'm not sure I like where this is going. 'What sort of platform?' I ask carefully.

A wide smile splits Mum's face as she squeezes my fingers. 'We want *you* to manage Sing It Back!' My expression must be one of incredulous horror as she tacks on smoothly: 'Just while we're away, a trial period—'

'No,' I say, getting to my feet. 'No way. Nuh-uh. No way.'

'Why not?' Dad looks genuinely surprised. The two of them spring up, full of concern.

I want to laugh. Instead I appeal to Dad's more sensible nature: no doubt this was Mum's harebrained idea. 'Come on, you can't possibly be serious. You know how I feel about the K word. It's not me, never has been. Plus I don't know the first thing about running a business.'

'Archie'll help you, so will Ruby.' Dad's talking about two of the bar's old-timers. 'We'll fund you through the whole time we're away; you've nothing to worry about—'

'Dad, *no*. It's too much of a commitment.'

'But haven't you been searching for this kind of commitment since uni?' Mum butts in, and Dad starts nodding. How come mums always talk you into destroying your own argument? 'You're always saying you want more responsibility, sweetheart. Well, this is your chance. You'll be in charge; it's just the sort of experience you need. And it's only a few months . . .'

I try a different approach. 'My heart wouldn't be in it. I'd do a terrible job. The whole place would collapse and die a horrible painful death.'

A look of hurt passes over my parents' faces, and I can't bear to think I've offended them. I'm about to qualify what I've just said when Mum says quietly, 'But that's what we're afraid of.' She looks to the floor. 'We're afraid that without you keeping its head above water, Sing It Back won't be here when we return.' Slowly her eyes meet mine. 'Please, darling. At least consider it. The bar is in such bad shape that it's a risk us going in the first place, but we have to take this chance. You must understand that.'

Of course I understand it. Oh *bloody* hell.

'I'll think about it,' I say reluctantly. 'I promise.'

A few seconds pass. Mum asks, 'Have you made a decision yet?'

'What? No, of course—'

'It's just we really ought to get going,' says Dad, glancing at his watch. 'We've still got a few bits and pieces to get in the car . . .'

Appalled, I remember the overflowing Bentley outside.

'You're going *now*?'

'Our ferry's at midnight and we've got to get up to Newcastle,' explains Mum, hurrying over to the table where there's a stack of navy blue lever arch files. She piles them into my arms. 'Here you go, darling – this is everything you need. All the information is in there: accounts, budgets, the lot. We know you'll do a brilliant job.' She kisses my head and I open my mouth, but no words come out.

'We did try to get hold of you earlier,' she says, smiling happily. 'We've been calling you all week.' Dad disappears into the kitchen to finish ransacking the cupboards.

I don't know if this is entirely true, but I do remember getting some missed calls a few days ago. I was too busy helping Lawrence rehearse his lines for some stupid audition, which I now really hope he doesn't get.

As if reading my mind, Mum adds, 'I'm sure Lawrence will be around to step in.'

I gulp. 'Actually me and Lawrence broke up today.'

'Oh, sweetheart!' Mum rushes to embrace me and the corners of the files dig into my chest. I have this overwhelming urge to spend three hours in the bath and then sleep for the whole weekend. 'What happened?'

'I don't want to talk about it, Mum.'

'But, darling—'

'I really don't.'

She hugs me again, longer this time. 'I'm going to call you as soon as we get there. I'm so sorry, poppet – if I'd known . . .'

I nod. 'It's fine.'

One more squeeze. 'I love you, darling.'

'Sapphy, we've got to get moving!' Dad charges through the living room.

'Your father never liked him anyway,' she whispers into my ear. Is this supposed to make me feel better?

'Hang on a minute,' I say, as in great haste the last of the bags are scooped up, kisses are planted on my cheeks and hair, and my parents are vanishing out the door. 'You can't just *go*. I mean, what about—'

'We'll call you when we get to Amsterdam!'

And with that, the door slams shut.

4

Things Can Only Get Better

They say bad luck comes in threes. Or is that good luck?

Whatever it is, when I wake up the next day I decide I am dying. Someone's got my head in a vice, and I'm so parched it's like my mouth's been given a colonic irrigation. I have an extreme desire for orange Fanta.

Pieces of the previous evening start to surface on the tides of my hangover. With a groan I remember my parents' announcement, then how after they left I spent all of five minutes despairing over the files before raiding their drinks cabinet and unearthing half a bottle of Bombay Sapphire, which I mixed with some tropical juice I found in the near-empty fridge. (I know: yuck.) Vaguely I recall staggering back to my Camden flat on the night bus, not forgetting to conduct the obligatory drunken phone call, though thankfully (and incredibly) not to Lawrence but to Lou, to whom I think I explained what had happened, in so far as anyone can explain anything with a horrendous volume of gin pickling them from inside out.

Bollocks.

I shower and get dressed. Right, I think as I sit on my bed, concentrating on not being sick. Plan, Maddie. Come up with a plan.

OK. Not happening. My brain can barely process what's happened over the last twenty-four hours, let alone work out how to deal with it.

Make a list. Make a list! Right. Yes. Good idea. I'll make a list.

I grab a pen and paper and start writing:

1. Make a list
2.

Um . . . This is tougher than I thought. I chew the end of my Biro before continuing.

2. Eat toast covered in so much Nutella it makes me feel ill
3. Call Lou
4. Despair over horrible ex-boyfriend and disastrous career prospects
5. Weep
6. Bang fists on floor

7. Howl like a caged animal
8. Lunch time? Eat lunch
9. Sort out whole entire life please god amen
10. Deal or No Deal

Finally I add 'Wake up' and 'Shower' at the top, so I can cross the first few off and feel like I've got started. Hmm. It's looking kind of OK up until the weeping part . . .

Quite astonishingly I managed to drag home the Sing It Back paperwork last night, so I lift one of the files from my bedside table and start flicking through. It's pretty haphazard, but that's to be expected: all the charts and tables are algebra to me, and there are some worrying-looking letters from the bank manager. Even so it doesn't take a rocket scientist to work out that the place is in deep shit. Everywhere I look there are numbers in deficit, red crosses, botched projections, unmet targets.

Lovely. Mum and Dad have left me to clean up a cesspool with nothing but a cotton bud. With a massive sigh I flip it closed, not knowing whether to laugh or cry. There's only one thing for it: *Takeshi's Castle* and chocolate spread.

♪

'They've done *what*?'

It's four o'clock on Saturday afternoon, a couple of hours before Sing It Back is due to open for another sleepy weekend. In the end I got stuck on number nine on my list, so decided to call a meeting with the bar staff. We're gathered round the table in my parents' flat, the scene of last night's horrendous revelation.

I hand Jaz a cup of coffee. 'Three months. So . . .' I smile weakly. 'It looks like I'm the boss!'

'I don't get it,' says Simon, running a hand through his dark-blond hair. 'Why didn't they tell any of us?' He pours milk into his drink and stirs thoughtfully. I can understand what Lou sees in him – if you like the quiet bookish type with the possibility of a battered Sartre in his coat pocket. He's got ambitions to one day complete a novel of his own, and working at Sing It Back means he's able to temp part-time, thus freeing up his hours to write.

'It ain't any wonder – look at the state of yer!' Archie Howard, Sing It Back's longest-serving employee – and, so the rumour goes, my parents' former hairdresser, though he's wise enough never to admit it – shuffles upright in his chair. 'Bless 'em, they knew there'd be this right old fuss with the lot of yer. So they're gone for a bit, it ain't the end of the world! You'll take care of us, won't you, pet?' He looks at me with crinkly eyes.

I try to appear confident. Privately I think my parents' failure to mention their trip is more likely down to an acute lack of organisation, but highlighting that doesn't help our plight.

'But Maddie doesn't know the first thing about Sing It Back – she hates it!' Jaz points out, fiddling with a gigantic scissor-shaped earring. I don't have the energy to feel offended.

'Then we'll all make sure we show her, won't we?' Archie pats my knee and I'm grateful for his reassurance. I just wish I had the same faith in myself.

'Hell*ooo*!' cries the final member of our party, a six-foot leggy blonde called Ruby du Jour, half stuck out the window with a fag in her mouth. 'What's with all the *drama*? Whatever happened to PMA?'

There's a silence. Simon looks embarrassed.

'Positive mental attitude!' shrieks Ruby. 'PMA! That's what I'm talking about, girls.' She grinds the cigarette out and slams the window shut, waving the smoke around with perfectly manicured hands. But blokes' hands, nonetheless.

Ruby du Jour is Sing It Back's much-loved resident drag queen. Her real name is Rob Day, an ex-backing dancer in his forties who worked for a time with the inimitable soul diva Bobbi Sanchez. Unable to leave the stage behind after Bobbi's career plummeted amid a drugs scandal, Rob hit the drag scene in the nineties and toured a handful of London's clubs with a brilliantly reviewed comedy act. He's really talented, or at least he was in his heyday – and the wonderful thing is you never know who's going to turn up at the club on any given night: Ruby is extravagant, exciting, extraordinary; Rob is sensitive, capable, trustworthy. I like them both in separate ways – it's like having two friends in one. Recently I've seen far more of Ruby than I have of Rob, though, and I miss him. He never 'came out' as Rob, only as Ruby, and I sometimes wonder if she's the only person he knows how to be these days.

'Look,' I say, 'we'll make it work. Trust me. I'll . . . I'll sort it out.'

'What's with all the negativity?' demands Ruby, coming to sit opposite me. She crosses her long legs. 'It's not like any of us are losing our jobs . . . are we?'

I shake my head. 'Of course not.'

'Then what's there to be upset about?' Ruby looks round

at the assembled faces. Simon shrugs. Archie raises an eyebrow. Jaz examines her neon-painted nails.

'The way I see it,' Ruby goes on, 'this is one hell of an opportunity. Not just for Maddie but for all of us!'

Jaz looks up. 'What d'you mean?' Curiosity gets the better of the guinea pig, too: with an enquiring expression, Andre emerges from her handbag. Is that a *monocle* he's wearing?

'I mean' – Ruby unclasps her clutch and plucks out a lipstick – 'that the club is in a sorry state. It's rock bottom. It's an embarrassment.' Blank faces. 'Come on, we all skirt around the issue—'

'We know you do, Rob,' Archie interjects gruffly.

'—but quite frankly the place is a *dive*.'

I hold my hands up. 'No offence, Ruby, but this isn't making me feel better . . .'

'Let me finish!' Ruby's painted eyebrows shoot up like a pair of brackets. 'My point is that it can't get much worse, can it?' Silence. 'Exactly. So whatever Maddie does *has* to be an improvement. If you ask me, we may as well make that improvement worthwhile.'

Simon looks doubtful. 'How?'

'Let's throw everything we've *got* at it!' cries Ruby, as though it's the easiest thing in the world. 'Why just cope, why just manage, why just' – she addresses me – '"make it work"? Why, when we can do so much better?' She applies a slick of bright red lippy and we all wait, transfixed. 'Archie, let's start with you. Shake up the old cocktail menu, it's nearly as ancient as you and it's crying out for a revamp. Market research, that's what you need to do.'

'Market you-what?'

'I can ramp up publicity,' Jaz chips in with a shrug, scooping Andre out and plopping him on the table. 'It can't hurt to print a few fliers and get some support going . . .'

Ruby extends a painted-red talon. 'Exactly.'

'I could update the playlists?' Simon suggests, looking to me for approval. 'Some of the stuff on there's pretty evil.'

'And *I*,' announces Ruby, 'will be working on a new cabaret act.' Everybody groans. 'What? What's wrong with my cabaret act?'

Archie shakes his head.

Ruby looks hurt.

'Hang on,' I say, 'Ruby's got a point.' And the more I think about it, the more she has. A little germ of hope is glowing in my chest, and the more I turn possibilities over in my head, the brighter it becomes. 'Ruby's absolutely right. We can do this.'

'Thank you very much!' Ruby says pointedly to the old man.

'And not just that,' I continue, warming to my cause. 'Why stop there? Why not turn the whole place around, make a completely fresh start?'

'I don't know what you've got in mind,' says Jaz, 'but it'll cost money.' She's pretending to look disinterested, but those big eyes betray a glimmer of curiosity – I know her too well.

'Mum and Dad left me a cheque book . . . though realistically speaking there'll be nowhere near enough in their accounts.' Suddenly I'm animated. 'I want to re-do the entire place from floor to ceiling. Let's change everything. If we can get it back to where it was fifteen years ago—'

'We'll throw a massive re-launch party for when they get back!' Ruby cries.

'Yes!' squeals Jaz, bobbing up and down in her seat. 'And we'll get posters done and invite Z-list celebrities and me and Andre'll get in the back pages of *Hello!*—'

'Yes! And—'

'Hang on a minute,' I laugh, my head buzzing. 'One thing at a time. I've got to look at ways of saving. I mean there's always taking out a loan, but to be honest my parents have kind of rinsed that option—'

'We'll help,' says Simon, nervously glancing round the table. 'I mean . . . won't we?'

'Of course!' Jaz grabs my hand. 'Trim our wages—'

'Nobody's doing any such thing,' I interrupt, clocking Archie's slightly relieved expression. 'This is my project and my responsibility. Nobody's giving me anything.'

Despite the seeming impossibility of what I'm suggesting, I realise I'm shaking. I can make this work. I can totally make this work.

'I'll move out of my flat,' I say, almost to myself. 'I'll move in here, then all my wages from Simply Voices can go into the bar. I'll be right on top of it that way, too – I'll need to be here to oversee the alterations—'

'But, Maddie, it's *hideous* in here!' Jaz's gaze darts across the walls.

I wave her away. 'It'll be fine.'

Ruby clutches my arm, like we're war-bound heroes about to storm the beach at Normandy. 'You can do this,' she tells me. 'You can.'

For a second my confidence falters. 'What about Mum and

Dad? I mean, what if I mess things up?' Yes, I want to do this for me – this is my chance to prove myself as management material – but it's imagining the look on my parents' faces that has me wanting to succeed.

It's Archie's turn to speak. 'If Rick an' Sapphy 'adn't trusted you, they wouldn't 'ave left you in charge.' He winks at me. 'Simple as that.'

Ruby squeezes my hand again. 'Don't you see what we're saying, Maddie? *Use* that trust.' She shrugs. 'You can make this happen.'

And do you know what? I believe her.

5

Saturday Night

At least I do until about nine p.m.

'Come on,' says Jaz, popping the top off a bottle of Corona, 'it's not *that* bad.' She takes a slug of the drink and sits down behind the empty bar. In moments she's back to flicking through her celebrity magazine.

'You think?' But my words are swallowed up by a ghastly shriek as one of the club's antique microphones blasts its feedback over a drunken rendition of 'Nine to Five'. The poor girl singing – one of only four here this evening – winces at her friends apologetically.

Jaz squeezes a wedge of lime into the neck of her beer.

Tonight her dress consists of mini laminated post-its with big black crosses scrawled over each one – I applaud her efforts even when there's no one around to admire them.

'Check this out.' She lifts her magazine and shows me the double-page spread.

I peer in. 'Ugh!'

All across Soho, bars and clubs like ours are pulling in the punters, raking in the cash, bringing in the custom. Jaz and I are examining a pop princess who performed on GMTV wearing an outfit made entirely of human hair. That's how busy we are.

The last time I set foot in Sing It Back was about four months ago, on Mum's birthday. Throughout the night I kept to the shadows, hid in the booths, never staying in one place for more than a few moments – in fact, at one point I remember hiding at the back of the broom closet with Lou, eating Frazzles and bitching about how Lawrence had failed to show up . . . I did *anything* to avoid my parents dragging me on to that stage. Especially when, at the end of the night, Dad took Mum's hand, knelt down in front of everyone and crooned to Stevie Wonder, with the bobbing head and everything. By 'everything' I mean he closed his eyes. God, yes, he actually sang the whole thing with his eyes shut. Argh.

But at least the place was sort of full that night. OK, it wasn't a typical Saturday and the guests were all my parents' friends, but there was at least an atmosphere.

I look around. Sing It Back is in a state. It's dark enough already but two of the overhead 'spotlights' have blown, leaving pockets of the room shrouded in almost-complete darkness. Every so often the dim light from a chipped mirror

38

ball swings reluctantly round, washing everything grey. The back wall is lined with booths, their mustard-coloured upholstery old and stained. Fringed lamps squat miserably on the tables, each bearing the name of an eighties act (Mum and Dad thought it was a genius alternative to table numbers, in the giddy days when they anticipated a kitchen opening up). In a foul clash the walls are papered poppy-red, peeling like sunburned skin. Cracked pink-framed mirrors punctuate the space; a huge wall-to-wall one, like you get at dance schools, is behind the raised area known as the stage. Whoever *wants* to see themselves singing? Isn't it bad enough hearing it?

A man brandishing a pint – one of the sole party of four – has taken to the mic. He's belting out a heinous rendition of Whitesnake's 'Here I Go Again', proving my theory that the only part of that song anybody knows is the 'Here I go again on my own' bit (which, for a lone vocalist, starts to feel a tad repetitive. Ah, there he goes again. And again. Please, not again). Every ten seconds the mic fleetingly cuts out and this woolly metallic boom wings around the bar. I feel like we're at the foot of the tripods in *War of the Worlds*.

'Mic!' the other bloke shouts, then what sounds like 'That's a shit mic.' I'm about to accept their criticism and refund the paltry sum we've made from their custom when I realise he's addressing the singer by his name. The good thing about terrible karaoke is that most people are too drunk to mind.

I sigh deeply. 'We've got a long way to go, Jaz.'

The door behind the bar opens and Simon backs in with a crate of washed glasses. After our meeting he and Jaz persuaded me to sit in on a typical weekend Sing It Back session, to get a renewed feel for what we were dealing with. In a first-ditch attempt to save money, I gave Archie and Ruby the night off: I had a feeling we wouldn't be at capacity.

'Cheer up, mate, it might never happen.' Simon grins as he starts stacking the shelves.

I smile back. 'What put you in such a good mood?'

He shrugs. 'Nothing.' Then he says, in a way that's a little *too* casual to be casual, 'How's Lou?'

My smile threatens to widen but I keep it in check. 'Oh, she's fine. Studying hard.'

He upturns a fan of wine glasses and expertly slots them into place. 'Psychology, right?'

I love that Simon listens – I can't even recall telling him that. 'Yep,' I say over a squealy version of 'I Will Always Love You'. 'You know she's doing this module where she gets to, like, read what other people are thinking.'

Simon makes a face as he squeezes past Jaz, immersed in some article about WAGS' interior decor. 'Psychology's different to telepathy, Maddie.'

'It's true!' I lie. 'Especially men. She can tell *exactly* what's going through your minds. It's all in the eyes, apparently, something about how often you blink when you're talking to a girl. Hey, I'll ask her next time I see you together!'

'Don't,' he says far too quickly. 'I mean, I wouldn't want to put her on the spot.'

As he busies himself I decide that if such a module really did exist, I'd have passed with flying colours. Simon *so* likes Lou!

'Go on then, what do you think?' he asks, swiftly changing the subject.

40

I frown. 'Of what?'

'Tonight. Bad as you thought it'd be?'

'Worse.'

Simon shrugs. 'Means the revival's going to be even better, then, surely?'

'Surely.'

The party of four's two-hour slot has come to a close. As they drunkenly pull on jackets and make their way out into the night, one of the girls trips over the stage, giggling as she lands on her bum.

'Cheers, guys. G'night.' I give them a wave, quashing the impulse to run over and hug them for being the only people prepared to give us their hard-earned cash.

Apart from one, that is. Moments later, in die-hard Sing It Back tradition, the man at the opposite end of the bar gets to his feet and dusts himself off. He's been here all night, as he is every Saturday, cloaked in the shadows and quietly drinking his Morgan's Spiced. Short and rotund, he has longish wispy brown hair that laps over an elaborate shirt collar. His chest is a great barrel, the buttons straining to hold him inside. His trousers are black leather.

Loaf.

Is this guy still at it? He's been propping up the bar in this borderline-creepy way for as long as I can remember, and from Simon and Jaz's bored reaction, I can tell his habits haven't changed a bit. With a roll of his eyes, Simon goes to clear the table of pint glasses while Jaz programmes the song in – always the same: 'Bat Out of Hell'. Apparently Loaf never buys a full session; this must be a perk for his never-ending custom. I don't want to sound brutal, but this is the sort of perk Sing It

Back could well do without. He'd better make the most of it while it lasts.

It's the sort of perk my ears could do without, too – that's if they're not already leaking blood. While Simon's loading up the dirties I watch, transfixed, as Loaf gallops through the first chorus, slamming his meaty chest with the passion of it, dropping to his knees in a move that comes so close to splitting his trousers I wince. At one point the karaoke machine jams, so it's stuck on 'Bat-ba-batbatbatbat' until it rights itself. Loaf doesn't seem to mind – if anything, it fuels his performance as his body jerks and shudders to the music.

Minutes later, it's over. There's a deafening silence. I feel like we've just come out of a wind tunnel. Jaz's hair looks even more wild than normal, as if she's had an electric shock.

Loaf gets up, straightens his shirt and slides some cash on to the bar. Grabbing his coat, without saying a word, he heads for the door.

'Who *is* that guy?' I ask when he's gone.

Simon shrugs.

'Don't you think it's weird?' I say. 'I mean, that none of us knows anything about him?'

Jaz pops a stick of gum in her mouth. 'Maddie, meet our only regular customer.' She picks up the fifty-pound note. 'S'long as he's not waiting around for change, I don't care who he is.'

6

Livin' On A Prayer

'What about these?' Lou presents a pair of my father's gold MC Hammer-style pantaloons. 'Help the Aged?'

I flop back on the bed. I'm tired, but every time I close my eyes I see Dad dancing to 'U Can't Touch This'. 'We're not chucking anything away,' I say wearily.

'But there's no *room* for your stuff!' Lou puts her hands on her hips, surveying the contents of my parents' wardrobe. 'Seriously, I've never seen so many clothes.'

'Yeah, well, I'll buy one of those storage things. You can get a plastic one for a fiver.'

Lou nods. 'I've got tons of those shoe ladder ones – I'll bring some round.'

I prop myself up on an elbow. 'Thanks, but I'm kind of hoping I won't have to cram all my worldly possessions into a rat-run of teeny-tiny holes.'

Lou sits down on the end of the bed. 'Tell me again why you're doing this?'

It's a week later and I've just moved into my parents' flat. Up till now I've been sharing a place in Camden with some friends from uni (Lou moved to London too late) but recently the place has turned into a glorified squat, what with people's boy-slash-girlfriends living there all the time, so I wasn't too cut-up to leave. I spoke to Mum about it a few days ago. The conversation went something like this:

Mum: 'Darling . . . *crackle spit crackle* [dodgy European pay phone] . . . happening for you?'

Me: 'I can't hear you very well, Mum. Is everything OK?'

Mum: [First part indecipherable] '. . . wonderful . . . *crackle* . . . lost his trousers! . . . Seven hundred, can you believe . . . *crackle* . . . Craig McLachlan's hair!'

Me: 'You keep breaking up on me, Mum. Listen, I'm crashing at yours for a bit to save money, hope that's all right?'

Mum: 'Of course, poppet . . . sensible . . . *crackle* . . . my special mayonnaise?'

Shortly after that we said our goodbyes.

'It's all going to work out fine,' I inform Lou, swinging my legs off the bed and padding into the kitchen. 'I'm not going to sit around on my arse just waiting for my life to happen.' I rummage about in the Sainsbury's carrier she brought round and fish out a bag of Maltesers. 'Thanks for the chocolate therapy,' I say, throwing six in my mouth at once.

'You look tired,' observes Lou, picking her way through the stacked-up cardboard boxes until she reaches the sofa. She tucks her legs up under her and hefts a dog-eared tome from the side table, scanning its bright yellow cover.

'*Business Management for Dummies?*' She shoots me a raised eyebrow.

I shrug. 'I tried to find *How to Take Over Your Mad Parents' Karaoke Bar and Save It From Dereliction for Dummies* but I guess they haven't published that one yet.'

Lou laughs. 'Oh, Maddie.'

I sit next to her, offering her my last Malteser – it's not my last Rolo, but the sentiment's there. She sucks it thoughtfully.

'Why don't you get some sleep,' she says. 'I'll unpack all this.'

It's tempting. I'm so tired I feel like I haven't been to bed in days. Which is sort of true: I've spent the past week drawing up official plans for Sing It Back and revising Mum and Dad's outlandish accounts. Even their budget for the bare necessities is way off! With their current business structure (impressed?), it'd be a miracle if the club still had running water in a month, never mind anything else. I can't have been going to sleep much before three every morning, hoping inspiration might strike in the small hours, trying to find ways of making the numbers add up, and even after that I've been lying awake fretting till the sun comes up.

'Do I look rough?'

Lou nods. 'Yeah. But who cares.'

I pull my hair into a ponytail. 'The costs are terrible,' I mourn.

'You knew that already, didn't you?'

'Not the extent of it.' I bite my lip. 'And, you know, it's one thing to keep the place going, but these plans we've got . . . I just don't see how it can work.'

Lou gets up to make tea. 'Have you sorted the loan?' she calls as she flicks the kettle on.

'I saw the bank yesterday – they're doing the checks now.' I put my head in my hands. 'But even then, Lou, I can't see it happening. The loan might help get the place out of debt but it's not going to make the sort of difference I'm thinking about.'

'Then scrap that,' Lou says reasonably, stirring the tea bags. 'All they wanted you to do was look after it. You don't *have* to do this re-launch thing.'

'I know.' I yawn. 'I just wish there was some other way . . . I know there's a solution out there, if only I could find it.'

Lou comes back in. 'What do the others think?' she asks, putting the tea down in front of me. 'Two sugars – you need it.'

'Thanks.' I take a hot sip. 'Who d'you mean?'

Lou's blonde head dips slightly. 'Oh, just . . . Ruby and that lot.'

I grin. 'If you're asking about Simon, yes, they're all behind it.'

Lou looks at me, wide-eyed. 'I wasn't!'

'Sure.'

'We have been talking a bit online.' She smiles shyly. 'He's really sweet.'

'I know,' I say, looking at her sideways. 'He's a nice guy. You should ask him out.'

'Maddie!'

'What?' I say, my karaoke troubles momentarily forgotten. I'm glad someone else's love life has a pulse – not that I've got time right now for the emotional vampire that is the post-getting-dumped dating process. 'Isn't that what people do?'

'I couldn't possibly,' says Lou primly.

'He likes you, Lou – I can tell. He's just shy, probably thinks you're out of his league.'

'Rubbish,' she announces, but I detect a hint of a smile. She reaches for the biscuit tin. 'I need a HobNob.'

I grin at her. 'Exactly!'

♪

That afternoon I shuffle into Sing It Back, ready to break the bad news. Ruby du Jour, clad in a leopard print jumpsuit and three-inch heels, greets me at the door.

'Sweetie, where've you been?' She gives me a fragrant hug and grabs my hand, leading me into the dank club. 'We've already started thinking about the new decor,' she babbles. 'Jaz has got some *fabulous* ideas off those WAGS. Not that you'd catch *me* sitting around at home all day, waiting for my husband to come home. Those footballers, honest to god, they get paid a fortune – and for what? Did you know Steven Gerrard's favourite meal is macaroni cheese?'

I slip on to one of the bar stools, blinking back fatigue. 'No, I didn't know that.'

The scene at the club breaks my heart a bit – and not for the usual reasons. Jaz and Archie are sitting in one of the mustard booths, scribbling on a piece of paper. The old man's face is aglow with excitement and even Jaz is focused on the task at hand. There's an array of different-coloured pens on the table, and every so often Jaz reaches into her hair to take one out – or put one back, I can't be sure. I wonder if she's got a whole stationery set in there.

'Hey!' she says as I pour myself a Coke. 'Check this out.' She holds up a large piece of cardboard bearing a badly drawn portrait of what I think is meant to be Andre the guinea pig. She's even used gold pen round the edge for a frame. 'I thought we could have these dotted around,' she suggests, 'like those head shots at the hairdresser's. It'll be really unusual – and Andre's got more than enough styles to carry it off.'

The guinea pig himself scuffles across the table, nose twitching as he inspects his portrait, fussy as a connoisseur. He's donning a silk waistcoat and socks. Honestly, what's the point of bothering with a waistcoat if you're not even wearing pants?

'Um,' I say, fiddling with the hem of my denim dress. 'Well, the thing is—'

'Now pay attention, Maddie,' says Ruby, tweezing out a stray false eyelash. 'Archie's got some fantastic concepts for the new drinks menu.' She leans across the back of the booth like a large cat. 'Archie, take it away!'

Archie clears his throat as he produces his own piece of paper, self-consciously showing his efforts. 'Well, I ain't much of an artist . . .'

Unfortunately I have to agree. The concoctions he's outlined, together with illustrations, are more round-the-bend than on-trend. One of them looks like an elaborate prawn cocktail, things sticking violently out of it at all angles,

48

coloured coral-pink – it could be, for all I can tell. As soon as I see the words 'Singapore Sing' I know we're in deep trouble.

'Wonderful, aren't they?' crows Ruby. Archie looks pleased.

'Obviously these are just rough,' Jaz cuts in. 'I was think-ing we could design a billboard, put it up outside, all lit up. Y'know, make a feature of it.'

Ruby nods happily. 'And you should see what Simon's put together for the playlists . . .'

I zone out, letting their proposals wash over me like a great big wave of doom. Andre is looking at me. The guinea pig knows the score. He can see the guilt in my eyes.

And then, in a moment of utter clarity, the first I've had in days, Andre scratches his miniature socks on the table and shuffles backwards, his bare bum wiggling. Crouching over the papers, never once taking his eyes from mine, he does a neat little poo right in the middle of the plans. That's it – I've got to come clean.

'We can't afford it, guys.'

The three of them turn to look at me. There's this awful silence I have to fill, so I jabber on. 'I thought I could raise the cash, but it turns out I can't. It's going to be much more expen-sive than I thought. I'm sorry. Really.' I bow my head. 'The plan's off.'

For a minute nobody says anything. Jaz throws her pen down and darts up from the table, rushing past me. I can't blame her – I'd probably be pissed off at me as well.

Ruby gets up and puts an arm round me. 'Oh, sweetie. It doesn't matter . . .'

A copy of *Spotlight* magazine – the weekly West End theatre journal to which Jaz subscribes – is thrust under my nose. 'I wasn't going to show you this,' she says, breathless, 'but whatever. If we need help, this might be our only chance.'

I frown. Jaz has circled an ad in the classified section in thick red pen.

'What is this?' I ask. Archie and Ruby come to peer over my shoulder.

Jaz can barely contain her excitement. 'Just read it!'

I take a deep breath and scan the words:

ATTENTION ALL LONDON BARS AND CLUBS!!!
ARE YOU STRUGGLING TO MAKE ENDS MEET? DO YOU WISH THERE WAS A FAST, EASY WAY TO MAKE MONEY AND GET BACK ON TOP?

I look up at Jaz. 'Yes,' I say.

She nods frantically. 'Read on! Read on!'

TOOTH & NAIL TV IS LOOKING FOR THE UK'S NEXT BIG REALITY TV SENSATION. DON'T ATTRACT HUNDREDS AT THE WEEKEND – ATTRACT MILLIONS. DON'T DELAY. CALL 020 078910

There's a brief pause while everyone digests this. It's the sort of high-strung, energised pause you get in films before something major is about to happen. Everyone's eyes are on me.

'Reality TV?' I look at Archie, then at Ruby, then at Jaz.

'Whatever that means,' says Archie, grabbing the mag

and inspecting it. Seconds later Ruby whips it from him, only to have it snatched off her by Jaz. Then it's thrust back at me.

'So?' says Jaz excitedly. 'What do you think?'

I read the ad again, then once more. I'm not sure what I think.

Three pairs of eyes are gazing at me: expectant, waiting, full of hope. What I do know is I can't let them down.

'I think it's worth a shot,' I say, beaming. 'What have we got to lose?'

7

Money Money Money

The sun is shining as I make my way down Bond Street on Monday morning, feeling like Melanie Griffiths in *Working Girl*. I'm wearing a black pencil skirt and a pretty sleeveless top, hopefully striking a balance between I Mean Business and Please Don't Ask Me Too Many Questions About Capital Pools. I even dared to raid Mum's jewellery box this morning and found a really cute vintage brooch.

Outside the tube station I double-check the address Evan Bergman's assistant gave me over the phone. Crossing the road, I head down an alley past a health food store.

A gentle breeze is blowing and it feels like summer: I

hope this is a friendly omen – to be honest I'm not quite sure what possessed me to do this. Reality TV? Hmm. I'm not the biggest fan. OK, I am partial to my autumn fix of *The X Factor* – but that's not *actual* reality TV, it's a proper competition that just happens to be on camera. Like *I'm a Celebrity*. And *Strictly Come Dancing*. And *Masterchef*. Oh, and *Britain's Got Talent*. Anyway, forget that. My point is that it's very different watching it than, well, being it. And yet here I am on the way to meet some hotshot telly producer about potentially starring in my own show. What on earth am I doing?

But this could be the only option Sing It Back has. I have to at least give it a chance.

A bit of a walk later and my feet are starting to hurt – I knew I should have changed into these heels when I got here – but then I spot a building that I think *must* be it. It's a modest four-storey townhouse with a white portico, sort of smart and shabby-looking at the same time. It just looks so . . . media.

Sure enough, there's a gold panel to the left of the door which reads TOOTH & NAIL PRODUCTIONS. I press the buzzer.

A gravelly voice comes over the intercom and spits out 'Tooth & Nail' in a way that makes it sound like the name of a teen slasher movie.

'Er, hi,' I say, leaning in. 'I've an appointment with Evan Bergman. Eleven o'clock.'

'Second floor.'

The door clicks open and I step inside. The hall is a vast white empty space, a black cast-iron spiral staircase winding up its middle, precise as a corkscrew. I ascend nearly on tiptoes, the points of my heels threatening to disappear through the ornate grill.

On the second floor a striking brunette is sitting behind reception, cradling a phone to her ear. She's wearing skinny jeans and biker boots, one of which is propped up on the desk. On her T-shirt there's a name tag with a handwritten *ALISON* scrawled across it in black felt tip. She shoots me a jagged look and gestures for me to sit on one of the leather banquettes.

I pretend to flick through a magazine. It's one of those trendy A3 ones consisting entirely of pictures of models wearing bin bags and looking cross. I search in vain for *OK!*.

Alison is nodding and *hmm*ing. When she hangs up she regards me stonily, her eyebrow raised. Clearly not one for talking, then.

'I'm here for Evan Bergman,' I say. 'I spoke to someone downstairs, but I'm not sure who. One of your security guys, he was quite gruff—'

'Actually that was me,' she growls. It's like the girl in *The Exorcist*. I must look alarmed because she adds, 'I'm sick. My throat's killing me.'

She doesn't look all that pleased to be here. 'Maybe you should go home?' I suggest.

Instead she grimaces. 'Boss won't let me.' The last bit catches and then she's coughing in harsh, hacking bursts till she's so red in the face I have to go and pat her on the back. I'm half worried she's going to projectile spew green stuff all down my outfit.

'Thanks,' she snarls. 'Bloody cold.'

'I'm sure he'd understand. You seem really poorly . . .'

Alison shakes her head and glances over her shoulder, presumably to check she's not being overheard. At the end of the corridor is a pair of sliding frosted doors.

'You seem nice,' she whispers hoarsely, 'so off the record, let's just say Evan's not the easiest person to work for.'

'I've never met him.'

Her phone rings and she picks it up. 'Yes?' She looks at me and gives a curt nod. 'Yes, she's here.' Cough, cough. 'I'll send her in.'

Alison hangs up. 'You're about to.'

♪

Evan Bergman is standing at the window with his back to me. He's holding his hands together behind him in the stance of a powerful man surveying his empire – even though the view out his office window is the back of a Burger King car park. Only when he hears the door go does he turn round and extend his hand.

'Maddie Mulhern,' he says, and his voice is smooth as silk, 'welcome. I'm Evan Bergman, Head of Production at Tooth & Nail. It's a great pleasure to meet you.'

The first thing I notice is his hair, which is an unnatural shade of purple-y black and sort of two-tiered, like a springy muffin. It seems to be slipping off the back of his head. I wonder if it's all real. His face is flat and wide and tanned like leather.

'Hello,' I say, trying not to take an instant dislike to him. When I shake his hand it feels soft and cool like raw dough.

Evan smiles at me with crocodile eyes. 'Please, sit down.'

His office is decked out in much the same way as the rest of the building, an exercise in black-and-white minimalism. His own desk and the chair I'm sitting on are made of Perspex, totally see-through, and the implied exposure makes me uncomfortable. The walls are covered in moody shots of New York and I search for a clue to this man's personality – a photo of his wife, child, Rottweiler (for I feel sure if he had a dog, this would be it) – but there's nothing.

Evan's own chair is plush leather. When he sits down it squeaks under his weight.

'Coffee?' he asks.

'No, thanks.'

Another smile. His teeth are capped and pearly white. 'I'm very happy you got in touch, Maddie. You don't mind if I call you that . . . do you?'

I shake my head.

'As you can imagine we've had a flood of applicants since we placed the ad. Let me assure you, this isn't an opportunity that comes along twice.'

I choose my words carefully. 'It's certainly very exciting. I'm sure it'll be wonderful for the right establishment.'

Evan leans forward. 'I suppose you're wondering why I've agreed to meet with you.'

It strikes me as an odd thing to say. 'Haven't you met with everyone?'

Evan laughs, throwing his head back so I can see the roof of his mouth, which is covered in tiny grooves, as if he bites down hard on things.

'Goodness me, no!' he cries. 'Maddie, I'm an extremely busy man . . . No, I *wanted* to speak with you, in fact I made a point of cancelling my morning's meetings – because I believe you have exactly what I'm looking for.'

'I do?'

'Yes.' He sits back and touches the tips of his fingers together like the roof of a house. 'My assistant told me the name of your club.'

There's a loaded pause. 'Right . . .'

The lids of his eyes come down like little hoods. 'Your parents own it, is that correct?'

Ah. Suddenly I see where this is going.

'That's right,' I say. 'But this has nothing to do with Pineapple Mist. Sing It Back is independent – in fact Mum and Dad aren't even here at the moment, they're on tour.'

As soon as the words escape I wish I could take them back. Evan's eyes actually light up.

'Really?' His voice is syrupy.

'Not for long,' I say, fumbling to unpick it. 'I mean, they'll be back soon, obviously—'

'But in the meantime, you're in charge.'

Another pause. Evan's fingers start tapping. He appears deep in thought, and he looks at me so intently and for such a long time that I swear I'm about to start laughing.

'Let's talk about the show,' he decides at last, standing up and clapping his hands together. 'I want to start filming ASAP' – he doesn't say the initials; he says it like 'ay-sap' – 'which means I want my people at the club as early as Friday. I'm not a man for hanging around, as you might already have guessed.'

I sit up straighter. 'Mr Bergman—'

'Evan.'

'—we haven't agreed to anything yet. I was hoping today would give me a better idea of what the proposition entails. It's a big commitment . . .'

'But you did make the phone call?'

I'm slightly baffled. 'Well, yes, but purely on a speculative—'

'There's little time for speculation in TV, Maddie.' The words have an edge of impatience. 'This isn't a go-away-and-think-about-it sort of an offer. Like I said, you'll want to grab this with both hands and hold on tight.'

He's still smiling but the words are hard. I meet his gaze, refusing to feel intimidated. Wait till I tell Lou about this – this guy's got to have a gazillion issues. Starting with the hair.

'Even so, I know the importance of formalities,' Evan says, adopting a softer tone. He perches on the end of his desk, his crotch level with my eyes. 'Think of it like one big happy family: you, the club – and us. Eight weeks, two months . . . a lifetime of success for your parents. And you *do* want that for them, don't you?'

I frown. 'Of course.'

'They're not getting any younger, there's retirement to think about . . .' He lets his words trail off, before resuming with gusto: 'The bottom line is you'll hardly even notice we're there. All you have to do is open your doors and let us document a few bits and pieces' – he says this with a casual wave of his hands, as if this aspect of things is incidental – 'and that's about the size of it. We'll fund the design, the renovations, the plans you have in mind.' Another grin. 'And I'm betting you have plans . . . ?'

I nod, feeling like I'm saying yes to more than the question.

'As I thought.' Evan rubs his hands together, satisfied. 'You're a woman who's going places. Every woman who's going places needs to have a plan.'

I'm not sure what to say to that.

I attempt to put the conversation back on track. 'There's going to be a privacy issue.'

Evan shakes his head, as if I've caught the wrong end of the stick. 'No, you see that's the great beauty of it. You'll carry on with your normal little lives and it won't occur to you to worry about the cameras. I guarantee you'll have better things to do. You'll have a club to run, remember? A very, *very* successful club.'

'Yes, but that's not really—'

'Maddie' – he smirks – 'we promise you a comeback beyond your wildest dreams and we'll deliver it. What else could you want? You must know the saying about looking a gift horse in the mouth.' He fixes me with a potent stare. 'Now don't tell me you're planning to look *me* in the mouth?'

I wonder if I should tell him that I've already looked in his mouth, in fact, and I didn't much like what I saw.

'We're offering to help you – and your parents – resurrect Sing It Back and make stars of you all. Just tell me how good that sounds.' He closes his eyes and breathes in deeply through his nostrils. 'Come on, tell me.'

'Uh . . .'

'Precisely. It's the best thing that could happen to you.' His eyes snap open. 'Isn't it?'

I feel like I'm throwing a Frisbee and it's never coming back. 'The publicity concerns me,' I grind on, beating my way through his nonsense. 'We want your help, but none of us,' I stop, remembering Jaz, 'I mean *most* of us don't want to be stars.'

Evan chuckles and shakes his head, as though I've missed something glaringly obvious.

'No, no, no: the *club* is the star of the show, haven't I made that clear? You'll just be . . . on the fringes. Obviously there'll be a certain level of interest generated in the people running the place, but the fascination will be with its revival. Isn't that what this is about?'

I'm not convinced. 'But it's reality TV – of course it's about the people.'

'Didn't our ad say we were looking for the next big thing?'

I nod.

'Well, then, you've answered your own question.'

I have?

'This is something new,' he goes on, 'it's revolutionary. I guarantee Sing It Back will never have known attention like it.' He returns to his side of the desk and opens a drawer, pulling out a steel-grey folder. He slides it across to me.

'What's this?'

'The contract. All the information, everything you need.' He narrows his eyes and I can tell he's sussing me out. 'You're a woman who likes to mull things over, I respect that.'

I wish he'd stop telling me what kind of woman I am.

He slips me his business card. 'Now I don't normally do this, Maddie, but I like you and I think you like me.'

Er . . . *what?*

'So I'm prepared to do something unprecedented. I'm

prepared to wait,' he glances at his watch, 'until six o'clock this evening.' There's a meaningful pause. 'You're first in a tremendously long queue. I'm sure you'll do the sensible thing.'

He rises, holding out his hand. This time when I take it it's hot and clammy.

'Please don't mention it, Maddie. The pleasure was all mine.'

'Um . . . sure.'

Evan's face looms in as he places his other hand on top of mine, holding it tight.

'Call me when you're ready to say yes.'

8

Love is a Stranger

When I emerge into reception the girl called Alison has gone. There's a young guy with a lip piercing in her place and he tosses me a disinterested nod as I hurry past.

Evan Bergman's folder is heavy in my arms as I pick my way back downstairs. I open it and haul out the bulky contract, holding the file under my chin as I flip through the first few pages. Scanning the general terms and not at all looking where I'm going, I push open the main door and walk straight into someone coming in.

Someone absolutely, totally and utterly to die for.

Words fail me. Until I realise I've spilled his coffee all down his shirt.

'Shit!' I say. 'Oh shit, I'm so sorry. Shit!'

Say something else, Maddie. Anything but 'shit'.

'Shit!'

'It's OK,' he laughs. Wow, he's properly gorgeous. He's the most gorgeous man I've ever seen. Ever.

'I really am sorry,' I gabble, and I know I'm acting like a dick. 'I wasn't looking where I was going.' I attempt to shove the contract back inside its folder and suddenly it seems about a thousand pages long, like bundling some thrashing animal back into its cage.

'Seriously, don't worry about it.' He looks at me and my legs go funny. He's quite a bit taller, with really dark hair and eyes the colour of slate. 'I've got another one upstairs.'

'Another coffee?' As soon as the words come out I know I'm taking my dickish behaviour to a new level of dickdom. 'I mean, otherwise I'll get you another, of course, since it's my fault. I know, I'll go buy you one, it's really no trouble. Where'd you go? What was it? Do you take sugar?'

Shut UP! Shut up shut up shut up!

He grins. He's got really nice teeth. 'Another shirt.'

An image of this man bare-chested isn't what I need right now. 'You work at Tooth & Nail?'

'For my sins.'

I swear I've seen him before. But maybe it's because he resembles fifty male models rolled into one with a splash of Johnny Depp.

'That's a nice pear,' he says, looking at my chest.

63

What? Ugh. I should have known he was too good to be true.

'Are you a fan?' he asks, and then I realise he's talking about the vintage pear-shaped brooch I pilfered from Mum's collection this morning. The fruit itself is modest, about the size of a Cadbury's Creme Egg, and made of silvery wire mesh. It's been set on a plain white square.

'Oh,' I say, flustered. Then I'm confused. 'A fan of what?'

'M People.'

I'm horrified. '*M People?*'

He nods, serious. 'Yeah, that's one of their album covers.'

For a second I'm speechless. 'It's *what*?'

'I used to work in music journalism,' he explains. 'That was quite an iconic look in the nineties, very distinctive.'

I want the ground to open up and swallow me. Thanks, Mum, I mean it. Thanks. Really, this couldn't be better.

'Yeah, it set a new trend in cover art,' he says. 'Less is more, you know.'

'It did?' I ask in a small voice. A Heather Small voice. *Arrrrggghhh!*

'You must really like them,' he says, and there's a twinkle in his eye that suggests he's trying not to laugh.

'I most certainly do *not*!' I puff.

'Not a big fan myself,' he muses, 'though I guess I can see it.'

I look down at the sorry brooch. 'It's not mine,' I say defensively, and even though it's the truth it sounds like the biggest lie I ever told. 'It's my mum's.' Could I *be* any more tragic?

'Well anyway,' he says, gesturing to his damp shirt.

Clutching the folder to my chest, I muster as much

confidence as I can. 'Yes, of course,' I sound ridiculously formal, 'I mustn't keep you. And listen, I'm sorry.'

He waves away my apology. 'It's no big deal, really.' Then he smiles at me again and he's got these lovely crinkly bits at the sides of his eyes.

There's a fraction of a second where neither of us moves. Just a fraction of a fraction, so that I'm not entirely sure it's there, before he moves past me and disappears inside.

I think I might have just fallen in love.

♪

So what if he thinks I'm an M People fan? It's not that bad, is it?

Focus, Maddie, I tell myself as I flip through the terms of Evan Bergman's contract, occasionally pausing to pick disinterestedly at my sandwich.

Yes, it's bad. It's very bad.

I'm sitting at a table in Vocalise, a neighbouring karaoke bar just round the corner from my parents'. I couldn't face returning to the club straight after my meeting at Tooth & Nail – there'd be way too many questions waiting there that I didn't have the answers to – so decided I'd stop off to a) scope out the competition, b) get through Evan's T&Cs without distraction, and c) give my wibbly legs a break after they (just about) carried me from my disastrous encounter with the World's Most Handsome Man.

But the contract's a blur. Every time I get to grips with one of the clauses it starts swimming before my eyes, and by the time I reach the end I realise I've just played out a mini fantasy involving me emerging from Tooth & Nail and *not* spilling coffee on him and *not* appearing to suffer from Tourette's and *not* wearing that stupid bloody brooch, and instead he maybe spills coffee on me and there's this moment where he awkwardly dabs at my pretty sleeveless top while thinking how beautiful I am and wishing he had the nerve to look me in the eye and maybe find the courage to ask me out . . .

So then I have to read the whole clause again.

'Can I get you anything else?' A girl with cropped dark hair and masses of eye make-up takes my practically untouched plate.

'No, thanks,' I say, wondering where my appetite has gone. Normally a crisis calls for some serious cake intake, but the combination of my unnerving meeting with Evan and my even-more-unnerving meeting with Mystery Man has me feeling a little sick. I'm desperate to call Lou, but I know she's at Simply Voices today – our Monday shifts never cross.

Nevertheless I'm impressed that Vocalise has table service. And it's not the only thing that's streaks ahead of Sing It Back. Even at three o'clock on a weekday afternoon they've got a handful of punters in – from their suits and shirts I guess they're on some kind of corporate team-building exercise – and the karaoke isn't sounding all that bad. This might be less to do with the party's singing ability and more to do with the state-of-the-art machines, spanking-new microphones and – unless my ears deceive me, as Cher's 'Believe' ramps up – is that a vocoding device? Phew.

The whole look and feel of the place is miles better, too. It's really cohesive, everything considered, everything intentional. Not like Mum and Dad's, where the overall impression is of something designed on a let's-throw-everything-at-it-and-see-what-happens basis.

The Subject agrees to all filming in relation to the Club . . . consents to cooperate fully in securing necessary footage . . . entrusts the Producers autonomy in the editorial process . . . approves creative direction . . .

I stir the twizzle stick in my lemonade. It doesn't *really* matter if he thinks I'm an M People fan. There's worse things . . . aren't there? It's not like I'd unwittingly accessorised with a ruby tooth and masqueraded as Mick Hucknall. Or said I liked Chumbawumba.

Camera crew will be awarded access to the Club and the Subject's professional space on a daily basis . . . the Club will be filmed and edited forty-eight hours prior to broadcast . . .

No, it's fine. He's probably forgotten that part of our exchange already. I mean, the rest of it wasn't a total car crash . . . was it?

In accordance with the terms of this contract, the Subject grants her permission . . .

I'm trying to zone out a particularly harsh number by Anastasia. I must have read this through a million times already.

I check the time on my phone: a little over two hours till Evan's deadline.

I'm torn. Half of me, the half I recognise, says no to the whole thing. It's a disaster waiting to happen. I don't know what I'm letting myself – and my staff – in for. It could all go horribly wrong and Sing It Back could be ruined for ever. Most of all, I hate the thought of being in front of the cameras – it's just not me. On top of that, Evan Bergman left me feeling distinctly uneasy: there's something about him I just don't trust.

But then there's the other half. Seeing Vocalise in its week-day glory, never mind what it must be like on a Saturday night, brings home the scale of the mountain Sing It Back has to climb. I don't know if we can do it without Tooth & Nail's help.

The singing party launches into a song by Four Non Blondes. Right, that's my cue to get out. Quickly.

Shuffling up my papers, I pay the bill and exit into the bustle of Frith Street, where the sky is looking dangerously like rain. I resolve to return to the club and talk it through with the others. After all, this isn't just my decision to make: it's everyone's.

Minutes later I'm fumbling with my keys outside Mum and Dad's. The SING IT BA K sign, a miserable rat-grey tubing in daylight hours, greets me like a sad dog that's been kept indoors by itself all day.

The club is shrouded in darkness. I kick my heels off.

'Simon?' I call. 'Jaz?'

No one's here yet. I switch on the lights and the ones still in operation flicker reluctantly to life, accompanied by an awful industrial *bzzz*. I slide into a booth and dig out the contract, as if staring at it some more is going to provide me with answers. Digging my mobile from my handbag, I dial Lou's number. It goes to answer phone and I consider leaving a message, before realising that by the time she gets it and rings back I'll already have gone over Evan's deadline.

I look at the clock on the wall. It's Gary Numan's face, pale and staring, a product of Dad's 'experimental art' phase (at least the 'mental' part rings true). Five-forty.

If only I hadn't run into Mystery Man – it's completely messed with my head. I haven't been able to focus properly all afternoon and it's all because of that stupid conversation. I've got to forget it – it's not like I'm ever going to see him again.

My gaze turns to the contract. Though he did say he worked at Tooth & Nail . . .

No, Maddie. That is the worst possible reason to get involved. It's not even a reason.

Suddenly there's a colossal BOOM! and one of the karaoke machines roars to life. I'm closer than I've ever been to wetting myself when I remember this is the one we've been having problems with lately. Otherwise I'd think we were being haunted by a poltergeist.

A Peter Andre-loving poltergeist, it turns out, as the opening bars of 'Mysterious Girl' settle into their stride.

With a deep sigh I get up and make my way over to the source of the noise. I punch some buttons in an attempt to kill it and there's a brief moment of reprieve when the thing cuts out, before the screen announces its next offering: 'I Wanna Sex You Up' by Color Me Badd.

'No!' I howl, furiously tapping the controls. 'Oh *god.*'

After I've tried every single combination of buttons I can think of, it's still going. I head behind the bar, searching for instructions, anything that's going to tell me how to kill the bloody thing. I call Simon but his phone's switched off.

'Bollocks!' It's on its third cycle now – it's only gone and *jammed*.

As I'm engaging in a last-ditch attempt to find an 'Off' button (why don't more things have 'Off' buttons? It'd make things so much simpler), I feel something cold tap my left foot. And again. My toes start to feel a little wet.

I look up to the ceiling, and a cool drop of water splodges bang in the centre of my forehead. It trickles past my hairline and into my ear.

Great. Now we've got a leaky roof.

The bulbs above me splutter and crackle. For a second they cut out completely and I'm left in the dark, alone with Color Me Badd, wanting to sex me up.

As soon as the lights are back, I grab my wallet and rifle through it.

It's three minutes to six. I fish out Evan's card.

After two rings, he picks up.

'Hello, Maddie.' I can hear he's unsurprised. 'You're just in time.'

'Good.' I take a deep breath. 'Because you've got yourself a deal.'

9

Causing a Commotion

I wake the following morning to the sound of someone hammering on the door. I'm in the middle of a dream where I'm being chased through the swimsuit section at M&S by Evan Bergman. I *know* it's Evan, even though I can't see him, but every time I turn round he's changed into Simon Le Bon.

Now he's calling my name. Except it sounds more like a woman's voice . . .

'Maddie?'

Bang bung bang. I open my eyes a crack.

'Maddie, are you in there?'

Yawning, I surface from the dream and check the time. It's barely past eight. Throwing off Mum and Dad's silky zebra print duvet cover (OK, but at least it's not a water bed), I pad out to the living room and open the door. It's my parents' neighbour and good friend Davinia. She's a professional socialite and gets photographed occasionally for being a friend of some minor royal, but if you ask her what she does for a living, she'll tell you she's a jazz singer. Davinia's been here nearly as long as my parents and is the perfect person to live next door – I can't imagine who else would put up with all the warbling.

'Maddie, I've been out here for ages!' she exclaims. 'What's going on?' Even at this hour, Davinia still looks immaculate. Her hair's wound up in a chic turban and she's wearing a strident shade of red lipstick that matches her floral Cath Kidston dressing gown. There are little wads of cotton wool between her freshly painted toenails.

I rub my eyes. 'What do you mean, "What's going on?"?'

'I *mean*,' she says, exasperated, 'there are people outside with cameras, lots of them. They're asking for you.'

'What?'

'Go and see for yourself. They've been here since seven.' She adjusts the turban with manicured nails. 'I ignored them at first, but then some man put his thing through the letter-box.'

'His *thing*?'

'You know – those big grey cotton buds they use for sound.'

I push past her, fleeing down the stairs in my Fido Dido pyjamas.

'You could have warned me!' Davinia sings from behind. 'I'm not nearly ready for my TV debut! Have you won a competition or something?'

I fling open the door. The first thing I notice is that I'm staring into the eye of a great big camera.

'What the hell is going on?' I cry, outraged. 'Turn that thing off!'

The camera lowers and I see a face I recognise. Alison, the girl from Tooth & Nail reception.

'What are you doing here?'

She scuffs her biker boots on the ground. 'Evan told us to get here – he's late.' Her voice is still scratchy but it's definitely better since yesterday.

'But what are you *doing* here? I mean, what's all this?' I gesture round at the equipment. 'You can't be filming already – we haven't even signed the contract yet.'

'Evan told us it was a done deal.'

My mouth falls open. 'Well, I guess,' I splutter, 'but nothing's been . . . formalised.'

'What needs formalising?'

I struggle. 'I'm not sure . . . Forms?'

'Forms.'

'I don't know!' I look to the other faces. 'Who are they?'

Alison rests the camera on her shoulder. 'This is Toby,' she says, 'first assistant director.'

A ginger guy with thick black-rimmed glasses and a nice smile leans in to shake my hand. Dazed, I accept it.

'This is Freddie, he's a runner.' Freddie can't be more than twenty. He's got an innocent look about him and floppy brown hair a bit like Lawrence's.

'And Nathan,' she finishes, nodding at a skinny guy with a lank ponytail and shifty eyes, 'our sound guy.'

'Hi,' grunts Nathan, chewing gum loudly.

'Did you just put your boom through my letterbox?'

'Beg yer pardon?'

'And I'm one of your camera ops,' says Alison.

I frown. 'I thought you were a receptionist.'

She rolls her eyes. 'I'm whatever Evan wants me to be . . .'

There's an awkward silence, during which Freddie looks at Nathan, Nathan looks at Toby, Toby looks at Alison – a touch dejectedly, I think – and Alison looks at the floor.

'Anyway,' says Toby, 'Evan wanted to move things forward. All right if we come in?'

'Er . . .' I check behind me. Davinia's still at the top of the stairs, excitedly mouthing something I can't make out. 'I'm not too happy about this, to be honest. I'd rather talk to Evan.'

'Aw, we've been waiting ages,' moans Nathan.

'That's not my fault,' I say. 'I didn't ask you to come.'

'Yeah, but we're here now . . .' God, he's sulky. If I didn't know better I'd say I had a bunch of moody teenagers at my door, not a cutting-edge fly-on-the-wall documentary crew.

'There he is!' cries Alison, pointing down the street, and it's the first time I've seen her even remotely enthusiastic.

I peer round the door. Sure enough, the big producer himself is strutting like a cockerel in our direction. He's wearing jeans and an open-necked coral shirt, exposing a triangle of tan-leather peppered with sparse chest hairs. The shirt is loosely tucked in and there's an impressive crocodile-skin belt on show. His hair is as bizarre as I remember.

Evan's arrival has an instant effect. Toby, clearly the authority figure in this motley crew, shoves his hands in his pockets and patiently awaits direction. Nathan removes the gum from his mouth and flicks it to the ground. Freddie keeps clearing his throat, as if he's too nervous to speak but, in the unlikely event that he is required to speak, he doesn't want to fluff his lines. Alison is the only one who doesn't appear uneasy – instead she looks positively . . . elated. That's strange – she was hardly his number one fan yesterday.

But Evan's all business.

'Maddie,' he pronounces, storming past the others and seizing my hand. 'It begins here.'

'Um, Evan,' I lower my voice, noticing Alison's miffed expression, 'could we have a word? You've caught me a little off-guard. I wasn't expecting you so soon.'

Evan gives a winning smile. 'Fear not, my little star. We're not filming anything today.'

'We're not?' Toby looks confused.

Evan doesn't bother turning round. 'Absolutely not – we wouldn't dream of putting you out. We just want to come and have a look around, get a feel for the place. OK with you?'

I suddenly remember I'm wearing my pyjamas. And shit, it's Tuesday: I'm due at Simply Voices in half an hour.

'Fine,' I say reluctantly, standing back to let them in. I hear Davinia rush back inside her flat and slam the door, the naughty child listening at the top of the stairs.

The crew bustle past. 'It's the door on the left,' I say, guiding them through. Evan brushes close to me and he smells of old mahogany furniture.

'Hang on a sec,' I say, 'let me grab the keys.' I take the steps two at a time and emerge seconds later with a bundle of metal trinkets in the shape of bass clefs and musical instruments. Hidden somewhere among them is access to Sing It Back.

'I should warn you it's a bit of state down there,' I say apologetically as I unlock the door. 'I don't even know if the lights are working.'

'Perfect!' says Evan, rubbing his hands together.

'I've got to make a couple of phone calls,' I tell him, mounting the stairs. 'I'll be with you in a minute, help yourself to coffee.'

Upstairs I ring Jennifer at Simply Voices.

'You'll have to get someone to cover for you,' she says, brusquely efficient, after I explain. 'We haven't seen enough of you lately, Maddie.'

'I know,' I admit, grabbing a clean towel out the airing cupboard, 'I'm really sorry. Things have been hectic since Mum and Dad went. I'll be in tomorrow – I promise.'

Minutes later I'm speaking to Lou.

'You've done *what*?' she cries, horrified.

'I know, I know.' I'm breathless after a breakneck summary of my meeting with Evan. 'But it's a good opportunity. And I said I was looking for a solution, didn't I?'

'Not this one!'

'Look, I didn't have much choice. It was all Peter Andre's fault.'

'What's Peter Andre got to do with it? And why didn't you call me?'

'I tried, you didn't pick up! Look, I'll explain everything

later.' I pad into the bathroom. 'Can you come over tonight? I'm getting the others round as well. Once I've been through the up-sides I promise you'll see it makes sense.' I cross my fingers behind my back, praying it's the truth. If I do a good enough job convincing them, I might start to feel convinced myself.

There's a pause. 'The others'll be there?'

'Yes.' I raise my eyes heavenward. 'All of them.' Then I remember Lou's not the only one with a ginormous crush. Without warning Mystery Man pops into my head – those eyes; that smile. 'I've got loads to tell you.'

'Fine.' Big sigh. 'So I guess you want me to cover for you?'

'Do you mind?'

She lets me hang, but I know she's going to say yes and I owe her one.

'Fine. But you owe me one.'

I flick on the shower. 'You got it. Love you.'

♪

Downstairs, Evan is looking decidedly like the cat that got the cream.

'This is wonderful,' he purrs, running his hands over the bar as though we're in a Porsche showroom and it's the paint-work on his dream car. 'It's just perfect.'

I sip my coffee. 'I wouldn't go that far,' I say, nodding to where Alison's trying to programme a song into one of the machines, which, after my efforts last night, has finally given up the ghost. 'In fact I'd say we were rock bottom.'

'But that's *why* you're so perfect.' He flashes me a smile.

I return it, wishing I could like him a bit more.

77

'Just sign here.' Slick as a snake, he unscrews the lid from a shiny racing-green fountain pen.

I look down to the contract between us, the dotted line awaiting my signature. Quickly I scribble my name, before I can change my mind. I've already changed my mind about fifty times this morning – and then changed it back again – so it feels a bit like tossing a coin.

'Whoa, this stuff is *old*,' announces Alison, flipping through our song lists. Freddie points at something and they both laugh.

'Yeah, we're working on some updates.' I turn round on my stool, feeling defensive. Sing It Back might well be a dump, but it's still *our* dump. 'I was thinking we could run some theme nights,' I suggest to Evan, 'you know, shake things up a bit.'

'We'll look after all that,' he says dismissively, easing the signed contract back into its leather wallet. 'The club's going to be unrecognisable when we've finished with it.'

Nathan, slumped in a booth, snorts. He mumbles something that sounds like 'It better be' and I decide then that I really don't like him.

Toby comes over. 'When we getting started, boss?' He pulls up the stool next to mine.

'The first show will go out in three weeks,' says Evan. 'First and last shows of the series will be broadcast live.'

I'm shocked. 'Three *weeks*? *Live?*'

Evan slugs back his coffee and I'm amazed he doesn't burn himself. 'This was always going to be a fast project,' he explains, 'I've got everything we need already in place. Kicking off with a live show will do wonders for publicity.'

Seeing my worried face, he continues, 'There won't be anything extra for you to do – just run the bar as normal. We'll have a presenter touring the place, showing people at home what's what, then after that the fun part: our cameras get free roam behind the scenes. The viewers will love it.'

'So we can get moving pretty quick?' Toby pushes at the nose of his glasses, a nervous habit I've seen him indulge in several times.

Evan pats his hair. 'Just as soon as I've made some preliminary changes.'

I look between them. 'Preliminary changes?'

'For starters, there's all the structural work.' Evan scans the walls. 'Your electrics are down and we're at risk of flood if we don't patch that up quick.' He nods to the damp mottling on the ceiling where all the water came in yesterday. 'Then I want karaoke machines that work – it's important we get as much dreadful singing as we can, the punters love a spot of ritual humiliation.' I expect him to laugh, but he says this without a trace of humour.

'Following that, a little brush-up on the interior,' he continues, and Toby nods obediently, 'just enough to bring the place to life.'

'But if the whole point is to chart our resurgence,' I ask, 'why do any work at all?'

Evan's words are brutal. 'First, what you've got here is something pretty nondescript. It's got potential, but as it is it won't get anyone excited. We've got to . . . embellish certain aspects, make a real statement. The fouler it looks on opening night, the better and more tasteful the contrast at the end of the series – we'll get stylists in to see to that over the eight-week period, it won't interfere with the club's opening.' He grins, but it doesn't quite reach his eyes. 'And second, Maddie, your parents are at serious risk of contravening a catalogue of Health and Safety laws. If I weren't on your side I could quite happily report you.'

Somehow I don't doubt that for a second.

There's an uncomfortable silence, which Toby fills. 'If we want Sing It Back to look the part, we have to help it along a bit,' he clarifies, his manner somewhat gentler than Evan's. 'Think of it like dressing a stage, or putting on make-up: all we're going to do is work with what's already there. The difference at the end will make it all worthwhile.' He gives me an apologetic smile.

Alison and Freddie select a Kylie number. It launches at deafening volume and I realise I forgot to tell them that the volume control's duff, too. Nathan, moody in his booth, clamps his hands over his ears and yells something obscene.

I turn to Toby. I have to shout to be heard over the noise.

'So hang on – if you're the first assistant, who's the director?'

The men exchange a brief look, but I can't work out what it means.

'Well?'

'Nick Craven,' says Evan finally.

I frown. 'Why do I know that name?'

Toby clears his throat. 'Nick used to work in serious documentary, but then . . .' Another glance at Evan, as if for approval. 'You remember the Rebecca Ascot affair?'

'I don't think so . . .'

'It was all over the papers,' says Toby. 'His career's not been the same since.' He shrugs. 'That's what you get for jumping into bed with a married woman, I guess.'

'The romance went public?'

'Sadly for him, yes. And for his future in TV. Rebecca was the wife of Pritchard Wells, Head of Commissioning at Channel 7.'

'Oh dear.'

'Exactly.'

I shake my head. 'So why is he working with us?'

Evan cuts in, smooth as a knife through butter. 'He's a good director,' he states – a little robotically, I think – 'needs a break. I'm not about to kick a guy when he's down.'

'As long as he doesn't try it on with anyone here,' I pronounce, aware I sound stuffy. 'I can tell you now, he won't have any luck.'

I'm uneasy: the idea of Evan Bergman playing Mr Nice Guy and helping out this man – or anyone, for that matter – doesn't quite ring true. Plus I'm not sure I like the sound of this Nick Craven, whoever he is. His implied friendship or connection to Evan unnerves me, especially if the two are heading up the project together. Something tells me I'm going to have quite enough to deal with already.

Evan takes another gulp of his drink, watching me over the rim of his cup with that reptilian gaze. 'Don't you worry about that,' he says.

♪

'Ooh I can't wait, I can't wait!' Jaz is dancing in circles and flapping her arms. She could actually be in danger of taking off, given the number of feathers sticking out of her hair. 'We're all going to be *famous*!'

It's early evening and I've called everyone over to Sing It Back to break the big news. Evan and his crew ended up staying for most of the day, drawing up targets, sketching out ideas, even calling up repair men, so I barely had time to order take-away pizza before the others showed up.

'Do you really think so?' asks Ruby du Jour, her eyes glittering. Well, she's *almost* Ruby du Jour – clearly the excitement had her rushing over here so quickly she forgot to put her wig on straight. Then, in a hushed voice, 'We're going to be celebrities?'

'Hang on,' I cut in, 'it's important we get this straight.' I look at Simon and Lou when I say this, because they've been the ones who've barely uttered a word since arriving. 'The impression I get from Evan is that we can make as much of our involvement as we like – the show's emphasis is strictly the club.'

'Fame never 'elped anyone,' interjects Archie, 'it'll make mugs of us all. I just want t'see this place busy again.'

'Which is exactly why we're doing it,' I say, pushing the rest of my pizza across the booth to Simon, who shakes his head.

'Is it?' he asks. 'I mean, this is going to have a serious impact on everyone.'

'Oh, lighten up, Si,' says Jaz, leaning across the back of the booth and ruffling his mop of hair. 'Take a risk for once. If you don't like it, Maddie can fill your shoes in a second.'

'Nobody's quitting, surely!' exclaims Ruby, hands flying to her face.

I raise my own hands. 'That brings me to the most important thing,' I say. I've thought long and hard about this, and it only seems fair. 'If anyone's uncomfortable with any aspect of the deal, there's no shame whatsoever in ducking out. The show's only on for two months and I guarantee you'll have your job back at the end of it. My priority is that everyone's happy.'

A short silence follows. Jaz reaches over Simon's shoulder and takes a slice of Double Pepperoni. 'Well, I'm happy,' she declares. 'And there's no way *I'm* walking. This is the best thing that's ever happened to us!'

'Or the worst,' says Lou. I shoot her a puzzled look and mouth, 'What's up?' but she quickly looks away.

'Neither am I,' says Simon. 'I like my job too much. And besides,' he smiles at me, mustering confidence, 'we're a team, aren't we? And every team has to put trust in its leader.'

'Hear hear!' Ruby adjusts her wig. 'Now, this calls for a celebration.'

'Yes!' squeaks Jaz, hauling up a reluctant Simon and dragging him over to the bar. 'Archie, why don't you try out some of those new cocktails? I for one could do with a *very* alcoholic drink.'

Archie rolls his eyes, but he indulges in a private little smile and I can tell he's secretly flattered. He shuffles up to join them.

'God, wait till you see this,' I say, scooting round to Lou's side of the booth.

Lou's playing with a pizza crust. 'What?'

'Archie's cocktails – they're mental.'

'Hmm.'

I turn to her, concerned. 'What's the matter?'

She's breaking the crust into tiny pieces. 'Nothing,' she says. She's a terrible liar.

'Come on, I'm going to get it out of you eventually.'

Lou makes a face and I see what's coming. 'I just don't get why you're doing this, Maddie,' she says. 'It seems really foolish. And not like you at all.'

I sit back, a tiny bit offended. 'I already explained,' I say. 'What's not to get?'

She shrugs.

'Seriously, Lou, it's our last option. I couldn't turn it down.'

'Hmm.'

'Look,' I snatch the crusts off her and chuck them in the box, 'I know it's the sort of thing I would have sniffed at a month ago. But that was a month ago, and this is now.' I pause. 'And maybe I'm sick of being the safe, reliable, *boring* daughter of my exciting, extrovert parents. It's time I took my own risks, see what that feels like for once.'

'You're not boring,' she says. 'And there's nothing wrong with being safe and reliable.'

'Maybe not. But I can't take the dreary road my whole life.' I laugh drily. 'Isn't that why Lawrence dumped me?'

'Lawrence is a wanker,' she says, and she catches my eye and we share a smile. 'Just as long as you know what you're letting yourself in for. I don't want to see you get shafted. This Evan guy sounds like a weirdo.'

'Yeah.' I rest my chin on my hands. 'But I'm hoping it's eccentric genius.'

'Maybe.' Lou glances over my shoulder to where Jaz and Simon are nattering at the bar.

'Imagine what he'd say to all this,' I muse.

She bites her lip, pulling her attention back to me. 'Who?'

'Lawrence.'

'Forget him,' she says, waving her hand. Then she grins at me wickedly. 'Haven't you got this other guy to think about?' As soon as Lou showed up tonight I dragged her off to tell her the details of my encounter with Mystery Man. I'm kind of hoping I'll run into him again. I mean, Evan's got to invite me back to Tooth & Nail at some point, hasn't he?

'I think I well and truly blew my chance there,' I say, and I only say it so that Lou can reassure me that's not the case.

'I'm sure that's not the case.' She peers over my shoulder once more. 'Maybe he found you charming? You know, in a kooky sort of way?'

'"Kooky"?'

'You never know.'

'What – after he'd lanced his third-degree burns and got "Moving On Up" out his head?'

She cringes. 'When you put it like that . . .'

I laugh, deciding to see the funny side. I've got better things to occupy my time than stressing about some bloke I'll probably never see again.

'Come on.' I grab Lou's hand and tug her up to join the others, just in time for Archie to thrust an extreme-looking Singapore Sing into her hands. Simon catches Lou's eye and smiles.

I look round the club. Jaz has put on The Human League and is trying to teach Andre the guinea pig to do the running man. Ruby du Jour is waving a cigarette around and lecturing a baffled-looking Archie about the bunions she's contracted from her stilettos. Simon's pretending to read a book, but keeps stealing glances at my best friend.

I'm not going to let them down.

For the first time in absolutely ages, it feels like I'm on to something. It's going to be brilliant. It has to be.

10

Under Pressure

Two weeks later, I'm hurrying through Soho in paint-splashed dungarees and a battered pair of Converse. God, I just *had* to get out of there.

I've just abandoned the Sing It Back renovations. I did feel a little like a general deserting her troops – Simon, gasping under the weight of a lighting stand, gave me a particularly worried look as he spotted me slipping out the door – but honestly, I've had a whole fortnight of this. One more minute of Evan Bergman yapping orders in my ear and I'd have bottled myself with a watermelon Bacardi Breezer.

We're days from live opening night and the past two

weeks have been a whirlwind. Everyone's been doing their bit at the club. As well as the crew from Tooth & Nail and my own staff, we've had painters and decorators in, builders, plumbers, electricians, engineers, interior designers, stylists, event planners, organisers, on-site developers, journalists, local news reporters . . . By this stage I wouldn't be surprised if a travelling circus had shown up, complete with bearded lady and human cannonball – maybe it could have caught Evan unawares while he was bent over tending lovingly to his mirror balls.

I turn into Berwick Street and pull out the list of items Evan thrust in my hand. There's a whole bunch of stuff to get in place before Friday. He wanted Freddie to run out but I managed to win myself a brief reprieve by remembering the name of a local supplier Mum and Dad have used in the past – Evan's been sourcing all sorts of fancy contractors for the new karaoke software, but there's no reason why we can't support small businesses for the accessories we need. Claiming I'd be only half an hour, I shot out the door before anyone could stop me. I feel like I haven't seen the real world in years.

Mixer amps – OK, I know what they are. *1000-watt moving head smoke machines* – Jaz suggested bubbles but according to Evan they're too passé. Unlike smoke machines, obviously. *Multi-coloured LED siren strobes* – I thought they were the ones you get on top of police cars before Evan smugly corrected me, something he seems to be fond of these days.

Since his arrival at Sing It Back, Evan's been on me like a rash – my own personal bout of psoriasis. He's taken over the club as if he owns it, and while I've got to remember that this is what I signed up for – that to a degree I must relinquish control – he's just so . . . dictatorial. He's been in my face for so many consecutive hours now that I see him when I close my eyes in bed (not ideal), and hear his officious bark in my sleep. I'm hoping he'll back off once filming starts, but somehow I doubt that.

Peeling off into a side road, I spot the retailer I'm looking for. I've never set foot in this place before, but I've heard Mum and Dad talk about it loads. There's a sign out front consisting of jaunty letters bobbing along the straight black lines of a musical stave. It reads: **ROCK AROUND THE CLOCK**. I hope it's got the kit I need: if this turns out to be a failed mission it'll totally look like I pulled a fast one.

There's a faded CLOSED notice in the window.

I check the time. It's midday – so much for rocking around the clock. Maybe the owner's on an early lunch. I peer in the foggy glass and can just about make out the cash desk, behind which sits a figure of indeterminate sex. It appears to be reading a magazine.

Gently I tap on the door. The bulky outline doesn't move, and for an awful moment I fear I've stumbled across a gruesome crime scene: some maniacal axe-murderer so desperate for a classic Gibson ES-335 that he nicked off with the goods and left a propped-up corpse slumped behind the till.

But then it moves, and even though I can't see its face I feel sure it's looking directly at me. Embarrassed, I back away.

Seconds later the door opens.

I can't help my reaction. I'm genuinely surprised. It's . . .

'*Loaf?*'

The man looks at me blankly. 'Sorry, what?'

I wonder if too much time at Sing It Back has started to play tricks on me. 'You're . . .'

He shakes his head. 'I'm . . . ?'

'You own this place?'

'And you own Sing It Back,' he counters. 'I know you – you're Rick and Sapphy's daughter.'

I nod. Much as I might dislike the fact, Loaf and I are chained together by an unbreakable bond: seeing now how dead his shop is, as dodgy old music establishments go we've got to have two of the very worst.

'Can I help you?' he asks. He's wearing his customary attire of black leather slacks and a frilly white shirt, his wispy brown hair creeping over the collar. He appears entirely without shame, as though I've never witnessed his frenzied alter-ego performing 'Bat Out of Hell' on a Saturday evening. Come to think of it, he must have missed us this past fortnight.

'I hope so.' I pull myself together. 'Are you open?'

He points to the CLOSED sign. The nail on his thumb is unsettlingly long, and there's a heavy gold signet on his little finger. 'What does it look like?'

I fold my arms. 'But you're here, aren't you?'

'I'm eating my lunch.'

'You shouldn't have let me in, then.'

'You shouldn't have been peering through the window.'

I sigh. 'Look, do you want our custom or not?'

He seems to consider it. Judging by the level of activity in the place I can't imagine he's inundated with the same offer every day.

'Come on then,' he says, stepping back to let me pass.

Inside there's a musty, though not unpleasant, smell, and it's bigger than I first imagined. An impressive array of instruments – guitars, keyboards, saxophones – backs into another, wider room housing an assortment of drum kits. Once upon a time this must have been spectacular, but everything has the air of having been left untouched too long, like the stillness you get in an unoccupied house. It might be the light streaming through the window, but every surface appears to be covered in dust, the lids of once-gleaming pianos dotted with fingerprints.

Loaf resumes his position behind the cash desk, where there's a greasy Subway wrapper paper-weighted by half a chicken roll. 'I suppose you've come to kit out Sing It Back for your *television debut*,' he says, delivering this last part with contempt.

I lean my elbows on the counter. 'This is what I need,' I say, producing Evan's list.

'Do your parents know about this?' he asks, taking a bite of his sandwich.

'About what?' As if I haven't the faintest clue what he's talking about.

'About Tooth & Nail.'

I put the inventory down in front of him. 'Do you have any of this or should I go elsewhere?'

He's eyeing me solemnly. 'You should be careful.'

I wait for him to elaborate, but he doesn't. Instead he feeds the straw into the top of a Capri Sun and slurps the entire thing in one noisy go, in a way that reminds me of this alien film I once saw where they all went about sticking rubbery antenna into people's heads and sucking their brains out.

'Why's that?'

'You don't know what you're letting yourself in for.'

I fight exasperation. 'It's OK,' I tell him, 'I've had that from everyone already. Rest assured this wasn't something I went into lightly.'

Loaf hesitates. 'Just watch your back, that's all I'm saying.'

'I fully intend to.'

He nods. 'Good. Because things might not be . . . quite what they seem.'

OK, this guy's *weird*. He's like the mad portentous garage owner you get in horror films set in the deep south, the one who tries to warn you about the local population of inbreds.

How on earth do my parents know him? I always thought Loaf was just some random who got drunk at the end of the bar. If only I could speak to them about it . . . but then how do I explain what I'm doing at Rock Around the Clock in the first place?

Dad phoned yesterday. We've been in touch several times since the deal with Tooth & Nail was finalised, and each time my omission of this glaring development has proved harder to conceal than the last. It's not that they're asking difficult questions – as far as the club goes I'm telling them everything's ticking over as normal – but I hate deceiving them . . . fibbing, faking, little white lies; whatever you want to call it, I'm not telling the truth.

I'm assuring myself it's because I want the surprise to be even greater when they return, but in truth I'm bricking it about their reaction. They left me in charge, yes, but they didn't ask me to broadcast their pride and joy to the entire nation. If it all goes wrong, what then? And the longer I keep it from them, the trickier it becomes to just drop it into conversation: *Oh, hang on, Dad – before you go, I wanted to let you know I've agreed to a deal with a TV company. Brilliant, isn't it? Not a big issue, we'll only be on telly every night of the week. That's right, I basically signed Sing It Back into someone else's hands. Ha ha. Oh yes, and you'll barely recognise the place by the time you get back. Really hope you like it!!!*

I mean, there's never an opportunity to get it in. Yesterday's chat, for instance – from Estonia, no less – went something like this:

Dad: 'Maddie, I forgot to tell you: we left some perishables in the fridge. Mum remembered when we boarded the coach this morning.'

Me: 'It's OK, Dad, I've sorted it.'

Dad: 'Anything exciting happening there?'

Me: 'No! Definitely not!'

Dad: 'Nothing at all?'

Me: 'Nothing whatsoever!'

Dad: 'How's the club?'

Me: 'Fine! Couldn't be better!'

Dad: 'And everyone there? How's Archie?'

Me: 'Great! Everyone's great! Same as always!'

Dad: 'That's wonderful, darling. Mum's struck up a friendship with Carol Decker. Did you know the two of them share the same birthday?'

Hmm, I probably *could* have dropped it in there somewhere, but trust me, it's harder than it sounds.

'I promise to be careful,' I tell Loaf gravely, thinking if

we can just get past this he might help me out with the stock.

But Loaf doesn't look convinced. For a moment he seems to think about expanding on his theme, but then decides against it.

Instead he snatches the list off me. 'Right, let's see what we can do.'

♪

When I get back, decorations are still in full swing.

Jaz pounces on me as soon as I walk in the door, clutching a bundle of paint brushes and with multi-coloured splodges on her face. 'I need your help,' she breathes, pulling me through the littered wreckage of power tools, bin bags and sawdust.

I can't argue with that. Jaz has taken this *artiste* thing to the next level: she's wearing a little black cap over her tumble of red hair, a stripy sweater and skinny jeans, and there's a white silk ribbon tied around her neck. She looks like a cross between a Pierrot clown and the star of a beatnik movie. She's brandishing a palette. What is this, a French master's atelier?

'Maddie!' booms Evan from the bar. He's busy bossing about a guy in white overalls who looks distinctly pissed off. 'Did you get what we need?'

'It's on order!' I yell over my shoulder, as Jaz and I duck under a step ladder and she yanks me to a halt.

I look up. Wow.

It's a portrait of Andre, and it's nearly bigger than me.

'Well, what do you think?' Jaz asks, her cheeks flushed.

I'm not sure what to say. It's a picture of a guinea pig in lederhosen. I suppose it's quite good, as pictures of guinea pigs in lederhosen go, but his facial expression unnerves me. Is he smiling?

I peer in closer. 'Is he smiling?'

'It's a half smile,' reveals Jaz, pleased with herself. 'Like the *Mona Lisa*.'

I try my own half smile. 'Exactly like it,' I agree, putting my arm round her. 'I'm impressed. Is Evan OK with it?'

'He said I could have this *one* patch,' she grumbles. 'And if he doesn't like it, he's painting over it.'

'Well, *I* like it,' I say, and looking at it again I decide that I do. 'It stays.'

We're interrupted by a kerfuffle over at the bar, followed swiftly by an almighty crash. I turn round to see Evan's large frame stumbling over. In an effort to break his fall he grabs the bar with both hands, swinging off it like a bare-bottomed monkey.

'Would somebody *get that rat out of here*!' he roars, red in the face, recovering himself. Andre the guinea pig scampers, oblivious, through the debris, clad in a mini hand-sewn Breton jumper and matching beret.

'He's not a rat!' objects Jaz, rushing over and scooping him up. 'He only wants to help. Don't you, Andre?'

Andre twitches his nose in assent.

Evan's attending to his spongy hair. 'He can help by leaving us all to get on with it,' he spits. 'This is no place for vermin.'

Jaz flounces off in a strop, muttering, 'Tell me about it.'

Over by the stage, Rob Day aka Ruby du Jour catches my eye and gives me a wink. It's a good job Rob's turned up for the renovations, as I can imagine Ruby breaking a fingernail or several and wailing at such pitch about it that the newly installed mirrors shatter into millions of tiny pieces (though they surely have to be reinforced to survive the menace of drunken karaoke). Plus it looks like Rob's equipped with an impressive array of DIY tools.

It's good to have Rob back. I remember what a handsome man he is under the big costume – he's got a really beautiful face, lovely cheekbones and kind, green eyes surrounded by long dark lashes. He's built like a dancer, tall and supple, and he moves easily, like a cat, full of grace. It's a pity he doesn't see what we see – and what Bobbi Sanchez must have seen, once upon a time – because without the big outfit he simply lacks confidence. Ruby's his mask, his disguise, his costume. It's as if he doesn't quite know who Rob Day is.

'How's it going?' I ask, watching him drill a smooth hole into the wall and dust it off.

Rob's voice is softer, quieter than Ruby's. 'Good, I think . . .' He leans in. 'Evan's a hard task master, isn't he?'

I make a face. 'Just a bit.'

'Did you hear what he said when he turned up this morning?'

I shake my head.

'He said, "Where's that drag queen I was promised?"'

'Oh, Rob, I'm sorry.'

He laughs. 'Don't worry about it; it was funny. And he never guessed it was me.' He flexes his arm and a not-very-impressive bicep pushes at the skin. 'Must be the pecs.'

I grin back. 'Must be. But seriously, I don't know where he gets off. I haven't even mentioned Ruby – and you mustn't feel you have to . . . play up to it, or perform, or anything. That's the wrong word, but you know what I mean.'

There's a glint in Rob's eye. 'She's dying to meet him.'

Archie joins us. 'All right if we 'ave a word?' he asks me in a hushed tone. 'In private?'

Clearly Evan's had the old man working to the hilt as well – Archie looks anxious and flustered, a bit disorientated. It's one thing to have the rest of us doing hard labour but I've really got to speak to him about this.

Rob and I exchange glances. He shrugs. 'Go ahead.'

'I've got some excitin' news,' Archie tells me once we're wedged among the boxes in the store room. 'Well, *I* think it's excitin'.'

'Great!' I say. 'What is it?'

'Well, it's a bit unexpected . . .'

I wait for him to go on.

'Turns out I've come into a bit o' money.' He licks his lips and I can see his hands are trembling ever so slightly. 'Quite a lot, as it goes.'

'But that's wonderful, Archie!'

'Yeah . . . cousin o' mine . . . passed away . . .' Archie's always been a mumbler, but now I can scarcely make out what he's saying.

'Oh, I'm sorry to hear that.' I didn't know Archie had any elderly relatives – but then why would I?

'. . . She left a bit o' cash behind . . .'

'She must have cared for you a great deal,' I say, touching his arm.

He looks up at me. 'So I'm quitting.'

The announcement is so abrupt that for a moment I don't think I've heard right.

'Archie, no—'

'I've made me mind up.'

A horrible thought occurs to me. 'If it's about the show, I promise you I'll—'

'It ain't nothin' to do with that.' He clasps my shoulders. 'Or with you. You're a lovely girl, Maddie, an' your parents should be proud.'

'But . . .' I'm at a loss. Archie's the longest-serving member of the bar, he's *always* been here. He's one of my parents' favourite people. I can't let him go.

'What can I do to persuade you to stay?' I plead, desperate.

He shakes his head, smiles a little sadly. 'Absolutely nothin', pet. I'm retirin' to a lovely cottage by the sea. It's what I've always wanted. Now I can afford it, I don't intend to wait a moment longer.'

I don't know what to say. But before I've had a chance to even think about it, the store room door slams open and Evan's in my face.

'What's going on?' he demands. 'Friday's only days away – this is hardly the time for a mothers' meeting.'

'I was just tellin' Maddie about my decision,' says Archie deliberately, sending him an odd look.

Evan's voice softens like ice cream in the sun. 'Ah yes, of course, of course.'

I'm confused. 'Evan already knows?'

Evan makes a show of almost closing the door, inferring we have his undivided attention, but I notice he refrains from shutting it completely.

'Archie came to me this morning,' he admits quietly. 'He's very sad about leaving you, and the club, and all his friends . . .'

Archie nods. 'I am.'

'We're sad to lose him,' I say, hardly believing the words even as I say them.

'It's a great shame . . .' Evan arranges his features into an expression of regret.

We all stand there in silence for a moment, like Archie's died or something, and then I see Evan's eyes flick to the old man. Immediately Archie makes his excuses and ducks back into the bar. As soon as he's out of sight, Evan brightens.

'But the great news is, I've already found a replacement!'

'You've done what?'

'That's right. In fact he's here now.'

I'm baffled. 'What on earth are you talking about?'

'This young guy dropped in earlier, while you were out, said he was looking for a bar job and heard about our plans here. I hired him on the spot. Happy coincidence, wouldn't you say?'

I open my mouth but no words come out.

Evan sticks his head round the door. 'Alex?' he calls.

In moments a tall dark stranger appears, complete with disarming smile and bulging biceps (and those big neck muscles that I always find off-putting, like he's got two loaves of bread sitting on his shoulders). He's handsome, but it's not the sort of look I find attractive – too plastic, and he's got more than a passing resemblance to Action Man. I know instinctively that he shaves his body hair.

Evan pulls him into the store, swiftly shutting the door. I feel like we're hiding from the teachers at school, having a sneaky fag at break.

I look between the two men. 'What's going on?'

Evan grins, exposing that dam of sparkling white teeth. 'Meet Alex,' he says, clapping the man on his chunky back, 'your new head barman.'

11

Suspicious Minds

'Can you believe it?' I splutter, chucking my tea bag in the kitchen bin. 'Suddenly I've got this random bloke working for me who I've never met before in my life!'

Lou scoops up her bowl of cereal and we head back to our desks. 'You could have said no,' she points out.

'How? We're going live in two days' time and there's no way Simon and Jaz can handle the bar by themselves. But then Alex doesn't even seem that experienced – he dropped a bottle of vodka last night trying to make cocktails. It was disastrous!'

'He was probably nervous.'

We slump down at our desks. The red light on my Simply Voices answer machine is blinking incessantly. It's going to be a long day.

'Maybe. It's a bit odd him starting just as Archie quits, don't you think?'

'I think Evan Bergman sounds like a control freak,' says Lou, spooning in her Cheerios with one hand while she checks email with the other. 'He's got to have the last word on everything. You have to stand up for yourself.'

Jennifer pops up from behind a partition, alert as a meerkat, and I'm just in time to stifle a yawn. I'll admit I've been slack these past few weeks – I've probably only done about sixty per cent of my allocated shifts – so it's little wonder that she's been watching me like a hawk. Flaunting evidence of my increasingly late nights is *not* a wise idea.

'You're right,' I concede. 'He's just so . . . convincing.'

Lou's phone rings. She munches her mouthful furiously before picking up, while I make a start on my mountain of mail, a bulging stack of jiffy bags and envelopes containing CDs and show reels from hopeful applicants. We're so inundated that we can't listen to them all, so it's my job to return to sender with a kind refusal. I try not to think too much about who I might be replying to: when once I overheard a snippet of an audition, the person speaking darted between so many accents and characters at such speed that it was like a case of demon possession and I half expected them to start growling away in Latin.

'Ohmygod,' says Lou, as I grab a bundle of rejections off the printer. She clamps a hand over her mouth.

'What is it?'

'It's Lawrence.'

I shuffle the papers. 'What about him?'

'Erm, do you really want to know?' She adds swiftly, 'Maybe I shouldn't have said anything.'

'Well, you have now. So come on – spill.'

'He's going out with Francesca Montgomery.' Lou clicks her mouse. 'Hang on a minute. Yeah, it says here they were spotted at Nobu at the weekend.'

'Who's Francesca Montgomery?' I ask, surprised by how I don't really mind. A couple of weeks ago I'd have been distraught, but I've been so distracted with Sing It Back that I haven't thought about Lawrence in ages.

'That theatre director.' Lou clicks some more. 'God, it can't be doing Law any harm, can it? According to this, she's considering casting him in her new play.'

I come round to look at Lou's screen. It's one of those celebrity gossip sites.

'Is that her?' I lean in for a closer look. She's quite harsh-looking, tall with a severe dark bob and horn-rimmed glasses. 'She's very . . . arresting.'

Lou raises an eyebrow. 'Maddie, she's about seventy.'

'No, she's not.'

We Wikipedia it. She's forty-eight. 'See?'

'That's nowhere near seventy!'

'And it's nowhere near twenty-nine,' Lou says drily. 'Don't try telling me this is an innocent case of love at first sight.'

We begin reading the article. Then Lou's clicking furiously on the little x to close the window – but it's too late, I've already seen it.

'They've been together for over a month . . . ?' I try to remember the exact date Lawrence and I broke up.

'Oh, Maddie.' She looks up at me. 'They've probably got it wrong – you can't trust anything these gossip columns say.' But I can tell that's not what she really thinks.

I'm crestfallen. 'You can't trust anything your boyfriend says either.'

Lou closes the window and swivels her chair to face me. 'All this proves is what a dick he is. You're a million times better than him.' She balls her fists. 'God! It makes me so cross.'

'*We* were together a month ago,' I say. 'Shit.'

'Clearly there's no real affection there,' resolves Lou, waving her hand as if to dismiss his new relationship, trying to make me feel better. 'Francesca wants him because he's young; he wants her because she might help shift his dead-in-the-water career. Plus it's a classic Freudian set-up and for that reason it's flawed from the outset, trust me. He's a nob, Maddie, OK? *He's a nob.* You deserve so much more.'

'I don't really care how they feel about each other . . .' I prod those vulnerable places to make sure – yes, I'm OK. 'I just can't believe he would do that to me!' I flop down in my chair.

Jennifer's face hovers above me. 'Everything all right over here?'

'Fine.' I begin stuffing the rejections into their envelopes.

'All set for bowling tonight?'

Oh *no*. I'd forgotten about the bi-monthly 'team-building' excursions they recently put in place to boost staff morale. I'll come up with an excuse.

'Maddie'll be there!' sings Lou.

'Who does Lawrence think he is?' I hiss when Jennifer's gone. 'An idiot, maybe, but a cheat? I always thought I'd be able to tell if someone was doing one over on me.'

'I can crumble a fish stock cube in his car radiator, if you like,' Lou says, tapping away.

'No, it's fine.'

'Dog poo through his letterbox?'

'No.'

'King prawns in his curtains?'

'Forget it.'

'Fine. In that case remember what he sounds like with haemorrhoids. I've got it on file somewhere if you need a reminder.'

♪

In the end Lou drags me to bowling, claiming I'm never going to feel any better unless my frustrations can be 'channelled into the physical world' or something. I think she means I need a drink.

We're on a team with Jennifer, our post guy and some bloke in Marketing I've never spoken to but who has the thinnest moustache I've ever seen.

'Maddie, you're up!' crows Jennifer, taking a hefty glug of her mango J2O. I don't know why she's so excited: every one of my previous six efforts have slid miserably into that gutter bit at the sides.

'Try a different ball,' suggests Lou, lifting a snot-coloured one with massive deep holes for the fingers and thumb.

'It weighs ten tonnes!'

'Yeah but you'll get more speed,' she explains.

'As I'm going down the gutter?'

'Come on, I'll show you.' She relaxes into a forward lunge and I burst out laughing.

'What?' She laughs back.

'Have you ever been bad at bowling?' I ask.

'Not that bad.'

'So you've never had to sit through someone else's demonstration of how bowling should look? Trust me, you don't want to.'

'But if you lean *into* it a bit more . . .'

'I know how it should *look*, Lou, I just can't *do it*!'

'Go for it, Maddie!' shouts the post guy as I clomp towards the lane in my red and blue clown's shoes.

There's an eight-year-old boy lining up his shot in the alley next to me. Our eyes meet.

He wants a challenge? Fine. He's got one.

I raise the snotty ball, staring hard at those white pins a mere arm's throw away, as if by sheer will I can secure victory. The boy takes his own aim, doing a brief hop-skippity-jump before launching himself like a firework, releasing the ball at the last minute and sending it shooting dead-centre down the aisle. It smashes into a strike.

'ULTIMATE DESTRUCTION!' somebody yells from his party – an older brother, I'm guessing, in a Space Invaders T-shirt.

I look behind at my own support team, feeling like a champion about to face the last hurdle. Everything's in slow motion. Jennifer's nodding. Lou's mouthing instructions. Post guy's got his face in a pint. That Marketing chump's already picking out his next ball.

106

But that's OK. Because I can do this.

I take a deep breath. *Focus*. It's just me and the runway.

Trotting a bit on the spot, I move into a run, lunge forward, extend my arm in that way I've been shown a million times before and prepare to let go . . .

Except I've run over the line. And for some reason I'm still running, my fingers wedged inside the ball. The bloody ball's stuck on my hands. And I'm still running. Why am I still running? I should stop. The pins are getting closer. I'm going to run straight into them. Perhaps if I knock them down manually it still counts as a strike—

And then I trip.

As I go flying the ball springs free, smacking into the lane and travelling the final few yards to the pins, where it slopes off to the sides and begrudgingly knocks one on its way past, which wobbles a bit before righting itself.

I land face-down. *Ow*.

The urgent sound of footsteps, hurrying, comes closer. Then Lou's crouching down next to me, her face alongside mine.

'Maddie! Bloody hell, what happened?'

'Did I get a strike?' I ask through my hair.

A pause. 'It doesn't matter. Get up.'

'I can't.'

'Are you hurt? Oh my god, can you feel your legs?'

'No.'

'No, you're not hurt, or no, you can't feel your legs?'

'I'm not hurt.'

'Come on then, people are looking.'

'I'm too embarrassed. Pretend I'm dead.'

'I'm having a conversation with you, Maddie. Clearly

you're not dead. Come on.' She hauls me to my feet and I shuffle red-faced back to the others.

'Foul!' yells Marketing Man, and I feel like saying the same thing back about his facial hair. Gleefully he punches my score of nil into the computer. The telly screen above our lane displays a pin with tears spraying out its eyes.

'Shouldn't those pins be crying if they *do* get knocked down?' I complain, hiding in the fifties-diner-style booth. The little shit in the next lane is laughing, and his older brother's laugh sounds like a hyena.

'You've got another turn, Maddie,' says Jennifer, like this is a good thing.

Lou takes it for me, and I get eight, which at least sends me off the starting blocks.

'Thanks,' I say. 'I hurt.'

She passes my wine. 'I think you landed on every single bit of your body. It was ugly.'

'I don't even know why I'm here,' I grumble, acting like the whole thing is totally below me and that there are plenty more important things in life than being good at bowling. Which there are.

'You're here,' Lou says, 'because there's no way I could have suffered it alone.'

'Apart from that.' I sip my warm, too-sweet wine. 'I should be at Sing It Back. I should be sorting stuff out for Friday . . .'

'Like what?'

'I don't know. I feel like I should be *mentally* preparing.'

Lou sits back. 'The best thing you can do is relax. Really, you'll just have to try and do as Evan says and act like the cameras aren't there. Or you'll go crazy.'

We mull this over as Jennifer bowls. She uses one of those slides on wheels and does a little victory dance when she knocks down three.

'This time in two days, Sing It Back is going live.' I shake my head in disbelief. 'I can't get my head around it, Lou.'

She gives me a weak smile. 'Look, I've been meaning to say . . . I'm sorry I've been crap about this Tooth & Nail thing.'

'You haven't.' I frown. 'You had concerns, but you were totally right to have them, and to tell me. I'd always want you to tell me.'

'Yeah, but I could have been more supportive. You've had a tough time and you made a brave decision.' She raises her glass. 'To Sing It Back – and to all the success it deserves.'

We clink.

'So now can you tell me what's really on your mind?' I ask, eyeing her over the rim.

'What do you mean?'

I roll my eyes 'Lou, I know you. Last time you were at the club you were weird. And it wasn't just the TV thing.'

Lou puts her wine down and turns to me. 'Do you think there's something going on between Simon and Jaz?'

I laugh, before I realise she's serious. 'No, god no, of course not. Why?'

'They seem close, that's all. It's stupid of me to care . . .'

'They are close,' I say, 'they're friends. Honestly, Lou, that's all it is. Jaz is *so* not Simon's type – and I can assure you Simon's not hers. I'd have noticed if it was anything more.'

'But you've been really busy,' she babbles, 'maybe you missed the signs.'

'Lou, seriously – if you like him that much, ask him out.'

'I couldn't!'

'Why not?'

She shrugs. 'I just couldn't. I'm too embarrassed.'

'You're saying this to the girl who just threw herself down a bowling alley head-first in front of half of Bloomsbury?'

She chuckles. 'That was quite bad . . .'

'Was it? I thought I looked pretty good.'

'Lou, you're up,' says Post Guy, giving Marketing Moron a high-five as they celebrate his seventeenth strike.

'Hey,' I say as she gets up, 'I've got an idea. Why don't you work shifts at the club?'

Lou looks uncertain. 'I don't know . . .'

'It's a way of getting closer to Simon, isn't it? And then you can see for yourself that there's zilch going on with him and Jaz.'

She lifts one of the balls, tries it for weight. 'What about Evan? It's kind of an awkward time to get involved, isn't it?'

'Evan won't come near you, you have my word. And to be honest we could do with all the help we can get.'

'Really?'

'Really. Plus Mum and Dad love you. They'd make you a full-time employee in a heartbeat, you know that.'

Lou hugs me. 'Thanks, Maddie, you're a star.' She beams. 'I won't let you down, I promise.'

12

Club Tropicana

I feel sick.

There's a real possibility that I might *be* sick. On live TV. On launch night. In front of a nation. On Evan Bergman's spongy head.

'Have you seen how many people are outside?' Jaz pulls back the blind a fraction and peeks out. 'Maddie, there's a *queue*. Can you remember the last time you saw that?'

I finish applying mascara – it's a miracle I got it on right with such shaky hands. I've eaten hardly anything today, which is making me feel really wobbly.

'I don't think I ever have.'

Jaz pushes Andre's nose against the window. They're in matching clothes tonight – floor-length (in Andre's case, claw-length) red capes and those weeny miniature top hats that look like they belong on a wedding cake.

'Somebody saw us!' cries Jaz excitedly, snatching the blind back across. 'We've been seen! OMG we've probably been papped!'

No being sick on Evan Bergman's head. No being sick on anyone's head. I can see the headline now: KARAOKE QUEEN SWAPS BANA-NARAMA FOR BARFARAMA.

'No, we haven't,' I tell her in a shaky voice. 'Nobody knows who we are and nobody cares. It's like any other night, OK? Business as usual, just like Evan said.'

She gives me a look. 'Yeah, except it totally isn't.'

I go into the bedroom and open Mum's wardrobe, hoping to find a belt to complement my dark blue maxi dress, but then I remember what happened last time I sampled these riches and slam it shut with a shudder. In my anxiety everything has taken on a faintly sinister hue, and when I check the mirror I can see Vanilla Ice looking disparagingly at me from his frame on the living room wall, arms folded, gaze dead-on, spoiling for a fight. (Not, in fact, unlike someone prepared to wreck a mic like a vandal.) I once heard that Vanilla Ice, post-chart-success, auctioned his toenails off on eBay.

'Be calm,' I say, padding back to Jaz and sounding distinctly *un*calm. 'We're not supposed to act any different, cameras or no cameras.'

'Is that why you're dressing up?' she asks with a sideways smile.

I rake a brush through my hair. 'I'm a hypocrite,' I declare.

'But when you're all done up like that I can't very well arrive in a sack, can I?'

Jaz takes me by the shoulders and looks into my eyes. 'It's going to be fine, Maddie.'

I breathe out slowly, my heart thrumming in my ears. 'I hope so.'

'I know so.'

'What if something awful happens? I'm wigging, Jaz – it's live TV. What if I'm sick?'

'Why would you be sick?'

'I feel sick. What if I'm sick on Evan Bergman's head?'

'What if whatever,' says Jaz in her warm-California accent, waving her hand dismissively. 'After this we'll get accustomed to the cameras being around and it'll be fine. Just focus on that and get through tonight like it's any other Friday.' Sensing this isn't quite enough, she adds, 'You're not going to be sick, Maddie, I swear.'

Outside I can hear whoops and yells – word of the show has spread locally like wildfire. Tentatively I finger the blind. Andre is scrabbling furiously about at the base of the window. Maybe he's caught his reflection and finally wants to end it all, but worries that his tiny cape might facilitate flight for sufficient time to break the fall and instead he'll wind up paralysed from the waist down, destined for all time to be dressed up and cooed over by Jaz with no means of escape.

'Dare I look?'

'Go on!' Jaz joins me.

The street is crammed with people, a great trail of them snaking right around the block. I can't believe my eyes. I forget my nerves for a moment and allow a rush of pure, unfettered excitement to wash through me. I imagine Mum and Dad's faces if they could see this. I *want* it for them, so very much. I want tonight to be just the beginning.

'I'd never have guessed it,' says Jaz softly. 'Pineapple, we salute you.'

I'm still not convinced by the name change – it feels too, I don't know . . . *current*. Evan wanted something snappy and memorable; a 'clean brand' that clearly signalled Pineapple Mist and tied into the name of the programme: *Blast from the Past*. He figured the nod to my parents' band name was fitting and, I have to agree, it works well visually, too: they've replaced the old battered sign with a snazzy new canary-yellow font and the accompanying neon fruit looks confident and refreshing. SING IT BA K has been relegated to one of the many cardboard boxes still in evidence in Mum and Dad's flat. I couldn't quite bring myself to part with it.

'Yoo-hoo!' Ruby du Jour pokes her blonde head round the door. She's ravishing in an emerald gown and bags of silver jewellery, her false eyelashes batting. 'Everybody ready for their TV debut?'

The nerves slam back with renewed force.

'Can everyone stop calling it that?' I snap. The others look hurt. 'Sorry – just a bit jumpy, that's all.'

'You look *gorgeous*,' Ruby tells me. She turns to Jaz. 'Er . . . so do you. Nice cape.'

'Andre and I are exploring a modern twist on *Little Red Riding Hood*,' Jaz explains proudly. 'It's the next big thing in fashion: I like to call it "Fairy Tales Reconstructed".'

'Did she wear a hat like that?' Ruby asks. 'It's ever so small.'

'Who?'

'Little Red Riding Hood.' Ruby tilts her head. 'Or Hat? Little Red Riding Hat? *Extremely* Little Red Riding Hat?'

Jaz throws her critic a withering look. 'I said it was a *modern twist?*'

'Come on,' I cut in before things get messy, 'we'd better get moving. Doors open any minute and Simon's down there all by himself.'

'He's got Alex,' says Jaz, adjusting her tiny headgear and doing the same to Andre's.

'Yeah, which means Simon's doing *all* the work.'

'You're too hard on him,' states Jaz, 'he only just started. Give the guy a break.'

'We did by hiring him.'

'I'd have hired him in a heartbeat. He is pretty sexy, don't you think? All dark and brooding.'

I choose to ignore that comment: Alex is sexy if you like men who're so muscular they look like they're made of a stacked-up pile of assorted-sized cardboard boxes. 'As far as I'm concerned, he's yet to prove himself,' I say. 'And so far, he's not a patch on Archie.'

Davinia's in the hall, hopping about like a flea. For someone who'd go to just about anything to get photographed (her most recent outing was to the launch of a dog perfume), this is as close to Mecca as it gets. She doesn't even have to leave the building.

'It's Chester Bendwell!' she squeaks, jumping up and down in her lime-green strappy sandals. 'I saw Evan showing him in!'

I fasten the backs of my earrings. 'Chester who?'

'Chester Bendwell! He presented *60-Second Haircut* – you remember. He's downstairs with all the crew. That moody camera girl with the dreadful wardrobe was taking him round.' She gasps. 'I bet he'll be doing all the voiceovers as well – can you believe it?!'

'Oh yes, Evan mentioned that,' I say, locking the door behind us.

'And you didn't tell us?' Davinia's voice has ascended to a pitch only wolves can hear. 'I've carried a torch ever since I saw him unplait that mullet.'

Ruby touches her arm. 'Honey, he's gay.'

Davinia's face falls. 'He is?'

'A sixty-second haircut?' Jaz is disgusted. 'What the hell is that supposed to mean?'

'It's a haircut that takes a minute or less,' simplifies Davinia, as if Jaz is the dumbest person on the planet.

'Duh,' says Jaz. 'Who came up with that ridiculous idea?'

'Don't sniff at it,' Davinia bristles, 'they got through twenty in a half-hour show. And they weren't *that* bad.'

Ruby's confused. 'Wouldn't they get through thirty?'

I roll my eyes. 'Come on,' I grab Jaz by the arm and peel her away from the fray, 'we've got our own TV show to attend.'

♪

It's going OK. In fact, I might even go so far as to say it's going *well*.

It's ten p.m. and the club is busier than it's been in years. Nearly every booth and table is taken and since we opened an hour ago it's been non-stop at the bar: Jaz, Simon and Alex are run off their feet. (Well, Jaz and Simon are – I keep having to

116

step in whenever Alex disappears out back, with no explanation as to where he's going or why.)

Even the karaoke's sounding good.

When I saw the fruit of our labours this morning, I actually felt quite emotional. While it's only the first rung of a long, long ladder, and the root components of the set are still there (including the Gary Numan clock – Evan was quite specific about that), everything is . . . bolder, confident, more audacious. The closest I can get to describing it is like a caricature. The foul upholstery's been buffed and scrubbed, boasting its gruesomeness to full effect; the mirror ball has been taken down and replaced with an even bigger, brasher one; the spotlights have been swapped with those siren thingies I bought from Loaf, shooting lurid pink beams of light across a polished stage and crowd of rowdy singers. The red walls have been re-papered in an even more aggressive shade of scarlet, the clash against the fuchsia mirrors truly startling. Revolting – and exactly what Evan wanted for the opening show. But despite this, for once in its life it looks deliberate, bothered about, like someone has taken care of it.

'It's wonderful,' I told Evan, amazed.

'It's tacky and awful,' he retorted matter-of-factly. 'Why'd you think I let that mad American loose with a box of paints? The place is so hideous it's a work of art.'

But nobody here tonight seems to care – they're having far too much fun. Right now there's a mob of people belting out Bon Jovi, a couple of guys on stage falling to their knees and pulling out their air guitars. For the first time we have variety on the song lists (i.e. more than twelve that actually survive the distance without skipping), even if Simon's a bit offended that people haven't taken to his revised list as he'd hoped. All the old favourites keep rearing their ugly heads: Take That, Queen, Madonna, the *Dirty Dancing* soundtrack . . . My theory is that people don't come to karaoke to look good or impress, or take themselves seriously; they just want to sing along to the songs they grew up with – the songs to which they laughed, cried, dreamed, lost, had their first kiss, fell in love, got their hearts broken.

And the best bit? I've hardly noticed the cameras. I've been too distracted to bother with them, especially not with manoeuvring myself into every single shot and hanging off anybody who happens to be in the frame (not naming names, Davinia). Evan was right: it does feel like business as usual. Well, *un*usual in the sense that we're actually doing business, but usual insofar as a regular night feels working with my friends.

'You seen Evan?' shouts Simon over the noise as we pull measures from the optics. He swipes a hand across his brow.

'No,' I say, shovelling the ice bucket and filling two glasses. 'I haven't seen much of Alex either – where is he?'

Simon takes cash and drops his tip into the communal pint glass. 'That's why I asked.' He gives me a troubled look. 'Every time Evan disappears, Alex does, too. He really doesn't know what he's doing, Maddie.'

'I've noticed.'

'He made a Long Island Iced Tea earlier – you won't believe what he did.'

'Put a tea bag in it?'

He frowns. 'How did you guess?'

'Two Guinness and four Sambuca when you're ready,

118

mate,' says a customer, leaning over the bar and flapping a twenty-pound note.

'You're kidding,' I say, amazed. 'And Evan hired him? Jesus.'

'Tell me about it,' agrees Simon, lining up the glasses. 'Thankfully I saw it bobbing on the surface before it went out. But, listen: Jaz and I need Alex here, good or not, especially if things continue to pick up. We need *someone*. You shouldn't have to keep filling in the gaps.'

'Actually,' I drop in casually, 'I've asked Lou to work a few shifts.'

'Oh.' He clears his throat. 'That's great.'

I shrug. 'Anyway, to be honest I'd much rather be here than out schmoozing with Evan. He wants me to do an interview with Chester Bender later' – I shudder inwardly – 'that's more than enough time in front of the cameras for me.'

'Have you seen him yet?' Simon lets the pints settle while he gets change.

I take another order. 'Who, Chester? Yeah, he's . . . extreme. His eyebrows are about three feet above his eyes. And he moves really quickly. I think he's wearing those trainers with tiny wheels on; all you have to do is blink and he's gone. He'll be at the bar one second and conspiring in a corner with Evan the next.'

Simon laughs. 'Don't you have to be, like, eleven to get away with those?'

'Guys, guys, guys!' Jaz ducks under Simon's arm. He draws her to him and plants a kiss on her hair. For a second I recall Lou's unease, before I remember they're just friends. 'Someone's put in a bid for my portrait of Andre!'

'What?' Simon grins. 'Are you serious?'

'Yes! Can you believe it?' The little hat on her head gives a jaunty wobble. 'Twenty-five pounds! He said he wanted Andre to pose for *The Birth of Venus* next – do you think that could work?'

'Sounds like a perv to me,' says Simon, taking another order.

'Jaz, stop selling Andre to art dealers,' I tell her, putting on my manager's hat. 'Alex is nowhere to be seen and we're drowning out here.'

Jaz puts a hand to her mouth. 'You're so right,' she says, full of remorse, 'what am I thinking? Andre would never do topless.'

'Just get back to work,' I instruct, 'I've got to find Evan.'

I'm lifting up the bar hatch and nearly slam straight into Alex (which at full speed might well have knocked me out). He regards me with a blank, unnerving expression. Behind him I can see Evan's springy hair illuminated in the raspberry strobe lights.

'Where have you been?' I ask.

'Out back,' he says flatly, shifting his considerable weight from one foot to the other. He's sporting a tight V-neck top that plunges to his sternum, and the hairless caramel cleavage going on between his pecs is probably bigger than mine. His expression is empty, like a walking-talking soldier toy that hasn't had its batteries put in yet.

'If you need to go out for a fag, just say.' I fold my arms. Something about this guy makes me really uncomfortable. 'But don't keep disappearing. Jaz and Simon haven't had a break yet and my count is you've had about five.'

'Isn't it fantastic, Maddie!' Suddenly Evan's with us,

florid-faced, the neck of his shirt tugged loose to reveal a gleam of sweat on his chest. 'It's looking great on camera. The team are catching everything!'

'Er, yes,' I say, momentarily disorientated as Alex slips past me and back to work. I'm annoyed with Evan for interrupting.

'Toby's happy,' he goes on, draping a meaty arm round my shoulders and pulling me into his hot armpit, 'the repairs we did are spot-on. Now, Chester Bendwell is live with the viewers at home; he's been taking them round, telling them everything they need to know so it all makes sense when we move to the nightly shows. They want to meet you, though, Maddie, so we'll come and grab you shortly.'

'What do I say?'

Evan doesn't seem fussed about that. 'Introduce yourself and say a few words, you know – tell them what it is you do; your name, obviously—'

'My name?!'

He looks at me funny. 'Yes . . . ?'

'My name's Maddie Mulhern!'

'I know it is . . .'

'Hey, Maddie! Check this out!' It's Jaz. I turn to see Alex brandishing a bored-looking Andre, trying to get him to take money off a gang of cooing punters.

'How cute is that?' she squeals. If I hadn't witnessed first-hand how dedicated Jaz is to that guinea pig, or how tenderly she takes care of him behind the scenes, I think I'd be tempted to phone the RSPCA.

Behind her, Simon looks distinctly pissed off. It's not like him to get annoyed with Jaz – or anyone, for that matter – but I can understand it: he's busy pulling pints while the others are more interested in pulling faces. It's nothing to do with the fact that Jaz and Alex seem to be getting on like a house on fire. Of course it isn't. Why would he care about that?

I haul a plastic crate from the bins and begin to load up the dirties.

'Ugh,' says Evan, sickened. 'Can't you put it down?'

'Evan, welcome to bar work,' I say drily. He's probably never had to lift a finger for anything in his life except typing in his multimillion-pound bank transfers.

'I meant the rodent,' he says bitterly, scowling at the shenanigans going on behind the bar. I'm about to come back with a smart retort when he abruptly moves off, his attention caught elsewhere.

I shake the dregs from a handful of glasses and pile them up, just as the opening strains of Whitney's 'I Wanna Dance with Somebody' kick off. I wonder how many times I've listened to someone sing this badly.

Except . . . You know what I was saying about people not taking themselves too seriously at karaoke? Well, this one's got to be a major exception. The girl on stage is wearing a tight top and jeans, a pair of severe black heels protruding sharply out the ends. She's moving like she's in a music video, without a trace of self-consciousness. The only time she appears aware of her surroundings is when she catches a glimpse of one of the cameras. I tell myself to get used to this: over the coming weeks we'll have plenty of wannabes descending on the club, hoping to catch the attention of some talent scout.

I lift the crate into my arms and push my way through the crowd, glasses head-high so I can scarcely see where I'm going. Normally the thought of stacking an industrial-sized dishwasher wouldn't fill me with pleasure, but the atmosphere in here is starting to give me a headache. I could do with some time out.

'Excuse me,' I tell the guy blocking my way. He doesn't shift so I push into his back a bit with the crate. '*Excuse* me.'

But instead of moving, he turns to me. Through the foggy glass I can just about make out he's dark-haired, but the image is vague and distorted.

'Hey,' he says. 'How's it going?'

I recognise that voice.

'This is heavy.' My arms are threatening to quit. 'Can you get out the way?'

'It's Maddie, right?'

I sigh – this guy isn't giving up. Do I know him?

'Uh, give me a sec,' I bluster, feeling harassed. I blow a strand of hair out my mouth. Shit, these crates are leaden – we're so unaccustomed to them being full that I feel like I'm lifting a teenager. I rest it on the bar and look up.

And I'm face to face with Mystery Man.

He's just as gorgeous as I remember. And he's wearing a suit. My god, he looks good in a suit. And even though I hadn't forgotten how grey and serious his eyes were, how dark his hair, my memory hadn't done justice to the impact of him in real life.

'Hi,' I squeak. Suddenly I'm conscious of the mess of my hair, the hint of sweat on my top lip, that livid-pink blotch I get on my chest when I'm embarrassed.

'Hi. The club's looking great, I'm really happy with it.'

'Er, thanks.' My heart's going crazy. 'Do you like karaoke, then?'

He laughs. 'Not a massive fan, I must admit.'

I laugh too, and it comes out very loud and brash. 'Me neither!' I exclaim, as though we've just discovered a surprising
shared horror of something really anodyne, like white bread.

'You're the one running a karaoke bar,' he smiles. He's
sexy.

'Well, I'm only doing it for my parents,' I explain, 'while
they're away. Between you and me, my worst nightmare would
be getting up on that stage.'

Mystery Man considers this. 'Yeah, it's probably mine too –
several disastrous episodes at school plays, it's put me off for
life. But it depends what I had to sing. Some are worse than
others. M People, for instance . . .'

It's my turn to laugh. Then, for what seems like ages, we
stand there looking at each other. It's unlike me to be lost for
words, but I really am.

'So what are you doing here?' I ask eventually.

He shakes his head, puzzled. 'What do you mean?'

'Well, if you don't like karaoke, and you're terrified of certain nineties pop bands . . .'

Now he looks uncomfortable. 'Didn't Evan tell you?'

My heart skips a beat. 'Tell me what?'

'I've been away this past fortnight,' he says, suddenly
sounding horribly professional, 'so I haven't been able to oversee the changes. I did ask him to pass on my apologies.'

My brain attempts to process what he's saying. It stands to
reason that Mystery Man knows Evan – they both work at
Tooth & Nail. But how does he know my name? And how
does he know I'm running the club? And, hang on a minute:
why *is* he wearing that drop-dead gorgeous suit?

I'm so wrapped up in these questions that for a moment I

forget where we are, or what we're doing – or that there's a camera pressed right in my face, with a hungry-looking Alison attached to its rear end.

'Alison!' I hiss. The red light is blinking and I know we're on air. What the *fuck*? Why is she filming this?

Evan marches towards us, cleanly into frame. 'Ah, I see you two have met finally,' he drawls, pleased as punch.

Mystery Man holds out his hand. It's a *really* nice hand.

Evan claps me on the back. 'Maddie, meet your director. I anticipate the two of you getting very close over the next few weeks.'

In a rush I know what's coming.

'I'm Nick Craven,' says Nick Craven.

Of *course* it's bloody Nick Craven.

13

Controversy

But there's a teensy problem: Nick Craven's reputation precedes him, and, if reports are to be believed, he's a complete and utter arsehole.

'Pleased to meet you.' I'm determined not to act like a dildo on both occasions we've met, and I'm painfully aware there's a camera hovering somewhere close to my face. Seriously, what *has* this got to do with Pineapple? And where's Chester Bendwell with his interview and his stupid wheelie trainers?

We shake hands and, though I hate to admit it, a little spark shoots up my arm. It's such a cliché, but the funny thing about clichés is that they always turn out to be true.

'You too,' smiles Nick, though I notice it doesn't quite reach his eyes. Nevertheless I'm eternally thankful that he doesn't mention our first encounter. I can feel Evan's eyes on me, drinking in the scene. It's as if he's waiting for something to happen.

'Excuse me,' I say, determined to retain (regain?) my professionalism. I drag the crate up with as much dignity as I can muster, which isn't much when I'm unattractively huffing and puffing under the weight of thirty bad-smelling beer glasses.

In the kitchen, alone at last and leaning back against the steel refrigerator, I gather my breath. Seeing Mystery Man again – and making the connection with his name – brings back my own memory of Nick Craven's misdemeanours. I remember it now: last year, it was. I *knew* I recognised his face. He was splashed all over the tabloids for publicly having it off with Rebecca Ascot, a high-profile anchor woman for Channel 7. They were pictured in a London club all over each other, then again in a black cab at the end of the night. He's cut his hair since – thinking about it, it was longer then, sort of down by his chin. Maybe he wanted a new look after the episode died down, an attempt to leave the past behind . . . or maybe it's because he used to be out in the field working on serious documentaries and lived in a tepee or something and had better things to do than cut his hair, like rescue children and baby seals and whittle miniature things out of wood . . .

Clever clogs documentary maker or not, Nick Craven was still named and shamed in every single media circle – a scandal that began by igniting the London papers but soon found its way national. Because Rebecca Ascot was married at the time to Pritchard Wells, the mega mogul network exec and head of buying at the major channel. Back then there had been a string of female celebrities in television who'd been treated awfully by their cheating love rat husbands, and this was a chance to take a woman to task for doing the dirty on her man. Add to that the fact that, if I recall it right, Rebecca Ascot was a few years older than Nick – and strikingly attractive.

Uh-oh . . . am I jealous?

Before I have time to analyse it, Evan follows me in, a gust of pervy aftershave wafting in his wake.

'That was perfect,' he announces, closing the door. 'You two have such chemistry.'

I put a hand to my forehead: my temples are throbbing. 'What are you talking about, Evan?'

'You and Nick—'

'I know *who* you're talking about,' I snap irritably. 'I'm just a bit confused as to why there was a camera in my face the whole bloody time? I've been put on the spot against my will and there was nothing I could do about it, save for making a scene and embarrassing myself on TV. It's really unprofessional, Evan – you should have introduced Nick and me before now. And besides, I thought the whole point of this was the club, not us – and certainly not *me*.' I know I'm going on about it – it's *so* obvious I fancy Nick. Could I make it any more obvious?

There's a pause. 'I wasn't aware the cameras were rolling,' he says flatly. 'They should have been with Chester – he was talking to the party who did "The Final Countdown".'

I don't believe him – about the not knowing, I mean, not about Chester and 'The Final Countdown'.

'I don't give a shit what Chester was doing,' I say, 'he could have been interviewing the Queen for all I care. I want to know why I was being filmed' – ooh, I'm pointing a finger now, like I'm in a courtroom drama – 'and what on earth Nick Craven has to do with it!'

Evan nods sympathetically. 'I'm not sure how it happened,' he says, shaking his head. 'I really don't . . .'

The door opens. It's Alison. She spots Evan and her face breaks into a grin, and it almost looks like she's going to embrace him, before her eyes land on me and the smile dies.

'Oh,' she says, obviously surprised.

'Hi,' I say, cross. Thankfully she's *sans* camera, but even so my hackles are up.

'Well, we can ask her ourselves, can't we?' Evan turns on Alison. 'Come on then,' he waves her in impatiently, 'shut the door.'

Alison does as she's told. 'What is it?'

'What on *earth* did you think you were doing out there?' he roars.

Alison looks genuinely bewildered. 'I beg your pardon?'

'That was a *travesty*!' Evan bellows. 'Filming Maddie like that when I expressly told you not to. What's the matter with you, girl?'

Alison's mouth opens and closes like a fish.

'You're to film Pineapple tonight and nothing but Pineapple, do you understand? We went through this just today – are you telling me your pea-brain can't retain information for longer than six hours?'

'Hang on a minute,' I cut in, alarmed at his tirade, 'there's no need to get personal.'

'But . . .' gulps Alison, 'but you said—'

'My point exactly!' shouts Evan. 'But you didn't follow what I said, did you?'

Alison regards him as if he's gone completely mad. 'We had a conversation this afternoon,' she says slowly, the colour rising in her cheeks, 'and you said we . . . well . . .' She tosses me a nervous glance, looks to the floor and says nothing more.

Evan's outburst appears to be over. I think he's really hurt Alison's feelings. Suddenly I feel sorry for kicking up such a fuss.

'Look, it doesn't matter that much,' I backpedal. 'I just want everyone to be on the same page about what gets filmed and what doesn't.'

'Of course,' concedes Evan, getting his breath back. 'Naturally.'

Alison looks positively furious. Her fists are balled at her sides and she's scowling at Evan from under her dark fringe with such vitriol that I feel like I've . . . well, like I've intruded on a lovers' tiff. Evan himself looks unperturbed.

A greasy head appears round the door. It's Nathan, the sound guy. 'Woss goin' on?' he grunts, idly chewing gum. 'Doesn't anyone care we're filming a show out here?'

'Quick debrief,' explains Evan, 'it's over now.'

Alison's still sulking. Nathan looks at her, then at Evan, and rolls his eyes.

'Chin up,' Evan tells her, giving her an awkward fatherly pat on the back. 'You're no good to us with a face like a baboon's arse.'

Now Alison really does look like she's about to cry.

I catch her arm as she's following him out. 'Are you all right?' I ask. 'What's going on?'

'Forget it,' she says miserably, glaring at Evan's back. 'It's stupid.' She looks at me as though she's thinking about elaborating, but then decides not to.

'Come on,' she says instead. 'Chester's waiting for you.'

14

When Will I Be Famous?

Lou folds one newspaper, slips it into her over-sized handbag and immediately opens another.

'According to this,' she says, flipping it out, 'Maddie Mulhern is "a buxom brunette with bags of bottle" – and look, here's a picture of you in front of the bar.'

I peer at the 'After Dark' feature, one of about twenty we've read on last night's live show (this one's titled PINE-APPLE: MIST CLEARS THE WAY FOR REALITY SENSATION), and scrutinise the photo. It's a still from my interview with Chester Bendwell. My mouth is open in response to a question, my hair's dishevelled and one of the straps on my dress has slipped suggestively off my shoulder.

'They make me sound like a wench!' I cry. 'And I look like one, too. Give me a push-up bra and a couple of tankards and I'll be in some Wild West saloon. God, I look gobby.'

It's Saturday morning and Lou, Jaz and I are in the dressing rooms at H&M. I'm struggling to get a basic cotton dress over my head – at least it appears basic, but each time I think I've figured out which arm goes in what hole, I find myself back at square one, tangled up like a squid in a net.

Jaz's face appears at the side of the curtain. 'Does that one say anything about me? What about Alex?'

Lou shakes her head, scanning the column. 'It's only a small mention anyway – they all are. I can't imagine *that* many people watched the first show. Wasn't it on Channel 30 or something?'

'It was TrueUK,' corrects Jaz, disappearing back inside to try on outfit number ten.

'It sounds like a dating line,' I say, struggling with the zips.

Lou opens another. 'It's like I'm reading about a different bar. I can't get used to it not being called Sing It Back any more – I mean it's OK, I guess, but the identity's totally changed. Don't you think your parents will mind?'

I'm trying hard at the moment not to think about my parents at all – except how thrilled and happy they'll be when they find out what I'm doing. Which, of course, they will be.

'It'll be fine,' I say, hoping I'm right. 'Evan had to twist my arm about it' – I twist my own arm trying to undo a pesky button at the back – 'but I can see it makes sense.'

Lou's eyes widen as she scans the feature. 'This one says you're a size eight!'

'Does it?' I ask before diving back into the material. 'They probably meant my feet.' Even so, I make a mental note to buy that paper more often.

When my head pops out the top, Lou is still wearing a disbelieving expression. 'There's no need to look *quite* so alarmed,' I say primly, lifting my chin.

'You have size eight *feet*?' squawks Jaz in the cubicle next door. 'But you're only tiny!'

'I don't have size eight feet,' I mutter, battling with the dress. 'Ugh! Lou, help me – this thing's got about fifty arm holes!'

Lou's the only one not trying stuff on – she's trying to save money, having bought way too many shoes last month – but Jaz begged me to come and, since I'd already promised to spend the morning with my best friend, I figured we could all do something together. Besides, I want Lou to see that Jaz isn't a predatory crush-snatcher and she's actually a really nice person. As with a lot of loud people, the mistake others make is that she doesn't have feelings or insecurities, things that make her vulnerable like the rest of us – probably, in fact, more.

Lou gets up and I can feel her tugging at the various zips and folds, but to no avail.

'It's stuck,' she proclaims. 'Is this your head?'

'No,' I yell blindly, 'it's my elbow.'

'Where's your head?'

'Where my elbow is.'

'Is this your nose?'

'Ow! You just poked me in the eye.'

'*This* is your nose.' She pinches the end of it.

'You're not funny, Lou,' I tell her, 'just get me out of this dress.'

'*I'm a Celebrity*,' Jaz's voice chimes happily, '*Get Me Out of This Dress!*'

I thrash about a bit more, before Lou says gently, 'It's a playsuit, Maddie. You've put your head up one of the leg holes.'

I stop thrashing. 'A playsuit? Isn't that what babies wear?'

'That's a romper suit. This is like a dress that looks like a top and shorts.'

Eventually, with Lou's help, I break free from the playsuit and step into it instead. It looks OK, but I could never feel altogether comfortable wearing something whose name implies enthusiastic participation in outdoor recreation and leisure, so I put it back on the hanger, change into my own jeans and top, and sit down next to Lou.

She's looking at a photo of Nick Craven – after his public TV appearance, the first in eighteen months, he's received a flood of coverage.

'Wow, he *is* handsome, isn't he?' she observes. 'But you know what they say.'

'What?'

'Once a cheat, always a cheat.'

I fiddle about with my mobile, pretending not to care. 'He didn't *actually* cheat, though, did he? It's not like he was with anyone at the time . . .' Lou fires me a look. 'Not that I'm defending him or anything. I mean, it hardly matters to me.' I study the photo. It's a side-on one where he's deep in conversation with Evan, sharp and smart in a suit but with an irresistibly sexy five o'clock shadow and slightly mussed-up hair. I feel a tug in my chest and try to put it down to the brie and tomato baguette I just hoovered up at Pret.

'Cheat or not,' I toss my phone into my bag, adopting a dismissive, couldn't-care-less tone, 'it's obvious he's good-looking *and* he knows it – he probably thinks he can jump into bed with just about anything! Well, not me!' I act affronted. 'Not that that's an option, of course it isn't – and even if it *were* I'd not be tempted . . . not that any such thing has been suggested, but just to make it absolutely, categorically clear.' I deliver a short, harsh laugh. 'No, I couldn't imagine anything *worse* than being seduced by such a shameless womaniser!'

'Hmm,' says Lou. 'Whatever you say.'

'I mean, it's obvious he's thinks nothing of shagging around,' I gas on. 'He'd probably sleep with Evan Bergman if he thought it was going to further his career!'

Lou stays quiet.

I'm aghast. 'You don't think . . . ?'

'Well, now that you mention it,' muses Lou with a naughty glint in her eye, 'why else did Evan hire him? It does seem strange given his reputation.' She takes a minute to mull it over before giving me a confident smile. 'But anyway, what do you care, right?'

I chew my lip. 'Right.'

Jaz emerges. 'Thoughts, please!' she says, giving us a twirl. She's wearing bright orange leggings with a pair of frayed denim micro shorts and a bikini top. All she needs is a scrunchie and a pair of DMs and we'd be in an episode of *Blossom*.

'It's very . . . loud,' says Lou, glancing up from the paper.

'Great!' trills Jaz, seizing this as unanimous approval. 'I can get the whole thing for under ten pounds.'

'Bargain,' murmurs Lou as she disappears again.

'Stop it,' I mouth, wishing Lou would make more of an effort. I know she isn't Jaz's biggest fan but I'm sick of playing the mediator.

Moments later, Jaz appears under a drift of clothing. 'Ready?' She grapples with the hangers and nearly trips over a trailing crêpey scarf.

'Ready.' Lou jumps up and takes a bundle, and I smile gratefully at her. 'Shall we all go grab a coffee?'

♪

'I swear that guy's looking at me,' hisses Jaz. 'This is it, Maddie: we're getting recognised!'

It seems trivial to point out that we're probably getting stared at because Jaz has a top on that reads LOOK AT ME, I'M FAMOUS! Instead I sip my tea.

'People don't care enough,' I say, 'it's only a karaoke bar. Surely there's only so much crap singing and dodgy furnishings a person can take.' I'm not altogether convinced even as I speak the words – in truth I was shocked this morning at how much coverage the show had secured. And there's a clear reason why: Nick Craven's first public appearance after Ascotgate.

'You'd better get used to it,' says Lou sagely. 'Of course people are interested: you've got Nick for one.'

'Swoon,' drawls Jaz, picking the pecans off her pecan slice with satsuma-coloured fingernails. 'He can direct *me* any time he likes.'

'Why did you get a pecan slice if you don't like pecans?' asks Lou.

'I like the pecan pieces inside; I just don't like the big pecans on top.'

'What's wrong with pecans?'

'The pecans on top look like brains. See?'

'Can everyone stop talking about pecans?' I nick Jaz's discarded pecans and pop them in my mouth. '*Blast from the Past* is only on for eight weeks – it'll be forgotten about five minutes after.'

Lou stirs her coffee. 'You do realise it's not *really* about the crap singing and eighties nostalgia.' She looks at me. 'Don't you?'

'That's part of it.'

'But only a small part. Evan wants you centre stage and anyone else he can rope in, too. It's a show about *people*, Maddie – most reality shows are.' She glances at Jaz. 'And some are more up for that than others.'

'But the focus is on the club,' I say, nodding decisively. 'That was Evan's point.'

'And you trust Evan, do you?' Lou reaches across and squeezes my hand. 'Look, all I'm saying is you've got to be prepared to enjoy the limelight for a bit – and not look terrified at the thought of someone recognising you.'

'I did not look terrified!'

'You kind of did.'

Jaz is immersed in one of the articles. 'It says here that

Chester Bendwell wants to give you a sixty-second haircut!'

'No, thanks.' I frown. 'What's wrong with my hair?'

Lou rolls her eyes. 'Nothing's wrong with it – the man's a fool. It's all self-promotion and you'd better get adjusted to it.'

My interview with the man himself was happily without incident. Soon after my flustered Nick–Evan–Alison encounter, I was thrust in front of the cameras and had Chester Bendwell's excited-little-boy-on-the-brink-of-wetting-himself face lurching into mine. All I could think about was Nick Craven, which, I suppose, was a blessing: I didn't have time to analyse the fact I was speaking to hundreds of thousands of viewers. I half expected Chester to refer to it and embarrass me further – I was convinced I'd had a sign over my head reading 'Yoo-hoo, over here, I fancy the pants off that man I just met!' – but he didn't, for which I'm thankful.

Instead he asked me all about the club: when my parents set it up, what the glory days were like (I probably fabricated a lot of this; I think at one point I said we'd had Marky Mark and the Funky Bunch performing – sadly, I don't think this is true), where my parents were touring now (good publicity for them, I hope) and, finally, why we'd chosen to invite the cameras in. The way he said it sounded like I'd opened my doors to a pack of vampires.

'It was OK, wasn't it?' I ask the others.

'You were great,' Lou reassures me. 'You seemed really confident! No one would have guessed it was your first time on TV.'

Jaz flips the page. 'You did look a bit . . . awkward when you met Nick Craven, though.' She says this without a hint of antagonism, which worries me: Jaz is known for speaking the truth.

'*Ugh*,' I put my face in my hands. 'Was it that bad?'

'No,' Lou says, 'it wasn't. Jaz is just winding you up.'

'I am not!'

'A part of me will never forgive Alison for broadcasting that.' I sit back, thinking about it. 'But there's something funny going on there, I know it.'

Jaz frowns. 'What do you mean?'

'Between Alison and Evan.' I run my finger round the rim of the tea saucer. 'When I first met her at Tooth & Nail she was clearly in a piss with him, then the next thing I know she's on my doorstep all soupy-eyed, then she's trying to please him and it's all Evan-this and Evan-that, and a week later he's shouting at her and she's throwing a sulk . . .'

Lou's mouth drops open. 'Are they having an *affair*? Yuck!'

'Evan's not *that* ugly.'

Lou shudders. 'Imagine it, though . . .'

'I'd rather not.'

'Brillo-pad hair, all that leathery skin . . . he's like a handbag with arms and legs.'

I giggle. 'Whatever he is, he's got some sort of hold over Alison. And I don't get the impression she's easily subdued.'

'Why's she doing it, then?'

I shrug. 'She works for him, she probably admires him. God knows what his agenda is, but my bet is he's been promising her all sorts. He gets a pretty girl in his bed,' I raise a mischievous eyebrow, 'and I'm talking black silk sheets *and* a ceiling mirror here, and she gets the thrill of sleeping with the boss. I just hope she knows what she's getting herself into. From what I can see he's constantly belittling her and making her feel bad. That's the way with men like him – it's all about control.'

Lou pretends to have a mouthful of sick. 'That's gross. Did you have to say the thing about the mirror?'

Jaz has gone quiet.

'What do you think?' I ask her.

She looks down at her lap. 'I don't know,' she says, trying and failing to be breezy. 'I guess it's complicated.'

There's an awkward silence, during which I curse my stupid big tactless mouth. I'm remembering why Jaz left the States in the first place – it was down to a very similar situation to the one I'm describing. How could I have been so insensitive?

'Oh, Jaz, I'm sorry,' I say. 'I'm an idiot.'

She shakes her head, attempts a smile. 'Forget it – it was a long time ago.'

Lou throws me a quizzical look and I resolve to tell her about it later – I can't imagine Jaz wants to get into the whole mess now. But it's another reminder that underneath all the hair and make-up she's just as fragile as the rest of us, and just as prone to heartbreak.

When Jaz first arrived at Sing It Back looking for work, she'd flown into the UK only a week before. Her dream was to act, to one day see her name in lights, to walk the red carpet – and she had very nearly made it. She'd spent the last three years in LA, where at first she'd been slowly but surely working her way up the slippery ladder towards stardom. But then she'd become involved with Carl. Carl was a self-made

141

Hollywood casting agent, who, rather than promote and celebrate Jaz, had, over the months they were together, gradually chipped away at her confidence and told her she was no good; that the parts weren't coming her way not because she'd just lost out by the slightest margin, or because the producers already had somebody in mind, but because she was lacking talent, ugly, needed her boobs done, her lips filled, her hair styled, her teeth straightened – whatever he wanted to pick on that day. He was a bit older than her and from the sounds of things a textbook control freak, set on tying her down and making sure he broke her low enough so that she hadn't the nerve to leave him.

Over time Jaz lost faith in her ability and avoided auditions – maybe she wasn't cut out for fame after all: if Carl was telling her so, and he knew the industry like the back of his hand, then perhaps she should listen. I don't know the exact circumstances of their break-up but by the end she was a wreck. As far as I can gather she did, thank god, finally find the courage to walk, and packed her stuff and boarded a plane without him knowing. She hasn't seen or spoken to Carl since, and I hope she never does.

Sometimes I forget this is Jaz's story: she seems so assured, like nothing can faze her, but there's a lot of insecurity buried deep. I think that's why she makes such a statement with her appearance – it's all to mask what she wants to keep hidden.

'How's Alex getting on?' Lou asks, changing the subject. Lou's good like that – sensing when people don't want to talk about stuff and moving things on like she hasn't noticed.

'Great!' Jaz brightens. She pushes away the rest of her

cake, though, so I don't think she's completely OK. 'He's really nice, he's awesome.'

'Hmm.' I make a face. Am I the only one who finds Alex unsettling? 'I'm not convinced, but Evan seems keen.'

'What's wrong with him?' Jaz pouts. 'He's so good with Andre.'

'He is good with Andre,' I concede, and I think we're now in the dangerous territory of beginning to refer to the guinea pig as Jaz's *child*, 'but he doesn't ever seem to do any work! And when he does, I can't believe he's got the bar experience he says he has – according to his CV he's got years, but I'd be amazed if he'd had minutes.'

'He seems fine to me,' says Jaz. 'I really like him.'

'That's one for each of you, then,' I tease, and Lou gives my shin a sharp kick under the table.

'Are you OK?' I ask innocently. 'Are you going into spasm?'

Lou blushes. 'Shut up, Maddie.'

Jaz looks between us. 'What?'

'Lou fancies Simon,' I tell her. 'It had to come out sooner or later, so there it is.'

'Shut *up*!'

'Well that's good,' Jaz fishes some cash out her wallet and slips it under the salt shaker, 'because Simon fancies Lou. He said so!'

I grab Lou's arm. 'Ohmygod. What did I tell you?'

Lou's tongue-tied, something I haven't seen before. She's gone very red and is trying hard not to smile, but I know she's elated.

'Lou, you have to ask him out!' I squeal.

'Between us, I think he'll ask you,' says Jaz, leaning in

conspiratorially. 'He said he was working up to it.' She turns to me. 'Simon's nervous. I think he's worried she'll say no.'

'But she won't, will she?' I nudge Lou and we both laugh. '*Will* she?'

'Maybe not,' she says, all happy and shy.

15

Love Game

'I suppose what I'm saying, Maddie, is that I'm looking for a little more . . .' Evan's tongue darts out and licks his lips, '*drama.*'

With a satisfied sigh, he eases back in his leather chair and narrows his eyes. I can hear a delivery van for Burger King reversing in the car park outside.

'More drama?'

'Exactly right.' Evan points a finger at me as if I've just had a Eureka moment – even if he's the only one who understands it.

A month has passed since I was last at Tooth & Nail, but so

much has happened in the intervening weeks that it could be years ago. *Blast from the Past* has been on for eight days now – I've watched snippets of the programme here and there but we've been too busy every night to catch a full episode – and Evan wanted to call me in to discuss 'format development'. As far as I'm concerned the format is perfect: what I've gleaned from magazine articles and peering over someone's shoulder on the tube promotes the club brilliantly: one paper described the club as 'King Kitsch and the Realm of Retro', which is great by me so long as Mum and Dad's name is getting back on the map. I'm feeling pretty happy about it, to be honest. What we're up to is unconventional, but it seems to be doing the job. It's even, dare I say it, *fun*. Though that's mainly down to working each day with a certain someone whose name begins with N and who's a clever director and who has the loveliest smile and the loveliest hands I've ever seen.

I'd be lying if I didn't say that part of me hoped Nick Craven would be at the meeting, hence this morning's five-times change of outfit. Eventually I settled on a pair of tight black jeans and a smart but sexy lace green top – I figured he'd always seen me in skirts or dresses so I wanted a change (I know: sad, sad, *sad*). Anyway, the only person getting the benefit of today's efforts is, unfortunately, Evan bloody Bergman.

'But everything's going well, isn't it?' I cross my legs and something in the set-up makes me think of *that* scene in *Basic Instinct*. Yuck. Forget that. Quickly.

'Toby seems pleased,' I say, 'and Alison. The ratings look good, you said so yourself.'

Evan spreads a pair of fattish hands across the desk. 'Ah,

but you're talking to a man with ambition. I won't settle for good if I can have great.'

'What are you suggesting, then?'

He goes through the motions of mulling it over, but I can tell he already knows exactly what he's going to say.

'I'd like to . . . help things on a bit.'

'Help things on?'

'Yes. I'm not convinced the cameras are catching what they need to.'

'I haven't had any problems with them,' I say. Alison and the crew have been with us nearly eighteen hours a day since launch night, but everyone's got so used to them now that we don't much notice any more. At first it was weird, but it's amazing how quickly you stop caring – especially when there's a tonne of work to be done. And that's the greatest thing: since we went on air, Pineapple has been so flooded with punters – Simon had to set up a ticketing system because we were turning so many away at the door – that the labour's been non-stop. We've also had stylists round to plan the next stage of updates: their ideas for the interior are super-exciting, I can't wait for Mum and Dad to see. When you're immersed in a job, you don't really care that Alison's following you about like a lost puppy begging for food. And anyway, only about two per cent of what they film goes into the final cut.

'No,' says Evan thoughtfully, 'no problems. But I wonder if we could step the action up a notch, give the viewers something to sink their teeth into.'

'Like what?'

He smiles. 'Take your argument with Alex, for example.'

I've been anticipating this. Ever since my fall-out with Alex the other day, I've been conscious that it's the sort of thing you see on reality shows all the time. Thankfully it wasn't a blazing, or a particularly interesting, dispute (I had to drag him aside for some stern words when he failed to place our stock order for the third time in a row) but it was enough to get Alison excited. Afterwards I realised the cameras had caught everything, but there was little I could do – especially with lanky Nathan in his customary pissy mood, refusing to engage in an adult conversation for more than five seconds. Besides, I didn't feel as though I'd acted out of line, and if viewers wanted the real-life workings of a bar, this was occasionally it.

'That shouldn't happen again,' I tell him.

Evan nods. There's a brief pause. 'But supposing I wanted it to?'

'You mean you want me to fight with Alex?'

'Not necessarily . . .' He links his hands behind his head and closes his eyes, as if we're two holiday-makers striking up innocent conversation by the pool. 'You must be wondering why I employed Nick Craven.'

The name makes my heart skip a beat – I really need to get a handle on that. 'Um . . . he's a household name?'

'Not only that . . .'

'He's a good director?'

The eyes fly open. 'That's right! And good directors . . . well, they direct, wouldn't you say?'

I choose not to say anything, because I know this is Evan's game: he wants me to feed him his very own argument – whatever that argument is.

148

'And the *very* good directors get the absolute best from their cast,' he barrels on. 'That's precisely what I intend to do here.'

I shake my head. 'You've lost me.'

Evan appears validated, as if he fully expected me to be this dim. 'I'll explain. Your friend, the blonde one who's been helping out . . . What's her name?'

I'm hesitant. 'Louise.'

'Louise, that's right. Very pretty, isn't she?'

'Yes.'

'And am I right in thinking . . .' he winks at me, and this small movement is more disconcerting than any words he could utter, 'that there's a little, how to put it, "chemistry" between her and Simon?' Evan doesn't actually do the finger quote marks round the word but he might as well – I can't imagine he's used it in any context other than when he was fourteen and it related to the periodic table.

'They like each other,' I say carefully. 'But we're all good friends.'

'Well, yes, of course, of course. Some more than others, perhaps.'

'Perhaps.'

'You see, Maddie – everybody loves a romance. You'd be working wonders for the popularity of the show if you could . . . let's just say, *encourage* this a bit.'

'Encourage what?'

'Louise and Simon. You know, chivvy them on.'

I can't help but laugh. What exactly is he hoping for, sex in the middle of the dance floor? Maybe Alex could oversee proceedings by warbling along to Another Level's 'Freak Me'? Oh my word. *Shudder.*

But it seems he's serious.

'I don't think they need it,' I say firmly, 'they're working things out for themselves. Let's leave it at that, OK?' What does he think I am? There's no way on earth I'm involving two of my favourite people in Evan's shenanigans – I'd die if I jeopardised what they might or might not have, and, aside from that, neither of them wanted to be part of this show in the first place.

Evan raises an eyebrow. 'So the romance is developing without our intervention?' He makes it sound like mould growing in a petri dish.

'It's not relevant, all right?' I'm surprised by the strength of my conviction. 'Like I said, just leave it.'

But Evan's deep in thought, and I can tell I'm not going to like what he's about to say next.

'Jasmine's a little firecracker, isn't she?'

'She's certainly a character—'

'I agree. She's a character needing a stage, a role . . . *direction*.'

God, he's good.

'So I was pondering whether,' his eyes switch to mine, 'we could introduce her to the mix, shake things up a little?'

'No.'

He holds his hands up in a gesture of surrender, though I strongly suspect Evan Bergman doesn't know the meaning of the word.

'Hear me out, now, Maddie, let's not jump to conclusions.' His voice is smooth, soothing, reassuring. 'This is what reality TV *is*. Surely you must realise that. Otherwise we'd be out on the street filming any old Joe who wanted to get his mug on the telly – the problem with that is, it wouldn't be *exciting*.'

150

Evan nods, liking what he's saying. 'I'm an entertainer. Well,' he clears his throat, 'of sorts. These days I entertain from behind the scenes; pull the puppet strings, if you like. You must know what it's like to exist in the wings, growing up with parents like yours.'

I nod, uncertain. There's a hint of bitterness to Evan's voice but I can't work out why.

'So I make things happen from afar,' he continues, 'it's my job and I'm good at it. But I can't make things happen without the cooperation of my cast, now, can I?'

'But we're *not* your cast.' I'm starting to lose my temper and don't want to fall out with Evan this soon into filming. 'We talked about this at the start.'

Evan doesn't miss a beat. 'Look, *Blast from the Past* is about the club, right? Just like I said. But you and your friends are *part of* the club, so you can't have one without the other. Understand?'

I resent his tone. 'I told you – I'm not risking Lou and Simon's friendship. That's the end of it. You can't convince me, so don't bother trying.'

Evan chuckles softly. 'You're missing my point.'

'Perhaps that's because you're not explaining it.'

'Very well.' Evan nods. 'Jasmine's participation will achieve the contrary: it'll make Louise and Simon realise how they feel about each other, push them into each other's arms and send them off into the sunset, happy ever after. Better? It's a classic love triangle. Those brain-dead morons slumped at home on their sofas, pudgy arms buried in a bargain bucket of KFC, are going to lap it up, just like piglets at their mother's teat: you mark my words.'

There's so much in that short spiel that disgusts me that I actually make a face.

'It's not happening, Evan. I'm not changing my mind.'

Evan heaves a big sigh and clicks his teeth, mindlessly shuffling the papers on his desk.

'Dear me, Maddie,' he says, shaking his head infuriatingly, 'you *do* have a lot to learn.'

♪

I'm really, *really* annoyed. As I emerge on to the scrum of Oxford Street, I decide my instincts about Evan Bergman were spot-on: I don't like him. At all.

We're scarcely a week into it and he's busy plotting sham romances already? Fine, we're doing a reality show, but isn't there a difference between allowing cameras into your life and actually orchestrating *scenes* and having to act and lie and mess people about? Especially when those people are your best friends? I can't even think about it. And Evan's assumption that I haven't a clue what the real world's about, when he's the one sat in Tooth & Nail Towers with his fake tan and his fake hair and his fake teeth – what's real about any of that?

Sorry. I need to calm down.

It's two o'clock. I decide not to go straight back to the club. Maybe I'll go sit in Costa and eat one of their giant flapjacks, or drop into Holland & Barrett to buy Lou some crystallised ginger (her new weight-loss initiative; apparently it's a super-food) or walk idly round Liberty and finger all the nice things I can't afford and pretend I'm Julia Roberts in *Pretty Woman*.

Or maybe . . .

For some reason it just pops into my head. Yes, that's where I'll go.

With renewed direction, I set off back to Soho, not really knowing why but unsure where else to head. There's an innocent reason: this is probably the person my parents have known the longest now Archie's gone, and in their absence I feel the need to check in with the old-timers, get my feet back on the ground and out of what I'm worried is rapidly becoming Evan's stage set. But I also remember what Loaf said the last time we met:

You don't know what you're letting yourself in for . . . Watch your back . . . Things might not be quite what they seem . . .

A shiver travels down my spine, despite the warmth of the late-May day. What did he mean? The bigger part of me dismisses his rants as the product of having a few screws loose: anyone who dresses as Meatloaf 24/7 and has a preoccupation with winged mammals taking to the skies has got to be a bit wrong. But my meeting with Evan has unnerved me: what if Loaf's not as crazy as I first thought?

Minutes later, I'm standing outside Rock Around the Clock. If anything it looks grimier this time – the OPEN side of the sign even more tattered and faded than its counterpart – and as before, it's empty apart from the lone figure wedged behind the till.

The bell tinkles self-consciously as I open the door. There's a smell I didn't notice before, like Heinz tomato soup.

'Hello?'

Loaf looks up from his magazine, spots me and immediately bundles it away, though not before I see it's a *Star Wars* comic. 'Hello.'

'Busy day?' I smile as I shut the door, meaning for it to come out friendly, but instead it sounds like I'm taking the piss.

'Actually I did make a sale this morning,' Loaf says, indignant. 'Admittedly the first in a while, but even so.'

'Wow!' Now it really sounds like I'm being sarcastic. 'What did they buy?'

Loaf tips his head to one side. 'Ah, they looked keen on the Rickenbacker 650S . . . then the girl had eyes on the Yamaha' – he gestures to a dusty-looking, but still very handsome, keyboard – 'but eventually they were taken with the Fender Electro Acoustic.'

I'm impressed. 'So they took it?'

'Well, not exactly. They left with a plectrum in the end.'

'Oh.'

'What do you want?' Loaf straightens his worn-leather jacket and pins me with a stare. 'I can't imagine you're wanting for too much these days, being a celebrity and all that.'

I fold my arms. 'I came to see how you are,' I say, which isn't a total fib. 'You haven't been into Pineapple since we started filming.'

Loaf seems to find this really funny. 'And you're surprised? You think I want to hop around with a bunch of fame-hungry teenagers desperate for five seconds on TV? No, thank you very much. Besides, it's a stupid name. That place is and always will be Sing It Back.'

'We changed it to match the series,' I explain, starting to think this visit was a bad idea. Evan's already made me feel like a stupid kid this morning – I don't need Loaf doing the same.

'You mean Evan Bergman changed it?' He tears open a bag

of prawn cocktail crisps and extracts one with his finger and thumb. His signet ring catches the light on its way past.

'You know what?' I turn to go. 'Forget it. I didn't come here for a lecture.'

'Wait!' Suddenly he's on his feet. 'Don't go. Sit down, please. In fact,' he looks at his watch, 'I'll close for a bit. We'll go through to the back.'

I peer nervously over Loaf's shoulder into the room beyond. I'm not sure I want to go anywhere with this person that's even remotely hidden from view.

'Come on,' he says, 'I'll make you a coffee.'

I'm about to politely decline when I remember Mum and Dad know him and have for years. What harm can it do?

Loaf turns the sign on the door and leads me out back, where a trio of chipped brown steps takes us down to a courtyard. There's an old bike propped up against the wall, one Wellington boot and a bin bag that's been attacked by foxes. To the left is a door with a number 9 on it, but it's loose on its screw and I wonder if it started life as a 6.

'My humble abode,' Loaf says, almost apologetically, as he fumbles to open the door. If Jaz and Simon could see me now, chatting with the local oddball and being let into his flat . . . well, they'd almost certainly call the police.

Inside, though, it's surprisingly nice, and not at all what I expected (which was probably something along the lines of the underground water cave in *Phantom of the Opera*, complete with rowing boats and candelabra). It's tastefully decorated, quite plain – quite *normal* – and there's no sign of those mucky tortoiseshell carpets that everyone had in the seventies and for some reason I felt sure would feature.

Loaf disappears into a little kitchen, banging mugs about and flicking the kettle on. 'Go on through!' he shouts. 'Door on your right.'

Ah, so this must be the living room. Seems all right: lots of vinyl; nice squidgy couch; old TV that looks like it needs a whack every so often to get it working; nest of wooden tables resting on animal-claw feet, but we'll forgive those; a glass decanter half-full of honey-coloured stuff, maybe sherry . . . ooh look, I'll just be a *teeny* bit nosy and have a peer in this cupboard—

'ARGGGGH!'

I'm face to face with David Bowie.

Or rather, a life-size mannequin of David Bowie, complete with Ziggy suit. He's gazing glassily at me from dead eyes lined with glittery pink make-up. Oh my fucking god – Loaf is a *freak*. I knew it. I've got to get out of here before he strangles me and stuffs me full of cotton wool or whatever those people who stuff roadkill use and puts me in a cage with dead buzzards and grizzly bears and sells my teeth to an Arab jeweller—

David topples out and smacks me in the face. I think I must black out for a bit, because the next thing I know I'm on the floor and David's rolling about on top of me in his slippery silver spacesuit. In a panic I wrestle him and get a mouthful of orange hair. Spitting, grappling, I attempt to push him away and end up grabbing blindly at a metallic shoulder pad and ripping it off.

'What the hell is going on?'

Loaf storms into the room and my heart stops in my chest. *I'm going to die.*

156

Loaf's lost it, a long time ago. He's a psycho, and now I'm trapped in his house. I'm trapped and nobody knows where I am. I could be rotting here for weeks before they find me. I'll be under the floorboards, buried alive next to a nude portrait of Morten Harket.

Please, god – what did I do to incur your wrath?

I should never have told Ginny Henderson at school that she looked like Ronald McDonald. (But she did.)

Now I'm going to die on a moth-eaten carpet with a life-size prostrate David Bowie.

Maybe if I lie really, *really* still, Loaf won't see me.

He sets the coffees down. 'Oh,' he says, as if there's nothing unusual about this scene in the least, 'you found David.'

Suddenly I can bear it no longer. 'GET HIM OFF ME!' I howl.

'What are you doing?' chuckles Loaf as David's lifted from me, dusted off and propped against the wall. 'Come on.' He extends a hand but I back away, wild-eyed.

'What the *fuck* is that?' I say in a trembling voice. I turn my face away; I can't look at David, I *can't*. But David's looking at me.

'It's David Bowie,' says Loaf. He proffers the biscuit barrel. 'Custard Cream?'

I'm speechless.

'Your parents commissioned him,' he says, amused. 'They commissioned a host of them for the club last year – we've got others on order, too: Freddie Mercury, Sinitta, Billy Idol, Robbie Williams . . . It's like a hall of fame. Not quite Madame Tussauds, but you get the picture.' He sips his drink. 'You OK?'

I'm slowly getting my breath back. 'Can you turn him round?' I gulp, sickened.

Loaf looks bemused, but he does as I ask. 'Oh no,' he says, inspecting David once the mannequin's forehead is safely resting against the wall. 'You've torn his outfit!'

'I thought he was attacking me!' I scramble to my feet and check my elbow, which is a little sore after I landed on it.

Loaf looks at me like I'm crazy. 'He's not real, you know.'

'I know that!' I splutter a defence. 'He just fell on top of me out of nowhere, what am I supposed to do?'

Loaf tuts and shakes his head. 'Not exactly nowhere, was it?' He takes a pew on the sofa and watches me over the rim of his mug. 'That's what you get for snooping around other people's things.'

Maybe he's right about that. Chastened, I sink on to a sorry-looking beanbag and immediately regret it – it's so low to the ground that my head's level with Loaf's knees and I have to look up to meet his eye. It's like story time round Grandma's house.

'So why are you looking after them?' I ask, feeling a little foolish at my outburst.

'Looking after what?'

'The models.' I nod towards the back of David's head, which might actually be creepier than the front – but I'm not about to turn him to find out.

'The finished products only started coming in a couple of weeks ago,' explains Loaf. 'I told your parents they could be delivered to Rock Around the Clock in their absence – they hadn't forewarned you so thought it wise to wait till they got back.' He hides a smile. 'Probably better that way, judging by your reaction. You should see the one they've ordered of Michael Jackson! Now that really *could* have been the real thing.'

I shudder.

'Have you told them about the show yet?' Loaf passes me my drink.

I shake my head. 'It's going to be a surprise.' I smile weakly. 'A good one, I'm hoping.'

Loaf doesn't say anything, just carries on watching me. 'And how are *you* finding it?'

I hug my knees. 'Fine,' I say honestly, 'until today. But whatever – I just wanted it to help the club financially – and it has. I mean, it is.'

'You've certainly got the numbers up if the papers are anything to go by.'

'Hmm.' I squint at him. 'You must miss it. You were in every week before. You still could, you know.'

Loaf laughs hollowly. 'I don't think so. I'm aware I'm an eccentric – and it's eccentrics like me that these reality shows eat for breakfast.' He dunks a Bourbon biscuit and sucks the liquid from it loudly.

When he's finished he asks, 'So what happened today?'

'Apart from getting mauled by David Bowie?'

'Apart from that.'

I sigh. 'Well, it's nothing really. I don't think. It's just that things have been great so far, really great, and I've been thinking how maybe the reality TV thing wasn't so bad after all. But now it's like it really *was* too good to be true, either that or I've spectacularly missed the point, because Evan Bergman – he's the producer at Tooth & Nail—'

'I know who he is.'

'—he's started going on about "stepping things up a notch" and giving viewers "something to sink their teeth into". Basically he wants me to engineer things so people – my friends – get pissed off, or upset, or argue with each other. And that's not something I'm prepared to do.'

Loaf nods. 'I can understand that.'

'So I'm just going to stand my ground. I'm not going to let Evan bully me.' I get to the bottom of my coffee and it turns gritty.

'Evan Bergman's a difficult man,' says Loaf. 'He's very convincing.'

'Tell me about it!' I splutter. 'Hang on a minute – you know him?'

Loaf checks the time. 'I should get back,' he says.

'But you know him?' It seems vital to find out. 'How?'

A pause before Loaf stands up. 'It was a long time ago,' he says, 'it's not worth going into.'

He collects the mugs and I notice his hands are shaking. What on earth is this about?

'All I'll tell you,' he murmurs, 'is what I told you before: look after yourself and watch your back. You've learned that for yourself today.'

'But what about Evan? I mean, if there's something I should know . . .'

He turns round at the door. 'That's all you need to know,' he says solemnly. 'For now.'

16

It's a Kind of Magic

It's raining the next day when Lou and I emerge from Simply Voices. We get drenched as we run for the tube, my pound-shop umbrella flipping itself inside out and filling with wind, threatening to carry us away.

'My hair's ruined!' Lou cries once we've ducked into the station. It's rush hour so we have to flatten ourselves against the wall to avoid being slammed into.

'You look gorgeous,' I say, catching my own reflection in the glass of a poster ad and not liking what I see – my own hair is like Lawrence Llewellyn-Bowen's. 'At least Simon's going to think so.' I flash her a cheeky grin.

'Wish me luck,' she says anxiously, patting her hair. 'Is my mascara smudged?'

'No. I'd say if you looked anything other than perfect, and you don't.'

Tonight is Lou and Simon's first date. I'm excited enough, so I can only think what she's going through.

'Good luck,' I tell her, as a guy with a massive backpack bumps into me – he apologises in French, 'but you won't need it. Do you know where he's taking you?'

'Just the pub,' she says. 'Thankfully he didn't suggest dinner – I'll have some scampi fries or something later. I can't go for a meal on a first date.'

'Why not?'

'I'm too nervous. And besides, I never know what to order. If I order a salad he'll think I'm a waif. If I order a steak he'll think I'm a pig – even if I really want steak, which I invariably do. And if I order something with garlic in – and practically *everything* has garlic in – I'll stink!'

'What, and scampi fries don't?'

'Good point.'

I laugh. 'Simon likes you already. You're friends, remember? It's not like a blind date – you already know he's a nice guy.'

'Yeah . . .' She squirms. 'That's why, though, I don't want to mess things up.'

'You'll be fine,' I say, hugging her. 'Call me first thing, OK?'

'OK.'

As Lou disappears down the steps, I lament that my parents'

flat isn't quite far away enough to warrant getting the tube. Instead I brave the elements once more and pray my tatty umbrella, which now resembles a dead crow's wing on a stick, survives the distance.

All the way home I think about Lou and Simon: I'm so happy they've finally got it together. And they will, I know, however tonight goes – they're made for each other.

Annoyingly, my thoughts turn to my own love life, or lack thereof. I wonder what Lawrence is doing now, but rather than feeling upset at his new relationship with that theatre director, I'm just annoyed at having wasted so many months with him. I still can't believe he was seeing us both at the same time! In truth I'm inclined to agree with Lou about the relationship with what's-her-face-Montgomery not being the greatest love affair in the history of the world: Lawrence is, I realise, too selfish. And it's far too like him to embark on something that's going to further his career to that extent. I don't want it to still sting, but it does a little. Not that he's dating someone new, but that the time we spent together was so clearly a farce.

I pass a bunch of people sheltering miserably under a bus stop and one of them meets my eye. This is happening more now: someone looks at me for a fraction too long, frowns a bit and nudges the person next to them, then by the time they've reached any conclusion about *Blast from the Past* I've already disappeared. Despite the size of the city, I feel more anonymous here than I would anywhere else: there are too many people and things to draw the attention away.

Everyone at Simply Voices has got over-excited about the show, too – I deliberately kept it to myself at first, maintained a low profile and didn't tell anyone, but when my identity got blown it only made the shock factor that much more. The most surprising is Jennifer, who, when she first caught wind of what I was doing, was pretty brutal about the fact it would wreck my life, ruin my parents' hard work, make fools of us all, etc., etc., but as *Blast from the Past* began to gain momentum – and popularity – did a quick backpedal and started getting me to sign things for her friends. It's all been quite flattering until she asked me for Nick Craven's signature and I realised then the true motivation behind her turnaround. As if I'd do that! I'd look like the biggest suck-arse on the planet. I told her she should come to the club and ask him herself, which brought her out in a rash and made her fumble hot-handed with a vanilla-iced cupcake till she dropped it down her silky peach blouse.

But even I have to admit that the show – and my involvement in it – is causing a stir. At the start I tried to resist it, thinking I could somehow fly under the radar, but of course that's impossible. Viewers have taken to the theme in a way I could never have expected. Evan says it's the kitsch nostalgia; Toby says it's the humour (despite the spangly new machines, it just goes to prove that karaoke can only ever sound terrible); Alison says it's the personalities – we've got some strong characters working at the bar; Nick says . . . well, I don't know what Nick says. He's been on-set – if that's the right term – for several days, but I haven't spoken to him much. His job is to make sure the cameras follow what action there is, and occasionally he'll ask us to move into a different part of the club to refresh the angle. But if I'm completely honest, I've been avoiding him: every time we speak I seem to make a tit of myself.

It annoys me that I care what he thinks, I reflect as I turn into our street. After all, who is he to pass judgement on another person's behaviour? I've never met anyone less qualified to do so in my whole entire life. He's a shallow go-getter. Yes, that's what he is. He's not at all nice, or charming – or even that handsome! He *tricked* me into believing he was handsome, by putting me on the back foot from the first moment we met. I've become far too carried away with the *idea* of what he looks like, when in reality he's not actually that fit . . .

Oh.

Except he is.

Because there, standing in the porch next door to Pineapple, with his hands in his pockets, is Nick Craven.

It's as if I've summoned him by sheer force of imagination, so when he sees me and waves, I experience a hot rush of you-found-me-out embarrassment. Had he not spotted me I would have turned right around and walked in the opposite direction.

What the fuck do I do now?

I go towards him. It seems to take for ever. I smile in what I hope is a friendly way, then don't really know whether to carry on smiling or stop smiling, but if I stop smiling I just have to wear this serious face and if I carry on I look like some sort of nutter. Do I keep looking at him, or is that creepy? Look at the ground? No, weird. Glance around in an interested way like I haven't walked down this street ten thousand times before? Even weirder. The umbrella has all but given up and is a serious threat to passers-by, so I bundle it up and stuff it under one arm. The bottoms of my jeans are soaked and I can only imagine what my top half looks like: all straggly hair and blotchy make-up. Why, oh *why* can't he turn up when I'm wearing my new Whistles dress and heels, and maybe talking on the phone to a friend, laughing and making someone else laugh, and I'll see him and be like, 'Oh, hi, Nick, give me a sec' while I laugh some more and he just looks on and thinks I'm so out of his league it's not funny, so what am I laughing at?

But it is funny. Ha ha ha. Because right now I look like something that's crawled out of a drain.

'Hey,' he says, 'how's it going?' He's shielded from the rain and looks utterly . . . beautiful, with messy black hair and wearing a lovely woolly dark-green jumper, the sort of jumper you want to hug.

I gesture to my own outfit. 'Soggy.'

Soggy. Got to be one of the most attractive ways to describe oneself.

But he laughs. 'Yeah, it's horrid.' A pause. 'I hope you don't mind me turning up like this.'

I shake my head.

'I'm not really here for work.'

'You're not?'

'In a sense I am, but not exactly.' He seems a bit awkward. 'Look, I get the impression we haven't got off to the best start.' He grins. 'I mean, the first time—'

'Yes, yes, we know what happened the first time.'

He nods, gathering himself. 'And there's stuff I've been meaning to discuss with you, so I wondered if . . . I mean, there never seems to be a good time to . . . well, you know.' He stops, runs a hand through his hair. 'Anyway, if you've got half an hour now, I'd really like to buy you a coffee.'

166

I'm taken aback. 'Now?'

'Yeah.' He frowns. 'Only if you've got time – or else we can do it another day.'

'No, no, now's good.'

To my shame, all I can think is: *Is this a date? Is this a date?* And then I tell myself off for being so stupid. Of *course* it's not a date. And I don't want it to be – because I know exactly what Nick Craven gets up to on his so-called dates with unsuitable women. Am *I* an unsuitable woman?

'I just need to grab a shower,' I say, despite myself already thinking about doing my hair and shaving my legs (why?) and using some of those expensive Jo Malone bath goodies that I was given three Christmases ago but was always too afraid to open. 'Give me ten minutes.'

'You live here?' he asks, glancing up at the windows of my parents' flat. The wooden blind, half-pulled, is sagging drunkenly across the window and there's a faded Wet Wet Wet sticker in one corner that, sadly, is just about visible. I think I scratched Marti Pellow's face out once when drunk.

'Er . . . yeah.' I unlock the door and he moves to follow me in.

My mind darts to the treasures concealed at Mum and Dad's. The photographs. The purple mirrors. The cello chair. I'm not ready to show Nick those delights quite yet.

'Wait here,' I instruct him, practically closing the door in his face.

'What? It's raining.'

'Like I said, I won't be long.'

'Come on, it's freezing!'

'There's a cafe over the road,' I suggest through the gap in the door, surprised by how rude I'm prepared to be if the circumstances are right. 'Back in a sec!'

Inside, I bolt up the stairs and nearly drop my keys, my hands are shaking so much. Davinia emerges from her apartment in a silk kimono, her hair done up in rollers.

'Maddie! Thank god. When do you want me downstairs this evening? Usual time?'

'Yes, yes, fine,' I say, pushing my way in.

'Evan told me Uri Geller's making a guest appearance tonight!'

'That's great.'

'Isn't it? Do you think if I ask him he'll bend my—'

'Not now, Davinia!'

'But—'

I slam the door. Right. Action stations. (*Action stations?* I must be feeling giddy.)

Fifteen minutes later I'm showered and dressed. I've never been a girl who takes ages getting ready and, besides, I'm only meeting Nick for coffee – it's not like it's a date and, even if it *were*, I don't want to give him the wrong impression. No, I've kept it simple: a (dry) pair of dark blue jeans, a coral-coloured top, quick brush of the hair and a generous lick of mascara.

I throw on a jacket and flee downstairs, stopping briefly to check my reflection in the hall mirror and slow my heart. It wouldn't do to emerge sweating and panting like a race-horse.

When I open the door I'm expecting to see Nick outside, and I panic for a minute before remembering I ordered him to wait over the road. Feeling ashamed at my earlier lack of manners, I cross and enter the little cafe. I spot him immediately, reading the paper with a serious expression and an almost-drunk cup of coffee in front of him.

'Hello.' I smile when he looks up.

'Hello.' He smiles back.

'Can I get you another?'

He stands up. 'I'll buy – but look, the sun's come out.'

I turn round. He's right. In all my haste I completely didn't notice. The rain on the road is glistening in the light of the late afternoon, all the world bathed in amber, and the lines of things seem clearer, more defined, like a painting.

'Let's go for a walk,' I say.

Nick gets the drinks and we head back out. It smells lovely, as only things do after rain. I'm conscious of him walking alongside me and the heat of the cup in my hand, the steam rising and warming my face. We peel off into the side roads because they're quieter, and I have to hurry to keep up with him.

'Do you always walk this fast?'

He doesn't reply. Instead he smiles and places a hand gently on my back. It feels like electricity.

Minutes later we emerge into Soho Square. Nick finds a bench and lays the newspaper down in sheets. Each one soaks up the wet, turns grey, and he keeps doing this till it's dry enough to sit. I blow on my drink to cool it down and watch the rest of the world hurry past in rush hour, feeling as if we're on an island in the middle, a still amid the chaos.

'Are you happy with how things are going?' Nick asks, and I'm reminded that despite my jittery feelings, we're only catching up about the show.

'Very,' I say. 'I met with Evan yesterday and he's pleased, too.'

A look of alarm passes over Nick's face, before he corrects it. 'Did he say anything else?'

I shake my head, deciding not to tell him about Evan's suggestions for creating more drama. Nick's the director – if he wants to come to me with a similar request he can have the balls to voice it himself.

'What made you want to do this?' he asks after a moment. Said in an offhand way, it wouldn't sound odd, but the way Nick says it seems off-kilter.

'We needed it,' I say carefully. 'The ad Tooth & Nail placed said it all.'

He nods thoughtfully.

'And really it's for my parents,' I prattle, uncomfortable with the silence. 'I want them to feel proud of it like they used to.'

Nick's face breaks into a grin. 'Pineapple Mist . . . happy memories.'

'Oh?'

'School discos. That and T'Pau.'

I groan. 'I think I can safely say I've *never* danced to that song.'

'Which one?'

'Mum and Dad's. How weird would that be? It's bad enough hearing it on Magic FM.'

Nick smiles, looks at me sideways. '"What You Do" is a classic. Come on, admit it.'

'Ooh ooh.'

He looks at me like I'm mad. 'What?'

'You missed the "ooh ooh" bit off the end,' I say, 'the bit in brackets. It's very important, that bit.'

'Oh, sorry.' He grins. He's *so* fit. 'But as the stuff in that era goes, your parents had one of the best.'

'Compared with what, "Agadoo"?'

'Shit, I forgot about that.'

'Exactly. These are the horrors I'm reminded of every day.'

Nick laughs, and it comes from deep inside, a proper laugh. 'OK, so top five singles of the eighties. You first.'

'Sure you want me to go first?'

'Sure.'

I reel them off. 'New Order, "Blue Monday". OMD, "If You Leave". Band Aid, "Do They Know it's Christmas"—'

'Come *on*. And to think you started so well.'

'What?'

'You can't have Band Aid.'

'Why not?'

'It's a Christmas song.'

'So?'

'It's cheating. It's like having Brussels sprouts in July.'

'You can't compare Bob Geldof to a Brussels sprout.'

'I can compare Midge Ure to a Brussels sprout. Same forehead.'

I giggle. 'Anyway, I disagree. Don't tell me you're vetoing a charitable cause.'

'Not fair.'

'Do you want me to go on or not?'

He smiles. 'Please.'

'The Boss, "Dancing in the Dark". New Kids on the Block—'

'No, sorry, got to stop you there.'

'Why?'

Nick looks disgusted. 'New Kids?'

'The first and original boy band.'

'Aren't you forgetting The Beatles?'

I shake my head. 'Not the same thing.'

'Some would argue with that.'

'I'm sure Paul McCartney wouldn't.'

'What, that he formed the inaugural mould upon which pop bases a lot of its ideals?'

'No, that he was the precursor to the Knight brothers and Joey-Joe McIntyre.'

Nick winces. 'When you put it like that. Anyway they were early nineties, so it's disallowed.'

'If you'd let me finish my entry, you'd learn that "The Right Stuff" was 1989.'

Another cringe.

'Actually it was "You Got It" and then "The Right Stuff" in brackets.'

'Are you obsessed with brackets, or what?'

'Yes. It's one of my main infatuations, along with spirit levels and isosceles triangles.'

'Fine, you win.' He hides a smile in his drink. 'And you've been asked that before, I can tell.'

'What?'

'The top five thing. OMD's the one you like best. Even if Orchestral Manoeuvres in the Dark is one of the wankiest names for a band I've ever heard.'

'How d'you know it's my favourite?'

'*Pretty in Pink*. The Andrew McCarthy effect.'

'*I* never fancied Andrew McCarthy.'

'Liar.'

'Really!'

'The other one, then.'

I shake my head. 'I just love that song.'

'You love it?'

'Yes, I love it.' I smile. 'Anyway, the list isn't definitive. Ask me again tomorrow.'

A cyclist rides past, wheels slick on the glossy road. We watch for a moment.

'Your turn,' I say.

'Do they have to be chart numbers?'

'Of course. Why, are you planning to hit me with something really obscure? I think I can handle it.'

'OK.' I notice his leg going up and down fast, like he's cold or nervous, I can't tell. 'Dexys Midnight Runners, "Come On Eileen". The Jam, "Going Underground". Marrs, "Pump Up The Volume". The Police, "Don't Stand So Close to Me". Phil Collins, "In the Air Tonight".'

'Phil Collins?' I nearly splutter out my tea.

'What?'

I pretend to be disappointed. 'You just didn't seem the type . . .'

'Come on! That's a serious drum solo.'

'All right, aside from that it's not a bad selection. And I suppose it's preferable to "A Groovy Kind of Love".'

'I like that one too.'

I laugh again.

'You think I'm joking.'

'What sort of music *do* you like?' I ask.

'Difficult question.'

'Not really.'

'You're not going to ask me for top three albums or anything, are you? I don't think I could answer that.'

'Favourite band of all time. You've got ten seconds to think about it.'

'Harsh!'

'Eight seconds.'

He warms his hands on the polystyrene cup. 'The Smiths. But don't hold it against me.'

'Why would I hold it against you?'

'You might.' He meets my eye and once again I think how dark and gorgeous his are, and for a second I feel like we're not talking about The Smiths any more. Self-conscious, I look away.

'How was it growing up with Pineapple Mist, then?' he asks, smoothly changing the subject. 'That must have been pretty crazy.'

I nod. 'It was. Fun, though.'

'I bet.'

'I always used to get jealous of my friends' parents, which sounds terrible – but things like holidays, I used to wish I could be like everyone else and come back after the summer and tell the class I'd been to France or Spain, or even that we'd had barbecues in the garden or anything . . . normal.' I shake my head. 'Instead we went traipsing round Butlins or Pontins or whatever, Mum and Dad performing that one bloody hit all through the holiday season to a load of disinterested punters . . . it was the same old story, year after year.' I think back. 'This was early nineties, so I guess there was an element of flogging a dead career. They never complained about it, though – they were still living their dream.'

Nick smiles. 'And now?'

'Now I wouldn't change it for the world. It was unusual, it was different; things you hate when you're young and value when you're grown up.' I put my cup down on the arm of the bench and rub my hands together to keep them warm. 'Also, it was fun. I made loads of friends, kids whose parents were doing the same thing.' I blow on my fingers. 'I always wanted a brother or sister but it didn't happen, so I loved that aspect of it. It's where I met Lou.'

'Lou's nice.'

'Yeah. Her folks were doing the same thing. They were in a foursome with another couple, sort of like Abba but not . . . I think they were called The Diamond Duos or something like that. Anyway, they were desperate for success – to the detriment of everything else. They never "made it" in the commercial sense, they never got a deal or anything, but they used to tour the circuit, same places as us. Lou had a rough ride of it. My parents are mad but they always took care of me; I always came first. Hers were too bound up in themselves to care.'

'That's sad.'

'I know. She always used to hang out with us. That's how we became close.'

'So you don't wish it were different? Your upbringing, I mean.'

'No.' I like that I don't have to think about it. 'I wouldn't swap it for anything. Even if they did force me to meet Timmy Mallett one terrifying summer at a festival in Scunthorpe.'

Nick laughs. 'We won't be seeing you on stage any time soon, then?'

'God, no!' I exclaim. 'I couldn't think of anything worse.'

He sits back. 'I'm with you on that.'

'You are?'

'Yeah. Much more comfortable listening to music than anything else – you'd have to take one of my limbs to get me to even hold a microphone. The dancing's nearly as bad as the singing.'

'It would be with a limb missing.'

'You're funny.'

'Oh come on, I bet you're a great dancer!'

'What makes you say that?' He straightens. 'My consummate poise and grace?'

'Ha.'

'"Ha"? If I didn't know you better I'd take offence.'

'We'll get you singing karaoke before the series is up,' I tease.

'Over my dead body.'

'You really think you'd be any worse than the people we get up there every night? The point isn't to *be* good. It's creepy if you're good.'

'I wouldn't be worse. I'd just deliver something . . . upsetting.'

'Upsetting?!'

'I'm not kidding. I'm really awful. Children will run screaming.'

I giggle. 'I'm sure it's not that bad.'

He shrugs.

'Anyway, enough of my story,' I say. 'What about you?'

'What about me?'

I almost regret asking. But I have to. There's a fist of happiness in my chest that feels like trouble, and I have to keep reining myself in every time I remember how he got here. Whether he's real or not. There's the Rebecca Ascot affair, the stuff that was written about him. Then there's the fact that, perhaps more worryingly, he's in Evan Bergman's pocket. I just don't know if I can trust him. I want to, but I can't.

'Well,' he smiles regretfully, 'I'm sure you know about my, er' – he clears his throat, goes a little red – 'status in certain circles.'

I fold my arms, only to keep out the cold but aware it looks defensive. 'Yeah.'

'Yeah.'

I wait for him to go on, but he doesn't. Instead he rubs his chin, his eyes dark and unreadable. I want to know more, and at the same time I don't.

'So you're hoping this gig might get you back on track?' I ask.

'That sounds callous.'

'Well, are you?'

He pulls at his earlobe. 'In a way, yes. Evan was . . . kind to give me the opportunity.'

'He approached you?'

Nick looks shifty. 'Yep.'

'So I guess you have to behave yourself this time.' I regret the words as soon as I say them. But he watches me like he's considering it properly.

'I guess so.'

There's a silence. I want him to confirm the thing with

Rebecca Ascot, or deny it. But then I don't really want to know either way. I want him to say that he thinks Evan Bergman's a weirdo, and reassure me that there's no hidden agenda. Quite what that hidden agenda might be, I haven't worked out yet.

'You cold?' he asks.

'A bit. We should head back.' I get to my feet before he has the chance to offer me his jacket. For some reason it would feel too . . . rehearsed.

'We should.' He stands and the easy banter of the last half hour disappears. 'Another busy night ahead, we hope.'

I laugh nervously.

'But you're happy? That's really why I wanted to chat – to make sure you're OK with how everything's going. No problems with anything?' He frowns a little. 'Or anyone?'

'Not yet.'

'Great.' He grins. Neither of us moves.

'Any problems, you come to me,' he says. 'I just want to make your life as easy as possible.' It reminds me of something Evan would say.

'Thanks.'

He smiles again. 'Shall we?'

I nod. 'Let's.'

17

Sealed With a Kiss

The girl on stage is doing that semi-squatting booty-shake thing that only looks good when Beyoncé does it. When the rest of us try, we could be a) someone's mum with a worryingly aggressive sex drive, or b) fitting.

Her voice isn't bad, or at least I don't think it is – it's difficult to tell with the distraction. Right now there's a serious possibility that we neglected to rewire the microphones sufficiently and she's actually being electrocuted.

This is typical Saturday night fodder. People come in even greater numbers at the weekend, desperate to claim their three-second slot on TV, deciding that if their appearance is outrageous enough they might make the edited cut – or at least glimpse themselves in the periphery of a shot. Actually hardly any of the karaoke gets broadcast: you often hear it in the background but the cameras are more interested in the patrons themselves, and in following us staff about. Personally I can't imagine what's so interesting about watching us clear tables and chat about nothing much (with the exception of Jaz and Andre, who have gained something of a cult status in *TweenGirl* magazine), but Evan says that 'mundane is the new extraordinary'. What that makes Jaz, then, I'm not entirely sure.

It's the following weekend and Divas Theme Night. I'm pleased I managed to get this past Evan, who's had an iron fist on proceedings since our meeting. He didn't seem all that keen on pursuing any of the ideas I had prior to agreeing to the show, but given that this was one of the reasons we got involved in the first place, I had to put my foot down.

We've got about six hen parties in tonight, heavily made-up, over-excited gaggles of girls and scarcely a bloke in sight. Earlier I spotted one buried in a crowd of screaming women and wearing an expression of pure terror, as though he'd just slipped unwittingly into the seventh circle of hell. Limousines have been rocking up outside, even a gigantic pink thing that looked like a school bus crossed with a pig. Jaz informed me it was a 'stretch hummer', which sounds to me like a pair of tights that haven't been washed in a week.

The Beyoncé impersonator leaves the stage to rapturous applause. So marks the end of that group's slot, and, on realising this, the girls are so distraught that one of our bouncers has to intervene and peel them manually off the mics.

'Just one more!' Beyoncé's friend cries. 'Just one Tina, I promise!' The bouncer is stoic. '"Nutbush City Limits"!' the girl babbles – desperate, wild, hopeful, as if this massive bald heavy's about to go, Oh, *all* right then, so long as it's not 'Steamy Windows'.

There's a scrum as the next lot hit the playlists. One of them produces a list of pre-appointed song choices – wow, that's efficient – and punches them furiously into the machine like some computer hacker in a heist movie. Everyone else is squabbling over the mics. (In my own experience of karaoke, it's a job to get anyone to go within two feet of a mic in the first half hour, so we must be doing something right.) Billy Idol winds up with barely a pause. A girl with bobbed brown hair takes to the stage with a tambourine and starts banging it with force.

'You can't have this!' Beyoncé girl complains, hands on hips, shooting daggers at the performers. 'It's a man!'

Man or not, I suspect Billy's one of the biggest divas going, so I'm not about to get involved. Plus it looks dangerously like a bitch fight might be about to unfold, and I'm ill-equipped to handle that at the best of times, let alone to a soundtrack of 'White Wedding'.

My very own diva slips into the chair next to mine. I'm hidden in a booth at the back, checking through our orders for the past week. They're miles above anything we were able to afford previously, and even then we're falling shy of our revised budget. For the first time in the club's history, we've got money to spare.

'Isn't this *fabulous*?' Ruby du Jour sips her cosmopolitan, depositing a red lipstick stain on the rim of the glass.

'Yup,' I say, glancing up at the girls doing Billy Idol. One of them looks uncannily *like* Billy Idol, which isn't, in fact, unattractive. 'It's pretty special.'

'It's unbelievable.' She chases her glacé cherry with an umbrella stick (glacé cherries? Umbrella sticks? I thought we were updating things). 'Rick and Sapphy aren't going to know what hit them!'

'Hmm.' I scribble down my monthly projection.

'How are they? I got a text from Sapphy last week but I couldn't make out what it said. Someone's keyboard exploded?'

'They're OK, I think.' I flip the file closed. 'Mum rang on Tuesday but we only got to speak for five minutes because they were having drinks with Kajagoogoo.'

'Kaja-who-who?'

'Not knowing will have absolutely no impact on your life whatsoever.'

'Have you seen the face on that?' Ruby sends a catty glance across the room, where stroppy Beyoncé is being drip-fed a garish green concoction by a sympathetic friend. Toby's hovering nearby with one of the cameras, Nathan's boom craning over them like something prehistoric. 'Hardly lady-like behaviour.' She sniffs and tends to the elaborate construction aloft her head: a blonde beehive with little red flowers wound into it.

I laugh. 'So where's Rob been hiding?' I'm referring to Ruby's male alter ego. Once it was easy to forget which was the original and which the costume, but lately Rob's nowhere to be seen. I have my suspicions why.

'Oh, this is all *much* too exciting for him.' There's a twinkle in Ruby's eye, but it's accompanied by a twinge of self-consciousness.

'You don't think he finds it a bit overwhelming?'

'Certainly not!'

I shrug. 'It *is* overwhelming, I'm the first to admit it – some days I could really do with a Ruby in my life.'

'You could?'

'Sure.' I consider it. 'Some days I'd love to try another version of me. And there's more than one side to people, isn't there? With Ruby you get to explore different parts of your personality – that's an amazing thing.'

She smiles. 'I suppose.'

'But Rob's just as important, remember?' I hope I'm getting my meaning across.

Ruby looks uncomfortable. 'He's not very – I mean, I'm not very – *exciting* without . . . Never mind. I can't imagine he'll interest many people out there, that's all I'm saying.'

'He'll interest me.'

'He won't interest Evan,' she says, and the tone she uses is so unlike Ruby that I turn to check she's OK. Of course she covers it with a smile.

'Has Evan said something to you?' I knew it!

'No, just . . .'

'Just what?'

'Only . . .' She clicks her teeth. 'He'd rather I was Ruby, that's all. Said it was good for TV. And the Rob thing is confusing, I know that. I can see his point . . .'

I frown. 'I guess I can see it too, kind of, but he's forgetting that this is meant to be a reality show. What's real about it if we're all pretending to be something we're not?'

Ruby gestures down at her dress with a sad sort of expression. 'Aren't I doing that already?'

'You know what I mean.'

'Forget about it, it doesn't matter.'

'The principle does. I'm sick of Evan issuing us orders. God!'

Alison swoops in, camera trained on the scent of scandal. Even though the idea is to carry on conversations as normal, I instinctively clam up.

'Well come on then!' says Alison, exasperated. 'Or this is going to be the boringest instalment of anything *ever*.'

'Didn't Toby catch the spat with Beyoncé?' I ask. 'You might still have time – she's been weeping for about fifteen minutes now.'

Alison whips round. 'Beyoncé's here?'

'Yeah. And Gaga and Rihanna. Needed the publicity, apparently.'

'I'm serious,' she moans, putting the camera down. 'Evan told us to get as much juice as we could, and all I'm going back with tonight is a load of drunk people singing and falling over.'

I raise an eyebrow. 'I hate to break it to you, but that's what tends to happen in karaoke bars.'

'But Evan wants *action*. He thinks—'

'Stuff what Evan thinks.'

Alison looks affronted. I wonder what Evan would think if I suggested lifting the lid on whatever's going on between him and his chief camera op – that's a little goldmine of action right there. Not that I would, of course. Because there's a little thing called privacy that Evan seems to have forgotten about.

Alex slips in opposite us, all chiselled jaw and plasticine

hair, a square foot of copper chest on show where his flimsy top falls open.

'Shouldn't you be working?' I demand. On cue Alison resumes filming.

'Just taking a break.' He regards me with flinty eyes. 'The others have got it covered.'

I check the bar. Lou and Simon are at one end, chatting and laughing and finding any excuse to be with each other. Their date went brilliantly. Lou texted soon after Nick walked me home, and when I saw her name pop up I knew it was either a complete success or a complete disaster. Just three words – 'I'm eating steak' – was all she needed to say. I did consider telling her about my chat with Nick, but in the end I chickened out. There didn't seem any point and, besides, I knew she'd be the voice of reason – and I wasn't sure I was ready to listen to reason just yet.

'Jaz seems moody,' observes Alex, running a hand through his Action Man crop. It's so rigid I'm surprised it moves.

'Does she?' I turn round. Jaz is clad in a torn denim 'ship-wreck chic' ensemble, with what appears to be a plastic crab caught up in the red seaweed of her hair. With her rodent side-kick in similar garb, I wonder if it's a 'modern twist' on *Robinson Crusoe*, with Andre as Guinea Pig Friday. She's laughing with a customer.

'Yeah' – he fires a purposeful glance at the camera – 'must be the Simon and Lou thing.'

I frown, deciding it safest not to comment. But Ruby beats me to it.

'What do you mean? She's not jealous of Lou . . . is she?'

'Of course she's not jealous,' I say firmly, just as Alex makes a face that suggests she is, in fact, extremely jealous. 'She's not.'

'I don't know about that,' Alex goes on. 'She was fine up until a few days ago when she found out they went on a date . . .'

I hoot with laughter. 'Come *on*,' I say, 'Jaz doesn't give a shit if they went on a date.' I look at the camera. 'This isn't going in, by the way, Alison.'

'Have you spoken to her about it?' says Ruby, touching my arm. 'Perhaps she *is* feeling a little hard done-by. They've always been close; it might have felt like a shock.'

'It wasn't a shock,' I tell them, 'because Jaz was integral to them hooking up in the first place. She was the one who told Lou he liked her!'

Alex looks momentarily stumped.

'Oh dear,' says Ruby.

'Oh dear what?'

'We all know why she did that.'

'We do?'

'It's a *classic* defence mechanism, my goodness: the forced brush-off. She's scared after what she went through last time.'

'Yeah,' agrees Alex, not having the faintest clue what we're talking about, 'that's right.'

'"The forced brush-off"?' I roll my eyes. 'What a load of old bollocks. There's no jealousy, take my word for it. And if anyone's still concerned,' I pin Alex with a stare, 'for I'm sure that's what this is all about, I'll have a word with her myself.'

'I know she likes him,' he blurts.

My head snaps up. 'What?'

'I know Jaz likes Simon. She told me.' His voice is almost

as robotic as his appearance. 'And she's really upset about them getting together.'

OK, *what?* It's tempting to tell Alex that if anyone secretly likes anyone on that bar, it's Jaz who secretly likes him, but I'm not about to give him the satisfaction – and anyway, it's all getting a bit confusing.

'I'm sure that's not the case,' I say. 'Alison, *will you put that bloody thing down?*'

Alex looks at me sideways. 'Think what you like.'

Disconcerted, I get up from the booth. Again I glance over at Jaz, who's busy serving drinks. The others are at the opposite end of the bar, working so close together they might as well be sewn at the hip. Alex is winding me up, he has to be. Why he insists on doing it in front of the cameras I have no idea.

Uh-oh. Someone's picked Mariah Carey. I make my way through the crowd to the strains of 'Hero' – and 'strains' is about the right word for it, since the woman on stage has gone completely red in the face. On all the twiddly bits (which is most of the song), she sounds like a toad gargling water. Why do people put themselves through this? I'll never understand.

I'm about to nip outside for some fresh air when I spot Nick Craven, half in, half out of the store room. He's standing in shadow, hands on hips, and it looks like he's talking to someone, but at this angle I can't make out who. He's wearing a crisp white shirt and I can see his tanned forearms (I go weak-kneed for forearms) and just have time to imagine what it might feel like to—

'Maddie, there you are!' An altogether different arm shoots

out from behind the bar and grabs me. It's Lou. 'I've got a favour to ask. All I'll say in advance is, don't hate me.'

I scrunch up my nose. 'What is it?'

'Sing something with me.'

I look at her like she's crazy. 'Have you lost your *mind*?'

She laughs. 'No. I've got a bet on with Simon that you won't. I mean, *he* says you won't, he says you never would, and I said, with a little persuasion, you might.'

'Lovely! Simon's won.'

'Wait!' She yanks me back as I'm making my escape. 'Just listen. Of course you're going to say no at first, but then I figured, I'm your best friend, aren't I? And if best friends can't pull in a favour or two every once in a while . . .' Seeing my appalled expression, she continues, 'Please! It's to prove a point. I can't have Simon thinking he knows you better than I do.'

'In these circumstances, he does.'

'Pretty please?'

'No.'

'But you'd be testing the boundaries of fear!' She tries the cod-psychology approach. 'We should continually test our boundaries, Maddie – otherwise fear becomes abstract, and we forget what it is we're really afraid of!'

'Sounds all right to me.'

'Didn't you see that episode of *Peter Andre: The Next Chapter* where he faces his fear of heights? He had to cross a tightrope in the mountains.'

'Did he do it?'

'Well, no, as it goes, he had to walk back down.' She nods. 'Actually he was totally freaking out, it was awful. But that's not the point.'

'You know I'd do anything for you, Lou,' I tell her solemnly. 'But I won't do that.'

I peer over her shoulder. From here I can see who Nick's talking to – it's Nathan, the greasy-haired sound guy. It looks like they're having an argument.

Before I know what's happening, Lou's got me by the hand and is hauling me on stage, her grip like a pair of cuffs.

'Make way, make way!'

'Lou, what the fuck are you *doing*?' I hiss, making a vain attempt to break free.

'It's good for you,' she tosses back over her shoulder. 'Thirty seconds, that's all.'

'I am never going to forgive you,' I declare, incensed, '*never*. Never ever *never*. The Contract of Eternal Friendship? It's burned. The Sisterhood Bracelet? Cursed. The Emergency Spinster Pact? Dead to me – *dead*, do you hear? The cats are all yours.'

I deliver her one of my notorious pinches, but to my chagrin Lou seems to be enjoying herself. She's built up immunity over the years to my pinching – when we were ten we spent many a productive afternoon testing each other's pain threshold and writing it down in a series of colourful charts. A*ha*. Now if I can just get her into a Chinese burn . . .

Everyone's looking at me so I plaster a reluctant smile on my face, deciding I've got two options: I can either hold a microphone and mumble something incoherent into it for half a minute, or I can conduct a sitting protest and kick and scream like a toddler being dragged from an ice cream van. Neither sounds especially appealing, but in the interests of salvaging at least a remnant of dignity, I'll go with number one.

But that's before I've heard what the current song is: Celine Dion's impassioned version of the Roy Orbison classic, 'I Drove All Night'.

Great.

♪

'Seriously, I was impressed.'

'Don't take the piss.'

'I'm not!' Nick's smile shines white in the moonlight. 'Especially that part where you coughed into the microphone, it really added something to the story.'

'Shut up,' I say, but I can't help my own smile. 'I was nervous.'

We left the club a while ago. Nick suggested getting some air shortly after my performance – if it can be called that: I just stood sort of rocking from one foot to the other like the only girl with braces at a school disco, occasionally warbling one of the low, more manageable bits while Lou chirruped over the top.

Once we're clear of the hectic Soho grid, complete with Obligatory Figure Puking in Alleyway, we emerge at Charing Cross and head down towards the river.

'But really,' he says, 'the cough was appropriate to the song.'

'How's that then?'

Nick puts his hands in his pockets. 'Well,' he says, 'consider the lyrics. It's about someone travelling through the night, right?'

'Right . . .'

'And he's so desperate for this woman he's prepared to go any distance – all he can think about is getting laid, never mind if his girlfriend's up for this surprise visit or not.'

'She probably didn't even bother shaving her legs when she had a bath that night.'

Nick nods. 'But Roy doesn't care, he just wants to get his own leg over.'

'Charming.'

'So it's a pretty sinister concept as it is. Throw in the part where this person – who, by the way, is never confirmed as being invited and might just be some random stalker – actually breaks into your room, creeps to your bedside and wakes you up god knows how, and you've got a full-on sex predator on your hands. For, uh, want of a better phrase.'

I laugh. 'Roy Orbison's a sex predator?'

'You know what they say about dark glasses.'

'Hmm. The thought of Celine creeping into my room freaks me out more.'

He imagines it. 'I see what you mean.'

'And the cough?'

'What about it?'

'What's that got to do with anything?'

Nick thinks it through. 'Every sex predator's got to have a cough, a really gravelly, pervy one. It warns you they're coming. Yours was pretty spot-on, I must say.'

'Thanks. But doesn't that defeat the purpose of being a sex predator? I mean, the whole point of Orbison's song is she *doesn't* hear him coming, whoever he is.'

'And that's a good thing?'

'When you put it like that, probably not.'

He lifts his shoulders, point proven.

'Fine. And of course that's exactly why I *did* cough – in the interests of an authentic story. It was nothing to do with the fact I haven't been ritually embarrassed to that extent since Mum dressed me up as Adam Ant and paraded me at Minehead.'

It's his turn to laugh. The sound of it draws something in me, and instinctively I take his arm. I half expect him to pull away, but he doesn't. It's not romantic, exactly, just a natural, friendly thing to do.

We walk down Villiers Street towards Embankment and pass the people spilling out of pubs; the pack of boys queuing for Subway; the crowd outside Gordon's wine bar, smoke from their cigarettes blooming and dissolving in the night.

Briefly I glance behind me, looking for what I'm not sure. Walking through Soho I couldn't shake the feeling of being followed – I've been thinking too much about what Loaf said, his enigmatic warnings. Either that or I've spent too long with the cameras in recent weeks. I must be getting paranoid.

'I saw you talking to Nathan,' I comment. 'Is everything all right?' I only say so to take my mind off it, but straight away I feel Nick tense.

'Everything's fine,' he says stonily. Instantly I regret mentioning it, and feel I should take my arm away but don't know how to without it looking deliberate.

I don't have to worry, though. As we pass through the station and take the steps on to Hungerford Bridge, he gets pulled away in the crowd. Couples hurry past after a night at the theatre, bodies close, their heads bent together. We walk in silence and then, halfway across, Nick stops and looks out at the river. Music from a nearby busker fills the balmy air, and I experience a rush of being in exactly the right place at exactly the right time.

I love the Thames at night. On one side Big Ben stands proud, his white face showing almost-midnight, a giant heart about to beat across the city; the Houses of Parliament, lit up gold, big as cathedrals yet intricate as jewellery; the Eye, its silver arc studded with purple, closing for sleep while it can. On the other, the Oxo tower with its bold red hat, the pearly dome of St Paul's and the bright buses crossing Waterloo Bridge. Above us, aeroplanes flash scarlet as they come to land at Heathrow. Below our feet, the cool black rush of the water.

'It's beautiful, isn't it?' says Nick.

'It is.'

We're shoulder to shoulder, leaning our elbows on the side and looking out to the east, where the orange wink of Canary Wharf pierces the dark sky.

'I came here with my brother once,' he says. 'Ages ago.'

He's deep in thought, and he's got the handsomest profile on earth (and I never really thought about profiles in that way before).

'You did?'

'Yeah. I was sixteen and he was . . . he would have been about ten.'

It hits me that I know nothing at all about this man . . . and why would I? I wait for him to go on, not wanting to interrupt for fear he'll pull back.

'Dad was working up here – he was always working.' Nick clears his throat. 'He couldn't get someone in to look after

Luke, it was short notice, so we had to come to the city – on a Sunday, I think it was, and wait till he was done.' A wry smile. 'We waited a long time.'

'So you just hung out?'

'Yes.' He smiles properly this time. 'We just hung out. At first Luke didn't want to be here – it wasn't his normal routine, it was . . . difficult for him.'

I'm confused. 'Why couldn't you stay at home?'

Nick shakes his head. 'Luke needed looking after, he wasn't well. To be honest he shouldn't have been left alone with just me.'

'Oh.'

'Mum went crazy.' He draws a hand across his chin. 'She hated Dad having him at the weekends, and he didn't even tell her. She blew up at me, said I was as irresponsible as he was. I didn't really get why she got so mad, but I do now.'

I stay quiet, not sure where this is going.

Nick's eyes are on the river. 'We stood right here, pretty much. It was winter, nearly Christmas, and there were lights strung up between the trees on the South Bank. Luke was so excited.'

I search his face. 'That's nice.'

'Yeah' – a faint smile – 'it was nice.'

'You must be close,' I say after a while.

'We were.' Nick's eyes are still and dark as the water. 'Luke died a few years ago.'

I touch his arm. 'Nick, I'm so sorry.'

He bows his head, shakes it a little, remembering. 'We knew it was coming,' he says, 'we knew he wouldn't be with us for ever. But even when you're prepared for something, you're not always ready, are you? I don't know how you can prepare your feelings. I don't think you can.'

'Of course you can't,' I say softly. 'It's so, so sad. I don't know what to say.'

He nudges me with his elbow. 'God, sorry – I don't know where that came from. It's just . . . being here, I guess.' A nervous laugh. 'Talk about dumping on you on our second date—'

Even in the dark I see his embarrassment at having called it that.

'I mean, not that this is a – er, you know, it's not like,' he scratches the back of his neck, 'well, anyway. Sorry.'

I put an arm round him. He feels warm and solid, safe and lovely, and I rest my head on his shoulder. We stay like that for a minute.

All I can think about is making him feel better; I can't bear for him to be upset. I say the first thing that comes into my mind.

'Can I tell you something? It's a secret.'

'What?' I can feel his breath in my hair.

'I'm not sure if I should . . .'

'You have to now.'

'OK. But you *have* to swear not to tell anyone. All right? And in doing so you'll be one of only a handful of people on the planet privy to this information.'

I can feel his smile. 'What is it?'

'First, you must promise you won't run horrified from this bridge.'

'I promise.'

'You can't throw yourself off either.'

'Deal.'

I pull away, look him in the eye. If I'm going to do this, I might as well do it properly.

'It's my name,' I tell him. 'It's not what you think it is.'

He grins, uncertain. 'Is this the part when you tell me you're actually a man?'

I laugh. 'What if I was?' He waves me away. 'No, seriously, what if I was?'

'I'd have just blown it, wouldn't I?'

'Would you? And to think this is just our second date . . .'

'Ah.' He rubs his chin.

'I'm not a man,' I say, acting affronted, before I remember what I'm about to confess and adopt a more humble approach. 'But some might describe me as . . . well, a freak.'

'A freak?!'

'Yes. You see . . .' I take a deep breath and close my eyes. 'Look, just ask me my name – it's easier that way.'

'But I already know what your name is.'

'Just ask me.'

'OK.' He grips my shoulders and I giggle. 'Maddie Mulhern, what is your name?'

I wait a moment, checking as I always do that I've got them in the right order. Am I really about to do this? Yes, it seems I am.

I blurt it all out in one go.

'MadonnaCherSinittaTiffanyEnyaCyndiLauperDebbie HarryPetShopBoysMulhern.' Then, idiotically, I add, 'Maddie for short.'

There's a very long silence. Every second is excruciating. I've still got my eyes closed.

'What's with the Pet Shop Boys?' Nick asks eventually.

I open one eye and squint at him. 'What do you mean?'

'I mean, it doesn't go with the rest of them.'

'It doesn't?'

'Of course it doesn't,' he says. 'For starters, they're blokes.'

'Well, I—'

'That part's just ridiculous.'

I'm surprised. 'That's it?'

'That's what?'

'You don't think it's a bit of a . . . mouthful?'

'Maybe. I might just call you Enya from now on.'

'Don't you dare!' Playfully I smack his chest.

'I'm kidding.' A beat. 'Now close your eyes again.'

'Why?'

'Just do it.'

His grip is still warm on my shoulders. The night fills with the low chimes of midnight, and my heart is pounding at double the time.

When Nick's lips meet mine and he kisses me, it's the most wonderful feeling in the world.

18

What's Love Got to Do with It?

'He *kissed* you?' Lou squeals, nearly spitting out her wine.

'Yes, he did,' I say, topping up my glass with soda. 'I wanted to break it to you in person. And it was without doubt the best kiss of my life.'

'But,' Lou splutters, attacking the remote to get the sound down on the stereo, 'but . . . *how*? I mean, you don't even know him!'

'Yes, I do.'

'Not really. I thought you thought he was a nob!'

'I did – at first. But then I changed my mind.'

Lou looks bewildered. 'Why didn't you tell me?'

'I just did!'

'That you liked him, silly. Last time we talked about Nick Craven you were slagging him right off to anyone who'd listen.' She points her finger at me. 'But I *knew* you were faking, I knew it!'

'He seems a nice enough bloke,' Simon chips in, glancing up from the book he's reading. 'Can't imagine why he's involved with reality TV, to be honest – he's too intelligent.'

It's Tuesday evening and we're round at Lou's flat in Finsbury Park, eating Doritos and polishing off a bottle of Pinot. Well, Lou is, mostly – I've got to be at the club in an hour. One thing I can say, this Tooth & Nail gig has been doing the world of good for my liver.

'He *is* a nice bloke,' I say. 'A really nice bloke.'

'What happened to him being a shameless womaniser?' Lou raises an eyebrow.

'He's not like that. I was wrong about that. Whatever happened with Rebecca Ascot is his business – he was probably going through a hard time.'

'You are so loved-up!' Lou grins, tucking her legs under her on the sofa. 'I've never seen you like this before.'

'It's not like we're going out,' I say quickly. 'It's very early days and I don't want to assume there's more to it than just a kiss, because that's all it probably was . . . probably. Don't you think? People kiss all the time and then they never see each other again! So I've already given myself a strict talking-to and I'm not getting carried away. I'm not jinxing it by imagining what might or might not be—'

'Wow,' says Simon, mercifully cutting me off. 'How can you be bothered to think about all this stuff?'

Lou leans over and ruffles his dirty-blond hair. 'It's why we've got bigger brains.'

'What, to fill it with all that rubbish?'

'It's not rubbish!' Lou cries indignantly, looking to me for back-up.

I make a face. 'It sort of is. I'm annoying myself with it.' I break a Dorito up into tiny pieces. 'Argh, why do I always have to *think* about things so much?'

'You're thinking about thinking.' Lou nods, sipping her wine. 'Stop it. There's more important things to think about.'

'I know, but I can't help it. If I could just stop thinking, then I'd realise that what I think I'm thinking might not actually *be* what I'm thinking – or, for that matter, what *he*'s thinking – and then I can try to work out what's just thinking and what's actually happening, when I'm thinking more clearly, and then maybe, if I did all that, for once I could think straight! I think.'

Simon rolls his eyes. 'Remind me again what there is to think about?'

I put my elbows on the coffee table and rest my chin in my hand. 'Well, it's just that it happened three nights ago and neither one of us has mentioned it, even when we're within ten feet of each other. Is that weird?'

'Yeah, but what are you meant to say?' Simon drapes an arm round Lou and pulls her close. '"I had such a great kiss – er, I mean time the other night. Fancy doing it again?"'

'I guess,' I muse. 'Though it is getting a bit awkward.'

'Of course it's awkward,' he goes on, 'because essentially

200

you're working together. If it was any other situation I'm sure he'd have called you by now. You're a catch, Maddie – Nick won't meet someone like you every day.'

I narrow my eyes. 'Do you want to be my new BFF now that Lou's officially struck off my Christmas list?'

He chuckles. 'Come on, everyone loved your Celine. Especially the coughing part.'

'OK forget it, you're struck off too.'

'I told you you'd get into trouble,' says Simon, fondly kissing Lou's head. It's one of those intimate moments between couples that, while it's not exactly a gross-out PDA, it definitely makes you feel like a spare wheel.

'That's my cue,' I say, grabbing my jacket. 'I've got to run.'

♪

On the tube I wonder if Simon's right: Nick and I are working together – it'd be wrong to act like anything had gone on between us.

Even so it feels like he's avoiding me – whenever I meet his eye, he immediately looks away; whenever I go into the bar, he's always on his way out; whenever I join the group he's talking to, he fluffs his words and makes some excuse to leave.

As the train pulls into King's Cross I try to focus on someone's discarded paper, but it's no good, I'm too distracted. Especially when I see a photo of Nick in the 'Last Night' double-page spread, emerging from Pineapple and shielding himself from the cameras.

I'm making it sound like he's being unfair, and he's not – he's just being professional, which is kind of the problem. I'd much rather he was straight with me: if he regrets the other night he should say so, instead of pretending it never happened.

Twenty minutes later I emerge at Covent Garden and decide to walk the rest of the way. I'm just passing French Connection when my phone beeps in my bag. I stop to dig it out.

It's a text from Lou telling me she's really excited for me, and she knows I was probably worrying all the way home. I smile when I read it.

There's another unread text in my inbox – it must have come in earlier and I didn't notice.

As soon as I see the number, I recognise it. I deleted the name two months ago but the digits are too familiar to forget.

Lawrence.

Hey Mads, how's things, was thinking of u this wkend.
Can we meet? L x

I stare at it for a few seconds, baffled.

Lawrence? *Really?*

This is odd. After I was so unceremoniously dumped, I didn't think there'd be reason for us ever to be in touch again. Clearly he's decided to extend the olive branch, but, looking at the message again, I'm not sure it's that simple. I'm confused by the wording and don't know how to reply. Rather than fire back something I'll later regret, I stuff it into my bag and carry on walking.

When I get back to the club, a couple of burly blokes are taking measurements for the new wall mirrors we're having fitted. Some of the themed tables we purchased have been delivered and there's a woman with a very tight bun issuing bossy styling instructions. She's wearing a nice dress I saw last month in Karen Millen but couldn't afford.

The crew are in evidence, as always, trailing Jaz and Alex around as they get things ready for tonight. Alison and Toby are chatting in a corner – he's gesticulating wildly but it's impossible to hear what they're saying.

'Hey, guys,' I say, tossing my bag down on the bar. 'What's happening?'

'Alex has come up with the best idea for a theme night!' Jaz grins, scooping up Andre and holding him out for me to see. She's wearing a dress that looks like it's made from sweet wrappers, and miniature red-and-white candy canes swing from her earlobes.

'Um . . . guinea pig theme?' I hazard, praying I'm wrong.

'No,' she says, like I'm being stupid, 'who does he *look* like?'

Andre blinks at me.

'*Beauty and the Beast*?' It's the first fairy tale that comes to mind.

Jaz clasps him to her chest, offended on his behalf. 'What are you saying?'

'Sorry, Andre,' I tell him, knowing it won't be enough just to apologise to Jaz. 'Go on, please. Enlighten me.'

She beams across at Alex, who smiles back. When his eyes meet mine, the smile drops. 'The Bee Gees!' Jaz announces gleefully. 'Everyone loves the Bee Gees, don't they?'

'I guess . . .' I frown, 'but what's that got to do with Andre?'

'Barry Gibb!' She thrusts him out again. 'You see it?'

I peer in closer. Andre's wearing a little blue sparkly waistcoat, there's nothing unusual about that, but now she mentions it there is a look of the lion-haired Gibb about him. She's coiffed his barnet at the front (god knows how: with a pipe cleaner?) and it's smooth and shiny as candle wax.

'You guys are getting on well, then?' I ask, looking between her and Alex and feeling just a little bit worried.

'Of course we are!' Pleased as punch, Jaz drops Andre back in his box and runs a cloth across the bar, humming to herself.

I'm rooting around in my bag to text Lou back when Nick emerges from the store. My heart thumps once, hard – I hadn't expected to see him today. He's wearing a dark green jumper, jeans and Converse, his hair messy and his eyes tired. Nathan trails moodily behind, his feet scuffing the floor like a sulky kid who's just had his Xbox taken away. When Nick sees me he gives a brief, nervous smile.

'Hi.'

'All right?'

'Yep.'

I feel Jaz looking at us and she not-so-surreptitiously jabs Alex in the ribs before dragging him off. My palms are so clammy it's making my phone feel like a bar of soap.

'You look knackered,' I say, trying the light-hearted approach but realising too late that it probably sounded rude.

'Yep.' He shoves his hands in his pockets and I see a muscle clench and relax in his jaw.

'What've you been up to?'

'Not much.'

'D'you have time to grab a tea or something?'

He clears his throat. 'Um, not now. Sorry.'

Wow, he really can't look at me. He's looking everywhere *but* at me – the floor, the ceiling, the walls, his own feet. I'm about to put both of us out of our misery and drift off on the pretext of making a phone call when we're mercifully interrupted (if silence can be interrupted) by the rumble of footfalls on the stairs.

Rob Day emerges, his face flushed. Nick, sensing an opportunity to exit, dives off. I try not to think too much about what this means, or the significance of whatever disastrous encounter just happened. What the hell is his problem?

'Rob!' Jaz reappears and puts her arms round him. 'We haven't seen you in ages!'

Alex looks confused, before remembering that Rob is Ruby and Ruby is Rob. When we first explained it to him he couldn't get his head round it. It took about half an hour and a very patient Jaz to force him to understand.

'Can I grab a word?' Rob asks me quietly so the cameras can't hear – luckily Alison and Toby are too busy bickering.

'Ooh, that sounds juicy.' Jaz slinks away, mouthing to me on her way past, 'Tell me later.'

'Sure.' I'm hoping whatever Rob has to say will distract me from Nick's presence hovering in the corner of my vision. For some stupid reason I feel like crying.

'There's someone upstairs for you – I didn't want to draw attention to it.' Rob glances quickly at the cameras.

'Who?'

'Follow me.'

I trail behind him up the steps and into the hall, where

there's a stack of unopened letters languishing on the mat. The front door is open and standing outside, leaning against the wall opposite, one foot crossed over the other ankle, is Lawrence.

He's wearing a primrose-coloured polo shirt with the collar sticking up. I always used to find that really preppy, and am glad to realise I no longer fancy him in the slightest.

'We, er, ran into each other on the way over here,' says Rob, giving me an apologetic sort of smile. 'I said I'd come find you.'

I nod to let him know it's OK, and with a final anxious glimpse at Lawrence, he ducks back inside.

Lawrence holds his arms out. 'Come here, Mads, it's been ages.'

'Hi,' I say, determined to be friendly but not up for physical contact quite yet. 'How are you?'

'I'm great,' he grins widely, 'never been better.'

He's had his teeth whitened, I think. And his hair looks different: it's still floppy and Hugh Grant-y but it's been put in rollers at the front like Raef from *The Apprentice*.

I stay where I am.

'Mads,' his smile doesn't falter, arms still outstretched, 'you're not going to leave me hanging, are you?'

There's a kerfuffle behind me and I can hear Alison's clunky boots making their way upstairs. Perfect.

'Alison, this is private. Can you leave us to it?'

I turn to Lawrence with a sorry-about-this expression, expecting him to look as awkward as I feel, but instead he's . . . well, the word that springs to mind is *preening*. He smooths a hand over his hair and pouts a little. Hang on, is he wearing make-up? I swear his eyelashes look longer and darker than normal, and there's an unnatural plasticky sheen to his skin. He bends one leg and nonchalantly rests a boater-shoed foot flat against the wall, turning his face to one side. In profile, the picture looks like a moody album cover. But it's less Morrissey and more Brother Beyond.

'Yah,' he drawls, waving the camera away, 'Maddie and I need to talk.'

'Lawrence, this isn't a good time,' I say. 'Could we catch up tomorrow or something? There's stuff I need to do.'

Now he turns to me, offended. 'Oh. Right. Sorry.' His eyes flit over to Alison and he readjusts his pose. 'I guess you're too busy now for old friends.'

'What?' I almost laugh. 'That's not true.'

'Too famous, then?' He smiles a little, which stops the comment being downright rude, but it's out of order all the same. He's put me on the spot and he knows it.

'Of course not,' I say, flustered. 'I just don't know if . . . well, you've caught me at an awkward time, that's all.' I nod subtly to Alison, hoping he'll catch on, but at the same time I've a niggling feeling that might be precisely the reason he's here.

'Did you get my text?' he demands.

'Yeah. About ten minutes ago.'

'I couldn't wait for your response,' he announces dramatically. 'I had to be here.'

'You did?'

'I did. Mads, you've got to hear me out.' Serious now, Lawrence comes towards me, his expression earnest. 'I've been working up to this for weeks.'

I back away, worried. 'Working up to what?'

207

'This.'

Oh. My. God.

Lawrence has dropped to his knees. I kid you not. He's on his knees, right there in the street in the middle of Soho, gazing up at me like an abandoned pet. Before I have time to object, he grabs my hands.

'I never had the guts before now, Maddie. Please listen to what I have to say.'

I'm struck dumb. I must be looking at him like he's gone completely insane, but even if I am it doesn't put him off his stride.

'I made a mistake.' He shuts his eyes, bows his head. 'A terrible, terrible mistake.'

Alison's blinking red light hovers in my peripheral vision, but I'm unable to pull away. All I can think of is how Lawrence's stance and countenance mirrors exactly a production I saw him in once at The Globe.

'Er . . . you did?'

Solemn, he nods. 'I did.' The words barely escape, his voice is so choked with emotion.

I'm about to say something, but after a protracted pause Lawrence gets there first. I have the impression that I don't actually need to be here: this is a monologue, and I could just as easily be a chair, or a hat stand.

'I should never have broken up with you.' He winces at the memory. '*Never.* It was stupid of me, a flight of caprice, an error of the highest order. It was . . .' Lawrence seems to sniff at the air, like a perfumier searching for that final note, '*misguided.*'

The eyes open, brimming with tears. 'I said some things I regret, god knows I did, Mads. I lie awake every night, torturing myself over and over, lonely and frightened and calling your name . . . just lying awake and thinking through those tangled emotions and how they tricked me, tricked *us*, and I *wish*, oh, how I wish I could turn back the clock and make things different. Mads, I wish I knew then what I know now.'

I'm one step off laughing. This needs to stop before the chest-beating begins.

'Lawrence, I don't think this is—'

'And what I know now,' he blathers, 'is that you . . . *you* are the love of my life.'

'Erm . . . I am?'

He shoots up, clasping my hands to him. 'That's right! I said it. Think of me what you will, I know I am flawed. I know there are things I can change, things I can do to make you believe in my lasting affection. But I'm human, Mads – I am only a man. And this human – this man – is telling you right here, right now, that he still loves you.'

Oh.

He's gazing at me, full of expectation.

'I thought you were going out with Francesca Montgomery.' It's the first thing that pops into my head.

'That's over now.' Lawrence searches my eyes. 'It was over from the start – I was only seeing her to get over you. And once I realised how I felt, I called it off without hesitation. I couldn't live a lie a moment longer.'

I stare at him.

'Mads, can you find it in your heart to give me another chance?'

I turn to Alison, camera strapped to her like a lifejacket.

'Show's over,' I tell her. 'Go back downstairs, I'll be with you in a sec.'

'But this is—'

'We'll talk about it later. And it's not making the edit, by the way.'

Alison pouts and slinks off, muttering something I can't make out.

'So you get to decide what goes in the show?' Lawrence asks as soon as she's gone.

'Um, sort of.' I rub my forehead.

'Maybe we should go inside,' he suggests, peering past me into the club. Then he looks up at the perfectly blue sky. 'You never know, it might rain.'

'Listen, Lawrence,' I say, 'I'm really flattered you've had this change of heart. I just . . . I mean, no offence, but I've moved on. And I think you were right in the things you said when we split – well, some of them, anyway. We're too different, I can see that now. And for me there's no going back. I'm sorry, really. It's best if you go.'

He blinks once or twice, as though he hasn't the faintest idea what I'm talking about, before slipping back into character.

'But there has to be a way,' he pleads. 'You're doing so well now, I can really see things changing for us. There was never that balance before' – he chuckles lightly, remembering the good old days – 'I was doing well and you . . . well, you weren't really doing *anything*, were you? But now we can be like partners, allies, helping each other to realise our dreams. Can't you see how great that would be?'

His logic confounds me. 'No, Lawrence, I can't.'

'Tell me you haven't stopped loving me,' he chokes.

Uh, this is awkward. I prepare to say something diplomatic but he beats me to it, pressing a finger against my lips.

'Shh,' he whispers, 'don't speak. What are words anyway? They're but a distraction.'

They're *but* a distraction? Was that from a Shakespeare play I saw him in? Is this actually a scene from Shakespeare?

But before I have time to decide, Lawrence's face is coming towards me at alarming speed, mouth open, eyes closed, and I have to act swiftly. I turn away and he ends up getting a mouthful of my hair.

Abruptly he pulls back. His face has changed, quick and sudden, like he's peeled off a mask. 'That's it then?'

I attempt to look regretful. 'I'm sorry, Lawrence. I don't want us to part on bad terms. I hope things work out for you, I really do.'

'Do I mean so little to you?' he whines.

'Of course not. We can still be friends.'

'I don't want to be friends,' he says tightly.

'I'm sorry,' I say again. 'I don't know what else I can offer you.' I feel like I'm selling bananas by the pound down the market.

One of Lawrence's eyes starts twitching at the corner. 'Let's just be honest about this, shall we?'

'About what?'

'Now you're on telly you've forgotten about the rest of us – that sound about right?'

'Absolutely not,' I splutter, insulted.

'But I'm not good enough for you any more.' His mouth is twisted. 'Am I?'

I wait before replying. I think about Pineapple, and how far it's come. I think about Lou and Simon, and Jaz, and Rob. I think about the time I've spent with Nick.

'No, Lawrence,' I say. 'You were never good enough for me.'

And with that, I walk inside and back into the rest of my life.

19

Little Lies

Family-sized tub of chocolate ice cream. Check.

Bottle of favourite red wine. Check.

Zero possibility of anyone calling me as mobile turned off. Check.

It's my first night off in ages. Jaz insisted I took it and I didn't put up much of a fight – the thought of cosying up on the sofa and watching TV to my heart's content was far too tempting. Only now I've stopped do I realise how tired I've been since the show began; I just haven't had a break. Though it's still all going on beneath me, tonight Mum and Dad's flat feels like a safe haven: no Evan Bergman, no Nick Craven, no cameras and, loveliest of all, no terrible singing (so long as I turn the telly up really loud).

Blast from the Past starts at nine, giving me just enough time to have a bath before settling down. I've only caught bits and pieces so far, but no doubt once the series is done I'll have ample opportunity to watch: Jaz has taken every imaginable caution to ensure we can indulge in a marathon viewing session at the end of it. It's the same for everyone – what we know of the show so far we've mostly gleaned in snippets from friends and family. Watching a full episode tonight is a wise idea.

My parents' bathroom is one of the more ordinary spaces in the flat, though that isn't saying a great deal. The loo seat sports a plastic cover, which might typically show an aquarium of fish, a deep-sea scene or some inoffensive design, but here displays a fetching headshot of Cliff Richard, his ears plugged with yellow headphones (a still from his video for 'Wired for Sound', the one where he's roller-skating through Milton Keynes shopping centre) and a surprised expression on his face, as if he's just been caught with his pants down – instead of, as may well be the case, catching someone else. I've been trying to remember to always leave the loo seat up, as I'm certain Cliff's eyes follow me about my business and I don't want anyone's eyes, least of all his, following me about my business when I'm in the bathroom.

Mum always uses those water bombs with flowers in that make your skin greasy, so I've done without bubbles. Now I'm in here, though, I rather wish I had. The bottom of the tub is sprinkled with semi-quavers, meaning that every time I move I think there's a family of cockroaches scurrying under

214

my bum. To make matters worse, on the opposite wall there's a large oval mirror, its frame dotted with tatty old *BIG!* magazine transfers. I remember plastering them on when I was eleven and to this day they're still there, an unsavoury reminder of the catalogue of my youth. Not only can I see my naked body lolling about in the bath, but Dieter Brummer, Corey Feldman and that thumb-sized Billy Warlock from *Baywatch* can, too.

Afterwards I wrap myself up in my big best fluffy white dressing gown, dry my hair and pour myself a good slug of vino.

Ten minutes before the show starts, the landline rings. At first I dismiss it as someone wanting Mum and Dad, then the thought creeps in that a terrible event might have befallen them in Eastern Europe, and before I know it I've convinced myself that their tour bus has overturned on a Siberian dirt track and they're being held hostage in a shack in the middle of a forest somewhere being forced to sing for their survival. I'd better pick up the phone.

'Hello?'

'Darling, it's me!'

'Mum! Are you OK? Are you in Siberia?'

'What? No, we're in Budapest.'

'Oh, that's good.' I twist the phone cord round my finger. (No, it's not a wireless: who in their right mind would get rid of a perfectly good handset donated to them by Nik Kershaw when he moved out of his neighbouring apartment in 1989?)

'What's happening at home?'

'Oh, same old, same old . . .'

There's a crackle on the line. '. . . voted third most popular act of the decade!'

'Who – you have?'

'Yes!'

'That's brilliant, Mum – listen, I've really got to go—'

'I heard about Lawrence seeing someone else, poppet. Are you all right?'

For a moment I'm completely thrown. What? Who? How? They're supposed to be safely bundled away in Siberia. They're not supposed to know *anything* about my life.

'What do you mean?' I enquire cautiously.

'I read he was seeing that Montgomery woman. We met her once, darling, and if it's any consolation she's not nice – a very severe manner, not at all friendly, not like you.'

'H-how did you find out about that?'

'Oh, I hope I haven't upset you, poppet. We were in Munich and one of our lot bought a German gossip rag – there was a picture of them together. I recognised him straight away, silly boy. And to think she's so much older than him!'

'That's all? I mean, it didn't say anything else about him or . . . or me? Or, you know, anything else?'

Mum laughs. 'You *are* a funny one. If it did, do you think I could understand it?'

I laugh too, relieved but with a twinge of guilt – I wonder if I shouldn't have just been honest with them from the start. What on earth are they going to make of everything that's happened when they get back?

'He's not with Francesca any more,' I say, steering us firmly on to that subject. 'And anyway, I don't mind either way.'

'Well, you say that, but it's always difficult to see an ex move on. I remember like it was yesterday the night I found out that Bryan—'

'OK, Mum,' I interject, wanting to catch the opening of our show and not relishing the chance to hear the intimate details of her previous relationships – especially not that one.

We hang up shortly after, once I've reassured her that I really am OK, and I settle down on the sofa and switch to TrueUK, just in time to see the closing moments of the previous offering, which looks like one of those sad budget *Schadenfreude* programmes about someone with three ears or a trunk.

I'm surprised at how nervous I am. I've watched the *Blast from the Past* credits before – they're like a cross between *Big Brother* but without the sinister eyeball thing (swapped with a sinister microphone thing) and, ominously, those of *Hollyoaks*. There's Jaz blowing bubble gum, me looking awkward (I remember the cameraman telling me to 'give it' to him, which begged the question: What is 'it'?), Ruby with a feather boa, Alex tossing a cocktail shaker in the air (on take twenty-three he managed to catch it). I notice Andre's now been given his own half-second slot, whiskers twitching as he scampers from left to right, and it makes me laugh.

The first ten minutes of the show is what I expect – Jaz and Alex discussing theme nights, Andre getting his hair done and footage from a *Shrek*-themed birthday party we had in a few evenings back. I'm annoyed to see that Alex is still banging on about the Jaz, Lou and Simon thing – it's almost like he's trying to antagonise Jaz over it, which surprises me because I thought they were close. Mostly I'm worried about Lou seeing it. I'm sure she wouldn't think any more of it than I do, but given her previous suspicions it's something we could do without.

I'm about to pop up to grab the ice cream when something

on the screen catches my attention. No, they haven't put it in. They *haven't*.

The footage is shaky, the camera rushing up the bar steps and out into the street. And then, right there, just as I saw him two days ago, is Lawrence. And me.

Hang on a minute: didn't I explicitly tell Alison to leave this out? The embarrassment factor's bad enough for me but it's Lawrence who comes off looking like a prize fool. I sit back down, worried, hoping it might switch to downstairs but knowing it won't.

Oh *god*. Lawrence is on his knees now. It's the other day word for word, everything that happened, from his ridiculous pleas to my own efforts not to laugh, which when broadcast on telly – oh dear – make me look like a total heartless bitch. What's more, it risks laying us open for a libel suit: while they've had the foresight to dub out (badly) Francesca Montgomery's name, it's obvious who we're talking about.

I'm FURIOUS.

I can't believe it! I made a point of talking to Alison after Lawrence left and expressly made her *promise* to cut that footage out – it's a breach of privacy; I could have them up for this. It's her and Evan who have final say on what goes in, so why on earth didn't they—

Ah, Evan.

Of course.

I'm about to grab my phone, call him on his mobile and tell him just how cross I am, when I stop, take a deep breath, and resolve it's in my best interests to watch the rest of the show, calm down and ring him in the morning. If I do it now I'll say something I regret, and professionalism might be the only thing I have over him right now.

One thing's for certain: it's about time someone put Evan Bergman in his place.

♪

The next day, I'm fuming.

I woke this morning feeling cranky and pissed off – so much so that I could barely eat my Coco Pops and watch *The Jeremy Kyle Show*, and that's saying something. It was double lie detectors, as well.

I'd lain awake for ages after going to bed, imagining all the things I wanted to say to Evan: how he must have known I didn't want that conversation to go in and not given a shit; how he probably did one over on Alison as well because she was too frightened to stand up to him. And, most of all, how if he'd gone against that request, what else of mine had been completely disregarded in his mission to give viewers something to chew on?

Eventually, in the small hours, I'd worked myself into such a state and was feeling so livid (as only you can when the rest of the world is blissfully asleep and you're not) that I decided to make a voodoo doll. I remembered Lou gave me this mini one a couple of years ago when a despotic old boss had unfairly docked my pay: you put it in a bowl of warm water and it grows to the size of a Barbie doll. Well, I'm ashamed to say I followed the instructions on the back, stuck a ball of cotton wool on its head which I blasted with some brown – through design or age, I'm not sure – nail polish I found in Mum's dressing table, and stuck it full of drawing pins. On waking this morning I was so ashamed that I wrapped it in seven plastic bags and took it to the big communal dumpsters round the back of BHS. (I could have weighted it down with stones and dropped it in the river, but that felt altogether too sinister.)

I'm doing my best not to think about all this now I'm actually faced with the man.

Evan's office at Tooth & Nail is flooded with sunlight. I'm squinting into the glare, and Evan, his back to the window, stares at me blankly from a face in shadow.

'You can't just disregard my wishes,' I say, once I've voiced my outrage at last night's episode. 'Some things are private, Evan – you have to understand that. If I didn't make myself clear on that point, allow me to now.'

I had imagined him apologising profusely, even pleading on his hands and knees for forgiveness (that was around three a.m., and sort of confused with the Lawrence-begging episode. I'll have to ask Lou about ex-boyfriends and authority figures with hair made of sponge . . . god, what's Freud going to make of that?). Instead he looks almost as tired as me, and distinctly unimpressed.

'Alison felt strongly about it,' he says flippantly, loosening the knot on his tie. 'She believed it was important to establishing your motivations.'

'What motivations?' I demand, outraged. 'As far as Lawrence goes, I have no motivations whatsoever!'

'We don't know you well enough, Maddie.' Evan shakes his head sadly. 'That's the feedback I'm getting . . .'

'Is that right? What are you going to ask me to do next, then – maybe I could organise a *Full Monty* staff strip?'

He leans back, the leather creaking beneath him. 'Not a bad idea . . .'

'Does Nick know about this going in? I'm sure he'd have something to say.'

Evan raises a sharp eyebrow.

'It wasn't Alison who was fussed about getting that in, was it?' I barrel on, knowing as I voice it that it's absolutely the truth. 'She understood fully when I talked to her about it – it was you who insisted, and she was too scared to argue.' My trump card surfaces from nowhere and blindly I grab it. Before I can stop myself it's fallen from my mouth. 'Because that's the way it goes between the two of you, isn't it?'

Instantly I know I've said too much. It's like that moment when you're pulling out the wrong block in Jenga and you're waiting for the whole lot to fall. So much for keeping it professional. I wish I could fold the words back into my throat.

Evan flushes under his tan. 'What exactly are you inferring?' His voice is low, controlled, and all the more scary for it.

'Nothing, I didn't mean anything by it.'

Evan locks me with that crocodile stare. 'I'd be careful what you say in future,' he says. 'I'm a very powerful man, you know.'

'I know.'

'Try saying what you mean, in that case.'

I'm not being cowed into a corner this time. 'I'm saying that if you want more drama, there are other places to get it.'

He narrows his eyes, prepared to call my bluff. 'There are?'

'I'm sure you can work it out.'

Evan watches me for an uncomfortably long time. 'Well,

you say that,' he says quietly, 'but ratings have sky-rocketed over the past week.'

'They have?'

'Yes.' He looks pleased, settling back. 'You don't think people are *really* interested in some washed-up old karaoke bar, do you?'

I'm shocked by his rudeness. 'I'm sorry?'

'It's the people they want to see.'

'But there has to be a line,' I maintain, 'and when we're not happy broadcasting something, it's got to stay out.'

Evan nods efficiently. 'Like your date with Nick Craven, for example.'

'I beg your pardon?'

Evan taps a hand on the desk, the metal *clack-clack* of his Rolex punctuating the silence. 'Your date with Nick, of course.'

I battle to keep my voice steady. 'What date would this be?'

Evan smirks. 'We had a camera follow you to Embankment last week – right after your debut on stage, which was quite a hit with viewers, I might add. Have you checked YouTube recently?'

'Tell me you're joking.'

'Quite the romantic scene.' He's chuffed with himself now. 'Nick really couldn't have planned it better. We're waiting for the right time to go out with it, take the viewers by surprise. Although I'm sure you'll agree the chemistry's been there between you from the start.'

My heart jumps into my mouth. 'You *filmed* that?'

'Just the crucial part.'

'Which was?' It comes out little more than a squeak.

'I doubt you need reminding.' He gives me a soupy expression. 'Often I think Nick missed his vocation – he shouldn't be hidden away behind the camera; he performs so well in front of it. Very convincing, wouldn't you say?'

I'm shaking. 'What do you mean?'

'Well, you didn't think any of it was *real*, did you?'

Silence.

'Ah, Maddie.' Evan chuckles. 'And there's me thinking you're an intelligent girl. You really believed him?'

I lift my chin. 'Why shouldn't I?'

Evan laughs drily. 'Let me put it this way: how do you think he managed to bed a married woman like Rebecca Ascot?'

I swallow. 'I don't think it was like that.'

'What do you think it was like, then?'

'I don't know . . . I—'

'By pulling the exact same tricks he pulled on you, that's how. He's a practised hand at it now – part of the reason he was so perfect for the job.'

My mouth is dry. 'He wouldn't have.'

But there's a chink of doubt appearing in my armour. It would explain why Nick's been so off with me. It would explain it fully. I was just another of his conquests, a desperate last grab at the publicity that could revive his career.

'Let me tell you, sweetheart – I know a hell of a lot more about that affair than you do. And, I might add, about this one.'

To my horror Evan pulls open his desk drawer, extracts a tan envelope and throws down a collection of stills of Nick and me. There we are, standing on the bridge, looking out at the river; him holding me by my shoulders; us about to kiss.

'You see,' he goes on, 'Nick was only acting on my instruction. I wanted you in the centre of things; the viewers wanted it too. So I told him what I required of him and he delivered, simple as that. And very well too, it would seem.'

'I don't believe you.' My voice doesn't sound like mine. 'Nick would never do that.'

Evan's cruel laugh wings round the office. 'Why do you think I wanted Nick Craven involved in the first place?' he muses. 'Because of his spotless record, his great profile? Hardly. It worked for him and it worked for me. This is his big opportunity, his way back. After the Ascot affair he was down and out' – a shrug – 'so I told him I'd hire him if he promised to play his part. He's been in it from the beginning, Maddie.' He speaks slowly, like this is a concept he's explained a thousand times and I still don't get it. 'This is how things are in reality television – don't tell me you're actually surprised?'

I'm biting my lip so hard I can taste blood.

I can't believe it was all a lie. I can't.

Not everything.

'I don't understand,' I say weakly. 'Why are you doing this?'

'Doing what?' Evan's eyes widen, offended at the accusation. 'I'm only sticking to my side of the bargain. It's all above board, Maddie, just look at the contract.'

Flashes of his clever wording come back to me.

. . . *Subject agrees to all filming in relation to the Club . . . entrusts the Producers autonomy . . . grants her permission . . .*

The fact that stupidly, idiotically, infuriatingly, I didn't read it through properly. I rushed into it. Because I was too busy thinking about something – about some*one* – else.

'I met Nick that day,' I say slowly, almost to myself. 'The

day I came in and you gave me the paperwork. I ran into him outside . . .'

'You did? What a strange coincidence.'

I can't get my head around it. That was planned too?

He grins, easing himself back and crossing his legs. 'Everything happens for a reason – wouldn't you say?'

Evan engineered the meeting, of course he did. He knew that having me bump into a handsome stranger outside Tooth & Nail would provide the bait he needed. Appallingly, he was right: I was reeled straight in. What's more, Nick agreed to it.

Or maybe that part was Nick's idea?

How could he?

'No more filming outside the club,' I tell him, surprised by how firm my voice is. 'I want your word. No cameras on us anywhere outside Pineapple.'

Evan makes a sucking sound through his teeth. 'I'm afraid that's not possible, Maddie,' he says. 'We're heading to the halfway point – you know I can't pull back on the drama now.'

'Even though your little affair's been blown out the water?' I snap. 'Because you might have wrapped Nick around your finger but you won't do the same with me.'

Evan laughs good-naturedly. 'Actually, I think a lovers' tiff could be just what we need.'

I grit my teeth. 'It's my club, Evan, and what I say goes.'

He leans forward. 'Or what?'

'Or . . . Or I'll . . .'

'You'll pay a fortune in lawyers' fees and never get anywhere, because we've got the contract on our side and you haven't got a leg to stand on?'

'I'll expose you.'

'And ruin your reputation, and your family's? "Daughter of Pineapple Mist Hits the Skids", just like every other teen with a famous parent who can't handle the pressures of growing up in the background. Sound about right?'

I shake my head. 'We're not like that.'

'So prove it. Play your part. We're in this together now.'

'I knew I couldn't trust you,' I say. 'I knew it from day one. And yet I still let myself get taken in by you. You've been lying from the start.'

He chortles, like this is just another scene he already scripted – maybe it is? – and it's all going nicely to plan.

'Let's just try to get along, Maddie, shall we? And we both know it's not me who's been lying to you. There's only one person who's been doing that.'

20

If I Could Turn Back Time

'Keep away from me,' I groan, turning into the pillow and burying my face in its reassuring plumpness. 'It's for your own good.'

Lou draws the curtains and an aggressive wash of daylight streams in. 'You've got a cold, Maddie, you're not a leper.'

I lift my head and squint at her. 'Leave me alone. I've a right to suffer.'

Lou gives me an exasperated look and heads into the kitchen. I hear her banging pots and pans around, then the radio snapping on and Vampire Weekend filling the flat.

It's four days later and I'm partway through a self-imposed stint of solitary confinement. I've had worse colds, but never one with such impeccable timing: reeling badly from my meeting with Evan, I just about managed to keep my head down at the club for one night – I still don't know how I'm going to make it through the remaining three weeks and can't bring myself to think about it – when the next morning I woke with a virus. I've been out of circulation since. Rather than feeling glum like I normally do when housebound, with only the lone mating caws of the *Loose Women* for company, on this occasion I'm positively grateful for the chance to draw the curtains and shut out the world.

Lou comes back in with a bowl of soup.

'Here you go,' she says, helping me rearrange my pillows and sit up. 'You OK?' She holds the back of her hand against my forehead.

'I'll be fine so long as I never have to leave this flat ever again in my whole entire life,' I say dramatically, loudly blowing my nose.

Lou sits down next to me, putting her feet up on the bed. 'It's not the end of the world, you know. There's only a few weeks left and then you never have to see Evan Bergman again.'

'He tricked me,' I say miserably.

Lou's well within her rights to say 'I told you so', and I'm grateful that she doesn't.

'Maybe,' she reasons instead. 'But you've got to look at the positives: the club's making tonnes of money – which is exactly what you did it for, remember? It's transformed, Maddie. You've made all your plans a reality!'

'A reality show,' I interject bitterly, spooning the soup into my mouth.

'You're just going to put an unhelpful spin on everything I say, aren't you?' She flicks channels on the telly. 'Ooh look, *Three Men and a Baby*'s on at four.'

I put the soup down. 'It'll only make me upset.'

'What, that you don't live in a massive New York apartment with handsome creative types and throw parties where it's acceptable to dance to Gloria Estefan?'

'No.'

'That the likelihood of you being in the same park as Tom Selleck, Ultimate Man, playing Frisbee and wearing high-waisted shorts is about a billion to one?'

I smile. 'That's moderately upsetting.'

'Well, then.'

'I'm just not in the mood for happy endings.' I pull the duvet up to my chin, determined to wallow in the full depth of my gloom. 'Especially not love ones.'

'Actually none of them finds love at the end,' explains Lou. 'Except they love the baby, of course. That's kind of the point.'

'Yuck.'

'God, you are in a foul mood, aren't you?'

I ball my fists and slam them down on the bed, stroppy as a child. 'I wish I'd never said yes to this in the first place, Lou. We're in a massive fuck-off mess now and it's all my fault.'

'Hey, everyone understands,' she says, kicking me gently.

'You think?'

'Sure. You've done the right thing telling them what's happening – now they know what Evan's up to they can decide for themselves how they want to be perceived. Getting all woe-is-me about it isn't going to help.'

'Ugh.' I pop a throat sweet out its foil and suck on it, ignoring her counsel. 'It's been a disaster from start to finish.' At Lou's raised eyebrow, I add, 'On a personal level, at least.'

Lou flicks channels idly. 'So I guess you don't care he's been walking round with a face like doom,' she says.

'Who?' I ask, feigning ignorance and not believing for a single second that she'll buy it.

'Oh, no one.' She settles on *Countdown*.

We both take a few seconds to work out the anagram. Lou comes up with 'Lavish' and I come up with 'Haves'. *Haves*. It's not even a proper word.

'I don't care, Lou,' I pronounce. 'He's dead to me.'

'That's a terrible thing to say!'

'What he did was terrible.' I sink down lower. 'He had me going the whole time.'

'But you haven't even heard him out,' she says. 'Don't you think you should at least see what he comes back with?'

I shake my head. I haven't told Lou about what Nick and I talked about on the bridge. If she knew he'd lied about that, she'd never speak to him again either.

'He asked me yesterday how you were. I think he knows something's up.'

'Good. He tried ringing last night but I ignored it. He's left it too bloody late – he's had days to call, even before all this blew up, and he didn't. Now I know why. He was probably receiving his next set of instructions from Evan.'

On cue my phone beeps and Lou and I look at each other.

'Pick it up, then!'

I reach over. I don't know what I'm hoping for. I'm angry and hurt and upset, and even if I don't want to hear it and I've already made up my mind, I still want an explanation.

But it's Lawrence.

'Ugh!' cries Lou, peering over my shoulder. 'It's Lawrence!'

Hey Mads, heard u were ill, coming over tonight to make u better. L x

Lou makes a pretend gagging sound.

'All right, all right,' I say, flipping the phone shut.

'He's tenacious, isn't he? I'd have thought he was well pissed off after your altercation last week.'

'I thought you weren't watching!'

'I just caught that bit,' she admits sheepishly. 'I had to turn it off when Alex kept banging on about Jaz liking Si. You don't think she does, do you?'

'No.' I blow my nose. 'I've told you before.'

Lou snatches the handset off me. 'You're not *seeing* Law again, arc you?'

'Of course I'm not.' I bristle. 'He's just been . . . phoning me. And checking up on me. And making sure I'm OK. What's wrong with that? I said we could be friends, didn't I?'

She reads the message again. 'But it sounds romantic, Maddie,' she whispers. 'It sounds . . . *menacing.*'

'He wants to make it up to me,' I say, patting down the duvet and lying back like a nerve-addled damsel in need of my smelling salts. 'And I could do with a little attention right now.'

'He didn't mind about your spat being broadcast?'

'No.' I yawn. 'Lawrence didn't mind at all.'

Lou snorts. 'That figures.'

'Well anyway,' I puff, 'what's wrong with enjoying a little grovelling? I deserve it!'

Lou looks confused. 'But I thought you hated him.'

'I never *hated* him,' I say patiently. 'I just didn't particularly *like* him.'

'That's the same thing.'

'No, it's not. And isn't a girl allowed to change her mind?'

Now she's properly worried. 'Not where Lawrence Olivier's concerned—'

'It's Lawrence *Oliver*.' To this day Lou believes she heard him on the phone once calling himself that – she's never let it go.

'Whatever. Aren't you forgetting how he behaved all the time you were together? And that it's very possible he cheated on you—'

'But we don't know that for certain, do we?'

'Oh, Maddie.' She shakes her head, despairing. 'Either you are suffering from a dreadful delusional fever or you're swapping one man's affections for another's.'

I try to focus on the numbers round – it's just not the same without Carol. 'Why would I do that?'

She props herself up next to me. 'Because you're feeling discarded. Nick's crapped all over you, and just because Lawrence happens to be taking a break from crapping all over you, you're happy to give him another shot – even if the chances of him crapping all over you again is almost a definite, and then you'll have had both of them crapping all over you.'

'Can we stop talking about me getting crapped on?'

232

'Sorry.'

'Besides, I'm not giving Lawrence another shot. I'm just saying he *did* break up with that woman for me, so he's got to like me deep down, hasn't he? I'm not a complete reject, am I?'

'Of course you're not.' She bites her lip. 'But listen – and I'm only telling you this because I believe, I *know* that you'd be making a mistake to trust him again – but I heard it was Francesca who dumped him, not the other way round. She didn't cast him in her new play and he kicked up such a fuss that she called the whole thing off.'

I sob into my tissues. Even that nugget of half-satisfying intelligence is a lie.

'And there's a rumour going round. It's bad, Maddie . . .'

'What is it?' I snuffle.

'Lawrence is so short of work he's been doing shifts at his uncle's butcher's.'

'So?'

'Well,' she winces, 'apparently he's been getting paid in . . . meat.'

I'm distressed. 'Meat?'

'Yeah. Like chops and things.'

'Oh *god*!'

Lou takes my hands. 'All I'm saying is that his motivations might not be entirely . . . honourable. That's all. He dumped you because he felt he was going places and you weren't – now it's the other way round he wants to claim his piece. It's dark, Maddie. And if you can't see that, then I have to tell you.'

'He's getting paid in *meat*?'

'That's what I heard.'

I blow my nose again. 'Fine. But even without the

233

Francesca Montgomery admission, he's still been there for me – and he knows me. Right now that's the kind of person I need—'

'You need someone familiar,' she says, 'and trustworthy – that's all. It's not Lawrence.'

'It's certainly not Nick,' I mumble. Thinking about him again sends me back into a pit of despair. 'I told him my name as well!' I howl.

'Oh for god's sake!'

'I know . . . I think I have Tourette's!'

'You don't have Tourette's; you're just a fool. I'd have thought you'd be more careful after last time.'

'I couldn't help it,' I lament. 'I thought I could trust him.' I remember that night on the Thames, how perfect it was – too perfect, it turns out – and a well of tears throttles my chest.

Lou puts her arm round me.

'And I guess those flowers are from Lawrence as well, are they?' She looks over at the sorry bunch of pink carnations on the windowsill, sad and droopy through lack of sun.

'Yes,' I sniff.

'I wonder how many sausages they cost.'

'Please don't tell me how many sausages I'm worth, I'm not sure I can handle it.'

'OK, OK.'

But I feel marginally better, at least for the minute, so long as Lou's here and we're watching *Three Men and a Baby*, and trying for the fiftieth time to work out if there really *is* a ghost by the window in the scene where his mum comes round, or if it's just a cardboard cut-out of Ted Danson in a top hat.

Lawrence turns up at five to six, a little after Lou's gone. I answer the door looking horrible. This is one of the (few) advantages to being chased by someone you're not interested in: it's quite fun to test how rough you can make yourself and still be desirable.

'Hi*yuh*,' he greets me, opening his arms for an embrace. One thing about Lawrence: he doesn't hold a grudge.

'Hey.' I sniff, and the end of my nose is sore and bright pink. My eyes are like slits and my hair's a greasy unbrushed hedge. There might be tomato ketchup stains down my T-shirt. 'Come in – if you're brave.'

Enthusiastic as a dog, Lawrence bounds in after me. 'I brought your favourite,' he says, holding out a pizza box. I open it. It's not my favourite at all, but I don't mention it.

'Thanks, that's really kind.'

'How are you feeling?' He perches on the sofa, leaning forward with the anticipation of a father whose child is off playing near a precipice. Under his coat he's wearing a peach linen shirt, dark blue jeans that have been ironed funny (or only just bought?) so there's a sharp crease down the middle of each leg, and toffee loafers.

'I'm OK, just vegetating.' I flop down next to him and drag a duvet over my knees.

'I caught the show last night,' Lawrence says with a serious frown. 'I'm concerned, Mads.'

'Let's not talk about the show.' I grab my box of tissues, annoyed that Lawrence has to bring it up within half a minute of arriving. 'I'm sick of it.'

'OK . . . What do you want to do, then, shall we go out?'

'Lawrence, I'm sick.'

'Oh yuh, sorry.'

'Are you going to take your coat off?'

'There's a great little coffee shop nearby, why don't we go there?' His eyes are bright. 'It'd do you good to get out the house for an hour, show the world you're still alive—'

'I don't *want* to go out!' Angrily I flip open the pizza box. 'And I don't want to *show the world* a damn thing about me right this minute, OK? I want to sit in, stuff my face with unsuitable food and forget about everything. Are you with me or not?'

Lawrence shrugs half-heartedly out his coat. 'How about tomorrow then? Shall we go out tomorrow? There's a restaurant I've been meaning to try . . .'

'Look,' I say, 'that's nice of you, but I don't know how I'm going to feel tomorrow. And anyway,' I think of the meat, 'can you afford it?'

He looks confused. I wonder if he's working out how many giblets he'll need or whether he was hoping I'd cough up like before.

'It's too soon,' I say, putting him out of his misery with a generic rebuff.

'Too soon after your fumble with that director, you mean?'

Great – I knew it was only a matter of time before that got out. Bloody Evan. I shove the box on the floor, my appetite vanished.

Lawrence reaches for me. 'I was worried,' he drones, 'that's why I brought up last night's show, I thought you'd want to talk about it.'

'It was on last night?' I groan. I love Lou for not telling me and I hate her at the same time. I expect it's splashed across the tabloids as well.

'Yuh.' Lawrence rubs his hands together. 'Look, Mads, I've got to say: I don't trust him.'

'That makes two of us,' I say drily, then immediately wish I hadn't. Lawrence pounces on it like a cat on a mouse.

'Oh yuh?'

'Never mind.'

'Are you seeing him?'

I don't know if it's just because we're discussing a disastrous romantic episode with another man, but when I look into Lawrence's eyes I think I see genuine affection. Is it possible he does still care, despite everything? He knows me – and what's more, he was *right* about me. I'm Maddie Mulhern, the quiet, careful one; the one who's best off backstage, not in front of the cameras, exactly like he said – because look where that leaves me? This is where I belong.

But does that mean I belong with him?

'No, I'm not.'

He exhales audibly. 'That's good. Because when I saw you two together—'

'Please be honest, Lawrence. Could you . . . on the bridge, I mean, could you hear anything we said?'

To my intense relief Lawrence shakes his head. 'Nuh, it was shot from a distance – it was just, you know,' he clears his throat, 'the significant bit.'

Phew.

There's a knock on the door.

'Leave it,' I say. 'It'll be Alison. She's been trying to get the cameras in here since the start, she's like a bulldog.'

'Maybe we should let them in!' Lawrence pats my leg, the other hand smoothing his already smooth hair. 'Just let everyone see you're OK.'

I baulk. 'Why on earth would I want to do that?'

'The viewers care, Mads . . .' He jumps up and pads over to the door, checking his reflection in the mirror on the way past. 'You can't just leave them in the lurch.'

'Lawrence, don't you dare.'

He peers through the peephole. 'Oh,' he says, bored, and his shoulders actually sag, 'it's just Ruby du Jour and one of her drag queen friends.'

'Fine.' I yawn, waving my hand in assent. 'They can come in.'

Lawrence pulls open the door and what looks like a bundle of Christmas wrapping paper rustles through. Ruby and Davinia – who, in Lawrence's defence, does bear a striking resemblance to her companion – are done up in almost identical dresses. I recognise Davinia's from a mobile phone launch party I saw her photographed at last year.

'Maddie, we need you back downstairs,' Ruby commands. 'This minute!'

With a fierce shake of my head, I burrow back into the sofa. 'I'm *ill*. Leave me alone.'

Davinia wrings her hands together. 'It really would be for the best . . . We need your help. Jaz is drunk.'

'So?' I say selfishly, unable to think of anything worse than facing that club right now – than facing Nick Craven, to be more specific. I'm mortified at having fallen for his hackneyed charms. 'I don't blame her. Anyway, I'm contagious.'

'I'll come,' chips in Lawrence, already going to grab his coat.

'No, Lawrence,' I say fiercely, 'you'll do no such thing.'

Davinia glances nervously at Ruby. 'There's going to be trouble,' she warns. 'Things are . . . kicking off.'

'I don't doubt that,' I complain, and I know I'm behaving like a brat. 'Things are kicking off for me as well, and there's no way you're getting me down there tonight.'

'But, Maddie,' Ruby comes over and sits down, 'we came up here because we need you.' She lowers her voice. 'There have been some . . . *developments* you should know about.'

'I'm sure there have!' I cry, unable to think outside my own predicament. In a millisecond I convince myself that Nick's been filmed snogging some other poor girl and this turns into everyone snogging each other and then it's a big revolting snogathon while I, the lone leprous pariah, rot away upstairs.

'Come on,' says Ruby, suddenly efficient and clapping her hands together in an awful way reminiscent of a primary school teacher who once forced me to eat corned beef and made the whole class stay behind till I finished every last scrap. 'Time to get you up and about.'

She and Davinia get to work, gathering up the pizza box and tugging at my duvet. Lawrence edges towards the door, primed for the green light.

'No!' I wrench the duvet back and for a moment it's me engaged in a tug of war with two gender-ambiguous fairy god-mothers, both forcing me to go to the ball. 'Just fuck off! Leave me alone! For god's sake, what part of that don't you *get*?'

Abruptly they let go and the duvet descends on me in a great cloud. I battle it off and two heavily made-up, sorely

239

disappointed faces appear over the top. I'm behaving like a selfish shit. And now I've hurt their feelings – Ruby's especially.

'If that's the way you feel,' says Davinia tersely, swivelling on her heel.

'Davinia, wait—'

Ruby doesn't say anything; she just looks at me. And that's a million times worse.

'One more night,' she says, pointing a painted fingernail at me – behind the big hair and make-up I can see Rob's gentle gaze, and I know this is serious – 'then you're coming back. You can't duck out of your responsibilities, Maddie. You started this. And now you've got to reap what you've sown.'

21

Waiting For a Star to Fall

The following evening, at seven o'clock, I force myself to emerge. Not just because it's about time I showed my face at Pineapple, but because Lawrence has finally cajoled me into going out with him.

Maybe it's a stupid decision, but the past few days have put things in perspective. I feel like I've been playing at being someone I'm not – parading myself on TV; taking the reins of a project I'm not experienced enough to handle; opening up to a man I know nothing about and finding out he's totally duped me – and sure enough I've been well and truly stung by it. I want my old life back. Plus I've realised that while I wasn't exactly *happy* when I was with Lawrence, I wasn't miserable either . . . and I was a damn sight better than I am now. Compared with how Nick's treated me, Lawrence is positively princely.

Not that this has anything to do with Nick Craven. Of course it hasn't.

Jaz is already there when I go downstairs. She looks sheepish when I walk into the bar, and isn't in her usual outrageous attire. Instead she's wearing a subdued pair of faded dungarees and her wild hair is tamed back in a ponytail.

'Hello, stranger,' I say, giving her a hug. 'Sorry for going AWOL.'

Jaz puts down her magazine and smiles uncertainly at me.

'You're not coming down with what I had, are you?' I ask, concerned. 'You look like you haven't slept in a week.' Jaz's eyes are red-rimmed and her complexion's pale.

'I'm OK.'

I can hear Andre scrabbling about inside his box. When Jaz lifts him out I almost gasp aloud: he's completely naked, no trousers, no hairpiece, no knee-high socks, nothing. I feel like I've just walked in on someone on the loo.

'Are you sure?' I'm properly worried now – I don't think I've ever seen Andre in his birthday suit before (I've seen him in every other conceivable suit).

'So is it a date?' Jaz's eyes are big and blue as she takes in my outfit – I guess I have made an effort, throwing on a figure-skimming grey dress and heels.

'It's not a date,' I say, smoothing down the skirt. 'I just want to get out of this place for a night, get back to some semblance of normality.' I sigh. 'I think I really upset Ruby yesterday. And Davinia. You haven't seen either of them, have you?'

Jaz shakes her head. 'Maddie,' she begins, hesitant, 'there's something I really have to tell you.'

'If it's about Nick Craven, I don't want to hear it.'

'Actually it's about me. You see, I've done something silly.'

My phone rings. 'Hang on a sec,' I tell her, rummaging about in my bag. Nerves flutter as half of me expects it to be Nick. My willingness to hear him out is rapidly dwindling: as far as I'm concerned his silence only confirms his guilt.

'Shit!' I say. 'Why can I never find anything in here?'

It's Lawrence. A brief conversation establishes he's already at the restaurant (early) and wants to know what 'aperitif' he should order. I'm not sure what an aperitif constitutes, so I go for a G&T. No doubt I'll turn up and Lawrence will be nursing a seventeen-year-old port. Or maybe a sherry. Last Christmas at his parents' manor (a pile in the West Country housing twenty King Charles spaniels and several turrets), I drank nearly an entire bottle of Tio Pepe and the next day offered to take the rubbish out and ended up surreptitiously puking into his mother's basil and thyme rockery. I never told him that.

'Sorry, Jaz,' I hang up, 'what were you saying?'

She looks flustered now, waving me away. 'Oh, nothing, nothing. You go.'

'Are you sure?'

'Yes, 'course. Let's talk when you get back.' She gives me a naughty grin, a shade of the Jaz I know. '*If* you come back.'

'Don't even joke,' I tell her, grabbing my bag and dashing upstairs.

Fifteen minutes later I arrive at Chez Sebastien, a little French bistro off Fleet Street. As the taxi pulls up I'm horrified to see a cluster of paparazzi mooching around outside, cameras at their sides, flicking fag ash on the pavement and scuffing their feet, bored. At first I think they must be here for someone else, but then I remember I'm no longer distinct from that wandering troupe of reality-TV-assisted D-list celebrities that Davinia hangs out with on a weekend. I'm one of them. I've sold my soul to the devil and the entire world is watching.

As soon as the doors open, they're on me, swooping to life, hectic as bats. How did they know I was here?

'Maddie! What can you tell us about Nick Craven?'

'Why haven't we seen more of you together? Are you in a relationship? What's happening between you?'

'Maddie, what's it like being part of the UK's most talked-about couple?'

I fumble through the glare and hurry inside.

To my relief I see Lawrence straight away, nestled in a dimly lit booth at the back. He's wearing a very smart charcoal suit, and instantly I regret wearing a similar shade of grey: we look like a couple of rats out for a cheese board. I wish I could reignite the spark of desire I had in the early stages of our relationship, when I used to feel butterflies at the thought of seeing him.

Fleetingly I remember Nick. That wasn't even a spark – it was a full-blown inferno.

'Mads,' he stands up and kisses me on both cheeks, 'you

look gorgeous. Come and sit down.' He pulls out my chair, but not far enough. I struggle to squeeze into the tiny gap, hoping he'll notice and put me out of my misery, but he's too busy scoping out the rest of the diners. Eventually I wedge myself in and pick up the menu, feeling more than fat enough already.

'Hi,' I say, deciding that once I get a glass of wine in my hand I'll feel better, 'you haven't been waiting long, have you?'

His smile's like liquid. 'I'd wait for ever.'

Talk about a Series of Unappetising Events. 'This looks nice,' I say, deciding that it doesn't matter that I don't feel with him how I felt with Nick. Nick's not the person I thought he was, so it's a waste of time thinking about it.

'Not as nice as you,' he says smoothly, raising his eyebrows over the rim of the open menu. I never noticed before how tidy his eyebrows are. I wonder if he plucks them.

The waiter comes and I order a salad for starters, then penne with courgette spaghetti. I hope it's not actual spaghetti, otherwise that's shitloads of pasta.

'And for you, sir?'

'Yuh,' Lawrence sits up straighter in his chair, 'I'll take the scarlops and choritho. Then I'll have the *sar*mon, hmm, yes, and a plate of fweets.'

'I'm sorry, sir?'

'Fweets.'

There's an awkward silence, before Lawrence grumbles, 'Chips,' and the waiter takes the menus away.

I hide my smile in the G&T. See? Nick's not the only one who can make me laugh.

'You were getting a bit of attention outside, then?' Lawrence asks, his eager face shimmering in the candlelight.

'I guess so.'

The wine arrives and Lawrence pours it. 'You'd better get used to it; the press are going mad over you. Who'd have thought it?' He chuckles. '*I* never reckoned you'd be doing something like this.'

'Nor me.' I sigh loudly, hoping he'll get the hint and drop it at that. But of course he doesn't.

'All that time you led me to believe you just wanted an ordinary life,' he goes on, 'and deep down you craved success – exactly like me!' He raises his glass. 'Cheers to that.'

We clink glasses.

'So I was thinking,' and his face suggests I'm going to like what's coming, 'perhaps I could make an appearance on the live final? You know, since I missed the first.'

'Lawrence, do you mind if we don't talk about the bar?'

He's confused. 'Why not?'

'I'm tired of it,' I explain. 'I just want to have a normal evening out, how things were before. Please?'

'How things were before?' He leans across. 'Maddie, are you saying . . . ?'

'I'm not saying anything. Let's take it one day at a time, OK?' I gulp back the wine. 'Lots has happened since the show began and I'm not ready to rush into anything. You understand that, don't you?'

'Of course, of *course*!' he says, dripping with empathy. 'I know *exactly* how it is. When you're so in-demand you just want to hide away and take a break from it all – you don't need to tell me about that!'

'OK . . . Thanks.'

'So I promise not to talk about the show.'

I smile gratefully at him as our starters come.

'But just as a last thing,' he harpoons a fleshy scallop with his fork (Lou once told me they were fish cheeks and I've not been able to eat them since), 'you wouldn't be against the idea *per se*, would you?'

'What idea?'

'Of me getting involved on the final night? Only to help you out, you know, take the pressure of live TV off a bit.'

It can't make things any worse, that's for certain. 'All right,' I say, picking disinterestedly at my salad, 'whatever.'

By the time the main course arrives, Lawrence is on his third monologue. I've barely been able to cram a word in edgeways and once again I get the impression he doesn't need me here at all; I could be a blow-up doll for all the conversation he requires.

'. . . So I said to her, "Look, if you don't want me for the new production, just tell me!" I mean I was going to split up with her anyway, because of you, but even so I'd appreciate a little *honesty*, stupid old bag . . .'

I find myself tuning in and out, smiling politely and nodding at the necessary junctures. Even the contentious subject of how he broke up with Francesca Montgomery doesn't really interest me.

Profiteroles seem to be the only thing for it, so I waste no time in ordering pudding. While Lawrence is digging into his crème brûlée I seize the opportunity to steer the conversation away from him.

'Top five eighties songs,' I say through a mouthful of chocolate. 'You first.'

Lawrence looks annoyed, like I've interrupted his train of thought. 'I'm sorry?'

'Favourite five singles of the eighties,' I say again. 'What are they?'

He's baffled. 'What the hell kind of question is that?'

I put down my spoon. 'It's just a bit of fun, Law.'

'It's Lawrence these days,' he corrects me.

'It's just a bit of fun, Lawrence.'

'It's stupid. You know I hate this music stuff – I never know what to say.'

'Come on, you always know what to say.' He brightens a shade at the compliment. 'Shall I start?'

'Fine, OK, whatever you like.'

I list my five and wait for his reaction. He's busy cracking the bronzed shell on his pudding and makes a sort of 'Mm?' sound when I prompt him for a response.

'Great,' he says. 'Great choice.'

'That's all?'

'Never heard of half of them.'

I pretend I don't mind. 'Your go.'

Lawrence pushes his crème brûlée away and tosses his napkin on to the table. Instinctively I know if he ever has kids he'll be annoyed if they spill something, or take up too much of his time.

'Must I?'

'It doesn't matter.'

'All right, all right – if it'll make you happy . . .' He sighs extremely loudly. 'What's that one about broken wings? I quite like that one. My dad's got it on one of his driving ballads CDs.'

'Mr Mister?'

'Excuse me?'

'"Broken Wings" by Mr Mister – that's the one you mean.'

'Yeah, that's the one.'

I grin. 'You really like that song?'

Lawrence throws his arms up. 'See what I mean?'

'It's a bit corny.'

'No, it's not. It's meaningful.'

'What does it mean?'

'Don't ask me. Birds don't like being in cages?' He's totally deadpan.

'Er . . .'

'At least it's not Pineapple Mist,' he snaps, on the defence.

'Pineapple Mist is plenty of people's favourite!'

Lawrence clears his throat, as if the conversation has become far too silly.

'Come on, let's get out of here,' he says, signalling for the bill. 'There's a great jazz place nearby with outdoor seating.'

I pull on my cardigan. 'Isn't it a bit cold to sit outside?'

'A little cold never hurt anyone,' he says, inspecting the tab. 'Right – you had the penne and I had the *sar*mon, which is a bit more expensive, but then you had a G&T and I'd already paid for my sherry separately, so that evens it out . . .'

'Lawrence, shall we just go halves?'

'No, no,' he rubs his chin, 'I'm not sure that's fair.'

'I'm sure it is,' I say, 'I'm not fussed.'

'I mean I think you owe more than me.' He pulls his phone out his pocket and finds the calculator bit, begins punching in the items. 'Bugger! I've messed it up.'

'Seriously, let's split it. I'll buy you a drink some time.'

'All right . . .' He shakes his head and slips his phone back in his pocket. 'Can you leave the tip though? Better do fifteen per cent since it's a smart place.'

By the time we get outside I'm not feeling in the mood to go on somewhere else, so I hail a cab and say goodbye to Lawrence on the street. He keeps looking around and seems annoyed, as if he expected someone else to be here.

'Bye then,' I say, opening the door. 'Thanks for, um, taking me out.'

Suddenly there's a man charging across the empty street, breathless, red-faced, brandishing a camera. 'Maddie?' His eyes widen as he claps eyes on my companion. 'Lawrence Oliver!' *Snap snap snap.*

Lawrence steps forward. 'The very same—'

'Bye, Lawrence.' I clamber into the car feeling like Paris Hilton without her knickers on, but not before he's grabbed me by the hand, a little painfully if truth be told.

'Can I kiss you?' he breathes urgently. 'I have to kiss you. I've been dying to all night. You don't know what you do to me, Mads.'

'Er . . . no.' I try to shut the door.

But he doesn't hear. Drawing me into his arms with surprising strength, Lawrence plants a big wet kiss on my mouth, and for a moment we're engaged in a very uncomfortable closed-lipped embrace, him trying for passion and me trying to get away as soon as possible but not wanting to embarrass him. The kiss can't last more than a few seconds but it feels like an eternity. At one point I peek and see that Lawrence is peeking too, except he's looking out to the side, where the man

250

with the camera is rapidly approaching. With our eyes open and our mouths closed the whole kissing thing seems oddly upside down.

I'm bright red by the time my taxi pulls away. I can see Lawrence in the rearview mirror, no longer alone but chatting to a small group of paparazzi, making elaborate hand gestures and for some reason filling me with dread.

♪

I've only been in the cab five minutes when I get a text from Lou. Two words:

Call me

Uh-oh, that doesn't sound good. It's unheard of for Lou to send a one-page text – she's forever blocking up my inbox with five-page-long messages that go into unnecessary detail about a coat, or a pair of shoes, or how someone was rude to her on the bus – and she never *ever* forgets to add kisses. I ring her back straight away, hoping I'm worrying about nothing, but as soon as she picks up I know something is seriously the matter. Lou's in tears.

'Lou? My god, what's wrong?'

'Where are you?'

'I'm in a cab on the Strand.'

A long pause. 'Can you get up here?'

Her voice isn't right. She sounds cold, removed. I've never heard her like it before.

'Sure – what is it? Are you OK?'

'Just hurry. I don't want to talk about it over the phone.'

When I turn up at Lou's flat half an hour later, I'm shocked by her appearance. She answers the door looking haunted, her cheeks puffy and her eyes swollen. My immediate thought is that the world is coming down with some dreadful killer virus – Jaz looked almost as bad when I left her earlier.

'What on earth's happened?' I ask, following her in.

She turns on me. 'Your fucking show, that's what's happened.'

I'm taken aback by her vitriol – Lou's always so calm, so reasonable. 'What do you mean?'

'I knew it would be like this,' she laughs bitterly, 'I knew it from the start – but did you listen? No.'

'Lou, you're going to have to help me out here,' I say, shaken by her outburst. I've never seen her so angry – at least not since I dyed her hair green in year nine – and it scares me. 'Slow down a minute and tell me what's going on.'

'It's too late,' she says, wiping her nose and collapsing on to the sofa. 'It's all messed up now. It's all ruined.' She puts her head in her hands.

Cautiously I sit down next to her. I consider putting an arm across her shoulders but something in her steely frame warns me not to.

'Lou . . .'

'You had to agree to this stupid show, didn't you?' she sobs. 'Even when I told you it was a bad idea and you hadn't thought it through properly. Because it wasn't just *you* who mattered, was it? It was the rest of us. But you didn't think about that, did you?'

I grapple for words. 'Of course I did. I—'

'Not enough,' she lashes. 'You didn't care that all our lives were going to be paraded in front of the cameras for all the world to see. No, never mind about that so long as you were raking in the money. Never mind what it's cost the rest of us!'

There's a horribly long silence. I feel like someone's punched me in the face.

'I don't know what you're talking about,' I say slowly, my heart pumping wildly. 'You have to calm down and tell me.'

She hugs her knees to her chest and another sob escapes.

'Simon and Jaz,' she snivels. 'They . . . they kissed.'

'*What?*'

'Last night, after I left yours. There I was, studying at home like some cross-eyed dweeb while he was off snogging someone else. And I knew it from the beginning, didn't I? I *knew* there was something between them. But you told me not to worry, that I was only making it up.'

I'm stunned. 'That can't be right. I mean, Simon and Jaz? It *can't* be.'

'And the best bit? It was all for the cameras, for a bit of attention. Because that's what reality shows do, isn't it? They ruin people's lives, their relationships . . .' she looks at me, full of heartbreak, 'their friendships.'

'Lou, hold on a minute,' I say, dumbfounded. 'I'm struggling to believe this. Are you absolutely sure? Simon's devoted to you, he always has been.'

Her body's shaking, she's properly crying now. 'Yes,' she mumbles, her voice thick with tears, 'because Simon told me himself. He came round here earlier tonight and confessed everything.'

'What did he say?'

She looks up at me with hard red eyes. 'He tried to get out of it, said she'd launched herself on him in front of the crew – god, I can't even bear to say her name – and there was nothing he could do.' She shakes her head. 'Why do men always say that? "There was nothing I could do" – of course there was, you prick.'

'And it was – it was caught on film?' Seeing Lou like this, I would honestly kill them both right now. This is a nightmare. It can't be real.

'Yup,' she sniffs, 'not for long, but long enough. All ready for broadcast, no doubt – that should push up your fucking ratings.'

'Lou, this isn't my fault.'

'Whose fault is it then?' she fires back. 'If you hadn't said yes to Evan fucking Bergman in the first place, we wouldn't be in this mess, would we?'

'Hang on a second, you know we've been done over by Evan – what am I meant to do about it?'

'But I never *wanted* to be involved!' she cries. 'And once upon a time neither would you – I guess you've changed, Maddie.'

'But you agreed to start working there!'

'And you promised, you *gave me your word* that Evan wouldn't come near me. Some word that turned out to be.'

I think I'm going to cry. Lou's hurt, I tell myself, that's why she's taking it out on me. But she's my best friend – I want to comfort her and she won't let me. I can't let our friendship get ruined over this, I won't.

'I'm sorry,' I say quietly. 'There was nothing I could do.'

She barks a harsh laugh. 'Oh, not you as well! It doesn't look like anyone's to blame, does it? Hey, maybe it's *my* fault! No one else looks like they're about to step up to the plate. Though I'd sure like to give a piece of my mind to that . . . that *cow*.'

'Maybe I should talk to her first,' I suggest, thinking if I can help she might remember we're a team and I'd never do anything deliberately to upset her. 'You know what she's been through with that guy in America – maybe she felt like—'

'Don't tell me you're prepared to hear her out?' she lashes, appalled. 'Not after what she's done. Everyone's got shit in their past, we don't all go around getting off with other people's boyfriends!'

Swiftly I clarify it. 'Lou, I'm on your side, a hundred per cent, but we have to find out what really happened. It just doesn't seem . . . real. I can't believe she would do that without good reason.'

'Good reason?' Lou glares at me. 'I suppose any reason Jaz gave you would be good enough, wouldn't it?'

'What's that supposed to mean?'

Lou stands up. 'I think you should leave.'

'What? Why?'

'I want to be by myself.'

'I'm only saying we should give Jaz the benefit of the doubt until we know—'

'Please.' She folds her arms, shut like a book. 'Just go.'

'But Lou, I'm sorry! Can't we just . . . I mean . . .'

She goes to the door. 'I won't be round at the club for a while,' she says, eyes on the floor. 'I can't face it.'

With shaking hands I pick up my bag. 'How long's a while?'

But she doesn't answer. Instead she waits till I'm standing outside in the hall, and then she closes the door.

22

What Have I Done to Deserve This?

The next twenty-four hours are terrible. Horrible. Possibly the worst of my life.

Lou's frozen me out. Our shifts at Simply Voices always cross on Thursdays so I thought I might at least catch her at the office, but no. By midday it was becoming clear she wasn't going to show up, and when I asked Jennifer, she told me Lou had had a family emergency and wasn't planning to come in till next week. I don't even know if this is true. I don't know anything about what's happening in her life, and even though it's only been one day, I hate it.

Three emails this morning say it all:

To: Maddie Mulhern
From: Simon Taylor
Subject: help

Hey. Lou said (yelled) that she told you.
It's not what you think. She hates my
guts. If you speak to her please tell her
I'm sorry and I love her.

To: Maddie Mulhern
From: Jasmine Rose
Subject: RE: we need to talk

Sure, I want to see you too. Three sounds
fine, hope ur OK xx

To: Maddie Mulhern
From: Evan Bergman
Subject: excellent news

Maddie
This week: RECORD VIEWING NUMBERS
1.5 MILLION tuned in on Sat
No hard feelings after our talk. Are you
back in circulation? We need you for the
final push. I know you won't let me down.
Evan.

Jennifer invites me to lunch, quizzing me on Nick Craven and asking me a load of questions I don't want to answer. Brusquely she announces she's on a diet and chooses one of those Pret 'no bread' sandwiches, which is the strangest food initiative on record. What's a no-bread sandwich? Not a sandwich – at all. Meanwhile I'm cramming a baguette and crisps down my throat, followed swiftly by a chocolate brownie chaser.

'Are you all right?' Jennifer enquires, no doubt regretting her decision to lunch with a shire horse. 'You seem . . . hungry.'

'I am hungry,' I say, reasoning that if Lou's not here then I'm eating for two.

'Why don't you go home early,' she says. 'We understand how frantic things are – why you're still opening envelopes and answering phones for us is beyond me.'

'Don't fire me!' I cry through a dam of bread. Then I mutter, 'This job's about the only semblance of normality I have right now.'

'We wouldn't dream of it,' says Jennifer. 'But the time will come when you'll leave us all behind – you're set for great things, Maddie, I've always known it.'

'You have?'

'Of course. You're your parents' daughter, how could you not be?'

That's if Mum and Dad don't disown me as well. Oh dear: they're coming home in three weeks. At this rate they're going to arrive at the flat to find me huddled in Dad's wardrobe among his 'piano' trousers, rocking back and forth and drooling, reciting 'Peter Andre made me do it' over and over again.

In the end I take Jennifer up on her offer and head back to the club after lunch. What I really want to do is avoid the place until the series has blown over, Lou's forgiven me and Nick and Evan are out of my life forever, but that's not going to happen. I have to face the music. (Sorry.)

Plus I've got to confront Jaz about what happened with Simon. A big part of me was tempted to ring last night and give her what for, but I was so upset after seeing Lou that I knew I'd only make things worse. Instead I emailed her this morning and asked to meet. I've no clue how I'm going to broach the subject, but she must know what it's about because she didn't seem in the least surprised. And judging by her lacklustre appearance the day after it happened, it doesn't take a genius to work out she's feeling like utter crap.

I'm so caught up in this that when my phone rings I pick it up without thinking.

'Yeah?' I say irritably, as I attempt to manoeuvre past a crowd of Japanese tourists drowning beneath a map of the Underground.

'Hi,' says the voice on the other end.

Oh.

And there was me hoping it wouldn't affect me when I talked to him again. My heart leaps into my throat.

It's Nick.

'Hi.' I peel off and disappear into Boots, where two blank-faced women gaze at me from the perfume counter. 'What do you want?'

'I want you to talk to me.'

I take a deep breath, attempting to slow my racing pulse. 'You could have talked to me before now.'

'I tried. I'm sorry, I freaked out.'

What is it with men? I wasn't asking him to marry me, for god's sake.

'I spoke to Evan,' he says. 'He told me you met.'

'We did,' I say, charging past the tampons. 'It was very enlightening.'

'Maddie, listen—'

I keep it light, brisk. 'There's nothing to say, Nick.'

'There is. It's complicated.'

'I'm sure. Why don't you try to explain it to me?'

There's a long silence, during which I think he's hung up. 'I can't.'

'So that leaves us where, exactly?'

'You have to trust me – it's not what you think—'

'But you can't tell me what *it* is . . . right?'

'Right.' To his credit he sounds suitably dejected, but for all I know this conversation could be scripted, too. Perhaps Evan's got a bug on me – it wouldn't be surprising.

'Sorry – not good enough, Nick.'

'Can we talk about this in person? Christ! Can I see you?'

I find the quietest aisle I can and pretend to peruse its contents. 'Just tell me one thing.' My voice is wobbling. 'Did he put you up to it?'

'Who?'

'Evan.'

Another silence.

'Be honest.' To my dismay a salty teardrop plops from my eye and trickles down my cheek. 'Did he put you up to . . . getting to know me?'

'Yes,' he says at last. 'He did.'

I have to get off the phone before the sob that's been threatening to strangle me all morning has its way. 'Thank you. That's all I needed to know. Goodbye, Nick.'

'Maddie, please—'

Nick's voice gets swallowed as I click the phone shut. My knees have gone to jelly and I have to sit down. I grasp the shelf in front of me and bundle back the armful of goods I've been idly handling. I can get over it now, I reassure myself. Now I know for sure, now I've heard it from Nick himself, I can get over it.

'Do you need some help, madam?'

I glance up. A friendly faced, slightly spotty Boots assistant is regarding me curiously. At first I think he must have a sixth sense – that or he knows a heartbroken girl when he sees one. Ah yes – I look at his name badge – young Atif's probably left a few girls broken and bloodied in his time. The bastard.

But then I see him nodding a little uncomfortably at the cluster of white packets I've replaced on the shelf.

LADY LEAK: *not all days are dry days*

FEMBUM: *for women who want to be free*

ASSOLUTION: *tell diarrhoea NO*

'Plenty of women find it upsetting,' he informs me, *sotto voce*, 'you're not alone.'

'Oh no,' I laugh, a touch hysterically, 'no, no, I'm not looking to *buy* any of this stuff, I was just . . . you see, I was on the phone and . . .'

Atif nods at me sympathetically. 'I understand,' he whispers. 'No need to explain.'

'Really, I'm not . . . leaky . . . erm . . . watertight . . . erm . . .'

Five minutes later I'm back outside Boots, eighteen pounds lighter and advertising a chronic bowel complaint.

♪

Jaz is waiting when I get back to the club. She gives me a massive hug as soon as I walk in and mumbles 'Sorry' into my hair. Then she holds on for so long that I have to tell her to get off while I at least put my bags down. Hastily I shove the pitiful Assolution into my handbag and zip it shut.

'Do you want a drink?' she asks nervously. She can barely look me in the eye, I notice. And she's wearing . . . trainers. I don't think I've ever seen her in flats, let alone something she could play sport in, and I'm not sure I like it.

I shake my head. 'No.'

'Maddie, I'm so sorry,' she gabbles, 'I've ruined everything, I know I have. I've been stupid, I made a terrible mistake. I wish I could take it back – please believe me, I'd do anything. Lou hates me, doesn't she? Of course she does, I'd feel the exact same—'

'Slow down,' I tell her, slipping into one of the booths and encouraging her to do the same. 'I'm not mad at you.'

She looks close to tears. 'You're not?'

'Just sit down, Jaz, you're weirding me out.'

'Sorry.' She does as she's told. For a minute neither of us speaks.

'Are you going to tell me, then?' I ask softly. 'What the hell were you thinking?'

Jaz exhales very slowly and for a long time, as if she's been holding her breath since it happened.

'I was drunk.'

'That's it?' I raise an eyebrow. 'That's your excuse?'

Furiously, she shakes her head. 'Of course not. I was drunk because I'd been drinking.'

'Yeah . . . ?'

'And I'd been drinking because earlier that day I had a phone call.'

This could take a while. It's starting to feel like that rhyme about the old woman who swallowed a bird to catch the spider and she swallowed the spider to catch the fly.

'From Carl.' She looks up at me. 'He's in the UK.'

I'm shocked. I thought Carl was still in the States, rotting in a gutter for all I care – but more likely messing up whatever poor girl had the misfortune to walk into his life next.

'What did he want?'

'He's here for a couple of weeks.' She bites her lip. 'I changed my number when I moved but he must have tracked it down somehow.'

'Why didn't you tell me?'

'I couldn't get hold of you. You were sick, you said you didn't want visitors.'

It hits me how selfish I've been. All because of bloody Nick Craven, I've been acting like a dick to all the people I care about – and what for?

'Sorry, Jaz,' I say, meaning it.

'That's not the point. The point is it threw me. And I started remembering everything he told me about myself: that I was a waste of space, ugly, useless, how I'd never amount to anything . . . It brought it all back, you know? Even though I thought I'd left all that behind.'

I nod.

'So I drank.' She looks guilty. 'A lot. And then the next thing I know Evan Bergman's telling me that he needs my help.'

'I bet he was.'

'And that we had to make up for the fact you were upstairs with the lurgy. And the thing with Nick Craven was off, because you'd started seeing Lawrence again.'

A deep weariness descends on me. 'It's not like that at all,' I sigh, 'but fine – go on.'

'So he told me to . . . you know, make something happen.'

I put my face in my hands. 'And how did he suggest doing that?'

'Well, he told me to . . . kiss Simon. Just for a second, because he said that's all it was, just for telly, and of course it didn't mean anything and everyone would understand that.'

'He told you that was how reality TV worked?'

'Something like that.' She squirms. 'And it's not an excuse, I know that – I do have my own mind and I could have said no. But I wasn't thinking straight and I just thought, Fuck it, what does it matter? It's only for TV.'

'It's only for TV . . .'

'Yeah. And Simon's my friend, and I've kissed friends before and it's meant nothing – I kind of didn't think it was that big a deal. And of course I'd barely landed on him – because that's how it was: he didn't play any part in it – when he pushed me off.' Her voice softens. 'But by then it was too late. Alison had everything she needed.'

I frown. 'This would be about when Ruby and Davinia came up to the flat?'

'Must have been. I can't remember, I was too out of it.'

I sigh. 'Oh, Jaz.'

'I tried to tell you!' she cries. 'Yesterday, before you went out with Lawrence.'

'I've been a nonce,' I say. 'I've been so wrapped up in my own problems I haven't noticed when my friends need me.'

A tear escapes out the corner of her eye. 'I feel awful,' she whispers. 'Simon won't even look at me. Lou hates me, I bet.' She checks my expression.

''Fraid so,' I tell her. 'But she hates me too.'

'I'm so sorry.'

I wave away her concern. 'There's more to it than this. She thinks I made a mistake by getting involved with Evan in the first place – and I'm thinking the same thing myself. I just didn't want to admit it.'

Jaz reaches across and puts her hand on mine. 'It hasn't been a mistake, not really – look around you.'

I scan the room. Pineapple is virtually unrecognisable from the Sing It Back of weeks ago. The money we've made has updated the fixtures and decor to meet the current trend (Toby ran a competition for viewers to design their own furnishings) – it's now more high-end boudoir than dead-end dive bar: glinting chandeliers bejewel the ceiling, a single obligatory 'mirror cube' at their heart; swathes of dark fabric closet each booth individually, lending an exclusive, VIP feel; elaborately framed mirrors stretch from wall to wall, glass surfaces shimmering like water; squashy couches line the space, shabby chic, alongside bespoke low-lying tables with stylised pineapples carved out of their centre. The revamped look has attracted a wider clientele, reaching out to corporate functions as much as it does to hens, birthdays, anniversaries, engagement parties. We've moved the club's profile into a new market and I'm proud of how far we've come. It just concerns me at what cost.

'I guess it's too late to stop the kiss going out?' I say, my stomach crunching at the thought of it being broadcast.

'I already thought of that,' Jaz despairs. 'Toby gave me Alison's number – she practically hung up on me. She told me she understood but that Evan would murder her if she edited it out.'

'So she refused?'

'I tried.'

'Hmm.' My mind's ticking over.

'Why?' Jaz's eyes widen. 'Do you think there's something we can do?'

'I'm not sure,' I say. 'But let me speak to her. I think I know what might swing it.'

♪

Alison's flat in Kilburn is on the ground floor of an insalubrious period property. The steps up to the front door are mapped with tangled undergrowth and there's a strong aroma of incense.

I'm instantly buzzed in without being asked who I am. Inside, the windowless hall is dark and quiet, and I trip over a bicycle tyre wedged against the wall. It's just possible to make out the number on the first door I come to, and I knock firmly on it, three times.

A tall man with a dreadful beard answers. The smell of

weed from inside the flat hits me like a wall. And something else – spaghetti bolognese?

'Oh. Hello.' He scopes me up and down with a lascivious grin. 'I know you.'

'Is Alison in?' I ask, folding my arms. There's a brown stain on his Pearl Jam T-shirt that doesn't beg analysis.

'Dunno.' He sticks his head round the door and yells to someone I can't see. 'Jon, you seen Al?'

Another man's voice comes back, muffled.

'She's outside,' he tells me, putting his arm up on the door-frame to let me pass. 'Come on through, you can get out the back way.'

'Thanks.' I squeeze past, trying not to press the entire length of my body up against his but finding it difficult. He doesn't seem to mind.

The flat's a tip – there's a crumpled duvet on the sofa and the remains of a Chinese takeaway lies scattered on the carpet. Half-drunk mugs of tea are dotted around the place. One of Alison's biker boots rests on its side by the TV. As I go past the kitchen, Jon, short with thick-framed glasses, regards me suspiciously as he stirs something cooking on the hob.

I peer down a crooked set of back steps. 'OK if I head out?'

'Go for it.'

The garden is small, completely overgrown and un-looked-after but quite romantic, with the late afternoon sun bathing the grass in a caramel hue.

Alison's sitting on one of two plastic chairs, the sort you find in school classrooms, her back to me. A haze of smoke lingers above her head.

'Hi.'

She turns round in surprise and flips her book shut. 'What are you doing here?'

'Toby told me where you lived . . . hope you don't mind?'

Alison drags on her cigarette. 'I was about to head to yours.' She exhales. 'What's new? Anything good on the Jaz/Simon front? We need something juicy since you and Nick fizzled out.' She sounds so blasé, it's almost inhuman. I try not to let it affect me.

'That's what I wanted to talk to you about,' I say. 'See, I need to ask a favour.'

'And I know what it is.' She throws her fag butt on the grass and blows the smoke out quickly. 'I'm not cutting it, Maddie.'

'There's got to be something you can do,' I beg. 'There has to be.'

She shakes her head. 'Sorry.'

'I'm asking you as a friend.' I sit down on the other chair. 'Please.'

'I can't.'

'Is it too late?'

A chill in the air makes her wrap her arms round herself. 'It's going out tomorrow,' she says flatly.

'Then we can still do something about it. This has hurt a lot of people, it's not right. Evan went too far this time.'

'And he didn't go too far with Nick?' she challenges. 'I would've thought you'd be more fussed about getting that cut.'

'You knew about that?' I sit back, shaking my head. 'Of course you did. Everyone knows about Evan's game – apart from the people he's playing it on.'

'It's not a game,' Alison says, completely without guile. 'It's just how TV works.'

'What about how people work?' I say. 'How feelings work? Doesn't that count?'

She looks at me like she hasn't a clue what I'm talking about.

'Anyway I didn't know about Nick,' I say briskly. 'About the footage, I mean, until it was too late. But this is different. I've still got time to do something about it.'

Alison draws out another cigarette and offers me one.

'No, thanks.'

'You'd have to talk it through with Evan,' she advises. 'And you know what he'd say.'

I choose my words carefully. 'I know what he'd say to me.'

My meaning hangs in the air a moment, and Alison slides me a narrow look. 'I'm not asking him, if that's what you're getting at.'

'I think he'd listen to you.' I feel my way, not wanting to scare her off. 'Wouldn't he?'

She pulls hard on her cigarette and doesn't reply.

'There's something going on, isn't there?'

Alison's gaze is fixed straight ahead. 'I don't know what you're talking about.'

'You and Evan,' I say slowly. 'There's something between you.'

She snorts with derision. 'I have no idea what you mean.'

'Come on, Alison, it's obvious. I knew it the minute you turned up that day with the crew. One moment you hated Evan, the next you were all over him. And I saw how his behaviour affected you.'

'How?'

'Too deeply for him to be just your boss.'

She turns to me, her face softer now. 'Does anyone else know?'

'I don't think so,' I say gently. 'Maybe.'

'Oh god,' she flicks the ash off her cigarette, 'I knew it would come out eventually. You probably think I'm an idiot.'

'It's not for me to say.'

'But that's what you think.'

'Who cares what I think? Evan's not my cup of tea, but that's irrelevant.'

Her body sags. 'I'm so relieved to talk to someone about it,' she blurts. 'No one else knows – my flatmates wouldn't understand, they're too immature. All they do is sit around playing *Arkham Asylum* all day and picking their noses.'

'That's what drew you to Evan? Because he's older?'

'The age thing doesn't matter,' she says. 'It sounds like a cliché, but I honestly don't mind the gap. He's sorted, he's focused, he's successful. That's how *I* want to be.'

I nod. 'That's how we all want to be.'

There's a short silence while we both consider this.

'I just hope his wife doesn't find out.'

My mouth falls open. 'His *wife*?'

Alison looks sheepish. 'Yeah.'

'He's *married*?'

She wriggles. 'Um . . .'

'*Alison!*'

'I know! I couldn't help it.'

'What? Evan overpowered you with his irresistible charm and good looks?' That was bitchy – Alison clearly finds him attractive, but then some people like scotch eggs: the world is a confusing place. 'Sorry, that was mean.'

'I really like him, Maddie,' she confesses. 'I think . . . well, I think I love him.'

Shit.

'When it first started it felt sordid—'

'It *is* sordid, isn't it? He's married!'

'They're estranged, apparently . . . He's going to leave her!'

'I bet.'

'Anyway it was never *meant* to happen. It's not like I got hired and then straight away I realised I fancied him. It was gradual . . . I helped him out with some projects, we ended up staying behind in the office after everyone else had gone home . . . And he paid me attention, you know? He seemed really *interested* in me, and my views, and what I had to say.'

'So he should – you're his employee. And that's why he's done an irresponsible thing. Forgetting for a second that he's married, what about you? I've heard the way he speaks to you.'

'He's not always like that,' she prickles.

'That's good.'

Alison grinds her fag out on the side of the chair and tosses it on to the grass. 'Do you think any less of me?'

'Of course not.'

'It's why I don't want to tell anyone. All the fucking back-lash.'

I tuck my leg up under my bum. 'You can't care what everyone else thinks. However much you might try to control it, people are always going to draw their own conclusions.'

Alison smiles uncertainly. 'Thanks for not judging. I know

it's a bit unconventional . . . I guess things don't always go the way you think they're going to.'

'You can say that again.' I rub my eyes, suddenly tired. There have been enough revelations over the past week to last me a lifetime.

'I'll talk to him,' she says.

I look up at her. Hope springs. 'You will?'

'Yeah.' She chews her lip. 'I can't promise anything, but I'll try.'

23

Let's Call the Whole Thing Off

It's Monday morning.

Jaz, Simon, Rob, Alex and I are at the table in my parents' flat. I'm reminded of the last time we were all here together – except it was Archie, then, not Alex; and Ruby, not Rob – and everyone was in a decidedly better mood. Looking round now, I can hardly believe it's the same lot. Jaz is sitting opposite Simon, gloomily doodling on a bit of paper, but they're refusing to look at each other (I can't work out who's more miserable, her or him); Rob has barely said a word to me since the night I blew up at him and Davinia; and I dread to think what's become of me – I feel like I haven't slept in a month.

Lou still hasn't called and I miss her like crazy: she's the only person I want to talk to. Even the sight of Andre in widow's weeds doesn't prove enough of a distraction. (Jaz has taken to dressing in funereal attire.)

'I'm pulling the plug on Tooth & Nail,' I tell them. 'I wanted you guys to know first.'

They exchange a few glances but no one seems surprised.

'Can you do that?' asks Alex. I didn't really want him here but he's been attached to Jaz's side like glue and I didn't know how to separate them without it seeming pointed.

'Of course I can,' I say. 'Why wouldn't I be able to?'

'Maybe we should just play it out till the end of the run,' suggests Rob, leaning back against a framed original Boney M album cover. It's a stunner: the foursome is rolling about on the floor, wrapped in chains and practically nude, and Rob's head slips neatly between the only standing member of the group, right beneath his glittery codpiece. 'Won't this be more hassle than it's worth?'

'Absolutely not. What's Evan going to do? At the end of the day it's my club – our club – and I'm taking back control.'

'But what about the contract?' mumbles Jaz. 'You can't just back out of it.'

'Look,' I say, 'Evan tricked me into signing in the first place . . . him and Nick Craven.' Everyone looks at me and I concentrate on not blushing, which of course makes me blush like a fool. 'But the ambiguity of those clauses plays both ways: he could argue his case based on the wording, but by the same token I can argue mine.'

'And you think you'd win in a fight against Evan Bergman?' Simon chips in grimly. 'I'm not sure I'd like to try.'

'You could always rip his wig off,' suggests Rob with a yawn.

'He doesn't wear a wig!' objects Jaz. 'Does he?'

Rob raises an eyebrow. 'Trust me – I know a wig when I see one.'

'Forget about the wig,' I say. '*I'm* going to try. It's my responsibility.'

Jaz throws her arms up. 'He'll only talk you out of it – that's his way! He's a snake. As long as it's going to get him what he wants, he'll tell you just about anything.' She glances swiftly at Simon and looks away.

I decide to voice what's been on my mind. 'Does anyone else feel like he's had it in for us from the start?'

A sea of blank expressions.

'Maybe I'm paranoid,' I chew my bottom lip, 'but since that first day I went to Tooth & Nail, Evan knew exactly who I was, who Mum and Dad were – it was as if he *planned* it.'

Simon frowns. 'But how could he? He placed the ad in the paper, didn't he? Anyone could have responded.'

'Yeah,' I admit, 'but that almost makes it more suspicious. Like he really struck gold with that, didn't he? What are the chances?'

Rob raises an eyebrow. 'You *are* being paranoid. Forget about it, for your own good.'

I notice Alex hasn't said anything in a while. His eyes are on the table and he's absent-mindedly picking the skin around his thumb.

'And you turned up pretty suddenly, didn't you, Alex?'

He lifts his head. 'Sorry?'

'That day Archie left. You turned up quick.'

'What are you saying?' demands Jaz. 'There's nothing wrong with Alex.'

'Hmm.' I narrow my eyes.

'Right place, right time, I guess,' Alex mutters, shifting in his seat. Then he elaborates in the manner of someone over-talking to reiterate a prepared story. 'I was looking for bar work, I saw your place, I walked in and that was it . . . Evan hired me on the spot. The rest is history.'

'But you weren't experienced,' I challenge. 'Not when you first came to us. In fact it looked to me like you'd never even worked in a bar, never mind headed one up.'

'Leave him alone!' cries Jaz, leaping to Alex's defence. 'Everyone lies on their CV. So what if he needed a bit of prac-tice?'

'A lot of practice,' mutters Simon under his breath.

I watch Alex for a minute, knowing there's more to his story but unsure what it is. It occurs to me that I've become too sus-picious recently.

'Sorry,' I say wearily, 'I'm being unfair.'

There's an awkward pause, which to my relief Jaz fills with one of her typical non-sequiturs. And to my greater relief, it has nothing to do with the club or wretched Evan Bergman.

'If you put Alex's first name with my surname,' she announces, holding up her bit of scribble-littered paper, 'you can make Axle Rose.'

'Except Axl doesn't have an E,' snaps Simon irritably.

'It doesn't?'

'Of course it doesn't.'

Jaz bites her lip. 'Never mind, I'm only being stupid. Sorry.'

There's an uncomfortable silence, before Simon says, 'If it did, you wouldn't get the Axl Rose anagram, would you?'

Jaz looks hopeful. 'What's the Axl Rose anagram?'

'Everyone knows what Axl Rose is an anagram of . . .' Simon looks round the table. 'Don't they?'

'I don't,' supplies Alex. Jaz shakes her head.

'What is it?' demands Rob.

But Simon chickens out. 'If you don't already know,' he says, flushing pink, 'then I'm not telling.'

At least this has got people talking. And I can tell Simon doesn't hate Jaz, not really – he's way too fond of her and they know each other too well. I suspect if Lou gave him the time of day then all would be forgiven, but of course that's looking highly unlikely for any of us. Especially since the infamous kiss went out on Sunday – Alison texted me to apologise; she couldn't get it past the boss, said he'd gone ballistic at her. I hope she's OK. I know she tried and I also know Evan Bergman is unlikely to conduct a favour for anyone, particularly if there's a bottom line involved.

Thinking about Lou watching it (though I'm certain she's been avoiding the show like the plague) breaks my heart. She's never disappeared like this before and I don't know how to handle it. She worked up to Simon for so long: I know she doesn't trust people easily, doesn't want to rely on anyone else (for a Psychology student she's remarkably adept at discounting her own abandonment issues) and so when they let her down it cuts deep. The frustrating thing is that the very person who wants to be there for her is also the last person she wants to see. I expect she's upset that I'm still hanging out with Jaz, and I can understand that, but what am I meant to do? We work together – and besides, she's my friend and you can't just call off a friendship the instant someone messes up.

Simon and Jaz are still bickering. Knowing Jaz she won't go to sleep tonight till she's either worked the Axl thing out or badgered Simon into submission.

Rob leans in, his voice gentle. 'Do you want one of us to come with you?' he asks. His eyes are concerned but relieved, and I understand then that it's what all of us want.

'No.' I shake my head. 'I'll do it myself.'

♪

I turn up at Tooth & Nail around lunch time, unannounced. I'm not expecting Evan to be there (and the coward in me half hopes he won't be), so it's a surprise when his receptionist tells me to wait on the leather banquettes and that Mr Bergman will be with me in a minute.

Perching on the edge of the sofa, with Evan's new receptionist (a pretty black girl with lots of silver jewellery) tap-tap-tapping away, I rehearse one more time exactly what I'm going to say. Not for the first time, I channel my inner Christina Applegate in *Don't Tell Mom the Babysitter's Dead*. She was just a regular girl like me, wasn't she? And when she got herself in too deep and the shit hit, she sorted it out and everything worked out fine. Yes. That's going to be me. Especially because at the end everyone forgives and forgets, she's praised for her entrepreneurial spirit *and* she bags the guy from Clown Dog who teaches her about grunions. Hmm. Apart from the bagging the guy part, then. But whatever, by the time I'm done Evan's going to wish he'd never messed with Maddie Mulhern – because while I may not be some hotshot telly producer, I *am* an intellectual being and I *won't* be taken for a fool.

Ooh! I spy a copy of *Take a Break* amid the trendy A3 magazines, no doubt left behind by some unsuspecting visitor, and land on it with glee. It falls open on the Top Tips section, and I have just enough time to read about recycling an old handbag by filling it with soil and using it as an outdoor planter when the door to Evan's office opens and a buxom brunette steps out into the corridor. She can't be much older than me, dressed in a foxy skirt suit and precarious heels, and is laughing like a schoolgirl. I hold the magazine up high to my face, peering over the top like a lame Jessica Fletcher, and watch, horrified, as Evan delivers a swift sharp slap to her bottom.

Somehow I don't believe that's his wife. And it's certainly not Alison.

Bastard!

The woman emerges into the lobby red-faced and flustered, before taking the spiral stairs down. New Receptionist is studiously pretending not to notice.

'Maddie Mulhern!' booms Evan, rumbling my *Take a Break* disguise but seeming unruffled by my surprise appearance. 'What brings you here?' He strides over and grabs my hand. His palm feels doughy and moist, and I withdraw my own quickly.

'I wanted a word,' I say, carefully replacing the magazine on top of its pompous counterparts, just to see the shadow of derision pass across his face, which, sure enough, it does. 'In private, if we can?'

The receptionist's eyes brush over me, and I have no doubt she suspects I'm the latest of Evan's conquests. Maybe she's one, too? The thought makes me ill.

'I'm in meetings all afternoon,' he says, a tad irritably. 'Regina?' He doesn't bother turning round to address her. 'Who have I scheduled for lunch?'

'No one, Mr Bergman,' replies Regina dutifully. 'Matt Howard at CVN called to say he was making an emergency trip to Gloucester: something about his wife tripping over a dog?'

'Hmm, yes, we spoke. She didn't trip over the dog; she sat on it.' He nods, remembering. 'She's very large, as I recall. And the dog is small. Was small.'

The information floats uncertainly in the air a moment, Evan gazing into the middle distance and Regina with her lips slightly parted, and me just standing there looking between them, before he snaps back to reality.

'Well then,' he says, crocodile grin flashing and vanishing, like the searching beam of a lighthouse. 'Isn't that a good excuse to take you out?'

'Really, Evan – this won't take a minute—'

'Walk with me,' he barks, taking my arm and leading me downstairs. 'I've been cooped up in a hot and sweaty office all morning. I could do with some fresh air.'

♪

It takes a good ten minutes before Evan decides on a suitable tea shop. He's particular about finding this one that does a special kind of cake (a tea cake? Evan Bergman? Wonders never cease), so we have to go traipsing round the back of Regent

Street, him striding ahead and me desperately trying to broach the subject I came here to address, but finding it difficult with only a burly shoulder to talk to. When we pass Hamley's for the third time in a row and someone outside in a jester costume blows bubbles in my face, I fight an urge to grab the nearest Beefeater teddy and strangle it with my bear hands. I mean my bare hands.

Eventually we come to a quiet little square around the corner from Reiss, and I promise myself that if this goes well I'll treat my wardrobe to something new. The idea gives me a boost, so as soon as we're sitting down – Evan picking the currants out of his buttered tea cake and me baffled as to why we've just chased this imperfect tea cake around central London – I brace myself for the announcement.

'Evan, I'm going to be straight with you.'

He looks up, but doesn't speak. They've provided him with a very small tea cup, the sort girls play with in Wendy houses, and when he wedges a fat finger in the porcelain handle I wonder if he'll ever get it out again.

My heart's galloping. 'I'm quitting the show,' I say, and to my relief it comes out firm and strong.

Slowly Evan replaces the cup in its saucer with a little tinkle. Then he dabs the corners of his mouth with a napkin. I wait for him to say something. He doesn't.

I feel the need to elaborate – despite the fact I know one of the best knacks in negotiation is to remain silent. I guess I'm not a negotiator.

'We've all been hurt,' I begin. No, that's not right: a man like Evan doesn't deal in emotions. 'What I mean is, we've been affected by . . . things you've done and . . .' Argh. Where's that speech I rehearsed a million times? 'Er . . . machinations . . . acceptability . . . unreasonable things . . . um, all in all, don't feel it's . . . well, not fair.'

That's great. Very grown up. I may as well stand in the middle of the cafe, stick my fingers in my ears and stamp the ground, shouting, 'It's not fair! It's not fair!'

'The club is grateful for Tooth & Nail's investment,' I go on, at last hitting my stride, 'but in my view there's been a great deal of dishonesty from the outset. On those grounds, Evan, I'd like to terminate the contract.' This last part comes out very fast, like the last well of water being sucked down the plughole.

I'm staring at the wooden table, my eyes fixed on a mark the boot-shape of Italy. I've said my piece; it's over.

Except it's not. Because Evan's still not doing anything.

For a second I wonder if the tea cake's poisoned him, and in a brief agreeable moment – though of course a completely evil and dreadful one – I wonder if he's choked on a currant and has just expired in his seat.

But that's before I realise he's laughing.

'Ah, Maddie, you're a funny girl,' he chortles, wheezing a little.

I don't get it. I look up, waiting for him to take me seriously.

But he keeps on laughing. 'Honestly, you really had me there.'

'I beg your pardon?'

He wipes his eyes. 'You're not serious.' Then, 'Oh, my girl, you *are*!' He tuts. 'You really think that's your decision to make?'

'It *is* my decision to make,' I say, looking him squarely in the eye. 'We own the premises and therefore without my permission you're unable to film there. No filming, no programme.'

Finally Evan appears to gather himself, spreading his large hands on the table and addressing me directly. 'You're right, of course,' he drawls, like I have trouble grasping basic concepts. 'But the problem is that you *have* given us permission, Maddie. That's what a contract is for.'

'There's a break clause,' I say, struggling to right myself in the wake of his indifference. This is not the reaction I expected. Frustration, definitely; anger, maybe. Possibly some begging for me to reconsider, to which I would have pretended to chew it over before sadly shaking my head, rising with great dignity from the table and leaving him weeping into his china cup.

He starts laughing again, longer and louder this time, so that several people at nearby tables turn to look at us. Then he stops, puts his tea and saucer aside and pins me with a stare.

'There *is* a break clause,' he says, voice thickened with enjoyment. 'And there's also a break clause fee. Are you telling me you want to pay that?'

'Yes,' I say, pleased the message is finally getting through. So what if we have to draw money down – Pineapple's making more than enough and, for the first time, I believe in our ability to sustain it, with or without the show.

'Lovely.' Evan sits back. 'In that case it's settled.'

My heart soars. That was so easy. Now I can tell Lou and she'll forgive me and be my friend, and everything can get back to normal. I'll never have to see Evan Bergman or Nick Craven ever ever again. 'Really?'

'Why not?' He smiles. 'I'm a rational man. I'm not going to force you to stay in a situation you're unhappy with.'

'Well,' I say, thrown by this unexpected fairness, 'that's good of you.'

'Shall we say Wednesday for the money?' The smile doesn't slip. 'That gives you a couple of days to rustle up the cash. A hundred thousand straight into Tooth & Nail Associates would be ideal, but on this occasion, because I'm fond of you, Maddie, I'll accept a cheque.' He tears a hunk of muffin with his teeth, releasing a clear buttery liquid that dribbles down his chin.

My mouth falls open. 'I'm sorry, *what*?'

'A hundred thou,' Evan says breezily, signalling for the bill and patting his pockets for his wallet, first the ones on his crisp linen shirt and then his suit trousers.

'Don't be absurd,' I splutter. 'That's silly money. You know we can't afford that.'

'You can't?'

'Of course we can't!'

'Oh.' He pretends to mull it over, before shaking his head sadly. 'Ah well, it looks like you're stuck with me for the time being, then, doesn't it?'

I flip. 'The contract said nothing about the fee being so high. There's no *way* I would have missed that – you're lying.' The old lady on the table next to ours is busy listening to everything: her hearing aid's probably tuned in to conversations happening eighty miles away.

But in truth I signed the contract when my mind was elsewhere – it could well have mentioned a break clause fee.

A 'sum to be determined' or some such, no doubt. Evan's got my hands tied and he knows it.

'Don't look so mad,' he soothes, like someone comforting a child who's just dropped their 99 Flake head-down on the pavement. 'Think how far you've come – you wouldn't have been in a position to offer *any* kind of break clause fee this time eight weeks ago!'

I glare at him. 'I wouldn't have had the need to, then, would I?'

'Let's not get hung up on the details.' He waves a hand dismissively. 'Think of it as paying for a service. You've paid for my ideas and, I think you'll admit, my ideas have in turn paid off for you.'

I shake my head. 'You're unbelievable.'

'You're too kind.'

'Everything the club is now comes down to the people who work in it,' I say. 'And that has nothing to do with you. All you've done is try to split us apart.'

He jabs a finger at me. 'The people who work in it! Precisely. When I arrived you were all nobodies, and now you're *someone*. Maddie, you never would have made the necessary changes – after all, I know what works for TV.' He feeds his arms into the sleeves of his jacket.

'What changes?'

'A bit of eye candy for the ladies on a weeknight, nothing wrong with that . . .' Evan places his hands on his stomach, sated. 'Better than some boring old fart, in any case. Who wants a fogey on the box on a Saturday night?'

I swallow. 'I hope you're not insinuating what I think you are.'

'All it took was a nice fat wad of cash,' Evan sneers, 'and dear old Archie was putty in my hands.' He's in my face, his voice a low hiss that releases intermittent bursts of saliva. 'They all are, sweetheart. It's about the money, every last penny of it. That's what drew you to me in the first place. Go on, admit it: it was the sweet, sweet smell of cash. All your precious Archie's guilty of is that he wanted the exact same thing. You wouldn't deny a man life's greatest pleasure, now, would you?'

'You paid Archie to leave?' I gasp.

'He was only too happy to oblige.'

'He was happy with us.'

'But happier elsewhere, with tens of thousands of pounds in his pocket. Why shouldn't he retire in luxury?'

I'm shaking. When Mum and Dad find out about this, they'll be so upset. They'll be distraught. Why didn't I see this before? They wanted to keep the club, yes, but not necessarily for the business – it was for the people they employed. Their friends. Their loved ones. It didn't matter about the cash. Why did I have to go and stick my stupid oar in?

'How could you?' I choke. 'You lied. You got Archie to lie to me, too.'

Evan rises to his feet. He calmly dusts the crumbs from his shirt, before bending down to deliver his last words. They drip into my ear like poison.

'I'd be careful if I were you,' he spits. 'I'm a very powerful man – I've worked hard to be where I am – and you're not being clever. It wouldn't be difficult for a man in my position to destroy years of your precious parents' hard work, now, would it? After all, it was *me* who facilitated Pineapple's come-back,' he jabs a finger at his chest, 'so it's *me* who can bring it back down. I could break you before I've even had my break-fast in the morning, Maddie: you and the people you care about. Have I made myself clear?'

My heart's thumping.

'Oh, and another thing. Never, *ever* again will you go run-ning to that silly camera girl so she comes knocking on my door in the middle of the night. Never. I've got a wife to think about, can you comprehend what that means? You play nice; I play nice. Understood?'

The bell on the door rings emptily to mark his exit, and then I'm sitting alone.

24

A Little Less Conversation

The man on stage has fallen to his knees, his face glowing with adoration and his hand proffering a small velvet box.

'I love you, Kylie,' he begins, as the final strains of 'Especially For You' tinkle all around. 'Will you marry me?'

Kylie (real name? I don't know what's more worrying – that this guy might actually be called Jason and Harold and Madge are about to emerge from the wings, or they've adopted these names for the purpose), a blonde woman of about thirty throws her hands up to her face and emits a high-pitched sort of whistle, like air escaping from a balloon.

'Of course!' she squeals, wasting no time in snatching the ring from his grasp. 'Yes!'

The cameras swing in to capture the wide smiles and glinting diamond, and the bar erupts in applause – though for me it's more to signal the end of an excruciating duet than the happy couple's news. (And anyway, I much prefer Angry Anderson's 'Suddenly' – Scott and Charlene's wedding song – but maybe they're saving that for the ceremony.)

No, that sounds horrible . . . but I suppose any declaration of love right now renders me the harbinger of doom. How come it's so easy for some people? How come some people just meet, go out, fall in love, get married, and that's all there is to it?

Nick keeps looking over – I can feel him watching me from the other side of the room, where he's busy in conversation with Toby. We haven't spoken since that phone conversation the other afternoon (which I now associate with intestinal problems, as if it wasn't bad enough) and frankly, I don't know what else there is to say. All I want now is to focus on the final seven days of the show and remember that after that I never have to come into contact with him again. It's fine. I'm fine. Head down, get on with it – it'll be over soon and I'll unpick the damage then.

'Aw, isn't it adorable?' sings Davinia, zooming up to where I'm standing by the bar and grabbing my arm. 'Look how in love they are!'

'If you like that sort of thing,' I sulk. The joyous couple are locked in a passionate clinch, and I consider striding up like a cross parent at a party that's gone on too loud and too long and pulling the plug, maybe replacing it with Radiohead and telling everyone to go home.

'Come on, it *is* cute.' She looks at me sympathetically. 'I know things didn't work out between you and Nick—'

'Davinia, can we not talk about it?'

'—but we all understand it's very tough for you at the moment. You're not yourself, darling . . . we're worried about you.'

I can't very well argue with that, having barked at her just last week. I should be kissing her feet for still wanting to talk to me – she's one of a dying breed.

'I'm fine,' I say instead. 'Honestly. I just don't want there to be any more trouble.'

Rob floats past with one of Ruby du Jour's red dresses swathed over his arm.

'Ooh!' Davinia trills. 'Is Ruby coming out tonight?'

Rob shakes his head. 'She's in protest,' he tells us. 'Turned a bit shy of late, as it goes.'

'How naughty!' says Davinia, patting the construction of curls on her head. 'I do love a spot of dissent among the ranks – it's terribly exciting!'

Something tells me Davinia hasn't fully grasped the situation: petrified of putting a foot wrong, we're all tiptoeing round the cameras like we've stumbled across a field of landmines (or maybe that's just me: unable to sleep, I seem to have been OD-ing on Minesweeper on my laptop in the small hours). As far as she's concerned, as long as we're on telly it's all a bit of fun, and for that I should be grateful: while the rest of us are pretending to carry on our lives as normal, Davinia really *is* enjoying herself. Which is nice – I'm glad one of us can.

'Those two seem to be getting on well, don't they?' Rob

nods to the bar, where Jaz and Alex are chatting as they get drinks together. I'm relieved to see Jaz is looking more like her old self. Tonight she's donning a T-shirt with a massive old-fashioned telephone printed on it in the Andy Warhol style, a papier-mâché receiver perched on her head like an Alice band. Very Gaga.

'She must bring something out in him,' I observe. 'He's never that animated with me. I always find it a bit like talking to a waxwork.'

'He's probably scared of you,' teases Rob, digging out a large carrier from behind the bar and stuffing the gown into it. 'Big bad boss lady.'

I'm tempted to reiterate the fact I didn't actually hire Alex – Evan did, right off the street. But that might bring up the whole Archie thing so I decide against it for now.

Kylie and Jason are slipping off the stage into the arms of their loved ones, drowning in a cacophony of congratulations and glasses of champagne. A sliver of gladness appears in the great dark cloud of the past few weeks. My own love life might be floundering on its back at the bottom of a well, but at least Pineapple has facilitated, in some small way, the happiness these two are sharing. I'm starting to feel almost better when from the corner of my eye I see Nick approaching. Uh-oh.

Rob and Davinia notice him too, and discreet as traitors they melt away, leaving me standing exposed at the end of the bar, a sitting target. I brace myself for whatever scripted bollocks he's about to deliver on Evan's behest. Probably the same thing he's been discussing with Toby.

But Andre comes to the rescue.

Or rather, Andre up someone's skirt comes to the rescue. There's a piercing scream as a large woman in a too-tight peach dress, halfway through a tuneless performance of 'Heaven is a Place on Earth', projects her glass-shattering alarm down the microphone. She falls backwards, caught from behind by an unfortunate man whose cheeks inflate with the strain. As they both crumple to the floor, something small, hairy and appearing to wear a skin-tight Super Ted costume darts out from under her and across the stage.

Then someone does something very silly. They say the R word.

'It's a rat! A rat in a dress!'

Pandemonium ensues. Women run screaming, falling over each other, trampling across fallen compatriots with spiky heels. The karaoke machine moves on: Michael Jackson's 'Ben'.

Jaz rushes forward before I have a chance to. We've had to be strict with her about keeping Andre in his little box behind the bar (celebrity guinea pigs needn't adhere to hygiene regulations, it seems) since filming began, but even now I know she's not really concerned about the shrieking masses; she just wants to make sure he's not hurt.

'Andre!' She's scanning the floor, desperate, as people clamber around her. Anyone would think a bomb had just gone off. 'Andre, come to Mummy!'

There's only one thing for it. And, mercifully, it's the very same thing that gets me away from the incoming missile of Nick Craven. I head on to the stage, grab the mic, and prepare to explain the presence of a guinea pig even I don't fully understand.

♪

It's gone midnight by the time I get back upstairs. There's an answer phone message from Dad, asking me to video a programme about Roxy Music that's on BBC2 tomorrow night. He says I can tape over the blank cassette marked 'Sapphy Does the Worm' – please god I never find out what that entails. And before you ask, yes, we do still have a VCR – even if my parents understood stuff like catch-up and iPlayer, I doubt they'd want to use it. The video's got its own remote and everything.

I crawl slugglishly into my Woodstock pyjamas (as in Snoopy, not the festival: I'm not my mother quite yet), check my phone a final time to make sure I haven't missed a call from Lou (I haven't) and make a cup of sugary tea.

I'm about to hole up in bed with a trashy magazine when there's a knock on the door. Thinking it's Jaz wanting to spill the gossip about Alex, I answer it without checking first.

It's Nick Craven.

An impossibly handsome, more handsome than I remembered in a dark grey T-shirt and jeans, his hair dark and messy, stubble on his chin and faint but troubled circles under his eyes Nick Craven.

I feel like my heart's being used as a punch bag.

'What do you want?' I ask as neutrally as I can.

Nick puts a hand up on the doorframe, and a delicious smell accompanies the movement. It's a familiar, comforting smell, like a box of clothes your mum put in the roof when you were twelve; like I've known it for longer than I've known him.

'If you're going to carry on ignoring me,' he says, 'I figured I had no other choice. Why aren't you taking my calls?'

'The other choice would be to leave me alone. I don't want to talk to you, Nick; I don't want to see you. Can't you let it go?'

He just looks at me. God, how he looks at me.

'Can I come in?'

'No.'

'I'll be five minutes. Please.'

I attempt to shut the door, but his arm is in the way. Suddenly I'm conscious of my tragic nightwear and hairy slippers and wish I could be wearing sexy plum-coloured lingerie, before telling myself off for bothering about what he thinks.

'There isn't anything to say.'

'There is.'

Meeting his gaze is like looking at the sun: even though I know I shouldn't do it, something compels me to try – and it burns. 'Not for me.'

'For me.'

Nick's tired, I can see. He looks like he hasn't slept in ages.

'Can I come in?' he asks again.

I've always liked to think I'm a good judge of character: the past two months have made me reconsider this. Nick's expression is direct, honest, fixed with intent – which doesn't make sense knowing what I know. As much for my curiosity as anything else, I decide to hear him out.

'Five minutes,' I say flatly, standing back to let him in. As he walks past a ripple travels through me and I hate myself for reacting that way.

Nick takes in his surroundings with a somewhat distressed expression: the portraiture on the walls, the imaginative furniture, the violet mirrors, the gallery of greats. It's difficult to tell if this is the standard reaction of anyone who sets foot in my parents' flat for the first time, or if he's just finding the words.

Finally he turns to me. 'Whatever you think about what happened between us, you're wrong.'

I fold my arms. I really wish I wasn't wearing these slippers.

'Whatever Evan's told you . . . it's not the full story.'

'Go on then.'

Nick exhales heavily, goes to sit down then stops. 'OK if I take a seat?'

'Whatever you like,' I say tightly. 'Don't make yourself too comfortable.'

He settles on the edge of the sofa, which lost its springs some time ago and sags wearily under his weight. I'm aware the angle he's looking at me from isn't the most flattering – I hope I'm not having a double-chin week.

'There's a lot I have to tell you, Maddie,' he says slowly. 'But there's also a lot that, right now, I can't.'

I tap my foot impatiently, remember the slippers and quickly stop.

'I did take you out because Evan asked me. He hired me because I was prepared to do that – I was desperate—'

My eyebrows shoot up.

'Not like that,' he hurriedly clarifies, 'not like that at all.'

'Right.'

'I hadn't had work in months. And I figured: if they're not

hiring me in light of my . . . past misdemeanours, why not try working for someone who'll hire me *because* of them?'

If this is meant to impress me, it's not.

'Evan wanted the romance and I agreed. Evan wanted the kiss, and I—'

'Sorry,' I interrupt with a harsh laugh, 'is this supposed to be mitigating?'

'But not there. Not then. I wasn't supposed to kiss you then.'

'Oh, right! Any preferred time and date you'd like me to show up?'

He closes his eyes. 'It took me by surprise, OK?'

'Me too. A really fucking horrible surprise, as it goes. And you were perfect for it, weren't you?' I can't help myself. 'I bet Evan couldn't believe his luck. I bet you couldn't either. So much for integrity, Nick.'

'There's more to it than that.'

'I'm sorry it's been such a hardship for you,' I choke.

'It hasn't. Not a second.'

'Then tell me what's so bloody complicated. Tell me what the problem is.'

Silence, before he looks down at his hands. 'I can't.'

I feel cold. 'Fine. I guess you're not the person I thought you were.'

Nick sits back, lifting the cushion from behind him to make way before realising it's an embroidered headshot of Noddy Holden. Gingerly he replaces it.

'I am that person,' he says, his dark eyes on mine. 'For starters, you've got to know the Rebecca Ascot thing was misunderstood.'

I wait.

'She'd been pursuing me for months. Every event I went to, she turned up; every time I got hired, she'd wangle it so her husband's channel was somehow involved; every party I was invited to, she claimed to have a mutual friend. She was . . . well, she was *stalking* me.'

'Please don't,' I say, spying my parents' Smash Hits 'Best Live Performance' award and just about managing to stop myself throwing it at his head. 'Don't make out like you're the victim of an unhinged woman who couldn't help herself. It's terribly dated.'

'I'm not making anything out,' he responds. 'She wanted to escape her marriage. She was miserable. I guess she picked me to help her – only she didn't bother telling me about it first. So here we are.'

'You were helpless to resist her charms. Of course. Sorry I've been so quick to jump to conclusions – clearly you were forced to kiss her and get photographed doing it.'

'In a way I was,' he claims. 'Rebecca organised the whole thing. She tracked me down at an album launch – of course I tried as politely as I could to ignore her, but even then she spent most of the evening draped off me – then as I was leaving she opened the door to my cab, climbed in and started kissing me. The paparazzi went mad and the whole thing got splashed around the tabloids the next day. That's all there was to it. When Pritchard Wells saw the evidence it signalled the end of their marriage – and of my career. So no prizes for guessing who came off worst. If I saw that woman again, believe me, I'd have a few words for her, though we both know any altercation would see me coming off as some bitter spurned lover. Sometimes you can't win in this game.' A short, dry laugh. 'You don't need me to tell you how things can get twisted to look a certain way.'

'And you've got the nerve to sit here and *complain* about that?' I shake my head in disbelief. 'Managing situations to your own ends is precisely what you and Evan have been doing to me. Come on, Nick, you have to see the irony.'

'I do. And I'm ashamed of it. But this job was the first I'd been offered in a very long time, and I promise you, I promise I never expected to feel—'

'You promise?' I realise I'm trembling, though with anger or upset or just plain coldness I'm not sure. 'How can you expect me to believe anything you say?'

'Because I'm asking you to.'

'Well don't bother.'

'I'm not a bad guy, Maddie. I'm not.'

'Then say what the matter is. What can't you tell me?'

A muscle pulses in his jaw. It's unbelievably sexy and for a moment I can't believe someone as beautiful as him is sitting here in front of me, in Mum and Dad's apartment no less, against a backdrop of Dave Stewart, Frankie Goes to Hollywood and The Boomtown Rats. But he's still a bastard.

'I guess it doesn't matter now,' he says, in a stiff voice I haven't heard before, 'since you're back with your boyfriend.'

I let him hang a second. 'I might be.'

He gives a brief, matter-of-fact nod. 'That's another reason I came here tonight. I have to warn you.'

'To warn me? About what exactly – getting involved with

you? Thanks, Nick, but you could have done it a few weeks back. That would've been much more helpful.'

'No. Listen to me. Evan has something planned for the live show. I don't know what but I fear it involves Lawrence Oliver. I heard him talking it through with Nathan last week. I'm worried for you – you don't know what that man's capable of.'

I blink. 'What are you talking about?'

'I think Evan wants to cause trouble for you next Friday.' He looks at me seriously. 'He's got it in for you, Maddie – don't ask me why but you've rubbed him up the wrong way and he doesn't like it one bit. That combined with smashing his ratings record is too much to resist.'

'What's that got to do with Lawrence?'

'God knows. That's what I'm concerned about.'

I try to find evidence that he's lying – a jiggling knee, a wandering eye – but he's addressing me directly. 'Lawrence and I have known each other for ages,' I say, uncertain even as the words emerge, 'he'd never do anything like that.'

'I had to tell you what I knew,' Nick ventures. 'It isn't much, especially in light of everything, but I couldn't stand by and let him ruin the work you've put into this place.'

I need to think about this. I need to be alone.

'Thanks for the heads-up,' I say briskly, going to let him out. 'But I can handle myself – and Lawrence.' I stand back. 'You should go.'

He doesn't move. 'Evan's ambitious,' he says.

I open the door. 'Like you?'

'I'm not ambitious, I was out of work.'

'That makes it OK then.'

'It makes it realistic. Not right, but realistic.'

I turn my head away. 'Please leave.'

There's a pause, during which I can sense Nick's mind ticking over. Maybe he's remembering his lines, or maybe it's just hitting home that I'm not listening to any more of his rubbish. I can hear the slow, dejected movements as he gathers his things, rises from the sofa and comes to my side, and I wonder if in a different lifetime we could be two people saying goodbye at the end of the night, kissing each other and not wanting to let go.

I'm about to close the door behind him when I stop myself. 'Nick, wait.'

He turns to me. 'Yes?'

'The stuff we talked about on the bridge that night . . . the things you told me. I need to know if you were telling the truth.'

His face is sad. He doesn't even need to say the words; I know the answer from his face and instantly feel sorry I asked.

'I never lied to you,' he says gently. 'How could you think I would lie about something like that?'

I nod. 'Sorry,' I say. And I'm trying not to blink because there's a pool of tears about to brim over and I don't want him to see me cry.

He reaches out. 'Maddie . . .'

But I shut the door and put my head against the wood, knowing he's only inches away but that we're a world or more apart.

25

Bat Out of Hell

By the next morning I've almost convinced myself that I've got nothing worry about.

Almost.

It's Saturday and we're six days from the final live broadcast. This time in a week, I tell myself as I make toast and sit down in front of a re-run of *Frasier*, it will all be over. Thankfully Mum and Dad aren't due home till the following weekend, which gives me time to throw water on the fire of any dubious publicity and try to regain a semblance of normality.

My stomach flips at the thought of Friday's finale. Even

without Nick's portentous words, if the first live outing was anything to go by I'm not convinced it's going to be the best night of my life. I'm hoping the proximity of the finishing line will pull me through.

And yet . . .

What if Nick *was* telling the truth? What if Evan really has got something dastardly planned, with or without Lawrence? How can I trust him?

These thoughts stay with me while I wash up my plate and make yet another cup of coffee. A signed photo of Bonnie Tyler takes pride of place above the sink and I decide to invoke the help of the Eighties Gods (by whom, contrary to popular belief, I don't mean Duran Duran): surely I've invested enough time and energy in this era that by some cosmic transaction it means I'm now able to reap rewards.

By the power invested in Bonnie Tyler . . . Hang on, that's not right. I now pronounce you Bonnie Tyler. No, wait a sec.

Our Bonnie Tyler, who art in Eighties heaven, hollered be thy name, thy songs be sung, thy hair be done on earth as it is in heaven; give us this day our waily spread (but not Simply Red) and forgive us our trespasses, as we forgive those who trespass against synth pop; lead us not into House Nation and deliver us from R 'n' B; for thine is the keyboard, the power ballad and the glory, for ever and ever. Amen.

It occurs to me that I haven't got drunk in a while – perhaps that's where I'm going wrong. Right now, though, there isn't anyone I particularly want to get drunk with . . . apart from the one person who's still not speaking to me. Lou.

I'm about to try ringing her for the four hundredth time

when a thought occurs to me, and I wonder why it hasn't struck me before. Maybe it's all this talk of approaching insanity, but once the idea's there it's difficult to shake off.

Loaf.

You don't know what you're letting yourself in for . . . Things might not be what they seem . . .

Hasn't he been warning me about Evan since the start? And didn't he say he *knew* Evan?

If anyone is going to have the answers, I decide, it's him. And I have to find out what they are. Even if, I concede as I hug the warm cup close to my chest, I might not want to.

♪

Rock Around the Clock is as dead as usual. The OPEN sign gazes reproachfully back at me as I push open the door, hearing the sad, lonely tinkle of the bell as I enter the shop.

'Hello?' My voice gets swallowed in the silence. 'Anybody here?'

There's an open comic on the cash desk, a bundle of keys and what appears to be a half-eaten blueberry muffin, so I decide Loaf can't be too far away. I have a sudden vision of his shop populated by plastic limbs, all those freaky model throwbacks he's got hiding in his living room, and feel a shiver travel down my spine. Mannequins should be reserved solely for John Lewis window displays, poorly scripted horror films and romantic comedies starring Andrew McCarthy (if the two aren't mutually exclusive).

I wonder about for a bit, have a stab at playing 'Blue Moon' on a handsome Steinway and, encouraged by this, see if I can remember the 'Für Elise' I learned at Grade 3 . . . I can't. So I muck about a bit with half-recalled theme tunes: the start of *EastEnders* (in essence a C major scale but a sure-fire crowd pleaser nonetheless) and that rousing guitar-solo anthem from *Top Gun* (RIP Goose), before I'm reminded of why I'm here. On the edge of my vision something captures my attention: a flounce of white material, appearing and dis-appearing, like a handkerchief being waved in distress. I flip the piano lid down and it shuts with a satisfying velvety *plunk*, then I stand up and make my way cautiously through to the back courtyard.

At the top of the steps I pause, open-mouthed. There *is* something out here in distress, but when I catch my own horrified reflection in the window opposite, I realise that thing is me.

Loaf is wearing a huge white kaftan, his wispy brown hair just licking the collar and his signet ring glinting in the late-morning sun. He appears to be practising some martial art (Tai Chi?), bending his stocky legs and drawing great circles with his arms, balancing and steadying, balancing and steadying. I'm sure it's a highly advanced mode of spiritual and physical exercise, a regime of absolute discipline and profound con-centration, but from where I'm standing it's Loaf prancing about like a dandy in a duvet.

'Er . . . hi?' I hazard, not wanting to interrupt but feeling way too creepy just watching.

But he doesn't turn round. And then it becomes clear why he didn't break off at the sound of my musical efforts – he's in some sort of . . . trance.

I stay there for what seems like ages, waiting. I'm rooted to the spot even though I know it's wrong, but it's like I'm in a wildlife documentary or something and I've just got unprecedentedly close to a rare and wonderful beast, and now I'm frightened to move in case I disturb its natural behavioural pattern.

Loaf's back is to me but I can see his facial expressions in the window, and my own slightly startled one floating behind. I decide it's all getting a teensy bit weird. I should come back later.

But just as I'm turning to go, I'm rumbled.

'ARRRGGHHHH!'

Loaf's eyes open – and when he catches both our reflections he stumbles backwards, one foot slipping on the cobbles and sending him flying. The kaftan lifts and billows like a parachute and I catch a very brief glimpse of a pair of chunky bare legs before he lands on his bottom with an almighty thump.

'I'm so sorry!' I gasp, my hands flying to my face to mark my genuine apology but also to stifle a laugh. It *was* kind of funny. 'Are you OK?'

'What the hell are you doing?' he blusters, shaking off my attempted help and scrambling to his feet. 'Couldn't you see I was having some . . . alone time?' He's gone very red. Against the white of his robes and the pastry-shade of his skin, it makes him look like a giant Cherry Bakewell.

'I'm really sorry,' I say again. 'I just came in and I thought . . . well, I didn't know where you were and then I saw . . . your dress and . . .' I tail off.

'It's not a *dress*!' Loaf vows, indignant. 'It's a toga.'

'A *toga*?'

'Yes,' he lifts his chin, 'for ease of manoeuvre.' Then he frowns. 'I thought I closed up for the afternoon.'

'The sign said you were open.'

'Well, I ought to close,' he says, flapping at the seat of his toga to get off the dirt. 'Custom's as slow as ever. And besides, I don't much go in for *uninvited guests* showing up whenever they feel like it.'

I nod. 'Understood. I'll drop by later.'

'No, no,' Loaf says, as if me backing out now would make this interruption not only an annoyance but also a complete waste of time, 'what did you want?'

'Maybe now's not the best time . . .' I venture. 'It's about the show.'

Loaf puts his hands on his hips. He looks like an angry Socrates. 'Come on then,' he urges, 'spit it out.'

'It's about Evan Bergman, specifically.' Even saying his name makes my tummy do a somersault.

He folds his arms and looks at me, a glint of inevitability in his eye, like a general who knew all along his prodigal soldier would return.

'In that case,' he says, 'you'd better come in.'

♪

Minutes later I'm in his Formica-laminated kitchen, sipping at cloudy lemonade through a straw while Loaf showers and changes upstairs. There's a box of Celebrations on the side and I help myself to a Milky Way, then another one, then I think, Oh, I'll just have a Mars. And maybe another Milky Way. I really hope Loaf hurries up or he'll come back downstairs and I'll be buried under a crispy avalanche of tiny chocolate wrappers. I decide to retire to the living room.

Loaf's got a good set of vinyl, from Dire Straits, Blondie

and T. Rex to more obscure seven-inch collectors' pieces. It's all here, from Musical Youth to Marilyn; from Bucks Fizz to Bronski Beat; from U2 to Ultravox, a veritable library all meticulously labelled and filed. Somewhere between the cautions to watch out for Evan and the impromptu tête-à-têtes with David Bowie, I'd forgotten what I knew about Loaf in the first place: that's he's an ardent lover of music. It's why he came to Mum and Dad's every Saturday of the year, without fail; why he sat through all that dreadful singing, just waiting for his turn . . . because, quite simply, he loved the songs. Until *Blast from the Past* got started, that is.

'Not found any nasty surprises this time, I hope?'

I spin round. Loaf's changed into a plain brown jumper and jeans, quite a departure from his usual elaborate attire, and in a flash I see a much younger, less eccentric man, and wonder how he came to this point in his life: owner of a lowly music shop that makes 5p a week, but proud owner of it nonetheless because it stands for the very thing he's passionate about. He'd rather sit in solitude all day with his crisps and his comics, among all those beautiful instruments, gathering dust and making no money, than be a millionaire and have even one of these records taken away from him.

'Unless you call Baltimora's "Tarzan Boy" a nasty surprise.'

Loaf smiles in the doorway. 'That's a matter of opinion.'

Compelled by my genuine interest in his story, I decide to get straight to the point. Gently slipping the vinyls back into their sleeves, I take a deep breath.

'I think Evan's plotting something,' I say, coming to perch on the edge of the sofa. Loaf sits down next to me, his expression troubled.

'What do you mean?'

'I mean . . . there's this guy, he directs the show, and I don't know if I can trust him, because . . . oh, it doesn't matter. But he said—'

'Nick Craven?'

I frown. 'I thought you didn't watch it.'

'I might have seen bits,' Loaf says, on the defence. 'Besides, you can't bloody miss it. It's everywhere! All your mugs splashed over the weeklies; I even saw your photo in my TV guide the other day, on the facing page to Simon Cowell!'

I lift my knee, rest my elbow on it and cup my chin in my hand. 'I know,' I say wearily. 'That's what worries me.'

'Go on.'

'It *is* Nick Craven.' I shake my head, not wanting to talk about it but knowing I must. 'We had something and then we . . . well, we didn't. I guess we never did. And now he's confusing me, telling me I've misunderstood, but the thing is I don't know whether or not I believe him and anyway, he *still* can't be straight with me for whatever reason so why should I care? He's been working for Evan Bergman – that much I do know because he admitted it – and he made me believe there was something between us when there wasn't.' I pause for breath. 'So now he's supposedly come good, he's maintaining that Evan's got some dreadful plan in place for the final live night – and worse still, that it involves my ex, Lawrence. If I'm being totally frank Lawrence *can* be a bit of a plonker, but I can't really entertain the idea that he'd be willing to sabotage me on live TV. Would he? I mean, we've had our differences in the past, but he wouldn't do that, he wouldn't

309

be so . . .' I chew my lip. 'Whatever, I can't go merrily on the word of some guy who's already lied to me and hurt me at the risk of one of the few friendships I have left intact – sort of. So I came here because I don't have anyone else to talk to, because it seems like all my friends are either pissed off with me, or they don't know where they stand any more, or they wish they'd never got involved in the first place, or they think I'm paranoid, or they might have agendas of their own, so I have no idea who to believe. And I figured if you *knew* Evan, because you said you did, that you might have an opinion on it – on whether I should trust him over Nick. Because I honestly have no clue!'

Loaf sits back and clasps his hands together in his lap. 'Finished?'

'Think so.'

He looks up at the ceiling for several moments, so that eventually my gaze follows his, as if the answer might have appeared there by magic.

'You want to know if I think Evan's capable of doing something like this?' Loaf's gaze slides back to me, and the way he says it fills me with dismay.

'Yes,' I say weakly.

'Capable of plotting something that will damage you, your parents and the club for ever more?'

I nod, queasy. 'And it's next week. Opening night was bad enough and we had a tenth of the number of viewers then. This is a big deal!'

'Why would he do it?' asks Loaf, in a way that isn't so much a question as a test. 'What's in it for him? Shouldn't he want the show to go off without a hitch?'

I laugh. 'God, no – he wants to go out with a bang: anything to get the viewers excited. He doesn't care about *me* – he doesn't care about any of us! Or Pineapple, he couldn't give a shit. He'll be well clear of us come Saturday and the more he pulls in the better his commission next time. He's jumping off a sinking ship and he figures if it's going down anyway, he might as well let off some fireworks.'

'Hmm.'

I tap my heel against the foot of the sofa. 'What do you know?'

Loaf stands up, walks over to the mantelpiece and runs his finger along its edge. He stays like that a minute, me watching his back and waiting for him to speak.

'I knew Evan Bergman a long time ago,' he says. 'A very long time ago.'

'You did?'

'Thankfully I haven't seen him in years.' He clears his throat. 'Fifteen, maybe twenty years. And if I never saw him again it would still be too soon.'

I slide from the armrest on to the sofa, not wanting to interrupt in case I put him off his stride. I grab a cushion and pull it to me, as much a comfort as a shield to whatever blow Loaf is about to deliver.

'I wondered if you recognised me,' Loaf says, his back still to mc. 'I thought you might – you and your friends always used to look at me funny when I came into Sing It Back.'

It wouldn't be right, or kind, to clarify exactly why we looked at him funny – though I still don't entirely approve of the 'Bat Out of Hell' thing. Nevertheless I'm sorry: rather than laughing at Loaf and mocking him, maybe I should have had

311

more time for our most loyal customer from the outset, bothered to consider why he might be how he is.

On cue Loaf announces, 'I wasn't always like this,' with such lonely bitterness that I half expect him to turn round having developed a hideous facial disfigurement and tell me nobody's ever loved him.

'You don't know my name, do you?'

'Er . . .'

'It's OK. Most people don't. Most people don't recognise me these days.' He turns to me, and I feel I should now be struck by some grand revelation.

'They don't?'

'No. I used to be different.'

Oh god. He *is* Meatloaf.

My voice drops to a scratchy whisper. 'Are you Meatloaf?'

'What?'

'Nothing.'

'My name's Gary,' he says softly. 'Gary Wishall.'

OK. Should I know who Gary Wishall is? Do you? Not wanting to offend him, I nod uncertainly. 'You are?'

He exhales, as if this is a secret he's been holding in for a long time, as if telling me now is a great relief. 'Yes. But in those days I became known as the Genie.'

It takes a couple of seconds for the penny to drop, but when it does it's all I can do not to gasp.

Wish Records. The biggest pop label of the eighties, a legendary hit factory with a flood of number ones to its credit; its founder on a par with Stock, Aitken and Waterman. I've heard the Genie talked about in certain circles, by Mum and Dad among others, by people all through my childhood as this borderline mythical, mystical figure with profound powers, like everything he touched turned to gold. And that must be where the name came from: acts would come to Wish Records and the Genie would grant them; make their dreams come true and send them soaring into the pop stratosphere.

'*You're* Gary Wishall?' My eyes widen. 'You're the Genie?'

He nods sadly. 'Once upon a time.'

'What happened?' I lean forward, practically on the edge of my seat. 'You just faded, you vanished – at least that's what they all used to say. No one knew where you were.'

Loaf (sorry – can't stop calling him that) rests his elbow on the mantelpiece. He waits a moment before responding. 'I had a shining career.' His voice catches. 'Until one man ruined everything.'

The name is on my tongue, poised for flight. But Loaf has more to say.

'It was the summer of '87. I was auditioning for a male duo, something to rival Hall & Oates, with the catch of Go West and the sex appeal of George and Andrew.' He gestures around a bit. 'I had my one guy – Lenny Gold, he won the Best Male Haircut of 1983. God,' he smiles, reminiscing, 'how we worked that perm . . .' – a fond chuckle – 'and I needed a match. Lenny was blond; I wanted someone with brown hair, a contrast, a yin to his yang. I was going to call them' – he closes his eyes – 'Two Shay.'

'Two Shay,' I murmur. '"Goodbye Lover". "Do the Rhubarb".'

'The very ones.' Loaf sits back down, and I can see his hands are shaking. He tucks them under his legs to steady them, or hide them, I'm not sure.

'I don't understand,' I say. 'Two Shay had three number ones. They were huge. And you put them together. You were responsible for it – the perfect match.'

'They were perfect,' Loaf rasps, 'Lenny and Don. But I saw none of their success. They sacked me as their manager – it was the death knoll in my career.'

'What went wrong?'

He shakes his head, scratches his chin. 'Evan Bergman walked into my life, that's what went wrong.'

'But what's Evan got to do with Two Shay?'

'Absolutely nothing – and that was the problem. That's why he made my life a living hell for eighteen months and sabotaged my career, my name, everything I'd worked for.'

I search his face. 'How?'

Loaf gathers himself. 'Evan Bergman – or Evan Bergamot-Laidislaw, as he was back then – was the son of the seventh earl of somewhere-or-other: I wasn't impressed by it so I don't remember. He was aristocracy, a rich, up-himself young toff, and I took against him as soon as he walked into my office. Acting like the world owed him a living; like he should be able to click his fingers and the rest of us would jump; like he didn't have to work for a damn thing – not like we'd all toiled, scrambled up from the bottom, reached for success with our bare hands because not everyone gets born with their fingers in a pair of silk gloves.' A pause while he catches himself. 'I'd placed an ad in the paper – much in the same way Evan drew you to him – advertising for a male pop artist to form one half of my duo. Evan responded to it. He was *desperate* to be a pop star, to be famous, to perform: I knew it as soon as I shook his hand. I could smell it on him, the hard ambition, the cut-throat drive – I knew then he'd do just about anything to secure victory in the charts. Because in that way a lot of privileged people have, his gripe against society was that society had never *given* him a gripe. He'd been handed everything on a plate since day one, and now he wanted to prove himself, to break away from the aristocratic label . . . and find a home on my label instead.

'He was good looking. Oh yes, he made a great match with Lenny – they looked wonderful side by side. But he couldn't sing a damn note . . . not one! I'm not talking about hitting a few bums and needing some extra help – we're talking circa Milli Vanilli here, after all – but there wasn't *any* raw material to work with. None. He could barely hit a middle C. And call me an opportunist but I'm also a music producer – I *care* about the industry, about nurturing talent and rewarding ability – and I don't believe in manufactured success when there's not at least a glimmer of genuine spark.

'So Evan auditioned and everyone at Wish Records was stunned . . . for all the wrong reasons. Of course he thought he had it in the bag, that we'd never refuse an aristocrat, least of all one who looked like he did. And I'm ashamed to say I did put him through to the final three purely because he looked so divine on camera, but a combination of his attitude and his acute lack of musical flair put paid to any shot he had at making it. We had to refuse.'

I'm amazed. 'How did he take it?'

'Badly. Let's put it this way: when I called him up to break the news, he told me his father was going to pay me a visit and blow off my kneecaps with a sawn-off shotgun.'

I gasp. 'He didn't!'

'He did. It was like *The Godfather* – simply ridiculous. Not to mention Evan was about thirty at the time, so I don't quite know what Daddy had to do with it.'

'What happened then?'

'We hired Don,' says Loaf. 'And Two Shay made it big. But I wasn't around to reap any of it.' He grimaces. 'Those boys were like sons to me – it broke my heart to let them go.'

I gesture for more. 'I mean what happened with Evan?'

'The last I spoke to him, he told me to . . .' He lifts his chin, appealing to some higher power. '"Expect it when you least expect it."'

'What's that supposed to mean?'

'It was supposed to make me fear for my safety, my reputation, everything I'd strived for – and it did. Because Evan took it upon himself to wreak his own brand of revenge.' Loaf shakes his head, smiles grimly. 'He just couldn't get over the rejection, couldn't understand why he hadn't been chosen: he was moneyed, from good stock, had the credentials – if not the talent. But that wasn't what Two Shay was about.'

'It wasn't?'

Loaf shakes his head. 'No. Two Shay was about *real people*, just like you and me. You never heard the lyrics to "Man2Man"?'

'*We won the race with mud on our face; we made the sound though we grew from the ground?*'

'Exactly.' He nods. 'But that's beside the point. Evan embarked on a dedicated hate campaign against me: it was subtle but lethal. Never mind the shotgun threat – by the end I'd have given anything for a couple of mangled legs. No,' he

316

chokes, 'instead he ruined me from the inside, using the contacts he had all across the industry. He broke into my office, copied my diary, my Filofax, my portfolio – he told clients and agents ahead of meetings that I no longer wished to represent them, that I didn't feel they could bring me the cash I required and so they were no good to me any more – people I'd spent years building relationships with. He sent me hate mail. He told anyone who'd listen, powerful people, influential people, that I was going mad, I was losing it, that I was having a nervous breakdown. And do you know what the worst bit is? I started to believe him. Because when I tried to get the authorities involved, Evan and his family were always there first. No one believed me. I wasn't eating. I wasn't sleeping. I wasn't working. Everything I did, he sabotaged. Every lifeline blew up in my face. Each time I thought I was making progress, he'd strike and I'd be right back at square one.'

'Two steps forward, three steps back,' I murmur.

Loaf nods. 'Paula Abdul. But in this case, opposites definitely *didn't* attract.'

'You poor thing.' I still can't believe it. Evan? Two Shay? I had no idea . . .

Mum and Dad must know. Of course they do! They never bailed out on him like everyone else did – because they're not like that.

'And the next thing I know, Evan's charmed these people, these circles' – he's seething now – 'the very contacts I'd spent *years* earning through hard work and sleepless nights and endless deadlines, and then all of a sudden he's got a blossoming career in TV and everyone's licking his feet. So then he begins his hate campaign in that field, too. And *everyone* believes Evan

Bergman because that's how he is.' Loaf laughs drily. 'He'll make you believe anything. He'll have an idea and make you think *you* thought of it!'

'That's why you haven't been into the club?'

'You've got to be careful – I know what he's like. He doesn't give up. He's evil. And he's got all the pieces in play at Pineapple, believe me.'

'I don't understand.'

'You'd better get with the programme, then – because it's already got with you. Listen to me, Maddie: Evan Bergman might have a glittering TV career but all he's ever wanted is to be on stage. He would have pitted himself against your parents. At the time Two Shay were formed – and he wasn't a part of it – Pineapple Mist was storming the charts. Evan attempted to tour the circuit for a while himself, under the name Poison Bergamot and the Dice' – he lowers his voice – 'until one especially embarrassing performance put an end to that.'

'Of course!' My hands fly to my face. 'I've heard of them! I'm sure they used to appear at holiday camps when I was growing up!'

'Very probably. Which means he would have performed not far from Rick and Sapphy – but of course he'd never have experienced anything like the success they achieved.' Here he looks at me meaningfully, and at last realisation hits me in the face like a cold slap.

'My god. You think this is all about some personal vendetta?'

'I wouldn't be surprised.' Loaf takes my hand. 'I think as soon as you walked into his office that day he knew he'd hit the jackpot.'

'He wants to sabotage my parents, too?'

What have I done?

'All I'm saying is that your Nick Craven might not be too far from the mark. Whatever Evan's got planned a week from now, I can guarantee it's not going to be pretty.'

26

The Final Countdown

Ruby du Jour glides into Pineapple late Wednesday afternoon. Just the sight of her lifts everyone's mood – it's been ages since we've had a sparkly Ruby in our mist.

'Gorgeous dress,' I say, taking in her floor-length emerald-green gown with sequin neckline. 'What's the occasion?'

'Well, honeys,' Ruby purrs, sliding on to one of the bar stools and crossing one long leg over the other, 'it's about time we all stopped walking around with faces like death. I don't care who Evan Bergman is – or once was – there are more of us than him and this is *our* club.'

Jaz helps her to a drink. 'You got that right.'

'When Maddie called a meeting today, I knew there had to be a plan.' She takes a sip. 'So what is it?'

Everybody turns to me, their faces expectant. 'I'm hoping there won't be need for a plan,' I say. 'But if Evan so much as tries anything, I'm beating him to it. One thing we have over him right now is knowledge. I've got enough dirt on that bloke to sink him for good.'

Jaz claps her hands with glee, an orchestra of colourful knuckle-dusters jangling on impact. 'Go, Maddie!'

Ruby frowns, the lapse in frivolity making way for Rob to emerge. 'Meaning what, exactly?'

I feel sick to the stomach at the thought of taking to that stage, but I don't tell them that. I'm their manager and it's my job to sort this out. If Evan's got something public planned then it's bound to involve him getting up in front of the nation – he's too much of a showman, I now know – and all I have to do is keep a close eye on him, gather my strength and have the guts to challenge him head-on. I'm keeping everything crossable crossed that it won't come to that. Everything.

'Meaning we've got all the stuff we need right here for a full-on defensive,' I say. 'Mics, a stage—'

'A soundtrack!' exclaims Jaz. 'How about "I Owe You Nothing"?'

'Hmm.'

'But you're terrified of that sort of thing,' says Ruby.

'What, Bros?'

'No,' she flaps her hands, 'the whole shebang. Stages, public speaking, *microphones* . . .'

'Tell me about it.' I see Jaz open her mouth. 'Don't *actually* tell me about it.'

'She's more terrified of what Evan might do,' Simon chips in. He raises an eyebrow. 'Right? Personally I reckon you should set the record straight anyway. Get up there first and rumble him once and for all on national TV – that'll show the world what he's been up to.'

'And come across like a total paranoid nutcase, pushed to the brink by an exposure I can't handle? No, thanks.' I shake my head. 'It would be just typical of Evan to want to make some ironic statement about the modern-day media breaking people like me down. Fuck it, maybe that's what he wants.'

'But what about all the stuff he's done?' Simon presses. 'Maybe, you know, there'll be people watching who want to know the truth . . . ?'

'Like blonde Psychology students with a hatred of lemon meringue pie? No. We've nothing to prove except to the people we care about, and that's something we'll do on our own time. Getting up there without need is just as bad as everything Evan's done to us. It's public spectacle.'

'If that's the plan,' says Simon, lifting his shoulders.

Ruby wrinkles her nose. 'It's not much of a plan . . .'

'It's all I have,' I say, a little snappily. 'What were you expecting, gunpowder?'

'I think it's sensible,' decides Jaz. 'And I think it's very brave to say you'll do it.'

'It's the least I can do,' I mutter.

'Evan's relying on the fact we're all afraid.' Simon pulls at the sleeves on his woolly jumper, unravelling a bit at the cuffs. 'He's convinced he'll get away with it, that's what pisses me off – never mind what he's done to us, what about what he did to Gary?'

Jaz pauses in plaiting Andre's hair. 'Who's Gary again?'

'It's Loaf!' cries Ruby impatiently.

'Ah.'

I roll my eyes: I've been through this about five times. As soon as I was done at Loaf's I explained the whole thing to them all – it's vital we know that we're not just dealing with a cut-throat TV exec, but someone potentially very dangerous – but I think I lost Jaz somewhere between double-barrelled surnames and Milli Vanilli.

'Look,' I say, 'let's not lose sight of the ideal scenario: that Friday night goes off without a hitch and we can all go home at the end of it and back to the rest of our lives.' I smile faintly. 'It might still happen.'

'What I want to know is how we're going to get Archie back.' Ruby raises her eyebrows at me questioningly. 'We never should have lost him in the first place.'

'P'raps he *wanted* to leave,' suggests Jaz. 'Do we know how much Evan paid him?'

I shrug, despair washing over me at the thought of dear Archie, and the fact I have no idea where he is and neither will my parents.

There's a brief silence while we all contemplate this. Then somebody speaks.

'I've got an idea how much he was paid.'

It's Alex. I'd all but forgotten he was here, he's been so quiet. I'm also able to count on the fingers of one hand the number of times he's volunteered information when we've all gathered like this – especially when it concerns Evan.

'What?'

Alex clears his throat. 'There's something I want to, uh, get off my chest,' he says, fiddling with the thin silver chain round his bronzed neck.

'What is it?' Jaz clutches Andre to her, his feet sporting little tartan fur-lined slippers (who'd have thought it? Fur on fur).

'You've all been so nice to me since I arrived.' He throws me a nervous smile. 'Well, most of you . . .'

I narrow my eyes. 'Why do I feel like you're about to prove me right?'

Alex blows out through his mouth. We notice that he directs the following at Jaz, as if it's only her reaction he really cares about.

'Evan hired me to replace Archie,' he confesses. A collective intake of breath whips round the booth and Ruby slams her glass down on the bar with such force it nearly shatters. 'Days before Archie left, he came direct to the modelling agency where I worked and booked me in under five minutes. I think he'd been here once and seen you all, and, well . . .' He trails off, before finishing feebly, 'Quickest casting of my life!'

'You snake!' Ruby puts her hands on her hips.

Jaz shrugs. 'I'd have done it.'

'I bet you would,' bites Simon.

'That's why you could never look me in the eye,' I say, shaking my head in wonder. 'You actively avoided me, you never gave anything away . . . I *knew* something was up!'

Alex looks sheepish. 'I'm sorry,' he says. 'At the beginning it was just a paycheck, but then I started to get to know you all and I felt really bad. Especially around you, Maddie – talking to everyone here brought home how much you valued Archie, and what was riding on this whole gig for your parents.'

'Oh, bring out the violins!' snaps Ruby.

'Hang on,' I say wearily, trying to be fair. 'Alex isn't to blame – he was looking for a break like the rest of us. He wasn't to know what Archie meant to the club or the nature of Evan's agenda. To him it was just a job.'

Alex sends me a grateful smile.

'And you really have no clue what you're doing behind a bar.' Simon shakes his head and gives a short laugh. 'That figures.'

'Sorry,' he mumbles. 'By the time I realised how much I liked you guys' – he and Jaz lock eyes – 'I mean really liked you, I didn't have the guts to say anything. It was never the right time and before I knew it you'd all sussed out Evan and I couldn't fess up without seeming like a traitor.'

'You couldn't resist the chance to get on TV, is that it?' demands Simon.

Jaz deposits Andre on the table, his feet slipping apart like a skier before he rights himself. '*We* couldn't, could we?'

'I always wanted to get on TV,' Alex goes on. 'Everyone said I should model, but really I wanted to act—'

'Same here!' trills Jaz.

'Doesn't everyone?' I mutter.

'—so this seemed like a good opportunity . . .'

'How much, then?' interrupts Ruby. 'How much was Archie worth?'

'I'm not sure,' Alex murmurs. 'At least twenty grand, maybe thirty . . . maybe fifty. I think . . .'

'*Fifty grand?*'

'That's enough,' I butt in, 'you don't need to explain, Alex. All that matters now is what lies ahead – and we need to be sure of two things. First, do you know anything about Evan and Friday? And second, are you with us or with him?'

Alex expands his sculpted chest. 'I don't know anything about Evan's plan, and that's the truth. What I do know is that Evan, Nick and Nathan keep disappearing for these "urgent chats" – but what they're talking about, I have no idea.'

I pretend Nick's name doesn't cut into me. 'And are you in or out? Our side or theirs?'

'In,' he says without hesitation. 'Yours. Whatever, I'm with you.'

Simon's sceptical. 'And we're meant to believe this guy?'

'I suppose we'll have to,' says Ruby, equally unconvinced.

But what choice do we have? I can't mistrust everyone – if someone says they're with me, I've got to take them at their word.

'We're in it together,' I say, my voice trembling, 'everybody here. There are five of us and one of him: Evan's not getting away with anything on Friday. Even forgetting what Loaf told me, I've got enough ammunition on his private life to stun the entire nation. If he fires any my way, it'll be him that goes down in flames.' Everyone stares at me. 'Or something.'

Tucking Andre under one arm, Jaz grabs Alex's hand. 'Come on,' she says, 'this calls for a celebratory song.'

'Oh *no*,' Simon moans, putting his face in his hands as they amble towards the machines, nattering about Alex's TV break.

It relieves me that Simon and Jaz are getting back to something like their usual banter – even if it is with that awkward way you do when you've got off with someone when drunk and neither of you especially wanted to.

Simon leans in and drops his voice. 'Have you heard from her?' he asks tentatively. The machine cranks up Phil Collins' 'You Can't Hurry Love'. I get a pang when I remember the conversation I had with Nick that day in Soho, and I squash it like a fruit.

'No,' I say. 'My guess is she's waiting it out till Friday's over – I would. She can't come back into this situation right now and I totally get that. Lou needs time, Simon, that's all. She'll come round.' I sound more confident than I feel.

'I hope so. I just want to get it over with so I can talk to her again. Then maybe she'll agree to see me, hear me out.'

'I've sent her texts explaining – and emails.' I sigh. 'Fuck it, what do I know any more? She hasn't written back to any of them.'

'Thanks, mate.' Simon runs a hand through his hair. 'I'm not giving up – I refuse to. Lou told me about her parents, how she was always second best, third best, whatever. That they never bothered about her, never wanted kids in the first place . . .'

'Yeah.' I miss my best friend so much.

'That thing two weeks ago,' Simon tosses Jaz a look, where she's busy teaching Alex how to hold a microphone, Ruby escaping from the situation with fingers in her ears, 'was pretty much the worst thing that could have happened.'

'No kidding.'

'She hasn't been into work?'

'I haven't been in myself,' I confess. 'In fact I've decided I'm quitting Simply Voices.'

Ruby slips in next to me. 'You're doing *what*?' she demands, concern etched on her face.

I nod. 'After the show's blown over I want to go away for a while,' I say. 'I think we could all do with a break, and I know for sure I need one.'

'Understandable,' agrees Simon, his mouth set in a grim line.

'Hopefully time away will give me some perspective on all this – and right now I don't feel like anyone's going to miss me much.'

Ruby hooks her arm round me. 'We'll all miss you, Maddie,' she says with feeling. 'How long are you going for?'

'I'm not sure,' I say. 'As long as it takes.'

♪

As soon as the others are gone and I'm back in the flat, I resolve to call Lawrence. I've got half an hour before the cameras show up and I decide to use it wisely. If Lawrence is a real friend then he'll understand why I'm ringing – and if I'm wrong, he'll get why I might be jumping to conclusions. Really I'm just praying it will put my mind at rest. Two days ahead of Pineapple's closing night, the more people I know are on my team, the better.

After a quick shower and two cups of very sweet tea, I dial his number. The first call fails but on the second attempt he picks up almost instantly.

'Mads!' There's a slight strangle to his voice, like I've caught him by surprise.

'Can you talk?' In the background I can hear the bustle of a busy shop. I have this image of Lawrence behind a meaty counter in rubber boots (or is that the fishmonger's?) with bright red hands and a stained blue and white apron, a giant pig's head staring vacantly over his shoulder with an apple stuffed in its mouth.

'Yeah,' he says, flustered, 'just got to wash my hands . . .'

'I mean if you're at work, don't worry—'

'I don't have a job,' he interjects swiftly. 'I mean, I'm in Soho, at an audition.'

'OK . . .' I say. 'It's just a quick call. There's um . . . something I need to ask you.'

'Yuh, what is it?'

'Look, please don't take this the wrong way, but—'

A loud bump on the other end of the line. 'Sorry, sorry.'

'Well, it's been brought to my attention that' – god, I sound like a dick – 'I mean, I've reason to think that . . .'

'Hurry up, Maddie, I'm freezing.' His teeth are chattering.

'Where are you?'

'Erm, outside.'

'It's sunny outside.'

'I've got a cold,' he snaps. I can hear a low industrial buzz and I wonder if he's standing in a fridge, surrounded by strung-up cow thighs. I'd better hurry up.

'You're coming on Friday, right?' I ask.

'Yuh . . . ?'

I dive in. 'Of course it's really silly but I just wondered if maybe Evan Bergman had been in touch with you about it without me knowing.' I laugh, high-pitched. 'It's stupid, isn't it? Of course he hasn't. I mean, why would he? But if he had, you'd tell me, wouldn't you? About Friday. If Evan had talked to you about Friday.'

Silence.

'Lawrence? You still there?'

'Sorry, yuh. No. I mean, no, never heard of him.'

'You've never heard of Evan Bergman?' I'm confused. 'Right now the whole *country*'s heard of Evan Bergman.'

'Oh, *that* Evan Bergman – sorry, right, thought you meant someone else.'

This is doing nothing to reassure me. Quickly I try to steer things back on track. 'Lawrence, answer the question. Evan's not spoken to you, has he?'

'Of course not!' A little shriek. 'I've really got to go, Mads. I've, um, got a meeting.'

There's a crackle on the line. 'I just lost you. Did you say something about meat?'

'No,' he blusters, 'what do you mean? What about meat?'

I wince into the phone.

'Gotta go,' he says hurriedly. 'See you Friday!'

And he hangs up, leaving me somewhat flustered and feeling decidedly worse than I did five minutes ago.

♪

I'm frantic in the bar that night, Alison trailing me round firing endless questions on how I feel about the show ending, about Nick, about my friendship with Lou, about Jaz and Simon and Andre and Alex – all of which I answer as diplomatically and as tersely as possible – when a text comes in from Mum.

I duck behind the bar and pull it from my back pocket.

330

Hello darling! Great news – we are coming home
a week early!!! Back on Sat. Can't wait to see
everyone. We know you've been brilliant –
we've missed you & the club like you wouldn't believe.
Looking forward to normality! Much love, Mum & Dad xx

Oh Jesus.

27

Don't Stop Believing

Breathe in. Breathe out.

Everything's going to be fine. Everything's going to be *fine*.

I practise my smile in the mirror and it wobbles a bit before falling off.

'I look like I'm crapping myself . . . don't I?' I turn to Simon, who's on his hands and knees poking about in Mum and Dad's drinks cabinet. He unearths a bottle of vodka, examines the label and then pours a measure into a waiting glass.

'Nah, you look fine,' he tells me, necking it. Then he pours another.

'You have to at least *look* at me, Si.'

He looks at me. 'You're fine.'

'I am?'

'Aside from the haunted blank stare of a woman confronted with the black moment of apocalypse, yes.' He holds the bottle out. 'Want one?'

I flump down on the sofa, not caring if I crumple the seat of my new stripy French Connection dress. 'No, thanks. I've hardly eaten anything all day; it'll go straight to my head.'

Simon makes a face. 'That's kind of the idea. Have you seen how many people are down there?' He shudders. 'It's a full-on mob.'

I groan.

'They were fighting earlier.'

'*Fighting?* What's there to fight about in a karaoke bar? Someone wanted Dead or Alive and they ended up with Def Leppard?'

'No,' he takes a final shot before replacing the bottle, 'on the streets. It's like *28 Days Later*. They're clawing each other's eyes out to get past security. Toby sorted a ticket system but they're all getting touted.'

I get up and peer out the window at the writhing masses below. It's the exact spot I was standing in with Jaz and Andre eight weeks back, waiting for the show to begin and having no clue what to expect. But I see now that those nerves were the fluttering kind; these are full-on kicking. What concerns me more? The fact that live broadcast starts in less than an hour; the fact Evan Bergman might be about to take Pineapple – and me – down for good; or the fact that Mum and Dad are coming home first thing tomorrow morning? My heart's banging in my chest like a drum; it feels like it's about to burst right out.

'Pete Burns showed up,' observes Simon, a little slurred. 'And that wine taster guy who does *Saturday Morning Kitchen*.'

I turn away from the window. 'What's *he* doing here?'

'Search me. One of Evan's cronies?'

'They have got similar hair.'

'Why are you so obsessed with Evan's hair?'

'I'm not obsessed with Evan's hair.' I fasten my own locks into a pony. 'It is weird hair, though, don't you think?'

'If you say so.'

'Davinia's going to be in her element,' I joke, seeking a subject that will take my mind off the fact I should've been downstairs an hour ago.

Simon nods. 'Last seen schmoozing with Chester Bendwell. I keep telling her it'll never happen. She's got more chance of going to bed with . . . I don't know, Jaz's guinea pig.'

'That's a nice thought. Does Andre get a say in that?'

'Any guinea pig in his right mind who walks about wearing tight leather slacks and showing off a hairy chest is hardly one to deny the ladies.'

'He isn't?'

Simon cocks his head, like I'm being dumb. 'Does the Pope shit in the woods?'

'Search me. Does a bear wear a white robe and head up the Vatican City State?'

'Ignore me,' he grimaces. 'I'm drunk.'

The door bursts open. Jaz, clad in an outrageous *Grease*-inspired catsuit with gargantuan silver belt and hoop earrings, shoots into the room and slams the door behind her. She backs against the wood, rigid as bamboo.

'Maddie, ohmygod thank *god* you're here . . . I think I just' – *pant-pant-pant* – 'I just saw . . . ohmygod . . . you won't believe—'

'*What*?' Simon and I cry in unison.

Her eyes meet mine. 'I just saw Carl.'

'No way.' I clamp a hand over my mouth. 'Where?'

'You know I told you he was over here? And that he called me the day that . . .' She looks guiltily at Simon.

'Yeah . . .'

'Well after that he just kept ringing' – she attempts to catch her breath – 'and obviously I kept ignoring it, because it's not like I want to speak to him ever again in my whole life but he just wouldn't leave me alone. And now he's here. Downstairs! At the bar! This guy ordered a Malibu and Coke and I could have sworn it was him. Except he's got shorter hair!' She throws her hands up to her cheeks, eyes wild. 'What the hell am I going to do, Maddie? *He's here.* What the fuck do I *do*?'

'Don't panic,' I tell her, taking her hands and leading her to the sofa. Having a new focus, a problem to sort out, spurs me to action. I don't have to be a passive spectator in this. It's my club and the people in it are here because I, in however round-about a fashion, invited them. Deep breaths – I'm in control. It's my party. And I'll cry if I want to.

'Who's Carl?' enquires Simon, baffled. 'And why's he drinking Malibu and Coke?'

'We'll explain later. Just get Jaz a drink, will you?'

Jaz descends on the couch, then immediately gets up again. 'What's he doing here? What does he want?'

'He wants to see you,' I tell her, as Simon shoves a tumbler into her shaking hands. 'But you don't have to speak to him – I'll ask security to take him out.'

Jaz shakes her head fiercely. 'No, don't. It'll only make things worse.'

'Don't worry, it'll be discreet.'

'Discreet?! It's live TV!'

I take her hands. 'Trust me.'

'I'm scared, Maddie.' She shivers. In her eyes is genuine fear. Whatever this guy did to her back in LA, I'm willing to bet I only know the half of it.

Simon looks between us. 'Will someone please tell me who Carl is?'

'It's a long story,' I say, just as Jaz bursts into tears.

'Hey, hey, don't cry!' Taking her drink, I manoeuvre her into a seat at the table. Instantly Simon's crouching down next to her, rubbing her arms, telling her it's OK. We both hug her and wait till she's able to speak.

'Do you want me to go?' Simon asks. 'I don't mind.'

I can see he does, in fact, mind – at the end of the day Jaz is his friend and she's upset. So I'm relieved when she shakes her head.

'No,' she says, and with the movement a tear plops out on to her hand, 'you should probably hear this.'

So she tells Simon about Carl, and he listens.

♪

Downstairs I can barely make my way through the throng to the bar, where Ruby and Alex are rushed off their feet serving drinks. I've only seen a photo of Carl once but I'd never forget his face: the slicked dark hair, sleek as an otter's back; the coal-black eyes and thin, reedy lips. I'm making him sound like a monster, at least in appearance, but he's actually quite good-looking – in a Robert-de-Niro-in-*Cape-Fear*, think-about-moving-and-I'll-saw-your-head-off-type way. I scan the bar, knowing Jaz is following behind, but I don't see him.

Despite the jumping beans in my tummy, I experience a stab of pride as I take in my surroundings. We did it. At the end of the series run, Pineapple looks nothing short of amazing.

Pink strobes illuminate my path across the main dance floor, white light glinting off shimmering glass surfaces, candelabra and giant mirrors. Music bleeds through the space, master to the chatting, dancing throng of revellers – neon make-up and extreme hairstyles; tiny skirts and sharp suits; long legs and raised arms; painted faces turned to the giant spinning cube, a solid mass moving to the thump of bruised beats spilling from the system. Karaoke hasn't got started yet – Toby and Nathan hired a DJ to take care of the first part of the night. I suppose they wanted to guarantee a note of credibility, before the squealers are let loose. Literally Let Loose? There's always hope – I was quite fond of 'Crazy For You'.

And tonight they're being let loose on a brand-spanking-new built-up stage. It's even got steps going up to it and a massive screen behind, so if listening to the warbles isn't quite enough you can get a hundred per cent zoom on their crooning features as well. Two elegant silver microphones stand tall on each side, stoically awaiting their time – though the shade of sophistication is somewhat tempered by an adjacent buffet of hot dogs and candyfloss trailing down one full side of the club, pressed up against the reflective wall so that a good half looks like it's covered in party food.

Wide-eyed cameras swoop like vultures over the crowd, broadcasting its subjects on to the huge screen behind, much to the squealing delight of those filmed. Is that Jordan's best mate being interviewed? I think I saw her on *Celebrity Come Dine with Me* last year – she's alarmingly orange with chunky knees and looks in danger of melting under the heat of the spotlight. Next to her is that Italian one from Blue – they're not dating, are they? Lou would know. I experience a pang of longing and wish she were here. She'd know what to do about Carl, about Evan, about Nick. Even if she didn't, she'd make me feel better.

'Maddie!' A flustered, stressed-out Alison tugs on my arm, her face screwed up in annoyance. 'Have you seen Evan? I've been searching for him all bloody night.'

'No, sorry.' Someone bumps into me from behind and drifts off without apology. Bollocks – actually I haven't seen Evan at all. I vowed to keep an eye on him and I've only gone and lost him already.

'He's ignoring me.' Alison pouts. 'He's been acting like a prick ever since that thing blew up between Jaz and Simon. Like it was my birthday yesterday and he forgot because he had to take his cat to the vet. Apparently! He doesn't even own a cat.'

'Oh! Happy birthday!' I congratulate her miserable face. 'Sorry, I didn't know.'

'Don't worry about it.'

'Maybe he just bought a cat . . . ?' I hazard, when what I really want to do is ask why on earth she cares about such a despicable person. I can't bear to tell Alison about Evan's other conquests, however many there are. I only hope I'm not forced to later.

'He hates cats,' she says grudgingly. 'He couldn't even be bothered to lie convincingly.'

'Makes a change,' I grumble.

She doesn't seem to hear me. 'It's because his wife's here,' she decides bitterly. 'I'm sick of it. He's told me countless times that they're only together for practical reasons – financial stuff, you know – and he doesn't love her any more. He's *always* telling me how he "can't stand one more minute". So why can't he get out? It's not like they have kids or anything.'

'Where is she?' I ask, curious despite myself.

Alison nods in the direction of the stage. By the central steps is an alarmingly short, round woman with cropped dark hair.

'She looks like Danny DeVito!'

'Not her!' Alison hisses. 'The blonde sucking a lemon.'

Alongside the shorter one is an extremely tall, thin, unhappy-looking woman in a minuscule white dress. Together they look like the aunts in *James and the Giant Peach*. It's hard to tell how old she is through all the plastic surgery – her mouth is more of a beak and the skin on her face is stretched to the edges like a trampoline. Skeletal legs protrude from a weeny skirt, thin and knobbly like Nik Naks. My guess is she hasn't smiled in about six years.

Toby joins us. 'Poor Mrs Bergman,' he observes, pushing the glasses on the bridge of his nose. 'I feel for her.'

'She looks like a bitch,' says Alison – quite harshly, in my view, given she's the one shagging the bitch's husband.

'Clearly she's not happy,' points out Toby, rather more fairly. 'Would you be?'

'Going to bed with Evan every night?' I splutter. 'Hardly!' Then I realise what a stupid insensitive thing that was to say.

Toby seems undeterred. 'Probably why she's had all that work done,' he suggests. 'It can't be easy being married to a serial cheat, feeling you have to keep up with all the younger, prettier models.' It's the first time I've seen Toby express anything except deference to Evan. He's normally so mild-mannered.

'I've got to find him,' breathes Alison, moving off.

'I've been trying to warn her,' Toby tells me solemnly. 'Evan doesn't care, he never did – he only cares about himself.' And he trails slightly pathetically after her, eyes searching the crowd through the thick frames of his glasses.

I spot the man himself almost as soon as they're gone, holding fort by the hot dogs (why didn't I think of that?), the gleam of sweat on his forehead and cheeks catching the sickly light. He's chatting to cameras, back-slapping someone with enthusiasm and taking huge, snarling bites from his bap like something feral that hasn't eaten in a week. Everything Loaf told me rushes back and a swell of anger rinses through my stomach. How can Evan carry on like he hasn't a care in the world? Like he hasn't ruined the career of a good, decent man, and isn't trying to ruin my parents, me and my friends – not to mention Alison! I ball my fists. Maybe I should follow Simon's advice. Maybe I shouldn't just wait to defend myself; maybe I should attack him first. What I wouldn't give to have the balls to get up on that stage, seize one of those microphones and tell everyone here – including his wife – just what he's been . . .

The man having his back slapped by Evan looks up and spies me. Oh, crap. It's Chester Bendwell. Evan's dead gaze follows his and when his eyes meet mine, a chill travels down my spine, making the hairs on the back of my neck prickle and burn.

In seconds (literally – he's wearing those trainers again) Chester's at my side, closely followed by his crew and their hulking great cameras. 'Maddie! *Fabulous* to see you!'

'You too.' I'm like a rabbit in headlights, one half of my brain on Evan and his proximity to the stage; the other on Carl, wherever he may be – and none whatsoever on Chester.

'Bet you hardly recognise Pineapple these days!' he exclaims wildly. A tiny piece of pink candyfloss is clinging wetly to his top lip. I say a few words in response, trying not to be put off by the features floating mere inches away, the bugging eyes and the commas of perspiration each side of his nostrils.

'And the Jaz and Alex romance?' he demands hungrily, dazzling me with a wall of bright white teeth – seriously, could he come any closer without actually *kissing* me? 'Can you tell us what's happening? We're dying to know. She got rid of Simon pretty fast, didn't she? Is he back with Lou? Or is she still mad? She must be seething!' He crows with laughter. '*I* would be. But never mind what I think! Tell us what you think, babe.' *Babe?* 'HAHAHA. What can you tell us about that, Maddie?' Chester sniffs hard. Bets in for how many lines he's just done in the loo.

'It's OK, we're all friends again,' I say, snatching the chance to pour water on the fire Evan's been so eager to fan. So what if people think I'm boring – they can decide for themselves what the truth is. It makes no difference whether I'm honest or not.

While Chester's babbling on, I steal a glance at the bar. Jaz has joined the others; Simon is working next to her and checking out every customer she serves. I'm glad she told him about Carl. It doesn't forgive what happened, but I think it helps explains it in part. She's been through a lot and it's messed with her head – but who's perfect? I'm not, that's for sure. Simon's wise enough to know that he isn't, either. And that he and Jaz have a great friendship that can, and will, survive a few seconds of stupidity.

'Maddie?' Chester brings me back to him with a warm, slightly sour gust of breath.

'Oh, sorry. What?'

We're distracted by an almighty screech on one of the microphones. Desperate, I crane to see over Chester's head, my heart galloping into my throat. The world turns in slow motion, the waves of the crowd seeming to part to pave my way through, luring me on to that stage, showing me what I have to do; that I must stand up in front of these hundreds of people and do what's right, I must challenge the man who's preparing to thwart me—

But it's just the karaoke starting, thank god. (Two months ago you'd have had to put a loaded gun to my head to hear me say that.)

And where is Lawrence, anyway? I haven't seen him. Maybe he's not coming, after all. Maybe Nick was wrong. And Loaf. Maybe it's all going to be OK. Maybe.

Someone from *Big Brother* five years ago spouts ten seconds of tripe into the mic about Pineapple Mist being Pineapple

342

'missed' (get it? Yikes), before the intro to 'What You Do (Ooh Ooh)' kicks in and the room screams and yelps in excitement as if they've never heard the song before. Chester seems to sniff at the air and pursues this fresh action like a pig snuffling truffles.

I'm just pondering Chester's lack of manners when I realise I'm not alone. Well, obviously I'm not alone, I'm in a room full of people, but I sense someone loitering behind me, stealthy as a cloaked assassin. I smell him before I see him – that nutty, slightly menacing aftershave – and his bulk just that fraction too close for comfort. Evan's fleshy arm clamps tight round my shoulders and pulls me close.

'Having fun?' he growls.

My first thought is, Phew, I know where he is. We might hate each other's guts but if I can just keep him distracted . . .

'Let's get a drink,' I say as pleasantly as I can.

But he's already on the move, tugging me along with him, pushing through the crowd, stretching his wide neck, searching for someone. Moments later I'm jerked to a halt.

'Nick, here's Maddie.'

And with that, I'm deposited with all the grace of a bag of shopping. Evan shoots off, swallowed by the masses as quickly as they spat him out. Nick looks just as bewildered as me. The people he's chatting with – two silky-haired women, I can't help but notice, with long legs and spiky heels – grudgingly melt away.

'Hi,' he says uncertainly.

'Hi.'

'You look lovely.'

343

'Thanks.' I keep my chin up, determined to be civil. 'I'd best get on—'

Nick grabs my elbow, peering over my shoulder, checking for the all-clear.

'Ow!'

'You've got to listen to me,' he commands, steering me into a corner.

I attempt to shake myself free, but he's too strong. 'Get off!'

'Give me a minute, all right? I wouldn't do this unless it was important.'

'Nick, don't, I'm not interested. Take your hands off me.'

'Maddie, you have to—'

'*Now!*' I jerk out of his clasp.

'If you'd just let me finish!' he hisses, backing me up against the wall. 'For fuck's sake, would you hear me out for once in your life? Can't you see I'm trying to *help you*?'

His face is inches from mine. I fight the sudden desire to kiss him. 'Go on then,' I say instead. 'Make it quick.'

'Evan wants you distracted, that's why he's brought you over. To talk to me.'

'Distracted?'

'Yes.'

'And you're sure you've got nothing to do with this? No cameras planning to show up any time soon?'

'For god's sake, I'm serious. Evan's about to—' He clams up. There's a blinking red light flickering close by.

I nearly burst out laughing at the predictability of it.

'What?' I demand. 'He's about to what?'

But it's too late.

A dreadful quiet descends on the crowd. Over Nick's shoulder I can see the stage, and on it a ghastly wiry-haired silhouette lit from behind, like the creature you think you see at your bedroom door when you're five and you wake up from a nightmare.

Oh no.

Oh *no*.

Evan's fat hands take one of the gleaming mics. I see him lick his lips, think I *hear* it, all that wet tongue and saliva. He takes his time, relishing the undivided attention.

He was desperate . . . to be famous, to perform . . .

Slowly Nick turns to face the stage as well. As he moves I catch sight of Jaz at the bar, and Simon, and Ruby. And I know what they're thinking: now's your chance, they're willing me – get up there now, before he says something, before he has the chance . . .

Do it now, a little voice instructs me. *Do it now while there's still time.*

I can't. I can't.

'Ladies and gentlemen, boys and girls,' Evan starts, like some horrifying travelling clown, 'I wish to take this opportunity to say a few words about the show. And what a show it's been!' There's a smattering of enthusiastic applause. '*Blast from the Past* has been a wonderful project for me – I think everyone here will agree it's been a roaring success. To Pineapple!'

Everyone raises their glass/bottle/sausage roll. Perhaps that's it. He might stop there.

Perhaps not.

'But all good things must come to an end.' The quiet settles once again. Evan savours the moment, shakes his head

345

sadly, inevitably. 'And on this occasion, I'm afraid that means more than just the series . . .'

The entire crowd is mesmerised, hanging on to his every word. He lets us wait, the consummate showman, before a gruff sound escapes his throat and he loosens the knot on his tie. I'm transfixed, rooted to the spot, unable to move.

'Anyone who knows me,' Evan booms, 'knows I am a man of integrity. And for that reason I am obliged to be honest with the people who have made me who I am today. That's you.' A nod to the mob, then the same to each camera in turn, taking his time, not rushing a thing. 'And I cannot let this show wrap without being completely truthful about what you've witnessed.' He shifts his weight, the head of the mic cradled in his palms like a precious gem.

'Now, I understand how reality TV works, it's my game,' he says. 'I understand how it becomes a family member, a best friend, a confidante; someone to share the highs and the lows; a strange, exciting, unpredictable – and yet absolutely reliable – creature that straddles both public and private, that generates gossip in the pub as much as it eases those lonely nights in. Believe me, as the show's producer – as *your* producer, I prefer to think – I appreciate the beauty of reality television more than anyone.'

Jaz is frowning at me. She's mouthing something but I can't make it out. Simon and Alex are making odd jerky movements with their heads, like, *Go on, you're up; it's now or never.*

But I can't. Now I'm here and it's happening, I can't bring myself to. I start to shake. A cold wash hits and falls down the entire length of my body, like someone's thrown a bucket of icy water over my head.

The man next to me takes my hand. Nick. I remind myself he's the last person I want with me right now, but his grip is so firm I can't prise free. Against my wobbliness he's like a rock, and to let go would be like abandoning my ship in a storm.

'So now I want to let you in on a couple of facts.' Evan rubs his hands together like a boy in a sweet shop. 'Call it a gift, from me to you, for your enduring loyalty – and a sign of my recognition that the people of this country have more wisdom than some might give them credit for. You see, *I* don't believe it's possible to deceive the viewing public.' His earnest face fills the screen, beamed into god only knows how many living rooms across the country.

A curious whisper ripples through the assembled company. A girl near us hisses, 'What's he on about?' and her male companion, a Jimmy Nail lookalike with a bolt through his eyebrow, shrugs. 'Beats me.'

'This may, at least initially, leave you feeling you've been . . . misled.' Evan pauses, putting his palm flat against his heart. 'Which is, of course, against everything reality television – and my production company, in particular – stands for. We seek the truth, and nothing but the truth, and where we can, we deliver it.'

Realisation dawns, and with it an exquisite rush of white relief.

Finally, Evan is going to come good. He's about to confess everything. How the thing between Simon and Jaz was fake. How he and Nick manufactured every last bit, all the supposed romances, including my own; that they scripted the lot. How Alex wasn't any part of the bar until days before broadcast and how they fired our longest-serving member in favour

347

of viewer numbers. How this isn't reality – it's about as far from reality as it's possible to get. How sorry he is for the manipulation and the broken relationships and the hurt he's caused. And I realise then, amid the daze of this glorious reprieve, that I *will* forgive him. Because it takes guts to stand up there and say what he's about to say: I couldn't do it when my moment was up. Evan Bergman is going to do the right thing. At last, he's doing the right thing.

'Now then . . .' He scans the audience. 'Where is she? Where's Maddie Mulhern?'

I'm about to raise my hand when Nick squeezes my fingers. 'Don't,' he whispers. 'Don't say anything.'

'But he's only—'

The spotlight hits me like a punch, flooding my startled face in clean, blinding light. Evan's expression hardens. His reptilian eyes glint like knives catching the moon. Something tells me he's not about to congratulate me.

'Maddie Mulhern has something to own up to. Don't you, Maddie?'

I do?

'This girl right here might have played the innocent all along, got you all on-side, but she hasn't been entirely honest with you, now, has she?'

Hundreds of faces turn to look at me. My mouth falls open, my mind goes blank. All I'm conscious of is Nick holding my hand. I want to run, but when I try to break free he pulls me back.

'Your dearly beloved proprietor,' Evan goes on, his voice hard as stone, 'has been hiding a ruinous agenda. She's taken every single one of you for a goddamn *fool*. You see, it has been brought to my attention – by a reliable source, I might add – that Maddie here plotted her "romance"' – he does the air quotes – 'with Nick Craven from the outset.'

A whisper of confusion snakes through the crowd.

'That's right!' he booms. 'Preying on his sullied reputation, she saw her chance at a quick rise to fame and she took it. It wasn't enough to be starring in the series of the summer, was it? Oh no, not for Maddie Mulhern. Ladies and gentlemen, it pains me to tell you that *nothing* you've seen or witnessed in connection with this relationship has been genuine.'

'No.' I shake my head. 'That's not true.' But my words are drowned out in the clamour of dissent spreading through the bar like wildfire.

'Now where *is* my source?' Evan scans the crowd, pleased as punch, a massive replica of his arrogant face plastered across the screen behind. 'Where is Lawrence Oliver?'

28

The Sun Always Shines on TV

I'm livid. I've never been so angry in my whole entire life.

Evan just accused me of his own crime. He's daring to pin this whole debacle on me.

That's it. Game over.

Summoning every last ounce of courage, I break free from Nick's grip and calmly make my way through the crowd. Instantly it stills, dividing to let me through, which makes me feel at once like someone revered and someone nobody wants to touch. Faces on either side, blank in the darkness, watch me with intent; the silence like mud, sucking at my feet, pulling me under.

At last I make the stage, take the three steps up and face my audience. The lighting dazzles me, blinding, so that my audience is little more than a dark swamp. My own hands appear in front of me, pale and ghostly, like someone else's hands. I take the other microphone from its stand, grip it hard and prepare to speak.

Stage fright hits.

The words disappear. Everything I wanted to say, gone, vanished, like a pebble dropped in water, that first hard splash and then nothing. Absolutely nothing.

I stare out at the room, the hum of expectancy trembling in the air. They're waiting. Evan's waiting. Smugness radiates from him like heat – he's got me exactly where he wants me. And I've never looked so guilty.

Someone takes the mic from my trembling hands. Only when he starts to speak do I realise who he is.

'It *has* been a lie,' Nick says. I look up at him and his face is blank, unreadable. Beyond him Evan's features rearrange themselves, delighting in the moment, waiting for Nick to corroborate his story.

It has been a lie.

Of course, that's it. That's *it*. The whole thing – maybe even the whole bloody series – has been designed to clear Nick's name, to make him the injured party and restore his reputation. It makes so much sense now, everything that he did and said and the whole thing with Evan, just an elaborate ploy from the start, the ultimate plan to get an injured man back on top – and after all the wondering and all the angst, the realisation hits me with something like relief.

That same relief restores my confidence.

'I'm not a liar,' I say. I'm surprised by how strong it comes out, despite the fact I'm the only one without a mic. 'I haven't lied about a single thing.'

Nick turns to me. 'I'm not talking about you.'

He's not?

'I'm talking about Evan Bergman.' He addresses the crowd. 'Nothing that man has just told you is true. Nothing he has told any of us since *Blast from the Past* went on air is true. He's manipulated you, the public, just as he has us. Don't believe a word he says.'

What?

But I thought . . .

Evan tosses a strange, high-pitched laugh into the crowd. 'Hold on just a minute—'

'I'll do no such thing.' Nick's voice is low, commanding, coming from deep inside. 'I've let you get away with this for long enough – worse still I've been a part of it. I've taken enough instruction off you, Evan, and I won't take a single one more.'

Evan's slack-jawed, the flap of wobbly skin under his chin quivering like a turkey's. But Nick's not finished yet.

'You employed me as your director,' he says, voice winging through the silence like a bird set free, 'and yet you've been directing me from the start. You say you believe that people out there should know the truth? That the viewers at home deserve your honesty? Then let it begin now, here. Admit it, Evan. Admit that this show was nothing but a scripted farce; a cleverly edited, entirely artificial charade.'

A collective intake of breath rises from the floor like a balloon.

'And that was your intention from the start. You don't care about television – not what's important about it: how information gets shared, how people are entertained, how knowledge is passed on, you couldn't give a crap about any of that. I've never met anyone who cares *less* about television – or about the viewers you claim to work for. What was it you called fans of reality shows only yesterday morning? "Brain-dead thickos gorging on human shit"?'

Evan's aghast.

'Is that true?' someone yells.

'What've we all been watchin' then?' another voice cries, distressed. 'What's the show been about?'

'Fucking reality TV,' a man with a black mohawk scoffs, 'could've told you it's a load of old bollocks.'

'You've conned the lot of us!'

'You wanker!'

The heckling gathers pace, the mob becoming ever more rowdy as people shove and push and shout over each other, fired by the injustice of it, drinks getting spilled and fists rattling the air, and from nowhere something hits the stage. I don't know what it is, but when a second swiftly follows, it hits Evan dead in the face, some sort of bun, making a cool wet slapping sound as it collides with his forehead.

Suddenly, unexpectedly, he's bald. It really does happen that way. The springy mop of hair just wafts off, like a kite on the breeze, travelling a short distance before settling on the stage. I half expect it to sprout legs and scurry off behind the screen.

'Even your hair's fake!' someone cries.

'Yeah! What else d'you want to tell us about?'

With renewed fervour the hordes refresh their attack, and there's a rapid surge towards the stage as people attempt to clamber up on to it, reaching for the mics, battling to have their say. I back up, panicked. Evan, red-faced and shaking, scrambles to retrieve the toupée. Mortified, he wedges it on to his head, pulling the sides down like flaps on a cap.

'*Stay back!*' he roars, eyes rolling, clutching the microphone to him like a crucifix against vampires. Surprisingly the rabble retreats, sweeping back like the tide on a beach.

'You really want to believe this man?' he spits, shooting daggers at Nick, his whole body shaking with rage. 'This desperate, washed-up has-been? He's been taken so far in by this floozy he can't tell his arse from his elbow, that's all it is.'

'I'm telling you the facts,' urges Nick. 'Evan Bergman is corrupt. He's corrupted this industry from the inside out.'

A sea of faces looks blankly from one man to the other.

'You moron,' Evan hisses, patting his hair frantically, struggling to regain control, 'you're even more idiotic than I thought. I gave you your only shot, you imbecile – and this is how you repay me? You're the one who came knocking on my door, crying into your cornflakes because no one else would come within three feet of you.'

Nick steps forward. 'And I regret it every single day.'

Evan pokes a finger at him. 'So if you want to be *truthful*,' he hisses, 'why not cough up the whole damn story?'

'Which rather disproves what you've just accused Maddie of.'

Evan must realise the corner he's walked into. He appears to think for a minute before changing tack. 'I was trying to help you,' he says, mustering conviction though his voice is feeble, 'trying to be honourable to a fellow of the industry—'

'No, you weren't. You were attacking a woman I care about.'

'Oh, spare me!' Finally Evan loses it, snapping like an elastic band. 'You're the one who came up with the bloody idea in the first place!'

The crowd gasps. My stomach lurches.

'Admit it to her, Nick, go on,' taunts Evan. 'Admit that you preyed on her as a last-ditch attempt to salvage your career, you pathetic *bastard*.'

'You misunderstand,' says Nick evenly. 'I'd explain it to you if I thought you were capable of grasping basic concepts of friendship and respect.'

'Try us out, sonny Jim,' Evan rasps. 'We might just surprise you.'

Sonny Jim?

Nick takes my hand, but I'm too confused, I don't know what to think. I pull away. I'm horribly aware of Nick and me up on the screen, my blotchy red face and quivering bottom lip, and I just really *really* don't want to be here. I want to be by myself or with Lou or with Jaz or with Mum and Dad, somewhere quiet and private so I can think things through. I don't want to be on TV. I never wanted to be on bloody TV.

'Look,' Nick begins, speaking slowly so I catch every word. His gaze is so intense that for a moment I believe we're the only people in the room. 'I started off with less than honourable intentions, OK? I admit it. Back then you were just a name to me, Maddie, part of a project I had to work on. Not because I wanted to,' an awkward laugh, 'to be completely honest I hate these kind of shows, but because it was all I was offered. So I took it. And as part of the contract I was obliged to participate in the . . . "storylines" Evan had in mind – he had plenty, he promised, and did I have any suggestions?'

He takes a deep breath and releases it gradually. 'I suggested a romance centring on the club's manager – I didn't know then it was you. Evan wanted me in the leading role and I hate to say, I didn't argue. Because it didn't matter to me then. If that's what Evan Bergman wanted from me, I'd do it. Only an eight-week gig and then it was over – perhaps I did have a future in TV after all; it was what I'd been trained to do, I'd worked hard at it and I deserved this break. I deserved it after what happened.

'But then I met you, Maddie . . . and the minute I met you I knew I couldn't go through with it. Well, I could . . . just not with the lying part.' He smiles. 'Because it turns out, after all, that I didn't have to lie.'

'Pass me the sick bucket!' Evan bellows, attempting to get the crowd on-side. But they're as rapt as I am.

'Shut up, Bergman!' a woman yells. 'Let the man speak!'

'I wanted out right away,' Nick continues, unshaken by the interruption. 'When we first bumped into each other outside Tooth & Nail, I promise you I didn't know who you were. When we met properly on launch night I instructed Evan the deal was off – I already knew you, I said, it wouldn't be right. And it wasn't. I liked you. Even if you liked M People.'

'I do not like M People!'

A lone voice rises from the floor. 'What's wrong with M People?'

'But Evan threatened me. He told me if I backed out of the arrangement he'd go straight to the papers and "fix me up". He had a sexting scandal he warned me he'd run.' A bitter laugh. 'I wasn't stupid, I knew where the power was. One more slip and that'd be it.'

'What the fuck is this?' Evan thunders. 'Suddenly everyone's developed a conscience? This is *TV*, people – what don't you stupid twits get about that? This is what we do! If you can't stand the heat, get out of the goddamn kitchen!'

'Cheryl and Mike would be ashamed of you, Evan. All of Bucks Fizz would.'

Hang on, I recognise that voice. It's Loaf – I swear it's Loaf.

'That was "keep out of the kitchen", you dimwit,' Evan tosses back, unaware he's addressing his old nemesis.

That's it – I have to get away. I don't care where I'm going or where I end up. I just want to be gone from here, far, far away where no one can find me. I've had enough. All the lies, the double bluffs, the propaganda – I can't take any more.

Jaz's red hair is shining at the bar like a beacon, a lighthouse I have to reach. I step off the stage and fumble blindly through the masses, the silence thick as fog. My legs are like jelly and my heel impales a bit of discarded pastry from the buffet, but I force myself onwards, thinking only of getting away, out into the clean air. The green EXIT sign is coming closer, blurry through the tears that are poised to fall, and when I reach it and push down on the handle, a cool slice of fresh July night pours in, filling me with hope. Briefly I glance back, expecting hundreds of eyes to be on me . . . but then I realise no one's looking at me. They're all watching Nick.

'Stop fucking filming!' Evan yaps, swiping the air in front of him. 'Show's over!'

'No.' Nick raises the microphone to his lips. 'I'm not finished.'

My hands come away from the door and I stay where I am. The spotlight bathes Nick in a warm golden hue, his remorseful face up there on the screen, and what strikes me is how long his eyelashes are, though I've never noticed before. At the side of the stage two camera ops exchange brief, nervous glances, before shrugging and returning to their positions.

And then, something unbelievable happens.

First, Nick goes extremely red. Then he opens his mouth. And then, like my worst nightmare and my best dream all rolled into one, a song comes out. 'If You Leave' by OMD, the song Molly Ringwald kisses Andrew McCarthy to at the end of *Pretty in Pink*; the song we talked about that day in Soho. And it's so, so embarrassing but so lovely that it's all I can do to stand there drenched in amazement, cringing for him and loving him at the same time. There's no music, just his voice. It's a poor voice, miserably flat, but at least he knows some of the words – and anyway, I know I'd sound worse. Without the electronic backing he's laid bare, and the lyrics sound sweet, vulnerable, led eyes-closed by their tune. It's hopeless. And full of hope. And excruciating. And perfect.

As he's launching into the chorus, I gesture for him to stop. I can't bear any more (I mean I really can't; it's terrible). Nick winds to a halt, and the crowd holds its breath.

'Come back,' he says simply. 'Don't leave.'

The ground starts to move beneath my feet, and I guess it isn't really moving and I must be walking, but before I know it my hand is in his. The entire room erupts with deafening applause, and when Nick pulls me on to the stage and kisses me on the lips, softly and with care, he smells so delicious I just fall into it and wrap my arms around his neck and for that moment it's only us.

'Turn that *bloody* camera off, you wretched cow!' Evan howls.

Nick and I pull apart, smiling nervously at each other. Alison, next to us, lowers her equipment and turns on Evan with revulsion.

'Do you know what, Evan Bergman?' she says. 'Fuck you. I've had enough.'

'Fine.' Evan waves her off like a bad smell. His huge face replaces Nick's and mine on the big screen. 'Go find another job. I don't need you anyway.'

'I mean I've had enough of *you*.' She waits to drop her bombshell. 'Of us.'

The excited murmurs surrounding Nick's performance die back, knocked by this fresh revelation. A buzz electrifies the air, the buzz of tension, incredulity, anticipation.

Evan barks a strangled laugh. 'In your dreams, you daft little thing.'

'Haven't you got the message yet, you *cruel old man*?' Alison mimics, camera down by her side like a costume she's just pulled off. '*No one here is on your side* . . . and for once that includes me.'

'Oh do shut up—'

'I won't shut up. Not this time, Evan. I'm sick of being the girl you just call up when you're bored, or your wife's not around, or you're at a loose end. I'm sick of being her.'

Evan gulps.

'And do you know what the saddest thing is?' Alison chokes on the words. 'I actually had feelings for you. How ridiculous is that? And I thought you might have feelings for me, too . . . at least you told me you did. But I'm not the only one, am I?' A dry laugh. 'No, not by a long shot.'

Finally Evan finds his voice. 'As if I'd look at you twice.' His lizard eyes rake Alison up and down with disdain. 'You're a mess. Toni, baby, don't listen to her.'

But it seems Toni has been listening to her. Because the next thing we know Evan's wife is storming on to the stage with her lemon-sucky face and Danny DeVito (who must be a best friend, or a sister?) following in close pursuit. She slaps her husband once round the chops – hard, so the wet sound ricochets through the hushed club – and tugs off her wedding band.

'Stick this ring *right up your own*, Evan Bergman,' she instructs him in surprisingly neat, clipped tones, pushing it against his meaty chest. 'I've put up with your cheating for years. *Years!* No more. It's over.'

'Toni—'

'You make me sick.'

'Baby, please . . .'

But it's too late. Evan swallows – I see his Adam's apple rise and fall like a bobbing float. A lost dog, he turns to Alison. Toby emerges from the wings and slips his arm round her shoulders. Alison turns away from Evan, close to tears, and I think then how she really did care, and how funny the heart is, and how it can't help who it loses itself to.

And then, just when I think it has to be over, a deafening crash thunders through the club. The doors fly open and through them travels an ear-piercing shriek, swiftly followed by a voice I know only too well.

Dad's.

29

Poison

'WHAT THE BLOODY HELL IS GOING ON HERE?'

Uh-oh. I haven't heard him sound like that since I was five and I made a potion out of all Mum's expensive hand lotions . . . down the loo.

My name flies out of the darkness. 'Maddie?'

Three hundred heads turn to look at me.

'Dad?'

Three hundred heads swivel back.

'Where are you?'

'Up here,' I say weakly, as Nick thrusts the mic into my hands. I give a little wave. 'Hi.'

'Up where? Who? What? What's *happened* to this place?'

'Um . . .' I say the first thing that pops into my head. 'Surprise!'

The main lights come on, flooding the room in harsh white light. Mum, her hair a plaited bush and reams of some material or other covering her frame like crinkly leaves, lifts a hand to her forehead and collapses back into the arms of the unfortunate person standing behind her.

Now I can see Dad's baffled expression. 'Maddie . . . ? Who *are* all these people? And what on earth has happened to Sing It Back?'

'They're um . . . they're here for karaoke.'

'*Karaoke?*' questions Dad, as if this is the most unlikely sounding thing he's ever heard.

'Yes. And I made a few, um, changes.' I attempt to sound bright, but my voice soon fizzles into a croak. 'What do you think?'

Mum's back on her feet now, clutching Dad's arm, her eyes wide. 'I don't believe it,' she breathes, her gaze sweeping across the room, taking it all in. 'I don't bloody believe it.'

'Look,' I begin to explain, 'what happened is—'

'Rick,' she turns to him, 'this is *brilliant*!'

It is?

'You don't need to tell me that!' Now Dad's beaming as well. What? I thought he was cross . . . wasn't he? But he didn't actually *say* he was cross. Maybe . . .

'Maddie, darling, there are *people* here!'

'Yeah,' I say unsteadily. 'You might know some of them actually. See, they're—'

'It doesn't matter who they *are*!' Mum cries. 'The point is that they're *here*! Someone get me a Chardonnay, for heaven's sake!'

Nick nudges me in the ribs.

'And, um, we're on TV,' I say into the mic.

They turn on me with vacant expressions. 'What?' says Dad.

'Yep!' I chirp with a note of hysteria. 'And it's been quite a show so far tonight!'

Mum, still beaming, looks like she did when I told her I passed all my GCSEs – I don't think she's registered what I've just said. Instead she flaps excitedly at the bar. 'Rick, would you look at that! It's all so . . . different! I love it!'

Dad doesn't move. '*We're on TV?*'

'Jaz, my darling!' Mum rushes over to the bar, dress flapping, and envelops Jaz in a monster hug. 'Simon!' She kisses him on both cheeks. 'Ruby, you gorgeous thing!' Then she whips back to Dad. 'Rick, don't you dare leave our guests out in the cold – bring them in to join the party!'

'What guests?' I ask. Right this minute I wouldn't be surprised if Robin Hood and his band of Merry Men strode through the door.

'We brought a couple of familiar faces back with us,' Mum explains happily. 'They became such great friends on tour – we just couldn't leave them behind!' She's talking like they've smuggled a pair of rabbits through airport security.

But when the mystery visitors emerge I see they're not rabbits at all. They're Don Jenkins and Lenny Gold. Better known as Two Shay.

On the other side of the stage, still on his knees, Evan

emits a startled gasp. His hair's slipping off the back of his head. His face is puce.

'*You!*' he hisses, staggering to his feet.

Ah.

'You ruined my life,' he spits at Two Shay, a maniacal glare contorting his features. 'You ruined me, you evil sons of bitches!'

'Well, there's no need for that,' Mum says, hands on hips. 'Rick, who is this man?'

Dad squints up at us, shading his eyes like he's looking into the sun. 'Darling, if I'm not mistaken that's Poison Bergamot.'

'Poison Bergamot?' Mum splutters. 'Don't be ridiculous! That man's long gone, no one's heard from him in years.'

Lenny Gold speaks up, tossing his lustrous caramel mane over one shoulder. Wow, it really is nice hair. 'It wasn't us, Bergamot,' he says in a smooth transatlantic accent. 'For the thousandth time . . . it wasn't us.'

'Who wasn't . . .' Dad blusters, 'What wasn't?'

'Explain yourself!' Mum demands. 'And if that is you, Poison, you'd better step right away from my daughter.'

'Butlins holiday camp.' Evan's mouth is twisted as he makes his way to the edge of the stage, taking the steps, dividing the crowd. 'Skegness, 1991. Remembering yet, boys? Ringing any bells?'

'Forget it, Poison.'

'The fans wanted me.' He moves slowly, eyes fixed on Lenny and Don as the audience disperses, peeling back, moving away. Nick keeps me close, though my instinct is to run down and throw myself in front of Mum and Dad before Evan beats me to it. 'They were calling my name,' he says, voice echoing in the loaded quiet, 'chanting my song – *they wanted Poison Bergamot*. But no, you couldn't have that, could you? You couldn't bear to see me succeed.'

'We told you, Bergamot,' Don yells, 'you're fantasising! *It wasn't us.*'

Evan shakes his head. '*Never.* You made me suffer out there, on stage, in front of all those people. I never should have worn it, I never should have trusted you; I knew it then and I know it now. My best metallic all-in-one, you rigged it. Didn't you? *Didn't you?* Admit it. All it took was a quick snip and my fate was sealed . . .' He gulps. 'Unlike my trousers.' An excruciating moment passes while he gathers himself. '*Two Shay*,' Evan spits the words, his voice spluttering to its death like an expiring car battery, 'you ruined my pop career, my lifelong dream . . . You *humiliated* me.'

Wait a minute . . . I remember this.

Do I? Yes. I remember this!

I was there. I must have been about six. And this memory, forgotten till now but the image gradually reassembling of an overweight, almost-bald man with a purple eye patch and make-up running down his face, his pale round bum suddenly, appallingly, coming into view, before he hauled up the seat of his silver suit and darted from the stage. The wardrobe malfunction to end all wardrobe malfunctions. Mum clapping her hand over my eyes. The laughing, baying audience.

That was Evan? *Evan Bergman exposed himself at Butlins?*

'For the last time,' Lenny runs a hand through his streaky hair, 'we had nothing to do with it. *It wasn't us*, Bergamot – how many times do we have to tell you?'

'Wasn't you?' Evan shrieks. He stops, fists at his sides, like a bull about to charge. I feel Nick slip from my side. 'Then who the hell was it? You were on right before me, you liars. You were the only other people in the dressing room!'

Mum's got one arm across Lenny's chest; one across Don's, like the world's most ineffective bodyguard. 'You stay back, Poison.'

But Evan's hurtling towards them now, his hair jumping off the back of his head, his little legs running like pistons down the length of the bar.

'BASTARDS—!'

Nick breaks his path, slamming into him and pushing him to the floor. Two bouncers descend on them both, hauling Evan up under his armpits, dragging him out.

'I could have been a star!' Evan roars, slamming a pink fist into his chest. '*Me!* I could have been a *star*!'

It's then I spot him. Loaf.

He's standing by the fire exit, one hand on the door, preparing to leave. But not before he's caught my eye.

And when he does, he winks.

Hang on a minute. Was *Loaf* at Skegness that year? Could Loaf have . . . ?

But before I have a chance to think about it, Nick's back by my side, gesturing for me to take the mic.

Right. There's only one thing for it.

'Mum, Dad,' I say, finally finding my voice and talking into it, firm and strong despite the fireworks of happiness and confusion and adrenalin exploding in my chest, 'welcome home. I think this stage belongs to you.'

And before Nick takes my hand, before 'What You Do

(Ooh Ooh)' cranks up, before Jaz and Alex and Simon and Ruby run to the stage to embrace me, before I hug Mum and Dad harder than I have in my life, I turn back to the fire exit.

Loaf has already gone, the door swinging shut on the dark clear night outside.

30

I Think We're Alone Now

'We're so proud of you, poppet.' Mum kisses the top of my head. 'How you managed to pull this one off I will *never* know.'

Gratefully I take the lurid green cocktail from her hands, a hasty concoction thrown together by Alex, and chuck a stinging slug of it down my throat.

'Even though I turned Sing It Back upside down,' I say, 'and in the process lost a treasured friend of yours, changed the club's name, prostituted it to the nation, brought Evan Bergamot-Laidislaw back into your lives . . . and did it all without asking you first?'

'Are you serious?' Dad grins. 'We never thought we'd see anything like it,' he gazes around in wonder, 'never in a million years. It's incredible, sweetheart, nothing short of a miracle.'

'We raised you to have your own mind,' Mum agrees. 'And when we gave you this opportunity we knew you'd do something spectacular . . .' she raises an eyebrow, 'even if we didn't *quite* envisage live TV.'

'To Pineapple!' proposes Simon.

Rob, handsome and smiling so the dimples in his cheeks come out, looks hopefully at my parents. 'If we can . . . to Sing It Back? I always preferred the original.'

'Do you know what?' Mum says, stirring her drink. 'I do, too.'

'In that case,' says Dad, 'to bringing back Sing It Back!'

'Original is best.' I smile at Rob, stripped of Ruby du Jour make-up, and he returns it ten-fold. 'Why change it,' I say, 'when it's already just right?'

It's well past midnight and, after the cameras have packed up and gone home, after Evan's been manhandled from the premises amid frantic whispers that he's going to be investigated by Ofcom – not to mention Two Shay's lawyers – and after the last of the straggling revellers have tailed off into the night, gossiping and speculating on the scandals set to explode across the tabloids tomorrow morning, only a few remain. My parents, tired and elated and overflowing with questions; Two Shay, nipping outside for a fag every ten minutes to get catty about 'that venomous little bitch', by whom I can only assume they mean Evan Bergman; Jaz, as inseparable from Alex as she is from a feather-boa-clad Andre, as the three of them snuggle up in a booth littered with party streamers and half-eaten vol-au-vents, reliving for the twentieth time the moment, at about ten p.m. if reports are to be believed, when Alex punched Carl (he, bursting with pride: 'And so I punched him!' Jaz, head bobbing in agreement: 'And Alex punched him. Well, pushed him . . .' Alex, affronted: 'He didn't push me back though, did he?'); Rob chatting animatedly to Mum and Dad, with just the faintest trace of Ruby du Jour on his cheekbones and eyelids; and Simon, grinning anxiously from ear to ear as he stands before us, occasionally shoving his hands in his pockets, then taking them out again, then shifting his weight from one foot to the other, then laughing too loudly whenever someone tells a joke. Most of all, he can't stop looking at Lou, who's sitting next to me on the edge of the stage, looking beautiful in a silky cream dress and matching every flirty glance of his with one of her own.

In the end, Lou came. She couldn't miss it, she said: after a lot of soul-searching she realised that she'd already missed me, and Simon, and all of us, for far too long.

'I'm so sorry,' she told me the second it was over, Mum and Dad warbling their hit in the background as Nick and I found our way unsteadily through the crowd. 'Can you forgive me?'

I hugged her hard for a long time. 'What on earth are you sorry for?'

'I overreacted,' she said, teary and emotional, 'it was unfair of me. I freaked out and I blew the whole bloody thing out of proportion. Listening tonight brought home how much you've had to deal with all by yourself and that wasn't right – I should have been there. You were going through a tough time and I wasn't around for you. I'm so sorry.'

'Come here, you nob.' I pulled her to me. 'Best friends always. Nothing's going to change that, never ever.'

And it's a very good job Lou did come. Because without her, the night could have ended quite differently.

'What was I meant to do?' She blinks at me now, the picture of innocence. 'Lawrence is a liability. A *drunk* liability.'

'You didn't need to lock him in a cupboard!'

Lou makes a face. 'Maddie, it was *so* obvious he only came back on the scene to claim his piece of the limelight. The minute he turned up tonight I knew he had a plan – I knew it!'

'OK, OK,' I concede, 'you were right.'

'I usually am.' Lou stirs the gaudy cocktail made personally – and without argument – for her by Jaz. She hates rum, but the fact she didn't tell Jaz this makes me think she's pretty close to forgiving her. 'And you have no idea how agonising it was seeing pictures of you two out; all that stuff they said about you getting back together. I just thought, Maddie's not *that* stupid, surely!'

'Hmm. For a while I think I was.'

'Well it's a good job you have a friend like me.'

I grin at her. 'I guess so. How else would I come up with genius ideas for disposing of ex-boyfriends, like luring them into broom cupboards and trapping them there?'

'How do you *work* this thing?' Mum is unsuccessfully punching the controls on the new karaoke machines, her and Dad circling them warily like they're creatures from outer space.

Seriously, though: I'm joking about it now but as well as being ridiculously happy that Lou came, I'm also ridiculously grateful. Because it turns out Lawrence was planning to corroborate Evan's story about me plotting the thing with Nick. His gambit was that he knew me better than anyone; that he was going to tell the nation how I'd dumped him ahead of the show to free up my time for a full-on seduction campaign (a concept I find laughable); and how I was so desperate to be famous that I'd do anything – or anyone – to make sure that happened. The hypocrisy of it baffles me.

But Lawrence couldn't quite pull it off. Panicking about executing his plan – and even more so after several intimidating meetings with Evan Bergman, who needless to say had promised him a starring role in a sitcom he had coming up – he'd polished off one too many vodkas before showing his face at the club. Five minutes in he'd bumped into Lou and, whether it was ill-thought-out relief at seeing a face he knew, sheer drunkenness or plain old arrogant Lawrence desperate to brag, he soon spilled his plan to get up on stage and 'do the right thing'. Well, clearly Lou deemed the right thing to be something else altogether, and moments later he was inside the broom cupboard, no doubt banging on the door and begging to be let out, every plea drowning in the cacophony of noise outside.

A thought occurs to me.

'Hang on . . .' I say, turning to Lou with an expression of alarm. 'Did anyone actually let Lawrence *out* of the cupboard?'

Lou matches my gaze with her own, her eyes like saucers.

Jumping up, we rush around the bar and out to the store. Exchanging one last look of simultaneous horror and exhilaration, the likes of which I haven't seen on Lou's face since we were seven and about to lift the lid on a dead vole Lou's cat caught and we'd kept in a shoebox for three weeks because Lou promised me she was learning a spell to bring it back to life – she hadn't, of course, it just really smelled – I reach for the handle and pull open the door.

Lawrence is inside, slumped like a sack of potatoes behind a mop and several rubbish sacks. His eyes are closed and he's drooling unattractively out one corner of his mouth.

'Lawrence?' I venture.

'*Yeurgh.*' He changes position, delivers a couple of grunty snores and turns away from the assaulting light. 'Mummy,' he whimpers, still dreaming, 'take me home.'

Lou clamps a hand over her mouth, stifling her giggle. I do the same and for a bit we just stand there trying desperately not to laugh.

'Lawrence,' I say eventually, prodding him with my foot. 'Get up!'

'Wha—' he moans, clutching his head, a mole blinking against the light. I wonder if this isn't too far removed from what that shoebox vole might have looked like had Lou's spell worked. 'Whozat?'

'It's me.'

Abruptly he sits up, Hugh Grant hair in a state of dishevelment and dribble patches down his shirt. 'Shit.' He looks around him. 'Where am I?'

'You're in the broom cupboard.'

He grapples about, slowly getting with the programme. 'But I've got to—'

'It's too late, Lawrence,' I say, folding my arms. 'Show's over – they've all gone home. I recommend you do the same before I consider selling my own story. Oh, sorry, I forgot: I'm not as desperate as you.'

'Maddie—'

'Come on, Lou,' I take her arm, 'he can show himself out.' Then I pause, turn back. 'And Lawrence?'

He gawks at me sullenly.

'Don't call me, OK?'

♪

Back in the bar, the first face I see is Nick's. He's laughing with my mother about something and I decide he's got just about the warmest, loveliest smile I've ever seen. I still can't believe what he did tonight. I still can't believe he's mine.

Lou squeezes my arm and heads back to Simon. Sing It Back is feeling the love – there's Mum and Dad, Jaz and Alex, Lou and Simon, me and Nick . . . and there's a distinct possibility of something going on with Two Shay, but I vow to keep my nose out of that one.

'We can't wait to watch the programme!' Dad cries as he and Mum finally get the machine working. 'Jaz has them all – thirty-four, I think she said?'

I cringe. 'Spare yourselves.'

Nick loops an arm round my waist as Mum oohs and aahs over the new playlists, finally settling on Stevie Nicks' 'Rooms on Fire'.

'I've just got one thing to ask you,' I say, putting my hands on his chest and looking up into his dark eyes. 'That day we met outside Tooth & Nail . . . that really wasn't planned?'

Nick pulls me close. 'Do you think I'd have worn such a good shirt if it was?'

I don't have time to grin before he's kissing me. And all the while he's kissing me I'm imagining that shirt and the good-smelling neck and the bare chest beneath and and and . . .

It's for definite. This one is for keeps.

31

Back For Good

One month later

Taxis never show up on time. In my world this exists as an indisputable fact, like always losing socks in the wash or never knowing the answers to the orange questions on Trivial Pursuit.

I'm sitting outside Sing It Back in the late-August sun, perched on my upturned backpack and contemplating buying another trashy magazine to accompany me on the flight. I've whipped through *Hey!* magazine at high speed, and I'm not just looking at the pictures (though admittedly I never read the true-life stories about breastfeeding piglets or having your woodwork teacher's baby).

The truth is I'm horribly addicted to reading about Jaz and Alex – and they're leading nearly every story on the major UK mags. The headline in *Hey!* this week reads WE MASSAGE EACH OTHER'S FEET – JALEX EXCLUSIVE! Not essential reading, I'll admit, but compelling nonetheless. And it's not just because they're my friends; it's because I know they're on cloud nine and loving every minute. Jaz, in particular – these days she's the country's number one reality TV star; she's got the nation hooked on her weird and wonderful outfits, her outrageous make-up . . . and especially her on-trend guinea pig. (Come to think of it, is anyone massaging Andre's feet?) Not only are the trio famous, the three of them are veritable style icons. I'm not entirely sure how Alex feels about sharing the limelight with a rodent, but he's so devoted to Jaz that I think he'd share it with a tree stump if that made her happy.

And I'm proud of her. On achieving the fame she so long desired, Jaz could well have stuck two fingers up to Carl and told the world what a nasty piece of work he was. Last we heard he'd slunk back to the States, complete with sort-of-black eye courtesy of Alex, and was hovering on the cusp of bankruptcy – the reason he'd come to find Jaz in the first place, it turned out. But she hasn't done any of that, and that's why she's the bigger person. Instead she's moving on with her life.

What their newfound celebrity does mean is that Jaz and Alex no longer work for my parents. It's kind of sad, but luckily I still see them all the time – and anyway, Lou and Simon, sickeningly (just sometimes) in love, have upped their shifts at the club. Lou quit Simply Voices on the same day as me, the idea being that she could complete her Psychology course in the day and pour cocktails to a warbling soundtrack at night. Simon has joined a writers' club and is having a stab at his first novel – he says it's going to be based on all of us, but frankly I don't know how you'd write about that without scaring people off.

I check the time on my watch. Damn! We've got to be at the airport in an hour, and so far there's no sign of transport or of boyfriend. Where is he?

The hot sweet smell of doughnuts drifts in from a nearby vendor. I'm going to miss London. And, though I never thought I'd say so, I'll miss Sing It Back as well. Sitting where I am now, just below the newly restored sign, complete with once-missing C, I realise there will always be a place for me here, no matter what. And I have to pat myself on the back for at least a part of the club's revival. This place isn't just my parents' future, it's mine as well – and it feels good to know it's secure.

Since the wrap of *Blast from the Past*, Mum and Dad have been enjoying a roaring trade: they've never known success like it. They've been inundated with offers for more TV series, fly-on-the-wall documentaries and reality shows, but say they're keeping the bar clear of this kind of exposure. (I think they decided this after reviewing each episode with far too fine a toothcomb – something I did warn them about. To their credit they resisted comment, but even they must be shocked at some of what went on.) I believe they're now considering an offer for their own daytime talk show – some journalist recently billed them as the next Richard & Judy. Sheesh.

Still, I know they would have given it all up in a heartbeat to have Archie back . . . and happily, now they won't have to. Because following Dad's frantic fortnight-long search – including a potential lead that saw him heading south to Eastbourne, to Bournemouth, to Dorset, to Cornwall – something miraculous happened. It was early on a Tuesday morning, just Mum, Dad and me having coffee downstairs, when Archie walked through the door, just like that, and put his cap down on the bar with the words: 'What the 'ell's 'appened to this place?'

Everyone was over the moon. Archie didn't retire in comfort, after all: quite the contrary, in fact. He'd just returned from a few weeks of exotic adventure on an all-expenses-paid Caribbean cruise, surrounded by beautiful women and every luxury he could imagine, sipping cocktails pool-side (no Singapore Sing, sadly) while he acquired a tan the colour of Yorkshire tea. So much for the seaside retreat, I thought, but we don't mention that. He, feeling only slightly remorseful at having taken the money and run ('What's a man goin' t'do? *I* knew I'd come back, even if you didn't'), put some of the money from Evan's fat cheque (and it was a *very* fat cheque, we later learned) into the new Sing It Back sign. 'Yer might not need it,' he said, 'but I want t'do my bit.' The rest went to a charity supported by his elderly cousin (who amazingly does exist, though whether she's still alive or not remains to be seen).

I check both ends of the street and fold the magazine into my bag. *Come on, come on, come on . . .*

A guy about my age with a Mr-Twit beard ambles past, checks out the name of the place and grins at me. I get that now – people recognising me and asking for my signature and stuff. It's nice, in a way, but it's not something I'll miss. I'm hoping once we get back the interest will have waned, which seems to be the way these reality things go. Not to sound ungrateful, but I like doing my Tesco shop in tracky bums and slippers and no one having a clue who I am, especially when I'm hungover and I need several bags of salt and vinegar Chipsticks and a paddling pool's worth of Dr Pepper before I can function properly.

Rob's been the luckiest of us in that respect – depending on how you look at it. He's put Ruby du Jour to bed for a time, says he wants to 'try being myself for a while'. It means he doesn't get recognised unless he wants to, which must be how Robert Smith from The Cure feels when he rubs off his red lipstick at the end of the night and brushes his hair.

I squint down the street. A figure is coming towards me, all messy dark crop and lovely blue T-shirt, his backpack slung over one broad shoulder. My heart does a happy little jig, as it does every time.

Nick has been just as fortunate – only today he was approached to work on a new Channel 12 documentary about the Suez Canal. Since the finale of *Blast from the Past* he's been in a position to cherry-pick jobs again, with the TV industry on its knees begging to collaborate. Especially since a host of other TV execs came forward with their own horror stories about Evan Bergman. Thankful, relieved, but most of all impressed, they're now full of admiration for the man they once scorned: a man who was daring enough to speak out. Even Pritchard Wells was reported as saying he was 'a credit to British broadcasting', and apparently, now it's safe to talk in favour of Nick, has been hearing rather different accounts of the night involving his ex-wife.

By the time he reaches me, Nick is wearing a massive grin.

'Sorry,' he says, kissing me on the cheek, 'I got away as soon as I could. Cab here yet?'

'Speak of the devil.' I smile, spotting the approaching car over his shoulder.

It pulls up and the driver gets out to help us with our bags.

'Off anywhere nice?' he asks, flipping up the boot.

Nick opens the door for me. 'Can't tell you,' he says, winking conspiratorially, 'it's a surprise.' He raises an eyebrow. 'Ready for your big adventure?'

I grin. 'Ready as I'll ever be.'

And I really am. I've had all sorts of amazing job offers over the past few weeks, the likes of which I never imagined in my wildest dreams I'd be turning down. Best of all is the variety: in one week alone I was approached for three presenting jobs (one of them for kids – not sure I could be *that* chirpy at five in the morning), a well-known TV personality asked me if I'd consider being her PA (hang on a sec – *me* consider *her?*), an upcoming reality show wanted me on board for 'concept development', and several London clubs came forward for my help getting their business back on track. But none have been quite right. *Blast from the Past* has made me re-evaluate things. My goal was always to work in the media, but the months I spent in TV have taught me to tread carefully: you can get in as much trouble behind the cameras as you can in front of them.

Anyway, I've got a swoon month with Nick to enjoy before I make my decision: a totally glorious, totally private, totally secluded month, with no filming, no obligations, no second-guessing, and nobody who has a clue who we are. I fully intend to enjoy every single second.

Nick's hand finds mine as the car pulls off. London washes past in a tapestry of colour, the brushstrokes of a city we're leaving behind.

That could be why I'm stalling – some of the offers I've received have been totally unexpected. I always assumed I'd stay in the wings, looking on, watching other people, helping them shine; never taking centre stage over backstage, just waiting for something to happen . . . an epiphany, a revelation, a moment.

One thing Evan Bergman's show taught me: there's more to karaoke than just the songs. Getting up there, holding a microphone and singing your heart out is more about having something to sing about than it is about being able to sing. That sort of confidence puts the don in Madonna, the beast in The Beastie Boys, the ultra in Ultravox.

And you know what Phil Collins said about waiting for this moment all his life (a little before, or after, the serious drum solo? I'll have to ask Nick).

Maybe, just maybe, this is mine.

It's time to get your karaoke on!

Turn the page for some karaoke-related advice and playlists from Ella Kingsley, author of *Confessions of a Karaoke Queen*

Ella's Top Five Karaoke Survival Tips

1. Eating ISN'T cheating

If you're a true karaoke legend at heart, you don't want to book your booth, warm up your vocal chords, tip back a bucket of wine on an empty stomach and promptly fall over comatose after twenty seconds of 'Born to Run'. No. You'll want to eat a big cheeseburger and fries before you do any of that. I'm not suggesting anyone should tackle a mic stone-cold sober but there's a difference between a touch of Dutch courage and the contents of a Dutch brewery. Fill yourself with good old carbs before you sing and you'll not only last longer but you'll sound better. Maybe.

2. Preparation is everything

A karaoke booth is like a Tardis. Somewhere between 'Like a Prayer' and 'Bohemian Rhapsody' an hour's slipped by and you've forgotten all those *really* great tunes you heard on Magic FM and now can't remember the name of. Avoid mind-freeze at the machine: there's no shame in writing your song list in advance. (Well, there is, but no one has to know except you and me.)

3. The heat is on

Be it in a bar, a booth or just a best mate's living room, karaoke gets one hot and bothered. Fact. Blasting out a classic tune at the top of your lungs gets the heart racing and the blood pumping, not to mention all the energy you need to jiggle your limbs around in the corresponding dance moves. 'All the Single Ladies', anyone? 'YMCA'? You get the sweaty picture. Wear breathable clothes in loose layers so you can peel off at will, and maybe just sneak a deodorant in your bag too.

4. No one likes a mic hog

You know you're a karaoke diva; your mum knows you have the voice of an angel; but don't force your friends to hear the entire back catalogue of ABBA sung by you and you alone. If you were at your ninth birthday party, you'd pass the parcel, right? Well now you are *slightly* older, the mic is that parcel. Bite your lip and pass it round after you've had your spot in the limelight. It's only fair. Plus, that way, you'll have reserved a bit of extra energy to really nail that top note on your next power ballad. And people will love that. Honest.

5. The morning after

If you've followed tip number one faithfully then you shouldn't be too hungover the next day – but that doesn't mean your voice won't be suffering. Not only were you singing super loudly last night but you were probably shouting over the music to your mates *and* the barman. And maybe you had a little sing-along in the cab on the way home. Who am I to judge? Anyway, soothe a raspy throat with hot water, honey and lemon and keep a pack of boiled sweets in your bag to suck on as essential karaoke medicine. You might find your legs are a bit sore too. That means that you probably went OTT with your Tina Turner staggering dance. Next time: warm down, ladies. Or wear legwarmers, whatever works for you.

Playlist SOS

Have you got karaoke booth blindness? Do you know that you want to sing but just not *what* exactly? Fear not, karaoke queens! Here are my emergency song lists in those key karaoke departments . . .

Boyband beauties
'Relight My Fire' by Take That
'Hangin' Tough' by New Kids on the Block – ripped Donnie
    Wahlberg jeans optional
'When Will I Be Famous?' by Bros

Rocktastic ballads
'Alone' by Heart
'Bohemian Rhapsody' by Queen
'Black Velvet' by Alannah Miles – it'll bring you to your knees

For the karaoke divas
'I Will Survive' by Gloria Gaynor – but your audience might not
'All By Myself' by Celine Dion
'I Will Always Love You' by Whitney Houston

For the vocally challenged
'Tubthumping' by Chumbawumba
'That's Not My Name' by The Ting Tings
'Come On Eileen' by Dexys Midnight Runners – dungarees,
   please

Strictly 80s
'Wake Me Up Before You Go Go' by Wham!
'99 Red Balloons' by Nena
'Tainted Love' by Soft Cell

Hens just want to have fun
'Dancing Queen' by ABBA – having the time of your life
'Material Girl' by Madonna
'Independent Woman Part 1' by Destiny's Child

Rapper's delight
'Ice Ice Baby' by Vanilla Ice
'Gangster's Paradise' by Coolio
'You Can't Touch This' by MC Hammer – Hammertime!